# MEN OF FIRE BEACH COLLECTION

## LORANA HOOPES

The Men of
**FIRE BEACH**

*Fire*
**GAMES**

Best-Selling Author
**LORANA HOOPES**

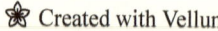 Created with Vellum

# NOTE FROM THE AUTHOR

Thank you so much for picking up this book. Though this was originally going to be titled The Cop's Fiery Bride, the suspense made me feel as if it needed a new look. Therefore, I decided to turn it into a spin off series. I hope you like this book. If you do, please leave a review at your retailer. It really does make a difference because it lets people make an informed decision about books.

If you are reading this book, you also qualify for a special bonus. Simply email your receipt or the first word of chapter 10 to loranahoopes@gmail.com and I'll send you a short PDF of Cassidy's time on the reality show. Just my way of saying thank you.

Sign up for Lorana Hoopes's newsletter and get her book, The Billionaire's Impromptu Bet, as a welcome gift. Get Started Now!

Cassidy Marcel gazed at the firehouse with trepidation. She loved her job, but she also knew firefighters. They loved to razz each other over everything, and her appearance on the reality dating show, Who Wants to Marry a Cowboy, would be no exception.

She'd gone on the show at the urging of her mother who was begging for grandkids, but Cassidy couldn't deny her biological clock was ticking as well. And it had come on suddenly. One day, she'd been content to be a single woman focusing on her career as a firefighter and the next, a desperate need to start a family had erupted within her. She'd begun dating again, but none of the men she had been out with fit the bill of what she was looking for – stable, self-sufficient, and a man of God.

So, when she'd seen that Tyler, the cowboy bachelor for this episode, was one, she'd re-considered her initial refusal and asked God for clarity. While she hadn't heard a loud voice in her head, she'd felt a sense of peace about it, and so she'd done the audition. And been chosen. And even felt a connection with Tyler. Until it became obvious that he had eyes for someone else. Now, she was back with a wounded ego, a bruised heart, and a feeling of confusion as she wondered if she'd been following her own will instead of God's. And she knew there would be teasing from her fellow firefighters.

Plus, she wondered how Captain Fitzgerald was going to react. The stony-faced Captain hadn't been her biggest fan before she took three weeks off; she assumed she would be even lower on his list now.

Inhaling deeply, she pulled her shoulders back hoping she appeared more confident than she felt. Then she opened her car door, tucked her dark hair behind her ears, and walked into the lion's den.

"Marcel, so glad you could grace us with your presence again." Billy Campbell, or Bubba, as everyone called him stood before her, a giant smile on his face. He was one of her favorite people in the firehouse. Originally from Texas, he had a heart bigger than his smile and was more like an older brother than a co-worker. "I didn't want you to feel like we didn't want you, so I thought this might help." From behind his back, he brandished a miniature black cowboy hat and held it out to her. Though small, it somehow sported sequins that caught and shimmered in the light.

Cassidy rolled her eyes good naturedly as she shook her head. She should have expected something like this, especially after the sugar incident last year. When Cassidy first joined the firehouse, they had celebrated by taking her out to a local dive that served decent food and boasted a karaoke night. None of her favorites had been available though, and Cassidy ended up singing Def Leopard's "Pour Some Sugar on Me." The next day, the guys had all presented her with bags of sugar throughout the day. Sugar wouldn't have to grace her grocery list for another six months at least.

"Haha, thanks, Bubba. I missed you too." She grabbed the hat knowing several more of these would be in store before the day was through. "Did I miss any excitement while I was gone?"

Bubba pushed open the door to the common room that doubled as a living room and the kitchen area. "Only if you count Luca's boycott of Deacon's Paleo meal plan."

"It's not a meal if there are no potatoes in it," Luca said speaking up from the couch. Luca was a Southern boy as well, and he believed every meal should include meat and potatoes. And chocolate. The man insisted that every meal come with a dessert which explained the extra twenty pounds he carried on his frame. Somehow though it didn't hinder him in his job. He was strong and agile and quicker than almost all of them. His eyes flicked up briefly from the television he was watching. "Oh, hey, Marcel, welcome back." He launched something at her without ever taking his eyes off the screen.

She knew what it was before it landed a few inches from her. Another miniature cowboy hat. This one was brown and had a tiny feather. Cassidy picked it up and flashed Luca a crooked grin. "Thanks, Luca. I missed you too."

"Forgive him. He didn't like the brownies I gave him with dinner last night, and he's still sour about it," Deacon said as he stepped around the island in the kitchen and toward her and Bubba. Strong and dark skinned, Deacon was the epitome of an oxymoron. His bulging muscles gave him an intimidating presence, but inside he was the biggest teddy bear. He pulled her in for a hug before brandishing his own miniature hat.

Cassidy chuckled as she took the hat though she had no idea what she was going to do with all of these. Though she had received a hat every time Tyler chose her to stay, the producers took them back afterwards to have for the next show. They had allowed her to keep the final hat as a souvenir, and though Cassidy wasn't sure she wanted to remember the show, she kept it as a reminder to never do something like that again.

"Brownies don't have prunes in them," Luca spoke up from the couch.

Cassidy lifted a brow at Deacon. "You made brownies with

prunes? Things really have changed in a month." It wasn't that prunes were completely out of the norm for Deacon. He regarded his body as a temple and rarely put anything processed in it, but he also wasn't one for sweets generally. He focused more on macronutrients and desserts rarely fit in his plan.

Deacon shrugged. "I thought I could slip some healthy desserts in on these guys. Keep them a little trimmer in the middle if you know what I mean." He patted his rock-hard abs.

"Might have worked too, if you hadn't eaten them as well," Bubba said with a deep laugh. "That was clue number one they had to be healthy. You really couldn't taste the prunes though, but man did they wreak havoc on my insides later."

"Okay, enough of that," Cassidy said shaking her head and squeezing her eyes shut. The image of a run on the bathroom was not the visual she wanted to have of her fellow firemen.

"Cassidy, oh my gosh, I'm so glad you're back."

Cassidy would have recognized Ivy's voice anywhere. Not only was she the only other woman in the firehouse, but her voice held just the slightest valley girl twang. On anyone else it might have been annoying, but Ivy was wholesomely sweet, down to earth, and as cute as a button. Her blonde hair perfectly framed her heart-shaped face, and big blue eyes sat above a perfectly-shaped nose that contained no trace of freckles, unlike Cassidy's.

Because Fire Beach wasn't a huge city, it made more sense to have the paramedics and the firefighters housed in the same place, so Ivy was often at the firehouse when Cassidy was. Dispatch usually sent both a firetruck and an ambulance to most calls though medical only calls were increasing which sent Ivy and the other paramedic out at other times as well.

Ivy attacked her with a hug before Cassidy was ready and the gesture jostled her full arms sending the tiny hats flying to the floor. Ivy's eyes widened as she released Cassidy and her petite hand flew to her mouth. "I'm so sorry. I was just so excited to see you. You don't know how awful it's been being the only woman here for the last month." She dropped to the floor to help Cassidy pick up the hats.

Ivy was teasing. Mostly. But Cassidy had been at the firehouse before Ivy arrived, and she remembered how hard it was being the only female. The guys didn't try to make her feel uncomfortable, but men and women were different. She'd been glad when Ivy joined to have another woman to talk to. "Don't worry about it. They're just silly hats, and I'm sorry I left you high and dry."

"Marcel? Is that you?"

Cassidy froze at the stern sound of her captain's voice. Having been recently promoted, Captain Darryl Fitzgerald was now all business. Every rule needed to be followed to the letter, and the teasing shut down when he was around. She snatched the hat and stood. "Good morning, Captain, what can I do for you?"

"You can follow me to my office. We need to have a chat."

"Of course, sir." Cassidy fought the anxiety clawing at her throat. Captain Fitzgerald was intimidating, but she had just returned. She couldn't have done anything too bad. Maybe it was about the hats. She would explain that the guys were just razzing her a little and then take them to her car so they were out of sight.

Cassidy's anxiety increased when Captain Fitzgerald shut the door to his office behind her. Closed door meetings rarely held a good outcome. Her hand rubbed the back of her neck. "Have I done something, sir?" She hated the slight tremble in her voice, but he controlled her future, and she loved her job.

"Sit." He pointed at one of the chairs opposite his desk and then walked to his own chair and sat down. Cassidy sat in the indicated chair and crossed her legs, then uncrossed them and sat straighter.

"I know that you had time saved up for this trip, but I need someone I can rely on in this firehouse." His steely eyes held hers as if daring her to challenge him.

Cassidy swallowed the knot in her throat and lifted her chin, hoping it came across as confidence and not sass. "I understand, sir, and I have no intention of going anywhere else anytime soon."

He leaned back in his chair and folded his arms across his chest. "That is good to hear, but to be sure, I am giving you some extra cleaning duties. You'll be in charge of cleaning the truck for the next month, and I want it sparkling at the end of every shift. Is that clear?"

Cassidy's mouth fell open, and she hurried to close it. She had no idea if he had the power to do that since she technically had done nothing wrong, but she wasn't going to argue with him. She loved this job and this house. No way did she want to go back to being a floater, so if he wanted her to wash the truck every day, she would do it. If he wanted to put her on kitchen duty, she would do that too even though her cooking left a lot to be desired. "Crystal clear, sir. I promise I am committed to this job and will do whatever it takes to prove it to you."

"Perfect, now we should discuss the mail situation." He steepled his fingers and regarded her with another cool stare. She was definitely on his list.

She furrowed her brow, confused as to what he could mean. "I'm sorry, the what?"

His eyebrow inched up his forehead. "You don't know?" Cassidy shook her head. "It appears you garnered a few fans while you were gallivanting on your show, and as they didn't know where you lived, they dropped your mail here."

Cassidy winced and bit the inside of her lip. No wonder he was angry. Captain Fitzgerald hated it when anything from the outside encroached on the sanctity of the fire house. "I had no idea, sir. I'm so sorry."

He waved a hand dismissing her. "It is what it is, but I want them gone from the firehouse at the end of your shift."

"Of course, sir. Um, where are they?"

He nodded to the corner of the room, and Cassidy turned spying a large brown bag that she hadn't noticed when they entered. Roughly the size of a burlap sack, it bulged and protruded as wide as appeared possible. "All of that is for me?"

"Yep, letters, gifts, you name it. I *suggest* you find a better place for it."

"Yes, sir." Cassidy pulled her shoulders back as she faced the mountainous bag. Since shift had just started, she might as well take it to the bunk room and go through it while there was time. She didn't need all of this cluttering her small apartment either.

The bag proved unwieldy but thankfully just enough extra sack remained at the top that she was able to drag it down the hallway and into the bunk room. Meant generally for sleeping when they worked long shifts, the bunk room held rows of two beds separated by half walls. A small table that contained only a lamp sat between each two-bed section.

She and Ivy shared the section at the very back of the room, and sweat rolled down Cassidy's spine as she pulled the bag to the bunk she normally slept in. With a sigh, she plopped down on the bunk and opened the bag. If Santa had been real, she would know exactly how he felt. She grabbed one of the envelopes and opened it.

*"Dear Cassidy, I saw you on the show, and I think we'd make a great couple. I love horses and roller skating. You can call me at 555-1324. Signed, David. P.S. If a woman answers, it's just my mom."*

Cassidy wrinkled her nose, shook her head, and laid the letter to the side. No need to keep that one. She wanted a man established enough that he lived on his own or maybe with a roommate. Rent wasn't cheap in the city, but moms were a no go. She wanted a man who had a good relationship with his mother but who didn't still live with his mother. She reached into the bag again. One down and only a few hundred to go. It was going to be a long afternoon.

Jordan issued his apology as he hurried into the office. "Sorry I'm late. We were chasing a lead."

"Of course you were," Graham said with a roll of his eyes.

Anger flared inside Jordan, and he lashed out at his brother. "They're missing kids, Graham. I think that's a little more important than whatever Dad may or may not have left us."

Graham held up his hands in surrender and Mr. Keyes, the attorney, cleared his throat as if hoping that might ease the tension in the room.

"It's no problem, Jordan, we were just getting started." Mr. Keyes adjusted his tie before placing his hands on either side of a stack of papers. "I'm sure you know that I called you in today for a reading of your father's will. Most of it is rather straightforward, but there is something I wasn't sure you were aware of." He picked up the top sheet of paper and scanned it before flipping it around to them. "Did you know your father owned a bar?"

"A bar?" Graham asked leaning forward.

"That's not possible. Dad was an alcoholic. Why would he own a bar?" Jordan asked.

"It hasn't been a bar in a long time. In fact, it hasn't been anything for a long time. I drove by the other day, so I would have current information for you both. It appears to be boarded up currently." He pulled a picture from the stack and slid it across the table to Graham who glanced at it before handing it to Jordan.

"So, we should try and sell it, right?" Jordan asked. He had no use for a bar or the rundown building in the picture.

"No, we can't sell it," Graham said shooting him an incredulous look. "Dad obviously kept the bar for a reason."

A reason? Jordan doubted it. Their father had spent most of his life so drunk that he rarely had a reason for anything. "He probably forgot he owned it and therefore had no presence of mind to sell it. What would we do with an old building?"

Mr. Keyes said nothing but shifted his gaze from one brother to the next as they argued.

"What would we do?" Graham turned in his chair to face Jordan, his face a picture of contempt. "We fix it up, give it new life, take it back to how it once was."

Jordan shook his head. Obsessed with focusing on the positive, Graham always wanted to fix things, even when the better option would be to stay out of it. "No way, I'm not opening a bar. I won't encourage drinking and enable the same behavior that claimed Dad."

"Fine, we'll turn it into a family restaurant then. A place where cops can hang out and have a sense of community." Graham had added that last part to try and persuade Jordan but he wasn't biting.

"I have no time to fix up a restaurant. Nor do I know anything about running a restaurant. And what about the money? Did Dad leave any money to fix this place?"

"Your father left you the proceeds from the sale of the house and he had a few stocks and bonds, but it isn't much."

And there it was. Their father hadn't kept the house in good enough condition to turn a profit and he hadn't thought about his sons' future either. He'd only thought about his next drink. "See? It isn't much. Probably not enough to renovate an old bar and turn it into a restaurant."

Graham folded his arms across his chest and turned away from Jordan. "I'm not selling. Dad could have sold the building years ago, and he didn't. That tells me it meant something to him, so I'm going to restore it with or without you."

Jordan turned fierce eyes on the lawyer. "Can he do that? Can he make me keep it?"

Mr. Keyes shrugged and offered an apologetic half smile. "He could offer to buy you out, but there is no stipulation that he has to sell."

Before he could say anything else, Jordan's phone buzzed. He swiped the screen and shook his head. Another kid had gone missing. "I have to go, but this isn't over. We are going to discuss this, Graham."

## 2

Cassidy blew out another exasperated breath as she surveyed the stacks of envelopes surrounding her. Who knew there were this many lonely men hoping to meet a woman they saw on television? Of course, they weren't all from men. She had gotten quite a few letters from women as well, mostly wishing her luck or telling her they were glad Tyler kept her around for as long as he did. There were even a few from young girls who said they wanted to be firefighters when they grew up too. Those made her smile. Firefighting was still a hard occupation for women to get into, but Cassidy enjoyed seeing the numbers rise each year.

"I was wondering where you went." Ivy's voice carried across the room as she approached. "Whoa, what is all that?"

Cassidy rolled her eyes and fanned her hands out. "This is my fan mail. Want to help?"

Ivy's blue eyes lit up and her smile shone with her exuberance. "Do I ever? I want all the juicy details, and you better not leave anything out." She pushed a few pieces of paper aside as she dropped onto the bed beside Cassidy and grabbed an envelope from the bag.

Normally, she loved sharing details with Ivy – the girls would often rehash their latest dates – but Cassidy didn't want to share the details of this experience. It reminded her too much of grade school when captains chose players for teams and there were always those kids who were chosen last every time. She'd been that kid once and she still remembered how much it hurt hearing every other name called. After that, she'd worked hard to improve her athletic skill so she wouldn't ever be the last one chosen again.

Being on the show had been similar. Her gut had clenched with every ceremony, and she'd sighed with relief when her name was finally called. The difference was, those women had not been her teammates but her competition. Eventually, there would only be one woman remaining, and while Cassidy knew that, she had still opened her heart to Tyler until it became clear he only had eyes for Laney.

"Not much to tell." Cassidy's eyes shifted back to the bag. She wouldn't begrudge the couple their happiness, but it was still a bruise to her ego and an experience she didn't want to relive. "Tyler wasn't really interested in any of us though I think we would have been good together."

Ivy stared at her, and Cassidy knew she was deciding whether to push it or leave the topic alone. Thankfully, she chose the latter. "Would you have moved to Texas for him and left all of this?" Ivy gestured around the room before tearing open an envelope and pulling out a letter.

Immediately, the heavy scent of cologne filled the air, and Ivy's face scrunched in disgust. She held the paper away from her face with one hand and covered her nose with the other. "Whew, I think whoever wrote this used half a bottle of cologne on this letter."

"Ugh." Cassidy waved her hand in front of her nose to try and lessen the stench. Axe. It would have to be Axe. It was her least favorite cologne and seemed to be the one of choice for most of the guys at her gym. The locker rooms always smelled of Axe when a class ended. "Don't even bother reading it. Just toss that one."

Ivy balled the letter up and tossed it across the room. It landed more than five feet from the trash can, but at only five foot three, Ivy wasn't much of a basketball player anyway. She shrugged and flashed a sheepish grin. "We'll get that one later, but I needed some air."

Cassidy took a tentative breath and nearly gagged. The stench still clung to the air. "We might need to get a fan. That doesn't appear to be dissipating."

"In a minute. First you have to answer my question." Ivy reached into the bag and pulled out another envelope.

"What was the question again?" Cassidy dropped her eyes to the envelope in her hand. She knew the question but was hoping Ivy might have forgotten.

Ivy put her envelope down and cocked an eyebrow at Cassidy putting on her best 'you can't fool me' expression. "You know very well what the question was, missy. Would you have moved and left all of this?"

"I don't know." Cassidy unfolded the letter she had opened and pondered the question. It was a question she had asked herself since she'd heard about the reality show. Her work was here as were her friends and her church, but if finding the perfect man meant moving, then she supposed she would do that too. "I love it here, but I'd also like to get married one day and start a family. If we had connected and that meant moving to Texas, I think I would have."

"You don't have to move all the way to Texas to get married. We have a ton of available men right here in Fire Beach, Illinois." Ivy wiggled her eyebrows suggestively and grinned at Cassidy.

If only that were true. "Yeah, men who want Barbie dolls like you not tomboys like me." Cassidy had never been the one guys flocked to of her friends. Generally, she was the one guys befriended so they could pick her brain and find out about her other friends. Whether it was her thicker stature or her job or her tomboy nature, Cassidy didn't know, but she was tired of being alone. Well, not entirely alone. She had her friends and her church, but those didn't really count. Not in the way she wanted.

"Uh, I think this stack here shows that's not always true." Ivy gestured at the massive pile in front of them and the papers on the bed around them. "I've never gotten paper cuts opening all my fan mail."

"Well, you would if you had been on national television." Actually, Ivy probably would have gotten three times as much fan mail. Cassidy still didn't understand how her friend was single except that she was picky. Every time she found a new man, she also found something wrong with him. She was beginning to wonder if Ivy even wanted a relationship.

Her eyes dropped to the envelope she had pulled out and she scanned the writing as she continued. "So far, there's been nothing worth writing home about in here anyway. I think most of them are lonelier than I am...." Her voice trailed off as she read the letter again.

"What?" Ivy asked clearly picking up on the change in Cassidy's voice.

Cassidy didn't want to read the words out loud. With a trembling hand, she passed the letter to Ivy who perused it, her eyes widening before she finished. Fear coursed through them when she looked at Cassidy again. "Does the captain know about this?"

Cassidy shook her head. "I doubt it. He gave me the bag, but all the envelopes were inside and so far, they have all been sealed."

Ivy bit her lip as she looked at the still mostly full bag. Then she pulled back her petite shoulders and exhaled. "Let's finish reading the rest and see if there are any more. Then, I think we need to think about showing this to him."

"I'm sure it's nothing," Cassidy began. She didn't want to make a big display out of it, especially on her first shift back.

"Maybe, but what if it's not? You can't mess around with this, Cass. This is your life we are talking about."

Ivy was right, but this was not how Cassidy had imagined returning to work. She was already on the captain's radar. This might send him over the edge, but if this stalker turned out to be real and not just threatening words on paper, it would be worse if she didn't tell him.

Jordan ran a hand across his stubbled chin as he stared at the run-down building. It was even worse than he'd pictured. Graffiti covered the walls and the boards over the windows. The building was brick, so the structure might at least be sound but who knew what would be waiting inside.

Jordan had spent the little time he had that afternoon trying to convince Graham to sell, but his brother had been adamant their father would have wanted them to re-open the bar. Jordan wasn't so sure. Their father hadn't even told them about this bar, much less run it the last thirty years, but then they hadn't spoken to their father much in the last few years. Not since their mother left him.

Jordan had been fifteen then and old enough to remember all the times their father yelled and hit and threw things. The broken glass, the black eyes, the lies. Graham, on the other hand, had only been ten, and either he had blocked out those moments or been so desperate for a father that he didn't care. Graham had visited their father several times when he had reached out to them and claimed he was sober, but Jordan couldn't stomach the man. How could a father do what he'd done?

With a sigh, Jordan stepped out of his car. His hand touched his side to make sure his gun was properly holstered. He went nowhere without it, and he'd worn it so long that he often felt incomplete if it wasn't strapped in its usual place.

Graham had said they would meet outside and go in together, but as Jordan was late and Graham was nowhere to be seen, he assumed his brother had started without him. Figured.

"I thought you were going to be here two hours ago." Graham's annoyed voice carried across the large room as Jordan pulled open the front door.

"Case ran long. What can I say? I'm here now." He shrugged out of his leather jacket and laid it across a table before rolling up the sleeves of his shirt. Then he placed his gun on top. His eyes scanned the room, but it was as bad as he'd expected. Old tables and chairs coated in a white layer of dust took up most of the space. The bar was a mahogany monstrosity that had probably been popular in the seventies if the orange and red colors of it were any indication. Shattered glass was all that remained of the mirror that had once stretched behind the bar. At least both of them would be going. Graham had agreed to not have a bar in the restaurant.

Graham put down his hammer and folded his arms across his chest. Fire burst from his eyes as he fixed Jordan with a fierce stare. "Are you saying my time isn't important? I had things to do this evening too, but I was here at five like we said we would be."

Jordan rolled his eyes, tired of this argument. Graham did this every time he was late for something, and okay, Jordan was late a lot, but generally for good reason. His job as an intelligence officer in the police unit often had him working crazy hours, but he wouldn't trade it for the world. Graham on the other hand sold insurance. Predictable was his middle name, and Jordan doubted he'd had anything planned except working on his computer which appeared to be his only hobby. Sometimes

Jordan wondered if they truly were related as they were so different.

"No, I'm not saying my time is more important." Though he was fairly certain it was. Graham wasn't getting criminals off the street; he was writing insurance policies and taking pictures. "I'm simply explaining why I'm late, but Graham, look around, man. This place is going to break the bank trying to fix it up. We should sell it and cut our losses."

Graham pushed his glasses up his nose and shook his head. "This is all cosmetic, Jordan. A little hard work and elbow grease will fix this place right up. As long as the walls are good, we'll have no trouble re-opening this."

Jordan bit the inside of his cheek to keep his frustration in check. He didn't want to spend his time fixing up this place. He had little free time as it was, but Graham had that gleam in his eye - the one that said he'd already made up his mind and nothing Jordan said was going to change it. Jordan supposed he could pull his big brother card and put his foot down, but Graham seemed to need this, and after years of looking out for him, Jordan still felt like he owed his little brother something to make up for his childhood. And if that meant opening a restaurant, he would find a way to make it work. "Fine, how do we tell if the walls are good?"

Graham picked the hammer back up and turned to the wall. "We remove this paneling and look inside the walls. Then we'll have a better idea of how much this renovation is going to cost."

"More than we have," Jordan said under his breath. Well, more than he had anyway. Graham made decent money selling insurance, but Jordan was paid by the city and few people got rich off a city paycheck. He grabbed the extra hammer and joined Graham at the wall. "What happens if what we find behind this paneling isn't good?" he asked as he jammed the back of the hammer into a space between panels. Images of termite eaten wood filled his mind along with the thousands of dollars it would take to fix them. "Then will you consider selling?"

"No, it will just mean it will take more money to fix it up. One way or the other, I am re-opening this place, Jordan."

Of course he was. It didn't really matter what Jordan said. Even though Graham was younger, he had always been bossy. It was probably one reason they did so few things together. Well, that and Jordan's schedule. As a special unit detective, he was basically on call most of the time. He worked a normal shift, but it wasn't unusual for his normal shift to turn into a much longer one if they caught a lead on a case.

Jordan wedged the hammer under a crack in the paneling and heaved. The wood screamed in protest - a high pitched squeal that was unpleasant to the ears but thankfully short. With a loud crack, the wood broke in half. Jordan pulled on the broken piece until it came loose from the wall. Then he tossed it aside and ripped the top piece off as well.

Jordan wasn't sure what he had expected to find behind the paneling having never torn any off before, but it certainly wasn't the rolls of paper he saw. "What is this, Graham?" He held the roll up for his brother.

"I don't know, but I have some over here too." Graham grabbed a roll from his section of the wall and motioned for Jordan to follow him to a table.

They unrolled the tubes and Jordan stared in disbelief at the image before him. "Are these…."

"Movie posters," Graham finished. "And they look old."

Jordan gazed down at the woman in flapper attire. "Old? These look like they're from the twenties. What was Dad doing with these?"

"Who cares? Do you know how much these are worth?" Graham asked. Excitement threaded his voice and Jordan could almost see the dollar signs in his eyes. Leave it to Graham to focus only on the money. "Come on, let's see how many there are."

Jordan followed Graham back to the wall. He hoped they might be worth enough to help with renovations, but he was still curious as to where they came from and how their alcoholic father ended up with not only a bar but rare movie posters paneled in the walls.

## 3

C assidy stood outside Captain Fitzgerald's office gathering her courage. She knew she had to tell him, especially if there was any possibility that the stalker might come to the firehouse and put her or her fellow firefighters in danger, but it didn't make the conversation any easier. He was already angry she had gone on the show. Cassidy had no idea how he would react to this.

"Come in." His gruff voice carried through the closed door at her knock. Was he like this with everyone? She had always felt he didn't really like her, but unless the man was psychic, he couldn't know she was at his door. Swallowing her fear, she pulled her shoulders back and entered the office.

In addition to being fierce and laconic, Captain Fitzgerald was a minimalist. His bookshelf sported more space than books and only one picture frame sat on his desk. Like the man himself, everything was neat and meticulous and in its proper place.

"Captain, can I have a minute?" Her voice was too quiet and what was with the tremble? Why did he have such a power over her? Was it simply because he was her boss?

His gaze flicked to hers, and his eyebrow arched on his stony face. "Marcel. I thought you'd be busy opening all your fan mail or cleaning the truck as I tasked you with doing."

Cassidy took another step in, forcing her eyes up from the worn carpet to the intimidating figure behind the desk. "I was, sir, opening the mail that is. I haven't gotten to the truck yet, but I will." Ugh, she was rambling, and her heart was thudding in her ears. She took a deep breath and tried again. "The letters are what I need to talk to you about. There were a few that stood out that I thought you should know about."

His piercing gaze fixed hers for a moment as if scanning her for a sign of weakness. Then he rolled his eyes and motioned her closer to the desk. "What is it then?"

Cassidy held out the three letters they had found that appeared to be from the same man. "The handwriting appears to be the same and the word choice looks consistent, so I'm fairly certain these are from the same guy. He seems to escalate, and while he might be harmless, I wanted to make sure you were aware of these. Just in case."

With a sigh, Captain Fitzgerald picked up the first letter and scanned it. His jaw tightened as he turned the page and his features grew stonier with each one. "Do you know this man?" he asked Cassidy when he had finished reading.

"No, sir. At least I don't think I do. I don't recognize the writing, and he didn't leave a name or a return address." Of course, she couldn't remember the last time a man had written her anything. A note, a card – it had definitely been a while.

"Wonderful, so we have no idea who or what we are looking for. You've put this firehouse in danger Marcel with your publicity stunt."

It hadn't been a publicity stunt, but Cassidy was not going to argue the point with the man. "I'm sorry, sir. That was never my intention."

"Be that as it may, you have. I'll bring this up in the next meeting and inform everyone to be on the watch for shady characters hanging around the house. As for you, if you receive anything else from this person or any unusual things start happening to you, I want you to call the police. I need your mind on the job and not on this."

"Yes, sir. I will." How she was supposed to keep her mind completely on work with the words from the letter running through her brain she wasn't sure, but she would try.

"Good. Now, I think it's about time you got to the trucks."

"Yes, sir." Cassidy took the clear dismissal and backed out of the office. It had been bad, but not as bad as she'd expected it to be.

"What happened?" Ivy asked when Cassidy returned to the bunk room. She had cleaned up the pile of mail and cleared the beds. Cassidy wondered briefly what she had done with all the other letters but decided she didn't care. She wished she could put the whole experience behind her and just forget about it. No, she wished she had never gone on the show in the first place.

Cassidy sighed as she sank onto her bunk. "He's going to share it at the next staff meeting."

"That's it?" Ivy's eyes grew wide with concern and her fingers tugged on a lock of her hair. Either a nervous gesture or a long-ingrained habit, Ivy pulled at her split ends whenever anything bothered her.

Cassidy shrugged trying to mask the fear she felt inside. "He seemed angry but not especially concerned. Told me to watch out for anything else strange and take it to the cops if anything happened. Then he told me to get to cleaning the trucks."

"Well, if he doesn't think it's a big deal, then maybe it isn't. He's been doing this job a long time, so he probably knows."

"Yeah, let's hope so. Anyway, I better get out there and get to cleaning." She wanted to clean about as much as she wanted to watch paint dry, but at least it would get her mind off this stalker for a while.

"Have fun with that. I'd offer to help, but I don't know the first thing about cleaning fire trucks."

"It's fine. It's actually a fairly tame penance for as mad as he was." Cassidy pushed herself off the bed and headed to the truck bay, but before she could even begin gathering the supplies to wash the truck, the alarm sounded.

"Truck 51, Squad 4, Ambulance 3, 2219 Eastside Street."

"You remember how to do this?" Bubba asked Cassidy as he hurried past her to his gear.

Cassidy shot him a withering look. "I think I can manage it." She followed him to the hooks that held their gear and pulled on hers. Donning them was like riding a bicycle, but she'd forgotten how heavy the extra equipment was. Still, she was determined not to show it. The boys needed no more ammunition with which to tease her. Hat in hand, she climbed up beside Bubba and took a deep breath to slow her racing heart. Then she closed her eyes and sent up a prayer for their safety.

"Whoa, hot date last night?" Alayna "Al" Parker asked as Jordan set his extra-large coffee mug down on the desk across from her. Her hazel eyes twinkled mischievously above her petite nose. With perfectly clear skin and long blonde hair, Al looked more like she was eighteen than her actual age of nearly thirty which helped with stings but annoyed her the rest of the time. She got carded everywhere.

Jordan blew out an exasperated breath as he collapsed into his chair and took a swig of coffee. "I wish. My brother and I inherited an old bar and we were up most of the night tearing off paneling and assessing the damage."

Al's eyebrow shot up. "You're keeping a bar?" She knew a little about his past and his father and was obviously shocked by this news.

"No, I'm keeping an old building that *used* to be a bar. Unfortunately. We're remodeling it to be a family-friendly restaurant sans bar." He rolled his eyes and downed another swig. Even this large triple shot coffee wasn't making him feel more alive. "Graham thinks it will be great."

"And what do you think?"

He shook his head as a frustrated laugh escaped his lips. "I think it's a money suck and we should sell it. I don't have time to fix up or run a restaurant. I barely have time to buy groceries for myself."

"So, why'd you say yes? Why not just make him buy you out?"

And there was the million-dollar question. "Because he's my little brother. Because he had a crappy childhood." Jordan had told Al most of his past already, so he knew this wouldn't come as a shock to her. "I've spent half my life looking out for him and trying to make him happy. I guess I'm still doing it."

"I could help," Al said with a shrug.

"You?" Al was tough, probably more than she needed to be, but he still couldn't see her hauling out old furniture and decorating the interior.

"Yeah, I grew up with two older brothers. I learned how to swing a hammer." She leaned closer and glanced around the small room, "and though I don't do it here, I know how to use a broom."

Jordan chuckled at her persistence. Not many of his other friends would volunteer to do dirty work. "All right, I'll keep that in mind."

"Where are we on the abduction cases?" Jack Stone asked as he entered immediately shifting the energy in the room. Though Jordan was sure it was his real last name, it was ironic how well it fit him. In his mid-fifties, Jack had a full head of salt and pepper hair that he kept immaculately cut - probably an old habit from the military. His face rarely displayed any emotion and even his voice was deep and gravelly. More importantly, he was good at his job, and he didn't like to lose.

Jordan tapped his phone to make sure he hadn't missed any last-minute messages before giving his report. "I spoke with my criminal informant, but all he could tell me was that he thinks he saw a kid matching our description leave Hyder Park with a man wearing dark clothing."

"That isn't much to go on," Stone said, disappointment in his voice. "How about you?" He turned his attention to Al whose thin shoulders pulled back as she sat straighter.

"I found a camera that might have gotten footage near where we think one of the abductions happened. I was planning on going there today to see."

"Good, the two of you do that." Stone walked to the white board where all their evidence hung. Though his gaze traveled over everything, it remained the longest on the pictures of the three kids – one girl and two boys. "Albright and Givens are canvassing the neighborhoods again and doling out advice to keep kids safe, but that's only going to last so long. This guy will strike again, and we need to find him before he does."

"Yes, sir." Jordan downed the last of his coffee as he stood. No time for more. He would have to hope his adrenaline would kick in and keep him awake. Across from him, Al grabbed her jacket as well and headed for the door. He hurried to catch up with her and followed her down to the car. Generally, he preferred driving but this was her lead, and he would let her run with it.

"So, your restaurant. Are you going to let me come help?" Al threw the question out nonchalantly as she reached for her seat-belt, but Jordan sensed something deeper behind it. He'd had the feeling she was looking for more than a partnership the last month, but he wasn't interested. He didn't have time for a rela-tionship and his mother had always impressed upon him that he should never date where he worked. Plus, his last one had gone up in flames, so he wasn't looking to jump into the fire again anytime soon.

"Yeah, maybe. It's still a mess right now."

She flashed a crooked smile at him as she turned the key and fired up the engine. "I don't mind a little mess."

Jordan knew that. While his workspace was always pristine, hers was often overflowing with papers. She called it creative genius, but he just called it a mess, and he had no idea how she found anything she was looking for. "I know you don't, but I'm not sure what the next step is. I'll definitely let you know when I have a better idea." Or not. He didn't want to do anything that might make her think he wanted more than a partnership. "So, where are we going?"

She glanced quickly at him before turning her attention back to the road. "A convenience store over on Fifth. It's near the school where we think one of the boys was grabbed."

Jordan could tell she knew he had changed the subject on her, but it was safer this way. Dating your partner opened the door for lapses in judgment that could get you killed, and if they broke up, it would make for a very uncomfortable work environment. "Good catch. I hope they have something."

༄ 4 ༄

Fatigue weighed on Cassidy as she walked to her car the next morning. Twenty-four-hour shifts were hard on their own, but add a fire into the mix and they were downright exhausting. Plus, she hadn't pulled a long shift in over a month. She hadn't thought her body would become out of sync so quickly, but it had. Normally, she would have three or four of these shifts in a row, but the captain had given her just one to let her ease back into the routine. She had the rest of the day to recoup and then she'd be back on shift tomorrow.

Cassidy opened the driver side door and threw her bag in before sliding into the seat, but as she shoved the key in the ignition, something caught her eye. Glancing up, she spied something white tucked into her windshield wipers. A ticket? But that made no sense. She was in the firehouse's parking lot and not parked in a handicapped space. A note? Ice trickled into her veins. Was it another message from the stalker?

On high alert, her eyes darted around the parking lot for any shadows or unknown strangers. Curiosity chomped at her nerves, but she wasn't going to get out of the car until she knew it was safe.

Assured there was no one else in the lot or at least not close enough to nab her in the time it would take her to grab the note, Cassidy opened her door and snatched the paper off the glass. Not wanting to take any chances, she clutched it in her hand until the car door was closed and locked again. Then she summoned her courage and unfolded the paper.

The handwritten words appeared angry and threatening on the single sheet with a definite hurried slant. Unsure if police would be able to gain much information just from the handwriting, she scanned for anything else that might be usable - an added symbol, a signature, a fingerprint smudge, but there was nothing. Nothing to give any clue who was writing this. However, the wording was consistent with the other letters - "I can show you that we belong together."

But it was the final phrase that set her heart thudding in her chest. "I don't know why you aren't responding to me, but if you don't believe me, I'll find a way to show you." The words alone held a chill but when added to the rest of the letters, the chill turned into flat out fear. And this hadn't come in the mail. It had been put on her car which meant that he'd watched her arrive yesterday when she came into shift. And if he knew what she drove, what if he followed her home? As much as she didn't want to, this was something the captain needed to know. However, as walking the parking lot no longer felt safe, Cassidy drove to as close to the front entrance as possible before hurrying out of the car and inside.

"Marcel, what is it? I thought I sent you home," Captain Fitzgerald said as she tapped on his door frame.

"You did, sir, but before I made it out of the parking lot, I found this." She held up the paper. "It's another note, and he left it on my windshield."

Captain Fitzgerald's eyes widened. Only slightly. But it was enough to increase the fear Cassidy was already feeling. If he was reacting, it meant he was worried, and if he was worried, she definitely should be.

"I'm calling Stone. It's time you told the police about this." Stone was the head of the special investigation unit. Cassidy knew little about him other than his fierce reputation implied his name fit him to a tee.

Captain Fitzgerald picked up the phone and dialed before Cassidy could speak, so she simply nodded and waited.

"Stone? It's Fitzgerald. I have a situation occurring over here. One of my firefighters is getting threatening notes, the latest one on her windshield while here on shift. Cassidy Marcel. Yeah, the one who was on the TV show." He paused and glanced at Cassidy. "Yeah, I can do that. Thank you."

He replaced the phone in the cradle. "Stone is sending someone over. You will stay here until he arrives and you will do what he says. Is that understood?"

Cassidy opened her mouth to protest. The fierce independent part of her wanted to tell Captain Fitzgerald that she didn't need some cop telling her what to do. However, she had to admit this stalker had her on edge and a part of her was relieved to have the police involved. "Yes, sir. I will."

After leaving the office, Cassidy wandered back to the bunk room to wait for whoever Stone was sending over. She knew no one in the special investigation unit, but if they worked for him, they were bound to be good. The man had a reputation for being thorough and hard on anyone who wanted to be in his unit.

"Marcel? What are you doing back? I thought the Captain sent you home." Bubba's voice carried out of the kitchen as she passed the common room.

She didn't want to worry him, especially since he acted like a big brother, but he would be more annoyed if she didn't tell him. With a small sigh, she changed her course and entered the kitchen. "Hey, Bubba. I, um, have to wait to give a statement to one of Stone's guys."

He set the towel down he had been using to dry dishes, crossed his beefy arms, and fixed her with a penetrating gaze that said she better spill all. "Why?"

Cassidy plopped down in one of the barstools across the counter from him and sighed. Her eyes focused on the Formica counter and the light gold sparkles sprinkled throughout it. "Because someone left a threatening note on my windshield."

"And?" Bubba should have been a detective himself. He seemed to have an internal radar that knew when there was more to the story.

"And since it appears to be from the same person who was sending me stalkerish letters while I was on the show, the captain wants me to report it." Cassidy spat the words out in a rush and waited for the tongue lashing she was sure he was about to dole out.

"As he rightly should. Why didn't you tell me about this earlier?" Though his voice held no anger, there was a clear expression of disapproval on his face at being left out of the loop.

"Well, to be fair, Captain Fitzgerald said he would mention it at the next staff meeting, and then we kind of got busy with the fire." Cassidy was making excuses, and she could tell he knew it, but she couldn't tell him the real truth. She could tell him she hadn't wanted to worry him which was partly true. She could tell him she hadn't thought it was a big deal which wasn't true at all, but neither of those was the real reason. The real reason she hadn't told him was because she didn't want him looking at her the way he was now. Like she couldn't handle herself. Like she needed to be rescued. Like she wasn't a real firefighter because she was afraid of something.

That last thought was stupid and she knew it. All firefighters were afraid of something. Besides, he probably wasn't thinking any of those things, but she was a woman in a man's field. She had to be better, she had to be stronger, and she hated that she wasn't.

"You should have told me, Cass." Disappointment clouded his voice and filled his stiff posture.

"I know." She dropped her eyes to the counter again. "I'm sorry. I thought it was nothing, just some random fan, you know? But when I found the note on my car, I knew it was more serious."

"Hey." He placed a finger under her chin and tilted it up. "I know you think you have to prove yourself here, but you don't. We know how strong you are. Don't do something stupid by trying to be a hero when your family is here to support you. Always."

Tears sprung to Cassidy's eyes. He was right of course. They might tease her, but these men put their lives on the line with her every time they went into a fire together. They trusted her inside the burning heat and would support her outside of it. "I won't. I promise."

"Cassidy Marcel, you have a visitor at the front desk."

Cassidy looked up at the intercom and shrugged. "Gotta go, but I'll fill you in later."

"You better," he hollered after her.

"Jordan, in my office a moment."

Jordan's head snapped up at Stone's command. Al shot him a wide-eyed look that held the same question his mind did. What had he done? He shook his head to tell her he didn't know as he pushed back his chair.

"Yes, sir?" he asked as he breached the doorway.

"Come in and shut the door."

Jordan pulled the door shut behind him and then sat in one of the chairs across the desk. He shouldn't be nervous. He'd done

nothing wrong, but Stone had the ability to send your heart thudding with just the tone of his voice. "What can I do for you, sir?"

"Captain Fitzgerald called. Evidently one of his firemen is
receiving threatening notes. He wants someone over there to
investigate it." Stone's steely gaze was meant to keep Jordan
from questioning his orders, but Jordan couldn't help himself.

"But sir, I'm in the middle of this abduction case, and
my CI-"

"We're all in the middle of this abduction case, but Fitzgerald
is a firefighter and we look after each other. If he says he needs
our help then we give our help. Is that understood?"

Jordan didn't understand why he had to go. This was probably the case of some lonely woman who'd been rescued and
was now suffering from the Florence Nightingale effect. It
happened to rescuers all the time. In fact, he'd had a few women
express their undying love for him after particularly dangerous
cases. Why couldn't Stone send Al or one of the other less senior
members? But it wasn't his place to question. Stone was in
charge. "Yes, sir. I'll go check it out."

"Good. She's waiting at the firehouse for you."

"She?"

Stone's brow arched as he regarded Jordan. "Yes, she. It's
Cassidy Marcel."

Jordan stifled a groan. "The one who was on the reality
dating show?" He never watched it, but Al did and when she
found out someone from their city was on it, she had regaled him
with a recap of every episode.

"That's the one. You have a problem with that?"

"It's just," Jordan ran a hand across his stubbled chin, "it's
probably just some lonely guy who is looking for a little fame.
Wouldn't I be more useful here working on finding these kids?"

"Would you feel that way if it were your mother or your
sister or your girlfriend?"

Jordan stifled a sigh. He still didn't want to spend time

dealing with a stalker, but Stone was right. If this had happened to a woman in his life, he would want the best person possible looking into the case and protecting her. "Fine. Point taken. I'll head over there now."

Stone nodded and turned his attention to his computer. The discussion was clearly over, and Jordan took his cue and left the office.

"Where are you going?" Al asked as he grabbed his jacket off the back of his chair.

"To the firehouse. I'm sure I'll be back soon."

"You want me to come along?"

"No, I've got this. Keep looking for more footage. I want to get this guy before we lose any more kids."

Twenty minutes later, he pulled into the firehouse parking lot. His eyes scanned the lot as he parked, but other than the car blocking the entrance, nothing seemed out of the ordinary. Was that an employee's car? Or had the stalking escalated? There'd been no call over the radio, so surely there wasn't a hostage situation, but then why was the car parked like that? It was a clear fire hazard.

He checked his gun as he stepped out of his car, but it was safely strapped to his side and nothing gave him cause to pull it as he crossed the parking lot to the front door. Unsure what he had expected, he was still taken aback by the door opening to a small atrium with a reception desk.

"Can I help you?" the woman occupying the desk asked.

"I'm Detective Jordan Graves to see Cassidy Marcel." He flashed his badge to assure her of his identity as he rarely wore a uniform. His work required him to blend in, not stand out.

The woman gave a perfunctory nod and picked up the phone. "Cassidy Marcel, you have a visitor at the front desk." She replaced the phone and motioned him to the few chairs in the room. "She'll be here in a minute. You may sit if you'd like."

Jordan preferred to stand. It was easier to be ready should anything happen, but he didn't have to wait long anyway.

"I'm Cassidy." A woman with long brown hair pulled back in a ponytail which accentuated her broad shoulders and slender neck approached him. She wasn't quite what he'd expected as little makeup graced her face though it was peppered with miniature freckles. She had the air of an athlete rather than the prima donna he'd imagined. A few papers were clutched tightly in one hand, but she extended the other to him in greeting.

"Detective Jordan Graves." He shook her outstretched hand wondering why she had gone on a reality dating show. Low self-esteem? A bet? Or was she one of those girls who looked low maintenance but demanded constant attention? He knew that type well. His last girlfriend had been one.

"Shall we go somewhere quiet so I can fill you in?" she asked. Her voice was soft and sweet and not at all like the princess-type voice he had expected.

At his nod, she led the way down the hall and into a conference room. When the door was closed behind them, he pulled out a chair and sat down. Might as well jump right in. The faster he finished here, the sooner he could get back to finding missing kids. "Okay, so tell me what's going on."

Cassidy sat across from him and straightened the papers before placing her hands on them. She took a deep breath as if summoning the courage to speak. "Yesterday was my first day back on shift. I took some time off to do a show."

"A reality dating show. I'm aware." He hoped she hurried this up because he wanted to get back to his investigation.

A pink flush crawled across her cheeks. "Yeah, a dating show. Anyway, when I arrived yesterday, I had a bag of fan mail. Captain Fitzgerald made me go through it and when I did, I found a few letters that gave me pause." She pushed the first few pieces of paper across the table to him.

Jordan picked the first one up by the corner and scanned the contents.

*Dear Cassidy,*

*I'm enjoying watching you on the show, but you deserve better than Tyler. In fact, I think we would be perfect together.*

The writer was clearly enamored with Cassidy but other than stating he felt they belonged together, there wasn't anything sinister in it. He set that page aside and read the next letter.

*Dear Cassidy,*

*Tyler wouldn't know a good woman if she were given to him on a platter. I know how to treat a woman better, and I would love the chance to show you.*

More of the same but still nothing to get upset about. He hoped she hadn't called him here just for these. Jordan glanced at Cassidy as he put that page aside as well, but her intense expression didn't give the impression she was simply seeking attention.

He turned his attention to the third letter, and his eyes widened slightly.

*Dear Cassidy,*

*I don't know what you see in Tyler. I would treat you so much better and I'll prove it when you return from the show.*

"Did you receive any letters on set from his guy?"

Cassidy shook her head as her bottom lip folded in under her teeth. "I don't even know who this guy is. While I was on the show, I had no contact with anyone, and I had no knowledge of who was watching. I didn't even know I was getting fan mail until I walked in the door yesterday morning."

He raised a brow at her but said nothing. She might not have known about it, but she probably enjoyed it. After all, who went on a reality dating show if they weren't looking for attention? "Is there anyone in your life who paid you extra attention before you went on the show? Anyone who gave you pause?"

Cassidy pursed her lips as she thought. "There's a guy who's a little odd in my apartment complex. He's always walking his dog and he tries to strike up a conversation whenever I'm around, but he seems harmless. Besides, wouldn't he just leave notes on my door if it were him?"

"Maybe, but if he's tried to get your attention that way and failed, he might try something like this. What's his name?"

"Dustin, I think." She dropped her eyes to the table as if embarrassed. "He told me once, but to be honest, I didn't pay much attention."

Jordan nodded. That didn't surprise him, but he couldn't fault her as he was guilty of the same thing. He knew there were women who'd talked to him whom he hadn't been interested in and had dismissed. It was something he was working on, but he certainly hadn't mastered it yet. "That's understandable. How about ex-boyfriends or men you turned down?"

A flush of pink spread across her cheeks. "I haven't had an ex-boyfriend in some time, and he left me so I'm not sure why he'd stalk me. There have been a few men who asked me out after I saved them from a fire, but I always said no and never heard anything else from them."

He wondered what her story was. She was pretty, not model beautiful, but attractive in her own way, and she appeared confident in her own skin – a quality a lot of women he had dated seemed to be missing. Maybe, like him, she was just too focused on her career right now, but then why go on a reality dating show in the first place?

"Do you remember any of their names?"

"My ex, sure, but the rest," she shook her head sadly, "I don't. I never really knew them in the first place."

Great. That didn't give him much to work with. "Well, the letters don't sound like your ex. They're worded differently, not like someone who knows you personally. Unfortunately, that doesn't help us narrow it down much. I'd say just keep your eyes open and be aware of your surroundings."

"There's more," Cassidy said. "Today, when I left, I found

this on my windshield." She slid the final piece of paper to him. "I don't know how he expected me to respond since he never left a name or a return address."

He picked it up and scanned the writing.

*Cassidy,*

*I know you're back in town, and now I can show you that we belong together. I don't know why you're not responding to me, but we will be together whether you know it or not. We belong together, and I'll find a way to show you. I'll be in touch soon.*

Okay, maybe he was being too hard on her. He doubted this was the kind of attention she had been seeking. The guy was escalating, and he could see why Captain Fitzgerald would want her to report it. "You say this was on your windshield?"

She nodded and her right hand lifted to tug at her earlobe. Nervous gesture? He had seen few people display that particular gesture, but she didn't wear earrings, so a nervous gesture made the most sense.

"He must be someone you've had contact with before, but it could have been any contact. Often stalkers build a relationship in their head over little things, so he might be someone you met in a store or helped at a fire. He thinks you had a connection, so he believes he's given you enough clues to know who he is. This note on your car means he was probably hanging around when you arrived. Do you remember seeing anything out of the ordinary?"

Another tug as her eyes darted to the side. "No, but I wasn't looking for anything. It was my first day back on shift. I was just glad to be here." She dropped her hand from her ear and folded it into the other one before fixing him with her dark brown eyes. They were rich and deep, the color of dark chocolate, and they held the tiniest hint of vulnerability. "What do I do?"

Jordan cleared his throat and focused his attention on the papers. He had no business reading anything in her eyes. He was too busy on his current case for anything else. "Unfortunately, there still isn't much we can do at this point. I'll take this in for processing, but I doubt they'll find anything. They're short for one thing, and while handwriting can tell us about a person, there isn't a database of handwriting to compare this with like there is with fingerprints. Do you have the envelopes they came in? Was there a return address?"

As a wince crossed her features, he knew before she spoke that she no longer had them. "No, no return address, but I think Ivy threw the envelopes away. I didn't think we'd need them."

Of course she hadn't. "Who's Ivy?"

"One of our paramedics and my friend. She helped me open the envelopes. There were a lot of them."

He glanced up at her. Was she bragging? Maybe his first impression of her being a diva had been right. "Okay, I'll follow up with her to see if we can get those envelopes back. There might be DNA if he licked them. In the meantime, I'll escort you home. He may already know where you live, but if not, perhaps a police tail will discourage him from following. I'll check out your place before you enter to make sure it's clear, and then I'll sit on your block for the next hour."

He reached into his pocket and pulled out one of his cards. They didn't hand them out often, but the simple card contained his name and cell number so that CIs or people like Cassidy could get a hold of him quickly. "If you see anything after that time, you call this number, and I'll be there. If something happens, we'll get a police detail on you until we catch this guy. Any questions?"

Cassidy turned the card over in her hands before flashing another disarming, crooked smile his direction. "I probably have so many, but I don't even know what to ask right now."

Jordan nodded and pushed back his chair. "That's understandable." Careful to touch the papers as little as possible, he folded them and tucked them in the Ziplock bag he pulled from his pocket. "I doubt we'll find anything on these, but I'll have the lab run it for prints anyway. Did anyone else touch it?"

Cassidy blinked at him. "Um, Captain Fitzgerald might have when I first showed it to him and Ivy touched the first few but not the one on the windshield."

"Okay, I'll get prints from all of you so we can rule them out, but let's get you home first."

Her eyes shifted to the side again and when they returned to his gaze, they held just the slightest hint of fear. "What if he follows us back and learns where I live?"

Diva or not, his heart went out to her. He knew what it was like to live in fear – he'd done it for the first fifteen years of his life, and while it made him who he was today, he wouldn't wish it on anyone. That helpless feeling was hard to ignore.

Jordan didn't want to tell her that if the guy had staked out her job and figured out her car, he probably already knew where she lived or how to find out anyway. "That's what I'm there for. The police presence should deter him, and I'll keep a watchful eye out as we drive. Don't worry. I'm good at spotting a tail."

With a determined set to her posture, she pushed back from the table, took a deep breath, and nodded. "Okay then. Let's go."

5

Cassidy felt a little safer as she walked to her car with Jordan behind her. He didn't advertise it, but she knew he carried a gun strapped to his side. She was no stranger to firearms having grown up with older brothers who taught her how to handle one, but she didn't have a concealed carry license. Perhaps she should look into getting one and brushing up on her training. Her experience was pretty limited to shooting coke cans off the trash barrel in their backyard growing up.

"Let me check your car first," he said as she pulled out her key fob.

She held it out to him and watched as he popped her hood and then her trunk. She hoped he didn't look in the backseat as she hadn't had time to clean it out since her return.

Cassidy had a tendency to be on the go so much that it almost appeared she "lived out of her car." Though she had a trash bag, wrappers and cups generally landed on the floorboards instead, and she'd lost count of how many items she had left in the car - coats, books, even her phone on occasion, so needless to say, it wasn't the neatest car on the block. And Jordan was handsome. His blue eyes stood out under his dark hair like blazing beacons, and the muscular tone of his biceps beneath his shirt sleeves had not gone unnoticed. She didn't want him thinking her a slob as well as a diva.

He hadn't called her that, but she had seen the look in his eyes. It was hard to miss since she'd received it from nearly everyone since returning. That look that assumed she had gone on the show for fame and wondered when she would flit off to the next opportunity.

She couldn't blame them, really. The same thought had popped into her mind when she first considered going on the show, but it wasn't why she had gone. And though she could tell them her real reason had been looking for love, it seemed silly now since she had come home empty handed. It was easier to let them assume.

Jordan dropped to the pavement and scanned under the car, then slid into the driver seat. After inserting the key, he paused as if listening for something. Then he turned the key. When the engine fired up, he exited the car.

"All clear. My car's just over there. Don't leave the lot until I'm right behind you. Then I want you to make sure you can always see me in your rearview mirror. Do you understand?"

Cassidy nodded though she wasn't sure if his words were easing her fears or ramping them up.

"If we get separated, pull into the closest lighted parking lot and wait for me. You have my number, so you can call and tell me where you are. I doubt that will happen, but if it does, do not get out of your car."

Yep, definitely ramping the fear up. Her heart thundered in her chest, but she was determined to appear calm. "I understand."

He waited until she was in her seat with the doors locked before sprinting to his car. After a similar check of his own, he fired up his engine, and she headed for the exit.

Even though she knew he was watching, Cassidy found herself peering out of the windows and checking the rearview mirror religiously. She saw nothing out of the ordinary - only his headlights, but there was still a part of her that worried this guy would follow and try something once Jordan was gone.

No lights were on in her apartment when she pulled into the parking space, but could he be hiding in the dark waiting to stab her? Or worse? She didn't want to think about all the things that could fall under 'or worse' but they filled her head anyway. Her heart fluttered faster in her chest.

She wasn't usually one to jump at shadows but this was such an unknown territory for her. As she'd told Jordan, there had been a few men who tried to hit on her at fires or the few times she had gone with Ivy to the hospital to check on patients, but none had ever gone farther than asking her out. They'd all taken her polite decline and turned their attentions elsewhere.

She opened her door to step out, but before she could shut her door, Jordan was at her side. His hand raked across his stubbled chin as his eyes scanned the area. "Let me go in first and check the place out. What number is it?"

"It's apartment A, straight ahead," she said pointing.

He followed her finger and then turned back to her. "Do you have a separate house key from your car key?"

"No, but I can take it off the ring." As she released the house key from her ring, her mind shifted to her house. Had she put everything away? The house was still a little messy from her whirlwind unpacking, but she thought she had at least put her undergarments in her dresser. And even if she hadn't, knowing she was safe was more important than worrying about him seeing her underwear.

"Stay in the car with the doors locked until I return. If you see or hear anything suspicious, drive to the police station and ask Stone to send help."

The fluttering in her heart increased. "Do you think he's in there?"

Jordan shook his head, but his gaze lingered only briefly on her as his eyes darted around the parking lot again. "I don't. I didn't see a tail, but it's always better to be safe than sorry in my line of work."

Cassidy swallowed trying to ease the fear gnawing in her stomach. "Okay, thank you." Then she climbed into her car and locked the doors.

Jordan waited until he heard Cassidy's door lock before continuing up the small walkway to her front door. He stilled his breath and listened as he inserted the key, but silence was all he heard. As the door swung open, he pulled his flashlight from his pocket and his gun from his holster. He preferred to search with lights on, but as he didn't know where all the switches were, this would do until he could find them.

The door opened to a simple living room. In the low light, he could make out a chair, a couch, and a small end table. He swung the light to the left and the right flicking on the light switch when he spied it. Nothing moved as the light dispelled the shadows, but Jordan took another moment to verify the surroundings before continuing into the house.

The room extended into a kitchen and a single hallway led away from the living room. Probably to the bedrooms and bathrooms, but he would need to check the kitchen first. From where he stood, almost all of it was visible, but a center island blocked some of his view and the rest of the kitchen resided behind a wall. Not a ton of places to hide but enough, and kitchens contained knives. He didn't want to be blindsided by a maniac wielding a knife.

Cautiously, he stepped forward keeping his ears hyper-aware

for any sounds. The small kitchen held no surprises other than a cluttered counter. How many appliances did one woman need? A toaster, a waffle maker, a blender, and a coffee grinder filled her counters. Did she use them all every morning?

Focus! He needed to focus. He was securing the house not dissecting the woman though she seemed like she might be an interesting one to dissect. He moved out of the kitchen and down the hallway. Three doors. All closed. He hated closed doors as they made it harder to get the upper hand on someone. With a deft twist, he turned the knob and pushed the door open, pointing his light and gun in at the same time, but this door held only a small closet. Stuffed to the brim with coats and shoes but nothing else.

The next door opened into a bathroom. Again, he was struck by the sheer amount of clutter on her counter. Bottles of product, a brush, and at least two hair appliances filled the small space. Maybe she was a diva type after all. Or was this a common trait for most women? His fiancé had also kept a ridiculous amount of beauty products in her bathroom, but then she had turned out to be a diva.... or at least not the woman he had thought he was marrying.

The last door must lead to the bedroom then and it was cracked. Had she left it that way or was someone inside? He heard no sound from inside, no shuffle, no rifling, no drawers opening and closing, so if someone was in there, they were either still or possessed ninja-like skills. With a swift push, he opened the door and crouched, but nothing flew at him.

After flicking the light switch on, he cleared her bedroom. While no one was inside, he'd have to ask her if she'd left it this way because it looked as if a tornado had touched down. Clothes hung out of overstuffed drawers and littered the bed. A half-packed suitcase sat in the corner begging to be emptied. How she could live like this was beyond him. His place was spotless, but perhaps some of that compulsiveness came from being a cop.

He slid his flashlight into his pocket but kept his gun out as he walked out of the house and back to Cassidy. She opened the door and stood when she saw him approaching, and he could read the questions in her eyes. Man, her eyes were like a mirror reflecting her inner emotions. He wondered if she knew how easy she was to read.

"All clear. There's no one inside, but it looks like your bedroom might have been tossed."

Cassidy's cheeks flamed as she dropped her eyes to the pavement. Her toe twisted a small half circle on the concrete. "No, that was me. I just got back from the show and haven't unpacked fully. It's not usually that messy."

Jordan held up a hand to stop her. He didn't care about her mess or her excuses. He wanted to finish this job and get back to finding the missing kids. "Make sure you lock all the doors when you get inside if they aren't already. The windows too. I'll sit down the street for the next hour. After that, call me if you need anything."

"Okay, thank you, Detective Graves. I know you must have better things to do than stake out my house."

"You can call me Jordan, and it's fine," he said cutting her off and shifting his eyes from her thankful gaze. "Just part of the job." But he did have better things to do. While he was sitting here watching for a stalker who probably wouldn't appear, another kid might disappear. Or worse.

## 6

Cassidy rubbed her eyes and tried to wake up, but the heaviness of sleep enveloped her like a suit of armor. She'd been too wound up to fall asleep, jumping at every shadow and every settling creak of the apartment even though nothing had been there. There'd been no phone call, no more threatening notes, but that hadn't eased her anxiety. And when an hour had passed and she knew Jordan was gone, it had only gotten worse.

At some point she must have fallen asleep as evidenced by her wrinkled clothes and dry mouth, but it certainly hadn't been quality sleep. She rubbed her eyes again. The light stung them, and her lids felt glued together. She would need a strong cup of coffee today in order to function.

With half-closed lids, she stumbled to the shower hoping the hot water would wake her up. Going into work tired was never a good idea, but for a firefighter it could spell disaster. She needed to have all her senses working in case there was a fire.

The water managed to clear some of the haze, and the two cups of coffee after finished the transformation so that by the time she had to leave for work, she felt a little jittery but fully awake.

Her eyes scanned the area as she opened her front door. She might not be a detective, but she could look for things out of place. Nothing appeared amiss though as she walked the few feet to her car.

"Hey, Cassidy."

She jumped at the masculine voice that came from behind her and nearly dropped her keys. "Hey, Dustin." Cassidy hoped that was his name as she turned around to find him leaning against the corner of her building, his dog beside him. If he was her stalker and she said his name wrong, would he get angry and attack her? More importantly, what was he doing at her building? She thought he lived a few doors down.

"I haven't seen you around for a while. Have you been busy with work?" He stared at her evenly as he waited for her to answer.

He didn't know she'd been on the show? She supposed that wasn't entirely surprising as she hadn't advertised it, but Ivy had been checking her apartment a few times a week. Had he not noticed her? She chose her words carefully, hoping to sound nonchalant. "Yeah, life has been busy, but that's the way it is sometimes, right?"

"I suppose, but I seem to have a lot of free time. Maybe we can hang out sometime when you have some?"

Not on his life. Or hers. But she couldn't say that out loud. Not until she was sure he wasn't her stalker. "Yeah, maybe. I can't right now though because I have to get to work. Don't want to be late." Before he could say anything else, she ducked into her car. As he watched her back up and turn toward the exit, she tossed him a wave hoping the fear she felt wasn't written all over her face.

"Everything okay, Marcel?" Bubba asked as she pulled open the front door of the firehouse twenty minutes later. He lounged against the reception desk with a cup of coffee in hand as if he'd been waiting for her, and he probably had. She'd probably find him around every corner until this stalker was caught.

"Everything is fine, Bubba. Nothing new to report." Although that wasn't entirely true, she didn't have any real indication that Dustin was the stalker. "No new notes if that's what you're worried about." She smiled and gave him a reassuring pat on the arm as she passed him.

"Sleep okay?" he pushed as he fell into step beside her.

Cassidy stopped and turned to face him. "Why do you ask?"

He pointed just below her eyes. "Just wondered if those dark circles were a fashion statement or something else."

She batted his hand away. "Fine. I didn't sleep well. It was a little hard to relax worrying that some crazy guy might try to break in."

"You could stay with me until this blows over if you'd like."

His words warmed her heart. She had known her friends were amazing, but she still hadn't expected this. "Thank you, Bubba, but I'm not going to give this guy the satisfaction of turning my life upside down. Besides, who knows how long it will be before they catch him. Jordan gave me his number to call if anything happened, so I'll be fine."

"Jordan, huh?" She didn't miss the teasing lilt in his voice.

Cassidy opened her mouth to tell him it wasn't like that – there was nothing romantic going on between her and Jordan er Officer Graves, but before she could, the alarm sounded.

"Truck 51, Squad 4, Ambulance 3. Fire in the Huntington Apartments. 412 Merriweather Lane."

Cassidy hurried to the bunk room to drop her stuff and then joined the others at the engine and quickly donned her gear.

"You awake enough for this?" Bubba teased as he grabbed his hat and stepped onto the rig.

Cassidy wasn't sure. The coffee was still coursing through her veins, but she didn't feel herself and didn't like it.

"Man, I hate apartment fires," Luca said as the truck roared out of the firehouse.

"Only because you hate stairs," Deacon pointed out. "If you ate a little better, you wouldn't hate them so much."

Luca turned his fiery gaze on Deacon. "I could take you any day, Jackson."

"Okay, let's focus on what matters here," Captain Fitzgerald said.

The men quieted and Cassidy reached up to touch the small silver cross that hung around her neck. It wasn't flashy, but knowing what it symbolized always seemed to calm her spirit. She sent a silent prayer up as the truck swung into the parking lot. Apartment fires were dangerous because there were multiple floors and they could give out at any moment. The possibility of falling to your death or being crushed when a floor caved in loomed in her mind.

"All right, it looks like the fire is on floor two. Marcel and Campbell, you take that level. Go door to door as quickly as possible and get the stragglers out. Sanders and Jackson, you clear the lower level. Witherspoon and Kalhoun, you take the third floor. Let's get everyone out alive, hear me?"

"Yes, sir," they shouted in unison before pulling on their masks and filing out of the truck. Cassidy followed Bubba into the main entrance. Her mother had once asked her how she could run into a burning building, but Cassidy rarely thought about it. It was her job, so she did it, but today the mask felt stuffier, the fire hotter.

Bubba motioned her to a back staircase that looked solid and intact and they made their way up it. The second floor was full of smoke which seemed to be coming from the apartment farthest away.

"Let's go quickly," Bubba said, the mask distorting his voice.

"Fire Department," they called out as they headed down the hall.

Cassidy pushed open the door on her right and entered the apartment. "Fire Department, call out." Her voice sounded muffled behind the SBCA mask. She cleared the main room and then headed down the short hallway. "Fire Department. Anyone here?" The sound of crackling flames filled her head, but there was no other sound. The bathroom and bedroom were empty as well.

"Anything?" Bubba asked when they met again in the hallway.

Cassidy shook her head. "I'll check the next one, but we better get some retardant on the last apartment before we lose it entirely."

"Our job is just to clear it. Let's finish up and report back to the captain."

With a nod, Cassidy pushed against the next door, but it didn't open as the others had. She stepped back and threw her shoulder against the door. It moved barely an inch, but it was enough to see that a body was blocking it.

"Bubba! Bubba, I need you," Cassidy yelled as she pushed against the door again. Moments later, she heard Bubba's footsteps behind her and with his force, the door moved enough. "Grab her and get her out," Cassidy said. "I'll make sure there's no one else."

Bubba glanced up at the fire. "Don't be long. We don't have much time."

"Just get her out of here." Cassidy continued into the apartment as Bubba pulled the woman out. "Fire Department, call out." Only the roar of the fire answered her. Sweat rolled down her spine from the pressing heat, but she continued through the apartment. The rest of it was empty as was the hallway this time when Cassidy re-entered and continued to the last apartment.

The unbearable heat pushed against her, but she had to be sure. She pushed against the door and nearly fell back from the wave of smoke and flames that roared out to meet her.

Cassidy pushed against the invisible wall of heat and called out. Flames licked up the walls and sweat rolled into her eyes sending a burning sensation that set her blinking. She turned to head toward the bedrooms but something on the floor caught her eye. A doll? Was there a child in here? Her head swiveled to the right and the left, but there didn't seem to be anything else indicating a child. No highchair, no gates, no other toys, but the couch appeared out of place. Cassidy crawled behind it expecting to find a child huddled there. Instead, she found a hole in the wall. What in the world?

Ignoring the encroaching flame, she crawled closer to the hole. Two leather straps hung from the wall and a bowl like a dog dish sat in the middle of the floor. What was this? A cage?

"Marcel, it's time to go."

Cassidy stood to see Witherspoon and Kalhoun standing in the doorway with the hose.

"There might be a kid. I haven't gotten to check the bedroom or bathroom yet."

"Captain said it's time. We'll keep our eyes open for a kid."

Cassidy cast another glance at the hole in the wall. She should obey the order, especially since she was on thin ice with Fitzgerald as it was, but something didn't feel right here. "I think it's a girl. Please."

"We've got this," Witherspoon said and motioned for her to get out of the way so they could fire the hose.

As they headed past her to cut off the flame, she grabbed the doll and exited the apartment. She had questions, and she was going to get answers.

"How was your babysitting gig last night?" Al asked with a smirk as Jordan sat down across from her.

"Who told you?" He certainly hadn't. After leaving

Cassidy's, he'd stopped by the restaurant and helped Graham clear out the broken mirror. Graham had sent the movie posters to a collector and secured a sizable sum from them which thankfully was going to pay for most of the renovations, but there was still a lot of work to do.

"Stone," she said with a shrug. "I asked him where you were, and he said you were checking out a stalker for Cassidy Marcel."

"Yeah, one she acquired while she was on that show you love so much, but it was a waste of time. Probably just some random fan. Anything new on the case?" He turned on his computer and waited for it to load.

"Not yet. I mean on one hand that's good news. No new kids taken that we know of, but we still have no idea where they are or how to get to them. Stone is getting anxious."

Jordan was getting anxious too. It didn't usually take them this long to nab whoever they were after, but this guy was slick. It was like he was a chameleon, changing every time so their intel was never good.

His phone vibrated in his pocket and he pulled it out expecting to see the number of his CI, but it was an unknown cell number. "Graves," he said holding the phone to his ear.

"Jordan? It's Cassidy."

Jordan stifled a groan. He couldn't deal with more stalker nonsense today. "Hey, Cassidy. Did you get more notes?"

"What?" Her voice held a note of confusion. "No, this isn't about the stalker. I need to know if you can investigate a scene."

Jordan's brow furrowed. Firefighters didn't usually call cops to investigate a scene. "I'm a little busy with a kidnapping case."

"I wouldn't have called if it wasn't important. I took it to Captain Fitzgerald first but he dismissed my concerns."

Jordan wondered if he should be doing the same thing, but there was a sense of urgency in her voice that gave him pause. "Okay, why do you want me to investigate a fire scene? What's going on?"

There was an intake of breath and then, "About an hour ago, we returned from an apartment fire. In one of the apartments, Bubba and I found an unconscious woman. He pulled her out and I continued to secure the apartment. That apartment was empty and I didn't find anyone else in the last apartment, but I found a doll."

So far Jordan was not seeing the sense of urgency or the need to call him. "Okay, so what? Maybe the people who lived there got out." Or didn't, but he didn't want to say that out loud.

"That's the thing though. There was nothing else in the apartment that suggested a child. No other toys, and there's one more thing." She paused for a moment and Jordan tried not to rush her. "As I was leaving, I saw the couch looked out of place. I thought a child might be behind it, but I found a hole in the wall instead."

Suddenly Jordan sat up a little straighter. A hole in the wall was odd but combined with the out of place doll, it felt a lot more suspicious. "Did you look in the hole?"

"Yeah, there were two leather straps as if someone had been tied up in there and a blue bowl like a dog dish. Captain Fitzgerald doesn't believe me that there might be something criminal happening there, so I thought I would take a chance and call you. I know you're busy and you don't know me, but -"

"Are you still at the fire house?" he asked interrupting her.

"Yeah, I'm on shift until tomorrow morning."

"Okay, tell me where the fire was and we'll go check it out." Jordan's gut was rarely wrong and right now it was telling him this might be worth looking into. He wrote down the address Cassidy gave him and hung up the phone after promising to call her with any information.

"Come on," he said to Al. "We need to go check out a fire."

"A fire?" Confusion colored her expression. "Isn't that a firefighter's job?"

"Yeah, it's something she said she saw at the fire."

Al's eyebrow lifted. "She? You mean the one you babysat

last night? Do you even know anything about her? Maybe this is just an attention getting stunt."

Jordan stared at Al. She wasn't usually one to pass judgment before getting to know someone, and he wondered if her attitude was jealousy of Cassidy's air time or the time she had spent with him. "Maybe it is, but what if it's not? What if there's another missing kid out there somewhere and we don't investigate it?"

Al rolled her eyes and sighed, but she grabbed her jacket. "Fine, we'll go check it out."

Though it was clear Al thought Jordan had lost his mind, she followed him to the car, and he filled her in on the way to the apartment complex.

"Are you sure it's safe to be here?" Al asked as they stepped over the yellow caution tape and entered the charred building. "Shouldn't we make sure the structure won't collapse before we walk about?"

Al was right. They should have someone with them who could verify the building could sustain their weight, but his intuition was telling him there was no time to waste. "We have to see if Cassidy was right before someone comes back and destroys the evidence."

"Okay, but you're going first."

The main floor appeared rather untouched by the fire but Jordan had no idea what the second floor would hold. When they came to the staircase, he placed his foot gingerly on each step waiting for it to fall out from beneath him. Only when it held, did he continue to the next step.

The second floor was definitely in worse shape. Remains of wall paper curled off the walls looking a little like eerie fingers reaching out to them and the smell of smoke still hung heavy in the air. Cassidy had said it was the apartment farthest back, so he headed that way hoping the floor would remain solid.

The door to the apartment hung off one hinge and a sea of black swam before them. This had to be where the fire started as it appeared to be the area most badly damaged. He scanned the room as they entered looking for any sign of children that Cassidy might have missed, but she was right. There was nothing. To his left, he saw the remains of a piece of furniture that must have been the couch.

"Do you want to tell me what we're looking for?" Al asked as she stepped lightly across the floor.

"Cassidy said there was a hole in the wall behind the couch and she thinks maybe someone was tied up in it. Someone small." He let the words hang in the air. "Like a child."

Recognition flickered in Al's eyes as she hurried to his side. "You don't think the guy we're looking for lived here, do you?"

"I think it's worth investigating." He stepped behind the couch hoping to see the hole that Cassidy had. The leather straps might have burned in the fire but maybe they could get DNA off the dish. All his hopes, however, were dashed when he saw the wall. The fire had burned the wall behind the couch completely. There were no straps.

"Do you think she was wrong?" Al asked as she surveyed the scene.

Jordan shook his head as he crouched down. He didn't know Cassidy well. It could be that she had an attention-seeking disorder and this was just another effort to fuel her ego, but then why become a firefighter? Yes, it got you attention, but it could also get you killed.

He pulled his gun from his holster and used the barrel to move the ashes around. Not knowing what else might be in the mess, he didn't want to take the chance of using his bare hand, but when his gun uncovered a hardened blue puddle, he forsook caution and grabbed the item.

"What does that look like to you?" he asked as he held the melted plastic up.

Al's nose scrunched in disgust. "A mess. What are you doing touching it?"

"It looks to me like the color of a dog dish, you know the plastic kind you buy at the store." Okay, so that was a bit of a leap, but he couldn't think of anything else that would be in the walls and look like this.

"So, she was right." Al's words were soft, breathy.

"It appears she was. Now, the question is... who lived here?"

# 7

"Okay, thanks for letting me know." Cassidy hung up the phone and sat down on the couch.

"Was that Jordan?" Bubba looked away from the TV which was playing the latest football game and wiggled his eyebrow at her. He was the only guy in the firehouse she had confided in before going on the show, and sometimes she wished she hadn't. Now, he seemed determined to make any guy she met a possible love interest.

Cassidy rolled her eyes to let him know how far off base he was although she couldn't deny she found Jordan attractive. She definitely hadn't missed how well his jeans fit his frame when he was crawling under her car or how sexy he looked with his gun drawn as he entered her apartment. "Yes, but it's not what you think. I asked him to check out the apartment from the fire earlier. He couldn't find the hole in the wall because the fire damaged it too much, but he did find a lump of melted plastic he thinks might have been the bowl."

Bubba let out a low whistle and turned his full attention to her. "So, what's the next step?"

"Jordan is checking with the landlord to see who rented the

apartment, but I think that will be a dead end. I'm going to check with Ivy to see if I can talk to the woman we rescued. She might be our only hope in finding this guy." Cassidy picked up the blackened doll she had taken from the apartment and sighed. "And this kid."

"She was pretty beat up and had a lot of smoke inhalation. It may be a few days before she can talk."

"I know. I just hope it gives us enough time."

"Marcel, isn't it about time to wash the truck?" Captain Fitzgerald's voice carried in from behind them.

"Yes, sir, I was just about to do that." Cassidy stood and tucked the doll behind her back. She'd tried to talk to the captain when they first returned from the fire, but he'd dismissed her concerns. He probably thought she was trying to get out of the work he'd placed on her, and though that wasn't the case, she hadn't wanted to argue with him.

"I'll talk to you later," she whispered at Bubba before ducking out of the room. She dropped the doll off on her bunk before heading to the bay. Some little girl was missing that doll, and Cassidy was determined to return it to her.

As she entered the bay, she hit the button to open the doors. At least it was a nice, warm day. She hated washing the truck when it was cold outside.

"Oh, hello, I was just about to knock, but I wasn't sure where the front door was."

Cassidy glanced up to see a man standing just outside the bay doors. He was nice looking in the nerdy Clark Kent way with dark hair, glasses, and a suit.

"Sorry, my car won't start, and I was hoping someone here might have jumper cables. I'm pretty sure it's time for a new battery but just haven't had time you know?" He shrugged and pushed the glasses up the bridge of his nose.

Cassidy sized the guy up. Normally, she would have thought nothing of a request like this. After all, the firehouse was nestled in a housing development, so visitors showed up often, but the ominous notes were still on her mind and going anywhere alone with a stranger, even one that looked like he couldn't harm a fly, didn't seem smart. Plus, the guy seemed vaguely familiar though she couldn't place where she'd seen him before.

"Actually, we have something even better. Just let me grab it and let them know where I'm going." She flashed him a small smile. "I'm supposed to be washing the truck."

"Sure, of course, thank you."

Cassidy stepped back inside and hastened to the common room where Bubba still sat watching the game. Luca and Deacon had joined him and all three were glued to the screen.

"Aren't you supposed to be washing the truck, Marcel?" Luca asked.

"Yes, and I'm going to start in a minute, but there's a guy who needs a jump. I just wanted to let someone know where I'd be." She emphasized the last few words hoping Bubba would catch her drift.

He glanced up and nodded letting her know he had her back and would come to check on her in a few minutes. It wasn't quite the reaction she had hoped for, but at least it was something.

She grabbed the battery jumper on her way back to the bay. "Okay, all set. Where's your car?"

"Just over here." The man led the way out of the parking lot and to the right. "Thank you so much. I'm supposed to be on my way to a meeting, and I thought I was going to be late."

"Well, this does take about ten minutes to charge the battery. I hope that gives you enough time."

He checked his watch which appeared to be a Rolex – the man had money or at least wanted to appear like he did. "It'll be tight, but I think I can make it. I'm glad it was you I saw first."

Cassidy froze as fear washed over her. "I'm sorry?"

"Oh, you probably don't remember. You checked the carbon monoxide levels at my friend Brian's house a month or so ago. I never got your name then, but I wanted to thank you. I had no idea you worked at this station. I'm Scott by the way." He held out a smooth hand.

Cassidy looked at it, not sure she wanted to shake it but even less sure she wanted to decline and risk angering him. She remembered this call. A nice house with a group of men watching a football game. One had complained of migraines and an odd smell, so they'd called in the fire department to make sure there was no carbon monoxide leak. It had been a routine call, and the men had all seemed nice and stable. She needed to get ahold of herself. The guy needed a jump. That was it. He'd given no indication of anything else. She was letting her fears control her. "Cassidy," she said finally shaking his. "This plugs into your cigarette lighter. You do have one, don't you?"

"Oh yes, it's not that new. It's this one." He unlocked the door of an older Ford Mustang and held the door open for her. "I probably should upgrade especially with this battery issue, but I just love older Mustangs, don't you?"

"Yeah, I guess." Cassidy wasn't much of a car girl. As long as it drove, it was good enough for her. "Here, you just plug this in and push the button." She handed him the device and stepped back. Her fear was probably unfounded, but harmless or not, she'd seen enough movies to know he could slam her with the door and cause some serious damage. Images of Kathy Bates from the old Misery movie flashed through her mind.

He plugged the charger into the port and flicked the power button before backing out of the car. "So, now we wait?"

"Yep, now we wait." The silence settled between them – heavy and uncomfortable. "So, what do you do?" She didn't need to know his occupation nor did she care, but small talk seemed less awkward than staring at each other in silence for ten minutes. However, she didn't want to let her guard down and give this guy a chance to overpower her if he did have nefarious intentions, so she leaned against the back door careful to keep a comfortable distance between them without drawing attention.

"I'm a financial planner. I set up IRAs and things like that. Boring but necessary." He flashed her a crooked smile and Cassidy returned it, mostly out of habit, but he did have a nice smile and it eased her trepidation a little. "How did you get into firefighting?"

Cassidy hesitated. Should she tell him? It wasn't anything too revealing and she couldn't see the harm in sharing. At least it would help pass the time. "On a bet actually."

Scott's eyes widened behind his glasses revealing eyes the color of a stormy sea. They were the most interesting color Cassidy had ever seen. "Really?"

"Yeah. I was in college and not sure what I wanted to do. There was this guy on my hockey team who thought women were inferior to men in every way, so he told me I couldn't make it through the firefighter academy. Not one to let him win, I had to try, and I fell in love with it. Switched my major to fire science, graduated, and here I am."

Scott shook his head and grinned. "Well, remind me never to bet you anything. I have a feeling you rarely lose."

Cassidy's smile faltered. Yes, she rarely lost, but she hadn't always won, and the sting of the one she lost still left its mark. That had been her last boyfriend, David. She'd spied him in a crowded restaurant, and after her friend dared her to ask him out, she had sidled up to his table. He'd been flattered and agreed, and their relationship had progressed quickly. To the point where she'd thought he would propose. She'd already planned the entire day in her head and the kids they would have after. Then, one day, he'd up and left. Said her job took up too much of her time and his secretary held his interest more.

"Have you had a fire today?" he asked glancing toward the firehouse.

"What?" Cassidy shook her head to clear the painful memory

from the past. "Yeah, we had one this morning. A fire at an apartment complex."

"Oh, dear. I hope no one was hurt."

Something in his tone bothered Cassidy though she couldn't place her finger on what. She glanced at her watch. The charger still needed another few minutes. "I don't think so, but I was only on one floor, and our paramedics handle injuries more than we do."

Scott nodded and glanced at the firehouse again. "Well, it sounds very exciting anyway. I bet it keeps you busy."

Cassidy watched his gaze slide to her left hand. Was he searching for a ring? Was this guy her stalker after all? How much had she shared? Too much? Suddenly, her heart began to pound in her chest. He'd made no move toward her, but if he did, could she run fast enough? Could she overpower him? She hated this feeling, this fear that every man she met might be out to harm her. Would she face this the rest of her life?

"Yep, a firefighter's life is busy. Pretty much work and sleep."

"That's too bad," he said holding her gaze. Could he see her fear? "There's more to life than work and sleep."

From inside the car, she heard the timer ding, and a feeling of relief washed over her. "Looks like you're all done. Why don't you try to start the car?"

Cassidy took a step back as Scott stepped toward her and then leaned into the car. The engine fired to life and he smiled at her. "What do you know? Thank you for your help."

"Sure. If you could just pull that machine out, I can put it back and you can be on your way." Cassidy tried to keep her tone even.

Scott leaned back into the car and then held out the starter machine. "Here you go. It was nice to meet you again. You're a lifesaver."

"It's what I do," Cassidy said with a forced smile. She took the machine and stepped back again, putting more distance between herself and Scott, but she didn't move any farther until he got in the car and drove away. Only then, did her breathing return to normal and her heartbeat begin to slow. She had to find out who her stalker was. There was no way she could keep living like this.

"Dang it," Jordan hissed in frustration as the computer came up empty again. He'd gotten the name of the renter from the landlord who'd confirmed he had rented to a single man, but so far that name had done nothing for the case.

"No luck?" Al asked.

"None. Whoever rented that apartment is a ghost. There's a million Michael Simmons, but no one with the matching social the landlord gave us, and the social is actually registered to a guy who died five years ago."

"Were there any cameras in the apartment?" Stone asked as he paced the room like a caged tiger. The movement raised the tension in the room which was already thick. The kids had been gone too long and they all knew the statistics, but none of them were willing to give up.

"No, it was too old," Al supplied. "None across the street either."

"Do we have anything else to go on?" The frustration created a hard edge in Stone's voice.

"There might have been a witness. Cassidy said they dragged one woman from the scene. I'm waiting to hear from her."

"Let's hope she knows something," Stone said as he scraped his knuckles across his stubbled cheeks. Usually clean shaven, the scruff accentuated his stress. "I feel like the trail is going cold and I don't like that. Not ever, but especially not when kids are involved." The slam of his office door punctuated his agitation.

"Cassidy, huh? Is there something going on between you two?" Al made the words sound innocent, but Jordan could tell from the sideways glance she shot him that there was more than idle curiosity behind the question.

"Not like that. She's a part of the case, that's all." But was that all? He couldn't deny there was something attractive about Cassidy, but no, the last woman he had opened his heart to had left him at the altar. He wasn't going to go down that path again any time soon.

"Okay, if you say so. Hey, you want to grab some dinner?" Al's abrupt shift took Jordan by surprise and he blinked at her a moment before he could form words.

"I can't," he said with a sigh. "I promised Graham I would help with the restaurant tonight. He wants to clear out all the old furniture and the monstrosity of a bar so we can start looking at interior designs." Although Jordan knew with Graham in charge there would be much less decision making and more informing of what the choice would be.

"So, how about we grab a pizza and I'll help. Broom, remember?" She wiggled her eyebrows and flashed a wide smile.

Jordan wanted to say no. He didn't want to lead her on, but having someone be a buffer with Graham might be nice. "Okay, but don't say I didn't warn you. The place is a mess."

"I'll consider myself officially warned. Come on, I'm starving." Al grabbed her jacket and headed for the door. Jordan had no choice but to follow.

After a quick stop at a local pizzeria, Jordan parked in front of the old building. The windows were still boarded up as Graham had suggested they fix the inside before the outside, so as not to attract vandals or thieves.

"Looks lovely," Al said in a teasing tone as she opened her door.

"Yeah, well, I told you. The inside is worse." He opened the door for her as she carried the pizza box.

"Late again, I see...." Graham's voice trailed off as he spied Al behind Jordan.

"Sorry, but we brought food. Graham, this is my partner Al. Al, this is Graham." Jordan took the box from Al as he made the introductions in case she wanted to shake hands.

"This is your partner?" Surprise and just a hint of disbelief filled Graham's voice.

Al leaned back and crossed her arms. "Is that a problem?"

Jordan squeezed his lips together and watched the scene unfold. Al's defensive posture was up and when she felt threatened, or in this case slighted, she was like a cornered raccoon who could claw your eyes out before you expected it.

Graham must have sensed it as well because he stumbled over his next words. "No, it's just he never mentioned you were a woman. With the name Al, I assumed..."

"Al is short for Alayna, and that's what you get for assuming."

Jordan chuckled as Graham's mouth fell open. Al might be small and look young – in fact, she had posed as an underage girl in more than one sting – but she was tough as nails and not afraid to speak her mind.

"I... I'm sorry." Graham stuttered over the apology trying to recover.

"It's cool. I guess Jordan doesn't talk about me that much." This time she turned her penetrating eyes on him.

With a shrug, Jordan brushed her accusation off. "To be fair, I don't tell Graham much about work. Now, I thought you said you were starving. How about we eat?"

"Yes, let's eat." Graham's face told Jordan that he would have questions to answer later, but right now he was glad to be out of the hot seat.

## ❧ 8 ❧

Cassidy grabbed her bag and headed for the door. Though there were showers and beds in the firehouse, nothing replaced the feel of her own pillow-topped bed, and after three days on shift, she was ready to be home and curl up in her own bed.

"Cass, wait up."

Cassidy turned to see Ivy hurrying her direction. Her pixie face sported a mischievous smile. "Hey, I met the nicest doctor at the hospital today. Tall, dark, and handsome. I think he'd be perfect for you and he's free tonight."

Cassidy tried not to roll her eyes as she sighed. She knew Ivy meant well, but her bruised ego was still healing from Tyler's rejection, and set up dates were usually worse than regular ones. Friends always meant well, but the added pressure just made the dates even more uncomfortable. "Not tonight, Ivy. I've been on shift for three days. I want a real shower and decent sleep in my own bed."

"Okay, but soon, right? You need to get Tyler out of your head and start dating again."

"I will. I promise. Just not tonight."

Ivy crossed her arms and narrowed her eyes at Cassidy. "All right, but I'm holding you to that promise."

Cassidy had no doubt she would. The girl was tenacious like a dog who wouldn't give up a bone. It was one reason she loved her. Most days. "I'll see you in a few days, Ivy."

The air was cool as Cassidy stepped outside the firehouse, and the last of the sun's rays stretched across the parking lot. Twilight was her favorite time of day as the colors reminded her of a fire, but a peaceful one.

"Hey, I was hoping I would see you again. I was just about to knock."

Cassidy jumped at the voice and clutched her bag tighter, her body tensing as it decided whether to fight or flee. To her right, a man stepped out of the shadows. The Clark Kent whose car she had jumpstarted.

"Sorry, I didn't mean to scare you. I wanted to bring you these as a thank you." He held out a beautiful bouquet of flowers as he stepped closer. "Thanks to you, I didn't miss my meeting."

"Oh, you didn't have to do that." Cassidy took a step back. He had to be her stalker. Why else would he have shown up again so soon? She ran through her options. There was a small can of mace in her bag, but she'd never get it out in time. She could throw her bag at him in distraction, but she doubted she could make it to her car before he caught her. Screaming was an option, but would they hear her inside the firehouse?

"I know I didn't have to, but it was an important meeting. Thanks to you I didn't lose the client. I was hoping maybe I could take you to dinner."

Dinner? There was little doubt in Cassidy's mind now. What would he do if she said no? Would he go crazy and attack her? He didn't look as if was carrying a gun or a knife, but that could be part of his ruse – look normal and unassuming to lure women into a sense of safety and then turn on them and take them down before they could run.

Cassidy wished she had a panic button on her phone that would alert someone, but there was no way she could make a move without arousing his suspicion. "I just got off shift and am pretty tired," she began, but she didn't get to finish because Ivy burst out of the front door excited and out of breath.

"Cassidy. The woman from the fire..." Her voice trailed off as she caught sight of Scott. "Oh, sorry I didn't know you had company."

Ivy wasn't Bubba or Deacon or even Luca and she certainly couldn't take this guy down, but at least there was safety in numbers. "Ivy, this is Scott. I helped him jump his car the other day and he was just stopping by to say thank you."

"And to ask you to dinner," he piped up.

Ivy's eyes widened as she looked from Scott to Cassidy. "Right, well, I'm sorry to interrupt." She stepped back as if she were going to re-enter the firehouse, but Cassidy wasn't about to let her do that.

"No, it's fine. I really have to go anyway, but why don't we exchange numbers and get in touch soon." Cassidy had no intention of giving him her real number, but she hoped she might get his. Maybe Jordan could run it through some system and let her know if he was legit or dangerous.

"Uh, sure." He pulled out his cell phone and tapped a few buttons. "Okay, go ahead."

Cassidy rattled off a number close to her own hoping Ivy wouldn't rat her out and then put his number in her contacts.

"At least take these," he said handing her the flowers, "and thank you again."

When he was out of earshot, Ivy tugged on her arm. "Do you think he's the stalker?"

Cassidy shook her head though she wished she knew. She didn't like thinking the worst about someone she didn't even know. She'd worked hard after David dumped her to focus on seeing everyone as

God did instead of seeing them through the burning hatred she felt for David. "My guess is yes. He comes out of nowhere asking for a jump and then shows up with flowers and a dinner invite?"

"Or he could just be a nice guy who is attracted to you," Ivy said playing the Devil's advocate, "but he probably won't be when he tries your number and finds out you gave him the wrong one."

Cassidy watched the car pull out of the lot and resisted the urge to shiver. "Just seems too coincidental to me. Plus, he gave me the creeps the day I helped him. He asked a lot of questions and stared at me."

"All things guys do when they're interested in you," Ivy said. "Maybe it has been too long."

"It didn't feel like interest," Cassidy said with another shake of her head, "but look, I'll see if Jordan can find anything out on him. If he's not my stalker, I have his number and can contact him and explain."

"If he listens long enough to hear your explanation."

Frustration exploded inside Cassidy, and she turned on her friend. "Whose side are you on anyway?"

An expression of hurt clouded Ivy's face. "Yours, of course, I just hate seeing you like this. You're scared, I get it, but not every new man you meet is your stalker. There are good guys out there, you know?"

"So, you keep telling me." Cassidy looked down at the bouquet of flowers in her hand. She hadn't wanted them in the first place, but after this conversation, the mere sight of them brought a sour taste to her mouth. "Here, enjoy these." She shoved them in Ivy's hands knowing she would have to apologize later but unable to deal with it right now. "I've got to call Jordan and get to the hospital."

Before Ivy could protest, Cassidy hurried to her car and started the engine. As she drove out of the lot, she dialed

Jordan's number. "Jordan? Meet me at the hospital. Our woman is awake."

Jordan found Cassidy waiting at the nurse's station for him. "She's able to talk? Does she remember anything?"

Cassidy chuckled and shook her head sending her dark hair swishing against her shoulder. She wore it down today, and it looked like chocolate silk. "I don't know. I waited for you before going to see her. Ivy asked them to call her when she woke up and she told me right before I called you."

"Okay, well, let's go see if she can help us." Jordan followed Cassidy down the hall to room 108 trying to keep his focus on the case and not the woman in front of him which was becoming harder with each moment he spent with her. They knocked quietly on the door before pushing it open.

A frail looking woman lay on the bed. Burns covered her face and arms, but though burns weren't his expertise, Jordan thought she'd been lucky. They didn't look like third degree burns.

"Ma'am?" Cassidy's voice was soft beside him.

The woman opened her eyes and stared at them. "Who are you?" she asked in a hoarse whisper.

"My name is Cassidy and this is Jordan. I was one of the firefighters who rescued you from the fire, and Jordan is a police officer."

Jordan stepped closer to the bed. "We need to ask you some questions about the fire. Did you know the man in 2D?"

"I can't say that I knew him, but I saw him a few times when his mail would get delivered to my apartment – 2B."

"Did you ever see him with a child?" Cassidy asked. "A girl maybe?"

The woman appeared to think for a minute. "No, I never saw

a child, but I suppose there could have been one living there. The mail I got had at least three different names on it. I just figured he was scamming the welfare system especially when I asked him about it and he told me to mind my business, but I suppose it could have been mail for other people who were living there. Never saw any others though."

Other names? Could they be lucky enough that he would have used his real name on one of them? "Do you remember the names?" Jordan pressed trying to keep his tone even.

"No, but I had just gotten some mail for him that day. I was on my way to give it to him when I realized I had forgotten a few other pieces that were sitting on my table. Before I could go back to get them though, something hit my head and the next thing I knew, I woke up here."

"Do you think the pieces would still be there? On your table?" These names would help them. Jordan was just sure of it.

"If the fire didn't get them. You're welcome to go in my apartment and look." She turned her eyes to Cassidy. "I didn't even know there was a fire. Do you know if my apartment was damaged?"

"Most of the fire was in his apartment. You might have smoke damage though. If you want, I can come back after we grab the letters and let you know."

Tears filled the woman's eyes. "Thank you. I don't have much, but a lot has sentimental value, you know?"

Cassidy nodded as if she understood, and Jordan realized she most likely did. Dealing with fires every day, she probably saw this reaction quite often from people.

"Thank you, ma'am," Jordan said as he stepped back. "You've been extremely helpful."

Cassidy followed him out of the room and fell into step beside him. "So, are we going back to the apartment?"

"We?" he asked. "No, I am going back to the apartment. You are going back to work or home or wherever you need to go."

Her jaw tightened and she pulled on his arm with a grip that was surprisingly strong and halted his step. "This is my case too. I'm the one who found the doll and the hole and called you." She ticked the items off on her fingers for emphasis. "I want to see this through."

Jordan thought about fighting her, but something flickered in her eyes. A defiant spark, and somehow, he knew she wouldn't take no for an answer. "Fine, you can come with me to the apartment, but then your job is done. The rest is on me, got it?"

She narrowed her eyes at him as if debating whether to push it further, but in the end, she agreed.

"Let's take my car there. No sense in taking two," he offered as they exited the hospital.

"Fine with me."

Jordan watched Cassidy as she climbed into the car and buckled her seatbelt. He'd assumed she was a diva when he first met her, but now he was seeing a whole new side of her. One that intrigued him but scared him as well. Especially because in small ways, she reminded him of Jasmine. That sense of confidence had been what drew him to Jasmine in the first place, but it had also been what tore them apart.

Now, here was Cassidy inserting herself into his life without even meaning to but making an impression nonetheless. However, he needed to keep those emotions locked down. He didn't need romance right now and certainly not with someone who ran head first into danger. No, if he ever dated again, he needed someone with a quiet job who was content to avoid danger. Someone he wouldn't have to constantly worry about and who could be content being married to a cop. A woman who was a firefighter was about as far from that as you could get.

The parking lot of the apartment was still deserted when they arrived. "I guess it will be awhile before they re-open this," he said as he turned the engine off.

"If they ever do," Cassidy said. "Fires like this often destroy the structure and then it's not safe to just apply cosmetics and go on like nothing happened."

"So, where are all these people living?" Jordan glanced up at the building as they approached the yellow caution tape and pictured all the people who must be displaced right now. Having rarely investigated a fire scene, he had never thought about the aftermath for those who might live there.

"Who knows? Hotels probably or with relatives. Sometimes they never recover and take to living on the streets. Those are the hardest ones to watch." She ducked under the tape as he held it up for her.

"I can imagine. You still like it though? Firefighting, I mean."

A crooked smile played across her face as he pulled open the door. "Yeah. I like helping people. Isn't that why you became a cop?"

"Uh, not really." Jordan debated telling her a story. One that didn't involve his troubled past, but he didn't want to lie to Cassidy. "I became a cop because my dad was an alcoholic who used to beat my mom. When she finally got the courage to take us and leave, I swore I would join law enforcement so I could stop men like my father in the future."

Cassidy's face folded in compassion. "I'm sorry to hear that. That must have been rough."

Jordan shrugged and turned away. "We all have our scars." He shouldn't have told her because now she was looking at him the same way everyone did who knew. With pity. He hated that look and decided to change the topic to get the attention off of himself. "What about you? Why did you become a firefighter?"

"A bet," Cassidy said with a chuckle as she followed him up the stairs. "You may not have figured this out about me yet, but I don't like being told I can't do something."

He snickered to himself; he had certainly picked up on that trait of hers. "I bet you were a handful for your parents."

A delightful laugh escaped her lips. "I was. My mother said I used to stick my tongue out at her with my lips pursed together. Said she could tell by my eyes."

Jordan tried to picture Cassidy as a young girl. Had she been a tomboy or more of a girly girl?

"Anyway," she continued jolting him out of his imagination and back into the present, "I dated a guy in college who told me I couldn't, so I decided to prove him wrong and fell in love with it."

And there was that hint of Jasmine again. Not so much what Cassidy said, but the way she said it. As if it was the most natural thing in the world. Jasmine had been confident like that. So confident in fact that she had even convinced herself she could be a cop's wife until the day of the wedding hit, and she'd realized she wanted more. More security, more time, more something that he evidently couldn't give. Was that why he had stopped dating confident women?

"Here it is, 2B. Let's hope her apartment wasn't too badly damaged." Jordan pushed the past from his mind as he opened the door to the apartment and stepped in. There was some charring from the heat on the walls and the items closest to them, but thankfully the fire had been stopped before it destroyed this apartment.

The only issue was the woman who lived here was a clutter freak, not quite hoarder level, but papers lay everywhere as if they had fluttered down from the sky like snowflakes. "She said the table, right?" Jordan asked.

A look of disgust crossed Cassidy's face as she nodded and took a step toward the kitchen table. Papers covered it completely acting as a makeshift tablecloth. "How did she eat in here?"

"Maybe she cleaned it off with each meal?" Though he doubted it from the look of the apartment. The place didn't look like it had seen a broom or a vacuum for quite some time.

"That seems like a lot of work." Cassidy picked up a piece of paper with her fingertips. Some orange stain covered it. "Or maybe she just ate on top of them." With a shudder, she dropped the paper to the floor. "I wish I had brought gloves."

Jordan did too. He had no idea what might be in all these papers and while he wasn't squeamish, the thought of a roach crawling across his bare hand sent a shudder down his spine. "Just be careful and look for anything with a male name on it."

"Like this?" Cassidy held up an envelope. "Isn't Jeremy Irons an actor?"

Jordan took it and read the name chuckling as he did. "Yep, I'd say our woman in the hospital was probably not named Jeremy nor a famous British actor." He set that one to the side and kept digging through the papers. "Here's another. Robert Bedford."

Cassidy gaped at him, her mouth hanging open. "*That* didn't raise any red flags?"

"I've seen a lot of weird names in my work," Jordan said. "People probably figure nothing's off the table anymore."

"What's the weirdest name you've ever come across?" Cassidy asked as she rifled through the pile on her side of the table.

Jordan thought for a moment. He'd met quite a few people who had the same first and last name – John A John or Charles Charles, but then he remembered the woman from the previous summer and smiled. "It doesn't sound weird if you say it, so I'll spell it. The name was spelled ABCDE."

The space between Cassidy's eyes furrowed as she set down her paper to look at him. "ABCDE? As a first name? How was it pronounced?"

Jordan chuckled as he remembered the lively woman. She'd been a handful. Dressed in bright colors and absolutely adamant she had done nothing wrong; she had tried to reason with Al and himself for five minutes before they managed to get her in the back of the car. "Absidee. Still an interesting name but not nearly as strange as the spelling."

Cassidy shook her head. "And I thought my name was weird. Growing up, I could never find it on those keychains or other trinkets that you buy at tourist shops. Not like my brothers who are named Wes and Paul. Pretty easy to find those, but the closest we could ever get was Cathy, which sounded similar but wasn't my name."

Jordan nodded as if he understood, but he'd never been on a vacation. At least not when he was young. When his parents had been together, his father either had drunk the money away or been too drunk to care about taking them somewhere. And after his mother left, she'd been too busy working two jobs to afford a "frivolous" vacation, but he could relate to how important a name was. Too many times, he'd wished his father would use his name instead of calling him boy. "How did you end up with the name Cassidy anyway? I mean it's pretty but definitely unique."

"My dad was a big Butch Cassidy fan, and I guess my mother vetoed naming either son Butch, but she liked that Cassidy was different." She shrugged. "So, there you go."

"Well, I think it's nice to have a unique name. I thought Jordan was like that until I went to school. Then one year I was in a class with three other Jordans. One boy and two girls."

A wide smile formed on Cassidy's face. "Yeah, I don't have that issue. Never met a boy with my name though I'm sure there might be some."

Jordan returned the smile and marveled at the ease of talking with Cassidy. She was not at all the diva he had first assumed she was and now he was even more curious why she had gone on the show. "Can I ask you something?"

Her eyes met his and he saw just the slightest hesitation in them. "Sure."

"Why did you go on the dating show? You seem so grounded and I can't imagine you enjoying all the hoopla."

"I didn't enjoy the hoopla, and I'm not, you know?"

"Not what?" Jordan asked confused. Had he missed something?

"I'm not a diva, and I didn't go on the show for fame."

His mouth fell open as he struggled to formulate an answer, "I didn't..."

"No, you didn't, but I could see it in your eyes. I didn't go for fame. In fact, I didn't want to go at all at first. When my mother suggested it, I thought she was crazy, but I've wanted to start a family for a while now, and though I dated, I wasn't meeting the kind of man I wanted to marry. So, I prayed about it and started to feel like God was leading me in that direction. That must have been my own ego though because it certainly didn't turn out in my favor."

"Maybe God wanted you on the show for another reason. One you haven't discovered yet." As he held her gaze, he realized he was suggesting that maybe she had gone on the show so they would meet. He should rephrase, explain himself. He didn't need Cassidy thinking he was attracted to her even though he was. Dating just wasn't in his future and definitely not with a woman who reminded him so much of Jasmine.

She held his gaze and electricity crackled between them. Her eyes had turned from a mirror reflecting her feelings to a microscope discerning his. Oh no, he was in so much trouble. He needed to fix this now. "I'm sorry I meant..."

She dropped her eyes to the table breaking the connection. "Edward Long."

He blinked at her sure he had misunderstood and unsure how the topic had shifted so quickly. "What?"

She held up an envelope. "It's addressed to Edward Long."

Edward Long? Why did that name sound familiar to him? He ran through the evidence he could remember from the case. His memory was good, and there was something just under the surface, but he couldn't place it.

"That's three aliases. Do you think there are any more?" Cassidy's nose scrunched sending cute, tiny wrinkles across the bridge as she surveyed the piles. Cute? No, he didn't need to be putting the word cute with her at all. He needed to rein his emotions in.

"I think we have to be sure. It shouldn't take us much longer."

"Okay, but then can we celebrate by grabbing a burger after? I'm starving."

Was she asking him out on a date? Though he wanted to say yes, dating Cassidy would be a bad idea. "I'm not sure that's a good idea."

"Oh, come on, Detective Graves, surely you have to eat?" The twinkle in her eyes matched the teasing lilt in her voice.

He should say no. He should tell her they would never work. She was too similar to the one woman who had managed to charm and then destroy his heart, but he was hungry. And he did need to eat. And he appreciated a woman who could enjoy a good burger. "All right. I do know a great burger place just down the road, but it's not a date." Maybe if he said it enough times, he could convince her as well as himself.

She held her hands up in surrender. "Got it. Not a date. To be honest, I think I'm avoiding dating for a while what with Tyler and now the stalker."

Right, the stalker. He still hadn't followed up with that. "Have there been any more notes?"

A cloud passed over Cassidy's face momentarily. "No. No more notes but something odd I was going to ask you about. The other day, a guy showed up at the firehouse needing a jump. It's not that unusual since we're in a neighborhood but there was something that seemed off about him. Then he showed up again today with flowers to thank me and a dinner invite. It just seemed…" her nose scrunched again as if debating the word she wanted to choose, "pushy, and I didn't get a warm fuzzy feeling from him. Do you think he could be the stalker?"

A need to protect her welled up within Jordan. If this guy was the stalker, he was getting brave showing up at her job and engaging with her, which could mean he was escalating. That being said, he didn't want to alarm her any further. "It's possible. I'd like to investigate him. Do you think you could describe him just in case?"

"I could, and I got his name and number. Well, his first name anyway."

She gave this guy her number? Was she intentionally stoking the fire?

"Don't worry," she continued as if reading his mind, "I gave him a fake number in return, but is there some database you can run his number through to see if he's a liar or something?"

A soft laugh spilled out of his lips at the thought. "Well, there's no database for that, but I can see if he has a record and if he's using his real name." Had he misread her attraction? Would she date this flower guy if he turned out not to be the stalker? Whether she would or not, this was just another sign that he didn't need to be pursuing Cassidy.

"All done over here."

He looked down at his pile and realized he was finished as well. "Let's go get that burger then." He knew he was probably playing with fire, but right now, he didn't care.

## 9

"This is your favorite burger spot?" Cassidy asked as they walked up to the open window of the burger truck. She hadn't expected an upscale restaurant but perhaps a sit-down place where they could talk. Nothing was around this truck except one picnic bench. Not even a table. They would have to hold the burgers in their laps.

"Don't knock it until you try it. These are the best burgers in Fire Beach. I'm surprised you haven't been here before." He approached the open window and quickly surveyed the short menu. "Do you trust me to order for you?"

Did she? Cassidy generally despised men ordering for her, but maybe that was because they never seemed to know her and always ordered something she wouldn't like. Somehow, even though she didn't know him well, she thought Jordan might have an idea what she would like, and if he didn't, then she would learn something about him too. "Sure, surprise me."

"Two peppered bacon burgers, two drinks, and a side of onion rings," Jordan said to the man in the open window.

Onion rings? How could he know she loved onion rings? Unless he did too. She'd felt a camaraderie with him both at the hospital and then again at the apartment. No, camaraderie wasn't the right word. She had felt an attraction growing between them even though he seemed determined to deny it for whatever reason. She wondered why. Was it his job? Hers? Maybe he couldn't date her because he was working her case. Or maybe he was going off her declaration that she didn't plan on dating? Why had she said that?

She shouldn't care what his reason was. Her heart was still healing after the interaction with Tyler, and a cop was not the kind of man she wanted to marry. Her schedule was already crazy, and though she might have to retire from firefighting if and when she became a mother, she wanted to be with someone who had a more stable schedule. Someone who wouldn't miss ball games and dance recitals. Someone who would be at church with her every Sunday. She couldn't see Jordan being that kind of guy, but that didn't diminish the attraction she felt.

"Here you go," he said breaking into her daydream and handing her a drink. Darn it, her daydreaming had distracted her and now he'd paid for the food. Did that make this a date after all? Should she offer to pay for her half?

"Could you grab some napkins?" he asked indicating the stash near the window with his head. His hands were a little full with the bag of food and his drink. "There's not much seating here, but there's a park just around the corner if you don't mind walking a little."

"A walk sounds good," she said with a smile as she fell into step beside him. She'd let the money slide for now. The evening air was cool as the sun began to set sending brilliant rays of yellow, orange, and red across the sky, but Cassidy's light jacket kept her warm enough.

A small park appeared before them, and though it held little more than a slide, a swing set, and a volleyball net, it did have a picnic table. Jordan waited for her to sit before sitting across from her.

"How did you find this place?" Cassidy asked as she scanned the park and began to unwrap her burger.

Jordan's eyes glazed over as he looked out toward the playground. "I used to bring my brother here to escape from life. When my dad started yelling, my mom would usher us out of the house. Partly to keep us safe and partly so we didn't know how much of a beating she was taking. This park was far enough away that we couldn't hear them and Graham enjoyed playing at it."

Cassidy placed a hand on Jordan's arm. "I'm so sorry. That's not the way a father should be."

"Don't I know it," he said with a derisive snort, "but it made me who I am today, and I think I'm a pretty good detective because of it."

While Cassidy knew that hard times and tragedies formed people, she wished stories like Jordan's didn't exist. She had been lucky. While her father worked a little too much when she was young, he was still there almost every night for her brothers and her, and forty years later, her parents were still married – not something most of the people she knew could claim.

"I think you're an amazing detective." She enjoyed the slight hint of pink that brushed his cheeks as she held his gaze.

Suddenly, his eyes widened and he slapped the table. "Edward Long."

"What?" Cassidy looked around expecting to see someone approaching them, but there was nothing but the approaching darkness.

"The name Edward Long sounded familiar to me when you said it, but I couldn't figure out why. But it was a name we were looking into on the case, and I interviewed him. I can't believe I didn't realize…. Would you mind taking the burger to go?"

Cassidy wrapped up her burger and tossed him a smile. "Nope. If it means you catch this guy, then I'm all for it." She had hoped to spend more time with him, but if there was a child in danger, their time could wait.

"Great." He had already tucked his burger back in the bag and was pulling out his cell phone. "Al? Do me a favor. Look up Edward Long and get me the address. I think he might be our guy."

He looked up at Cassidy. "Can you write an address down for me?"

Cassidy looked around but she had no pen and no paper. What she did have was her phone. She quickly opened the notepad app and hovered her finger over the face as she waited expectantly.

"I'm with Cassidy." He rolled his eyes. "It's not like that. We just came from the apartment fire. Al, we'll talk about this later. Just give me the address. 452 Wheeler Avenue. Thanks."

Cassidy typed the address into her phone as he rattled it off and suppressed the urge to ask him about the odd conversation, especially since it seemed his partner didn't approve of her. She didn't think she'd even met his partner, but now did not seem the time to stir the pot.

"Let's go. I'll drop you off on my way." He was already two steps ahead of her, his toned legs taking long strides. She hurried to catch up with him.

"Take me with you."

He stopped long enough to shake his head. "No, it's too dangerous. I don't know what this guy is capable of."

"But you said you interviewed him already. He knows you and probably won't let you in without a warrant. Do you have a warrant?" Cassidy hoped she was right. She watched a lot of the Law and Order type shows with the rest of the guys at the house, but she certainly wasn't versed in the law.

Jordan's eyes shifted as he ran a hand across his chin, and Cassidy knew she had him. "No, I don't have a warrant. Okay, what are you thinking?"

"Let's run back to the station. I'll grab my gear and show up as a firefighter. Tell him there was a gas leak reported and I just need to check his apartment. You can be waiting outside."

"I don't like it," Jordan said with a slow shake of his head. "You aren't trained for operations like this. If something happened to you…"

Cassidy placed a hand on his arm trying to ignore the emotions that ignited within her at the simple touch. "It won't, but Jordan, we can't let the guy get away."

He looked down at her hand and then back into her eyes. "Fine, but we do it exactly as I say. You understand?"

"You bet."

Jordan still couldn't believe she had talked him into this. It was dangerous and if anything went wrong, Stone would have his head. However, Cassidy was right. This guy was sly and this might be their only chance to catch him.

"Okay, just like we went over, do you understand? You walk the place pretending to check for carbon monoxide and look for any signs of the kid. If you see anything or he appears jumpy, you use the code word."

Cassidy issued a swift nod before turning those eyes on him. Though fear flickered in them, determination overshadowed the fear and Jordan's respect for her grew a little more. She was out of her element and about to do something potentially dangerous, but her shoulders were pulled back in resolution.

"I'll be in that doorframe," he said pointing to one down the hall, "until he lets you in. Then I'll move to be right outside the door, but you'll still have to speak up."

"Okay, let's do this." She adjusted her helmet and then faced the door. Her bulky uniform made her appear larger, but Jordan was very aware of how unprotected she was. He sent up a prayer for her safety and his own as he ducked into the doorway.

A moment later, he heard the sharp rap of her knuckles and then her words, "Fire Department, open up," in a clear commanding tone.

"Yeah, what do you want?" Jordan could tell from the clarity of the voice that the man had opened the door. He wanted to look to see if it was indeed the man he had interviewed earlier, but he didn't want to chance being seen.

"Sorry, sir, I need to check your apartment. There's been a carbon monoxide leak reported in the building and we need to clear all the apartments." Jordan marveled at how firm her voice sounded. If she was scared, she wasn't showing it.

"I'm busy."

"It will just take a minute, sir, but you have to let me in. Carbon monoxide can be deadly if you breathe it too long."

"Fine, but hurry up. I've got things to do."

Jordan heard the swish of her pants and knew she had entered the apartment. Now, the only question was whether Edward Long would close the door or not. He forced himself to count to ten just in case the man chanced a glance down the hallway and then he peeked around the doorframe. A sliver of light escaped from the doorway. He had left it ajar.

Careful to keep his footsteps as quiet as possible, Jordan moved down the hallway until he was outside the door. The conversation inside was muffled, but thankfully he could still hear it.

"Have you experienced any headaches, sir?"

"No."

"Is there anyone else here in the apartment with you?"

"Why does that matter?"

Jordan's breath caught at the harsh tone of the man's voice. Cassidy had better lay off the questions.

"I just wanted to make sure no one was having headaches,

sir. The first sign of carbon monoxide poisoning is generally a headache, then vomiting, then dizziness. Most people pass out, but if it gets to that point, it usually means brain damage or death."

She was good and Jordan breathed a little easier when Edward's voice came again softer this time. "No, there's no one else in the house. Are you almost done?"

"Yes, sir, I'm almost finished."

"Hey, what are you doing? Get away from there."

Jordan tensed and tightened his grip on his gun. She must have seen something, but why wouldn't she just use the code word and get out.

"Sir, I was just going to check the cabinets. There's no need to pull a gun out."

Oh crud. The guy had a gun. That was his cue. Waiting any longer might get Cassidy shot. He took a deep breath before jumping through the cracked door and leveling his firearm on the man. "Fire Beach Police Department. Drop your weapon. You're under arrest."

As he'd hoped, his entrance drew Edward's attention away from Cassidy, but now he swung the gun Jordan's direction.

"Drop your weapon," Jordan repeated. He did not want to fire on this man. Not in an apartment building where bullets could go through walls and not with Cassidy so close.

Edward lowered his arm as if he were going to comply, but then a cold gleam appeared in his eyes and his arm shot back up. Jordan watched the scene as if in slow motion knowing he could either fire and risk getting shot or get out of the way but not both.

He was a good shot, but firing could injure Cassidy or the kid as he still wasn't sure what she had seen. Plus, Edward's bullet might hit him as well, but getting out of the way might give Edward time to turn the gun on Cassidy.

Before Jordan could decide, he saw Cassidy's leg shoot out

and connect with the flesh right behind Edward's knee. As the man stumbled, his arm jerked up and the piercing sound of a gunshot filled the air, but it gave Jordan the time he needed. Sprinting forward, he tackled Edward to the ground and kicked his gun away. Edward protested and attempted to throw Jordan off his back, but the attack had caught him off guard and Jordan was able to wrestle Edward's arms behind him.

"Edward Long, you're under arrest," he said as he secured the handcuffs.

"What for?" Edward asked belligerently. "She's the trespasser. She was snooping in my apartment."

Cassidy walked over by the cabinets and pulled at the paneling on the wall revealing three small children trapped inside. "For kidnapping would be my guess."

"I'm going to say we can probably tack on human trafficking," Jordan added as he gazed at the children who huddled together and stared at Cassidy with fearful eyes. He hated the terror that covered the faces of these children, but he was relieved that all of them had been found. It didn't often work out that way, but Long must have been waiting for more money or had issues getting them offloaded. Whatever the reason, he sent a silent thank you to God for watching over the two boys and girl who couldn't be older than eight before spouting the rest of the Miranda rights at Edward Long.

"I'll bet we'll even be able to add on assault and arson, won't we?"

Edward turned his head and snarled up at them. "That woman had it coming. Always knocking at my apartment. She should have just left the mail in my box or under my doorstep."

"You might want to take that right to remain silent," Jordan said as he reached into his pocket and pulled out his phone dialing the numbers to reach dispatch. "This is Detective Jordan Graves with the Special Investigation Unit. I need two ambulances and a backup to transport a prisoner to 452 Wheeler Avenue. Call Stone."

Cassidy crouched down and addressed the kids in a soft voice. "Don't worry guys. You're safe now. I'm a firefighter. See my uniform? Can you come out?"

One at a time, the kids crawled out of the small space and clutched onto Cassidy. Rage roared inside Jordan and the urge to punch the man beneath him fought to escape. How dare this man take these children from their parents? How dare he try to sell them for money? How dare he keep them shut up in the walls like animals?

But punching the man wouldn't solve the problem and it would probably frighten the children even more than they were. So, he wouldn't. Instead, he turned his attention to Cassidy. "You did good." She was impressive, and as much as he still feared losing his heart again, his objections were beginning to seem less important.

She shook her head and squeezed the children tighter. "No, we did good."

## 10

J ordan watched the paramedics load the children into the ambulance before turning to Cassidy. "How did you know they were in there?"

Cassidy shook her head, but she didn't look at him. Her focus remained on the children. "I didn't for sure. I saw that the paneling was separated from the wall and it just reminded me of the hole I saw at the fire. When he got jumpy as I approached it, I knew he had to be hiding something."

Before Jordan could tell her how lucky she was Edward hadn't fired on her, Stone approached. "Good job, Jordan. We'll get the kids reunited with their parents tonight and I'll see if we can get our friend here to talk. He can't be working alone." Stone turned to face Cassidy. "I hear we owe this break to you."

"Oh, I don't know if you can attribute the whole break to me." She smiled up at Jordan. "Jordan was the one who remembered the name and came in with guns blazing."

Stone lifted an eyebrow as he glanced from Cassidy to Jordan and back again. "Yes, well, he's lucky things turned out the way they did. Next time he should remember to call for backup though."

Jordan took the criticism with a nod. He knew there would probably be another stern reprimand in his future, but he was grateful Stone didn't do it in front of Cassidy.

Stone turned his attention back to Cassidy. "Thank you for the help you supplied in this case. I'll make sure your captain knows about it. Word on the street is that he wasn't too happy when you took time off to do your show, but maybe this will allow him to ease up on you. Jordan, why don't you take tomorrow off? I think you deserve a rest day."

"Thank you, sir." Jordan wasn't sure he'd get any rest though. Graham had texted him earlier asking him to meet to go over the interior layout of the restaurant, and he still needed to investigate Cassidy's stalker.

Beside him, Cassidy spoke up. "Um, before you go, sir. I have a doll that belonged to the girl at the firehouse. I'd like to get it back to her. Do you know how long they'll be at the hospital?"

"I'm not positive, but if you get it there tonight, I'm sure it will get to the owner." With that, Stone walked back to the squad car that held Edward Long.

"Not the talkative type, is he?" Cassidy asked.

Jordan chuckled. "Not really, but he is good at his job." He turned to face Cassidy and his breath caught as he gazed into her eyes. He'd felt something in the apartment when he'd seen the gun pointed at her. This fear of her getting hurt. And he'd reacted without thinking, which was dangerous. He should break contact now and run, but his body wouldn't move.

She returned his stare, and her lips parted as if begging for him to kiss them. His body screamed at him to take her in his arms and do just that, but he muffled the shouts and told himself they would never work out though he was no longer sure exactly why. "It's getting late. I should probably take you back to the hospital."

The sparkle in her eyes dimmed, and her mouth formed a

thin line. Jordan knew he had hurt her. He hadn't meant to, but a little hurt now was much better than a lot of hurt later. "Look, Cassidy, I'm not good at this stuff..." His voice was stilled by the placement of her lips against his.

For a moment, he was too surprised to react, but then his brain kicked into gear and his hands moved from her arms to her neck, his fingers tangling in her hair. Her hands pulled at the back of his neck as if trying to draw his face closer. Then suddenly, she pulled back.

"You want to tell me you felt nothing?" she asked when the kiss ended. Her breathing was irregular and he could hear the pounding of her heart. Or his? He was no longer sure of anything it seemed.

He opened his mouth, but he couldn't tell her that he'd felt nothing. Nothing was definitely *not* what he'd felt. A spark of heat flowing from his head to his toes and an overwhelming sense of peace that hadn't graced him in a year – those he had felt, but was it enough? Was it enough to throw caution to the wind and give love another chance?

"Never mind," Cassidy said before he could find words. "I shouldn't have done that. I know relationships that begin from dangerous situations rarely last, but I just couldn't help myself."

"I just..." He should tell her, explain his hesitation, but the words wouldn't come. He wasn't even sure what his hesitation was any more. Was he really worried she would be like Jasmine? "I can't right now."

"It's fine." She stepped away from him, crossed her arms over her chest as if building a wall between them. "Can you just take me back to the firehouse so I can get the doll? Then you can drop me at the hospital."

"Cassidy, I..." but he had nothing. He wasn't ready to open up the past yet and that meant closing this door. For now. With a sigh, he led the way back to his car.

"Is that Jordan?" Ivy whispered with wide eyes as Cassidy grabbed the doll off her bunk.

"Yes, now stop staring. He's going to think something's wrong with you." Cassidy's voice came in a hushed hiss. She was still berating herself for kissing Jordan. What had she been thinking? Well, she hadn't. That was the problem. She'd been swept up in the moment and following her heart and just like with Tyler and David, she had put it out there only to get it rejected. Again.

"Something is wrong with me." Ivy began to fan herself with her hand. "My heart is beating like crazy, and I feel like someone turned up the heat. Ooh, girl, he is fine on the eyes."

"Stop it," Cassidy said swatting her friend's hand. She'd made a big enough fool of herself tonight; she didn't need Ivy making it worse.

Ivy snapped out of her teasing banter but wasn't done with the topic yet. "He's so handsome. No wonder you didn't care about the doctor or the jump start guy."

Scott. With all the excitement of finding Edward Long, Cassidy still hadn't given Jordan the information on Scott or Dustin for that matter. Would he still look into her stalker? Or would he pass her off to someone else to avoid the tension that now lived between them. "Yes, he's handsome. He's also waiting for me, so we'll discuss this more later."

"Have fun." Ivy flashed her a wink and a mischievous smile.

Cassidy shook her head as she returned to Jordan who stood in the doorway of the bunk room looking uncomfortable. "Sorry about her," she said in explanation, "Ivy means well, but sometimes she gets a little…"

"Zealous?" he finished for her.

"Yeah, that would be a good word, but I got what I came for, so let's get back to the hospital before they release whoever this belongs to."

As they drove to the hospital, Cassidy debated whether to bring up Scott again or not. She didn't want to worsen the mood, but her stalker was still out there. As she opened her mouth to broach the topic, the hospital came into view on their left. It could wait.

A different woman was working the station this time, but Jordan's badge granted them admission. The children's rooms were all in a row, and Cassidy and Jordan popped their head into the first one. A small girl was asleep in the bed, but her parents sat vigil by her and they glanced up.

"Sorry, we didn't mean to disturb you," Jordan said before they could say anything. "I'm Detective Graves and this is Firefighter Marcel who found your daughter. We're looking for a little girl who might have lost a doll."

Cassidy held the doll up and the woman brought her hand to her mouth. "That's Baby. Sophie's been crying for her since we got here. Where did you find her?"

"I found Baby at the scene of a fire," Cassidy said, her voice choked with emotion. "I'm sorry she's in such bad shape, but she's actually the reason we found the children."

A soft sob escaped the woman, and her husband wrapped an arm around her shoulders. "I'm sorry," he said wiping a tear from his eye, "we're so grateful. It's just a lot to take in."

"It is," Jordan said stepping forward, "but there are places that can help." He pulled out his wallet and handed over a business card. "This place has great counseling for situations like this. Please don't hesitate to use them."

The man nodded, and Cassidy stepped forward and handed the doll to the woman. "I don't know if she'll still want it since I'm sure it doesn't look the same, but you can tell her how brave Baby was."

"Thank you. Thank you for finding our daughter."

"You're welcome." Though Cassidy sometimes saw survivors after a fire, this case felt different. Heavier. More rewarding.

"Is it always like that?" Cassidy asked as they stepped back into the hallway.

"When the outcome is good? Yes."

Cassidy didn't ask what it was like when the outcome wasn't as good. She'd seen that first hand as well. They walked in silence back to the parking lot and to her car. "You didn't have to walk me out," she said.

"Actually," he sighed and jammed his hands in his coat pockets, "I did. Cassidy, I need to explain."

Her heart began to pound in her chest as she leaned against her car. Jordan stepped closer closing the distance, but Cassidy didn't move. Even when his fingers touched her cheek and tucked a strand of hair behind her ear, she didn't break her gaze from his mesmerizing stare.

"You caught me off guard tonight, Cassidy, and that is hard to do."

"I'm sorry…" She didn't get to finish the apology as his finger touched her lips silencing her and sending waves of emotion through her body.

"I've spent a lot of time building up emotional walls. My last relationship ended in the worst way possible. She thought she wanted to marry a cop, but on our wedding day, she realized she didn't and never showed."

Cassidy's eyes widened, but she said nothing sensing that he needed to continue and get whatever he wanted to say off his chest.

"I haven't dated since." His fingers slid down her neck to the top of her shoulder. "I thought I was done with love, but you awakened something in me with that kiss. I just need some time to process. Can you give me that?"

Cassidy nodded. She didn't want to give him time. She

wanted to pull him to her and taste his lips again, but if time was what he needed, she would give it. "Jordan, before you go. I know Stone gave you tomorrow off, but if I send you Scott's information, can you look into him when you get back to work?"

"Of course I will. I want any information you have on the guy in your apartment complex too, and Cassidy?" She stared up at him mesmerized by the look in his eyes. "If anything else happens – letters, phone calls, a feeling - I want you to call me. No matter what time it is. Don't let this thing between us stop you from calling. Promise?"

"I promise."

He raked a thumb across her cheek. "Good, now go home and get some sleep. I'll call you tomorrow." His lips touched against hers, softly, not like their first kiss, but the simple touch still sent a shiver down her spine. There was no doubt in her mind. She was falling for Jordan Graves.

He waited until she was in her car with the motor running before he walked back to his own car. With a smile on her face, Cassidy pulled out of the parking lot and began the drive back to her house. It was still early, not even six. Maybe she would take a long bubble bath before cooking dinner and then curl up with a good book.

But her smile faltered as a bang sounded, and her car began to pull to the right. Had she blown a tire? How? She'd seen nothing in the road. With all her might, she yanked the steering wheel to the left but it was no use. The car was stronger than she was and continued to pull to the right. She fumbled for her phone hoping to dial 911, but as she got it out of her pocket, the car hit the curb, and the phone flew from her hand and landed on the floorboard. Cassidy had no time to grab it though because at that moment, something rammed her from behind and her head slammed on the steering wheel.

11

"Why do you look so cranky?" Graham asked as Jordan shrugged out of his coat and laid it across the bar.

"What do you mean? This is how I always look." He took his gun out of the holster and laid it on the jacket.

Graham shook his head as he pulled out a blueprint design and spread it on the table. "No, you look meaner today. More agitated."

Jordan sighed and paced away from the table. He hadn't slept much the night before as he'd lain awake thinking about what to do with Cassidy. His mind would list all the reasons they would never work out, but then his heart would speed up just thinking about her. "It's this woman, Cassidy. She's a firefighter, and she's amazing. Even helped me solve the big kidnapping case I was working on."

"So, what's the problem? She sounds perfect for you."

Jordan ran a hand through his hair and let out an exasperated breath. "The problem is that she reminds me of Jasmine, you know, the other woman you thought was perfect for me."

Graham's head shot up, a hurt expression on his face. "Hey,

you can't blame that on me. She was perfect for you. If you hadn't been a cop."

Jordan threw his hands up and rolled his eyes. "But I am a cop! And what happens if Cassidy turns out to be the same?" He didn't think he could put his heart out there again.

Graham folded his arms and leaned back. "Okay, so that's the worst that could happen. What's the best that could happen?"

"What?"

"I mean if she doesn't turn out to be like Jasmine, what could life be like?"

Jordan shook his head and raked a hand across his cheek. "I don't know. She's a firefighter and I'm a cop. Our schedules would probably never work. And her job is nearly as dangerous as mine. That's no way to raise a family."

"But?"

Jordan frowned at Graham. Why was he pushing this? "But when she kissed me, I felt alive. For the first time since Jasmine."

Graham shrugged and leaned back over the blueprint. "So, I guess the question you need to ask yourself is if it's worth it. Are the fears and the hardships worth feeling alive again?"

Jordan narrowed his eyes at his brother. They didn't talk about their dating lives much, but the last he knew his brother was single, so when did he get so insightful? "When did you get your counseling degree?"

Graham glanced up. "I didn't. I'm actually sharing something Dad said to me before he passed."

Jordan tensed at the words. He wasn't sure he wanted any advice from his father.

"Hear me out," Graham continued holding up a hand. "You know he tried really hard to be sober the last few years. He wasn't perfect, but he was trying. One day, he told me he was having a hard time. Only he wasn't talking about women. He was talking about his next drink. He could stay sober and live with the pain of what he'd done, who'd he'd hurt, or he could let the drink take that pain away."

Before he could stop the words, Jordan opened his mouth. "What did he choose?"

"He chose to feel the pain, to own up to his mistakes. I know you don't want to be like him, but he wasn't all bad, Jordan. He let alcohol take ahold of his life and that ruined him. Don't let the fear of heartbreak do the same to you."

Jordan wanted to argue, but what Graham was saying made sense. Fear wasn't the same as alcohol, but he could see how if he let it control his life, his opportunities, that it could have the same hold on him. He walked to the table and scanned the blueprint. "You might be right."

Graham leaned forward as well. "I know I'm right. Anyway, all I'm saying is that you can't live your life in fear. What if this firefighter is the one you're supposed to be with and you never give her a chance? Now, can we pick an interior design?" Graham pointed to the blueprints spread out on the table. "I'd like to get started on this as soon as possible."

Jordan chuckled at his brother's abrupt switch in topic. Now that he'd had his say, he was all ready to get down to business. "Yeah, just give me one second to call her and see if she can meet up later."

Having made the decision to give love a shot, he suddenly couldn't wait to see Cassidy again. He pulled out his cell phone and dialed her number. At nearly nine thirty in the morning, he expected to hear her voice pick up, but the phone simply rang. And rang. Until finally her voice mail clicked on. He listened all the way through it and then left his message. "Cassidy, it's Jordan. I was hoping maybe we could get together today. Please call me when you get this message." He hung up, briefly wondering where she might be but sure she would call him back when she received the message.

"Okay," he said walking back toward Graham. "Show me what you've got."

Cassidy moaned as she struggled to open her eyes. Her head hurt though she wasn't exactly sure why. In fact, her whole body felt stiff and sore. She touched her forehead wincing as her fingers pressed on a raised bump. Where had that come from?

Then it came back to her. She was on her way home from the hospital when her tire had blown and then something had hit her car. She'd hit the steering wheel which explained the bump on her head, but why wasn't she still in her car?

Was she in the hospital then? Her eyes opened the rest of the way and she took in the room – what little of it she could see in the dim light. She was in a bed, but this was not a hospital room. The dark walls were nothing like the sterile white of a hospital, and the one window in the room was boarded over allowing only a sliver of light into the room.

She pushed herself to a sitting position gritting her teeth against the pounding pain in her head. There was nothing in the room beside the bed and a pail against the wall. Was that where she was supposed to relieve herself? The door was solid metal except for a rectangular panel that appeared to open and close. This wasn't a room. It was a cage. Her stalker must have found her.

When the throbbing in her head lessened, Cassidy stood and walked to the window. The boards were nailed on the outside, so she couldn't even try to pry them off from in here. She supposed she could try to break the glass and push on them, but she didn't know what the noise might bring. Also, there was no way to bandage herself if she cut herself on broken glass from the window, and she had no desire to bleed out in this depressing room.

Fear tightened in her chest. How was she going to get out of here? She wasn't expected at work today so no one would even know she was missing until tomorrow unless they found her car. And even if they did, how would they know where to begin looking for her? She didn't even know where she was.

A scraping sound drew her attention back to the metal door. "Who's there?" she called out. "Where am I?"

There was no verbal answer, just a gloved hand appearing with a bowl. Cassidy couldn't even tell if the hand belonged to a man or a woman though she suspected a man. Not wanting to give her captor the satisfaction of knowing she was hungry even though she was starving, she simply waited.

"Grab the bowl." The voice was deep and gravelly, but also machine like. He was altering his voice.

"No. Let me out of here."

"You will eat," the voice commanded.

Cassidy crossed her arms enjoying the power it gave her even though her captor couldn't see them. Her stomach ached and rumbled displeased at having missed dinner the night before, but she wasn't going to let him know that. "You can't make me."

"Suit yourself." The hand let go of the bowl and it dropped to the floor. The bowl didn't break, but the contents, which looked like runny oatmeal, spilled out on the floor. Then the rectangular door closed.

Cassidy walked back to the bed and curled her knees to her chest. She would have to eat sooner or later or she wouldn't have the strength to attempt an escape if the opportunity arose. Tears filled her eyes and a vice closed on her throat. How was she going to get out of here?

She turned her face to the ceiling and did the only thing she could do. She prayed.

## 12

J ordan glanced at his watch. Four hours had passed since he called Cassidy and there had been no reply. Was she angry at him for the day before? Had she been called into work? Work. He could call her work and see if she was there. Jordan typed the firehouse into his search engine and dialed the number that popped up.

"Fire Beach Firehouse, how may I direct your call?" the woman on the other end asked in a pleasant voice.

"Is Cassidy Marcel on today?"

"I'm sorry, sir, I can't give that information out." The pleasantness had dropped from her voice and she was all business now.

Of course, he should have known they wouldn't give out personal information. "I apologize; this is Detective Jordan Graves with the FBPD. I'm investigating her stalker case and need to speak with her, but she isn't answering her phone. If she's there, can you connect me?"

"I'm sorry, Detective, she isn't on shift today, and I haven't seen her."

Jordan hung up the phone without saying goodbye and

chewed on his bottom lip. Maybe it meant nothing. Maybe she'd decided to unplug and lay low, but he didn't think so. His gut was churning again, and it was telling him something had happened to her.

"What's wrong?" Graham asked as Jordan paced the room.

"I'm not sure. Cassidy hasn't returned my call, and I'm worried about her."

"Dude, maybe she's just busy." Graham rolled up the blueprint they had chosen and secured it with a rubber band. "I think you're overreacting."

It was possible, but Jordan didn't think so. His gut was rarely wrong, and right now it was twisting and turning into knots. "Maybe, but I met Cassidy because she had a stalker. What if he found her? What if something happened to her?"

A look of sympathy crossed Graham's features. "We're done here. Why don't you go see if she's home and lying low?"

"Thanks, man." Jordan strapped his gun back in place and shoved his arms into his jacket. It was ten minutes to her apartment and each minute seemed like eternity. He was tempted to throw on his lights and sirens to get people to move out of the way, but this wasn't an emergency. Yet.

A broken lamppost appeared on his right and snagged his attention. He didn't remember seeing it before and while it might mean nothing, the hair on the back of his neck now stood at attention. He pulled the car over and stepped out.

The dent in the lamppost held a streak of red – the same color as Cassidy's car. His eyes dropped to the ground, and he spied broken plastic and streaks on the curb as if tires had rubbed against them. There had obviously been an accident here but where was the car?

Jordan pulled out his phone and dialed Stone.

Stone's gruff voice filled his ear. "Jordan? I thought I told you to take the day off."

Jordan shook his head. He didn't have time for explanations.

"You did, but, sir, I think something's happened to Cassidy Marcel. Can you see if DOT transported a wrecked vehicle from 72$^{nd}$ and Trosper last night or this morning?"

"Hold on. I'll check." This was why he liked working for Stone. The man knew when to ask questions and when to trust his officers. "Yeah, they towed it this morning to lot A. Said no one was inside."

"Thank you, sir. I'll be in touch soon."

Jordan jumped back in his car and turned it around. Lot A wasn't too far away. He just hoped he would find some answers there. "Hold on, Cassidy, I'm coming."

Cassidy stared at the walls around her and wondered how much time had passed. Her watch was missing, probably taken, and she didn't have her phone. She had nothing but silence and four walls.

For a while, she had prayed, but soon her words ran out. Not that she thought God wasn't still listening – she was sure He was – but she could only ask Him to save her so many times. Then she'd tried to sleep, but hunger had started gnawing its way up her stomach. The smell of the runny oatmeal on the floor hadn't helped.

The sound of scraping metal came again and Cassidy hurried to the door hoping to catch a glimpse of the room outside. She didn't know what she'd do with the information as she had no way to get out of the room she was in or tell anyone where she was, but the tiny room was closing in on her, and she needed to know there was more out there to regain her sanity.

"Please, let me out of here," she said as she squatted down to try and see out of the rectangle. A pair of legs clad in denim appeared before another plate of food filled the window. This time a sandwich and a bag of chips.

"I can't let you out until I've convinced you we belong together." The voice was still altered but Cassidy was sure she'd heard it before.

"You've convinced me," she tried. "We belong together. Now, please let me out."

"Nice try, but I haven't yet. Take the food."

Well, it had been worth a shot. "No, I'm not taking anything from you. You'll have to watch me die in here and then we'll never be together."

"You will eat." Once again, the plate dropped and the window slid shut. The sandwich landed in the oatmeal – guess she wasn't eating that – but the bag of chips managed to avoid the brown mess. Cassidy had no intention of breaking them open right now, but they were bagged. It would be harder to poison something bagged, so she plucked them up and took them to the bed. Chips weren't enough to sustain energy for long, but she was not going to die in here.

## 13

Jordan opened the door of Cassidy's car and tried not to dwell on the worst-case scenario as he spied the dried blood on the steering wheel. She'd probably hit her head or her face, both of which tended to bleed more than other areas. It was clear from the car that something had hit her from behind, probably pushing her into the lamppost.

There was no other blood on the seat or anywhere else which gave Jordan some hope. He moved farther into the car searching for anything that might give him a clue as to what had happened to her. Nothing in the seats caught his attention other than the fact that her bag still sat in the passenger seat.

He opened it feeling as if he shouldn't be snooping in it but knowing it was necessary. Her wallet was still there and when he popped the snap, he saw her credit cards and cash still inside. So, this wasn't a robbery. He hadn't thought it was but finding this confirmed it.

A glance in the backseat revealed nothing new there either, but Jordan hoped Cassidy would have left him some clue if she could have. He backed out of the car and bent down to check the floorboard. There his eyes landed on her phone. He plucked it off the mat hoping he would be able to access it. She had never sent him the text with the information on the possible stalkers and now it might hold the only clues.

He pressed his finger to the power circle, but the keypad screen came up. Darn it. He didn't know her well enough to have any idea what her password might be, but he knew someone who might.

After examining the car one more time to make sure he hadn't missed anything, Jordan shut her door and hurried back to his own car. Ten minutes later, he pulled into the firehouse parking lot. He just hoped Ivy would be working.

The same woman he had met a few days before was at the desk. "Can I help you?"

"I need to speak to the paramedic. Ivy something or other. I'm sorry I don't know her last name, but it's important I speak with her."

His eyes must have shown the frazzled sense of urgency he felt in his bones because the woman picked up the phone and paged Ivy Hopkins.

She appeared a moment later, her blonde hair pulled back in a loose ponytail and a quizzical expression on her face. "Jordan? What can I do for you?"

He held out Cassidy's phone and watched as Ivy's eyes widened. "Do you know how to unlock it?"

"Why do you have this?" Fear threaded her voice and her eyes darted around as if she thought he might harm her.

"Cassidy's missing. I found this in her car. She never sent me the information about the possible stalker, but she said she had the man's name and number in her phone. So, can you open it?"

"Um, I think so. She told me what it was once." Ivy grabbed the phone and closed her eyes. Her face scrunched in thought. Jordan wanted to shake her and tell her to hurry up, but he knew that would accomplish nothing, so he waited. Ivy's eyes popped open and she tapped a few numbers in the phone. "No, that's not it." She tapped the screen again and a triumphant smile lit up her face. "Got it."

Jordan snatched the phone from her and clicked on the message icon. There was no draft to him, so she hadn't even started forming the message yet. He supposed that made sense since she had been taken before she got home, but it didn't keep him from kicking himself for not getting the information from her before he let her go.

"What was the guy's name?" As he scrolled through her contacts, he realized she had never told him the guy's name. Why hadn't he asked better questions?

"The guy who stopped by here with the flowers?" Ivy asked.

Jordan's eyes shot to her. "Yes, did she tell you his name?"

"Yeah, his name was Scott. I was there when she exchanged numbers with him."

Scott. He flicked the scrolling arrow to get to the eses. Yes, there it was. He took out his own phone to take a picture of the number. "Could you describe him?"

"Of course. He was handsome, but kind of nerdy with the glasses and all."

"Great, I need you to come to the station with me and describe him to a sketch artist. What about the other guy?"

Ivy's forehead furrowed as she shook her head. "What other guy?"

"The one at her apartment. She said there was a guy who seemed odd at her apartment complex. One who walked his dog and stared at her."

"Dustin? I'm pretty sure he's harmless. He's always walking his dog outside. I spoke to him once or twice when I was checking on her apartment for her." Suddenly her eyes widened. "Oh my gosh, could he be the stalker?"

"I don't know yet, but I'm going to investigate them both."

Ivy's face paled and her hand covered her mouth. Jordan knew that look. "What?" he asked.

"I just… I thought they were friends, so I talked about her when he asked. Like he wanted to know why I was there and I told him I was watching her apartment while she was on the show. Did I do this? Did I get her kidnapped?" Her eyes took on a vacant stare.

Jordan had no time to console the woman, but he knew she was beating herself up. "We don't know who the stalker is yet, so stop blaming yourself and let's find this guy. Can you come to the station with me now?"

"What?" Ivy blinked a few times bringing her eyes back into focus. "Yes, just let me tell Captain Fitzgerald what's going on. I'll be right back."

As she dashed off, Jordan checked his watch. Cassidy had been missing for nearly twenty-four hours and he didn't want it to be any longer. He had to find her.

Cassidy's stomach rumbled again as she turned on the hard bed. The light in the room was fading which meant evening was approaching. Her mouth was dry from not drinking all day and she could already feel the lack of food taking a toll on her. How much longer would she be here? Had anyone found her car yet? Did they know she was missing? Would Jordan hunt for her? He'd admitted there was an attraction but then he'd said he needed time. What if that meant days? No, she couldn't think like that. She needed to stay focused and positive.

The rectangle slid open again, but this time Cassidy didn't scramble over to try and peer out. She knew the view was limited and she didn't want to give this guy the satisfaction of seeing her. "Dinner."

"I'm not hungry," Cassidy said though the ache in her stomach protested.

"You will eat."

She had tried begging and lying. Neither had worked, but Cassidy wondered if bribery might. "I'll eat if you'll tell me who you are."

"You shouldn't have to ask," the voice growled.

Ouch! She'd touched a nerve, but she wasn't going to stop now. She wasn't sure what she would gain by knowing the identity of her captor, but she needed to know. "But I do. You're disguising your voice and you haven't shown me your face, so how would I know who you are?"

"I sent you the letters."

"Yes, but you didn't put your name on them or a return address, so how could I know it was you?"

"I left you other gifts." The agitation in his voice increased with every answer, but Cassidy felt fairly safe locked in this room.

"At the fire station?" There'd been a few gifts in the bag, mostly chocolates which she had thrown out even though she loved chocolate.

"No, on your doorstep."

Cassidy sucked in her breath. So, he knew where she lived. That had to make it Dustin unless Scott had followed her home without her knowing it. "What gifts? I never received any on my doorstep." She thought back over the last few months, but she couldn't remember anything being outside her door.

"You're lying. You did get them and after everything I've done for you, I can't believe you're saying you don't remember or that you kissed that guy. I know you didn't mean it, but I'm the only guy you're supposed to be kissing." He dropped the plate spilling the soup and bread onto the floor before slamming the rectangle shut again.

So, he'd seen her yesterday with Jordan. That made sense. Seeing her kiss another man would probably push him over the edge enough to abduct her, but that still didn't tell her who *he* was. Her gut was telling her it was Dustin, but what had he meant by gifts? She hadn't been lying about that; she'd never received any gifts at her apartment. At least not that she knew of. She lay back on the bed and tried to go over every interaction she had ever had with Dustin.

Generally, she saw him on her way to or from work when he'd be walking his dog outside. There was the one time he'd offered to wash her windows, but she'd declined. She hadn't wanted him that close to her windows, and the landlord had a company that came out once every few months to clean up the outside of the apartments.

The gifts still bothered her. What if he had put the gifts on the wrong doorstep? But Dustin knew which apartment was hers; she was sure of it. Did that mean it was Scott then? Maybe he'd followed her to the parking lot but hadn't seen which building she entered? That didn't make much sense though because if he was stalking her, why wouldn't he watch her walk all the way inside?

He just hadn't given her enough clues to be sure, but Cassidy would keep trying.

## 14

"**J**ordan? What are you doing-" Al's voice faded as she spied Ivy behind him. "Who's that?"

"This is Ivy Hopkins. She's a friend of Cassidy's and a paramedic who works out of the firehouse. Cassidy's been taken, and she's here to help identify the possible suspects." Jordan sat down at his desk and turned the computer on.

"Whoa! What?"

Jordan could understand Al's confusion, but he didn't have time to explain it. He typed the cell number into the database and waited for the information to pop up. Scott Cline 5554 Wagoneer Avenue.

"Is that him?" Ivy asked peering over his shoulder.

"Is that who?" Al asked coming around the desk to see the computer.

"The guy who came to the firehouse," Ivy said. "Evidently, Cassidy gave him a jumpstart and then he showed up later with flowers and a dinner invite, so we think he might be her stalker."

"A possible suspect," Jordan corrected, "and I don't know yet. Let me put this in the DMV site and see if there's a picture." Jordan pulled up the website and plugged in the information. A moment later, a picture filled the screen. He turned the monitor toward Ivy. "Is it?"

Ivy nodded. "Yeah, that's definitely him. Is he the stalker?"

"I can start a background check, but it's going to take some time to get results back. In the meantime, I'll visit Scott's home and see if he'll talk to me. Then I want to stop by Cassidy's apartment and see what else I can find out about Dustin. You don't know his last name, do you?"

Ivy's head shook slowly, sadly. "I don't. I never asked much about him."

"Can you at least tell me what he looked like?"

Ivy shrugged. "Bland. He has sandy brown hair, about your height, thin. Nothing that would stand out. Maybe I should go with you to help identify him."

"No, you're staying here. The landlord should be able to help." He glanced at his watch. It was after five. "Except the office is probably closed. Do you have the landlord's number?"

"No, but I think it was on the door for emergencies. I know it was on Cassidy's fridge." She reached into her purse and pulled out her keys. "I have her apartment key if you need it."

Jordan stared at the key. He didn't want to go in Cassidy's apartment. Not without her permission and not with the emotions running rampant through his body right now. "I'll take my chances on the number first. If it's not on the door, I can find it out another way. Al, call me when the background on Scott Cline comes in."

"I'm going with you."

"No, I need you here to give me the information. Cassidy's already been missing nearly a whole day. We have to move fast and that means I need someone I can trust getting me the information I need."

Al held his gaze for a minute as if debating whether to argue with him or not. "Fine," she said and sat down in his vacated seat.

"Thanks Al. I'll get you a complete name as soon as I talk to the landlord." He headed for the exit and pushed open the door.

A few minutes later, he turned left on Wagoneer and pulled to a stop in front of 5554. An old Mustang was parked in the driveway, and Jordan hoped that meant Scott Cline was home.

The door swung open to reveal the man from the photos. "Scott Cline?"

"Yeah?" The man's voice was hesitant as his eyes scanned Jordan's face.

"I'm Detective Graves, and I need to ask you a few questions about Cassidy Marcel." Jordan pulled his jacket aside to display his badge.

The man's eyes flicked down to the badge and then back up to Jordan. "Who?"

"Cassidy, the firefighter you brought flowers to."

Scott blinked, nodded, and pushed the glasses up the bridge of his nose. "Oh, okay. I don't really know her. She helped me jump my car and I brought her flowers and asked her to dinner. I tried calling the number she gave me, but it was the wrong one. I just figured she wasn't interested."

"Unfortunately, she's gone missing, so I'm hoping you can tell me where you were yesterday."

Scott's eyes widened and he took a step back. "I didn't have anything to do with that. I was at work all day yesterday. You can check with my office. I had another big meeting, so I was there at seven a.m. and didn't leave until after nine p.m."

Jordan ran through the timeline in his head. He had left Cassidy before six p.m. and she had never texted him which made him think the accident had occurred shortly after she left him. "Can I get your work information to verify?"

Scott rattled off the information and Jordan plugged it into his phone. He would have Al verify it, but his gut told him Scott was not the man.

"Listen, I hope you find her, but if you do, tell her I'm no longer interested. I don't need this kind of drama in my life." He stepped back and closed the door.

Jordan fought the urge to knock on the door again and give the guy a piece of his mind, but that would do nothing to help Cassidy. This guy didn't seem to be the captor and the timeline didn't fit. He was a jerk but nothing more. Which meant that the best suspect right now was Dustin.

While it was possible he was dealing with a total unknown person, the statistics behind stalking suggested it was someone who knew Cassidy, and Dustin asking about her was a classic sign of stalking which made him wonder if this escalation was his fault.

Could Dustin have been at Edward Long's apartment or the hospital and seen them kiss? If he had, it might explain the abduction. Dustin would have been angry that Cassidy was seeing someone else and that might have led to the aggressive behavior. If that was the case, Jordan was responsible for this event. He had put an innocent woman in danger, and he had to make it right.

"Dustin?" Cassidy banged on the door and hollered at the top of her lungs. "Dustin, let me out of here so we can talk." She still wasn't positive Dustin was her stalker, but after reviewing what she knew, the scale tipped in his favor. "Dustin?" She pounded again and the rectangle slid open. "Dustin, let's talk about this."

"So, you finally realized it was me." His voice modulator was gone, and Cassidy recognized the voice immediately. The sound had never given her warm fuzzies but it sent shivers down her spine now.

"I did, but I still have questions for you. I was hoping you could answer them. I know you don't owe me any explanation since you've done so much for me already, but it would help me." Cassidy hoped she was hitting the right buttons. She'd never had to deal with a stalker before, but the cop shows she watched stated stalkers usually made up stories in their heads of what they thought happened.

"What do you want to know?"

"Why did you send the letters to the firehouse? Why not leave them on my doorstep?"

"Because you never said anything about all the other letters I left on your doorstep. When I heard you'd gone on the show, I thought maybe if I sent the letters to your work, you would know how serious I was."

Other letters? Cassidy had no knowledge of other letters. "I never got them, Dustin – the ones you left on my doorstep. I'm sorry; I would have acknowledged them if I had." She probably would have run to the police and filed a restraining order, but she would have acknowledged them.

"I don't believe you," he roared and pounded on the door with such force that Cassidy took a step back. "I told you in those letters how much I loved you and how we belonged together and you went on that stupid dating show anyway. That's not how you show love."

"You're right, but I promise you that I never received any letters or gifts from you at my apartment. I only got the letters and gifts at the station and since you didn't sign them, I didn't know who to thank. Please, can you let me out so we can discuss this?" Cassidy held her breath as she waited. She didn't know what she would find on the other side, but it had to be better than this tiny room.

"I'll think about it." And then the rectangle closed again and Cassidy was left in the silence once more. Only now, the light was officially gone, and the room was dark. Dark and silent. She didn't know how much longer she could take it.

## 15

**J**ordan pulled into the apartment parking lot and parked in front of the darkened office. He hoped the landlord's number was on the door. Twenty-four hours had already passed and Jordan knew the statistics were grim, but he'd beaten the statistics with the children. Maybe he could beat them with Cassidy too. He breathed a slight sigh of relief when he saw the small note on the door that held the landlord's name and phone number.

He punched the numbers into his phone praying the man would be home.

"Hello?"

"Is this Bob Warnke?" Jordan asked.

"It is. What can I help you with?"

"My name is Detective Graves with FBPD and I need to ask you a few questions. Can you give me your apartment number or meet me at the office?"

"I'll be right there." The phone clicked in Jordan's ear and he ended the call and placed it back in his pocket.

A minute later, a man with fuzzy white hair and a bathrobe

shuffled up to him. "I'm Bob. Sorry, I generally retire pretty early. What's this about?"

"It's about one of your tenants," Jordan began. "Do you have a Dustin who rents here? About my height with sandy brown hair? Always walking his dog?"

"That's my nephew, Dustin Gibbs. Has something happened to him?"

Jordan dodged the question and posed his own instead. "Do you know where he is, sir? It's important I find him."

"I'm sure he's in his apartment. Come on, I'll take you there." The man shuffled down the sidewalk to a building two down from Cassidy's. "His apartment is B, but what's this about?"

Jordan knew he needed to tread softly. He didn't want to alarm the man and have him shut down. "I believe Dustin may have information about a missing person I'm searching for."

The man blanched and dropped his eyes as he fumbled with the keys. "Please tell me you don't mean Cassidy Marcel."

A vice squeezed Jordan's heart and he balled his fists to keep from shaking the man. "I do mean Cassidy. She went missing yesterday. What do you know?"

Bob's hands trembled as he flipped through the key ring. "You have to understand Dustin isn't quite right in the head. He's a good kid, but sometimes he gets fixated on things. I saw him talking to Cassidy one day and the next morning I saw him by her apartment. He had left a flower on her doorstep. I didn't want her to freak out, so I took the flower. I thought Dustin would let it go, but he seemed to become obsessed with her. He left at least three more items on her doorstep – notes, flowers, candy."

Jordan's blood boiled in his veins. This man had known and done nothing? "Why didn't you tell Cassidy?" If he had told Cassidy, she could have done something. She could have moved or filed a restraining order. She could have at least known what she was up against.

Bob offered a small shrug. "I didn't think he was dangerous. He never has been before, and I've known him his whole life. In fact, I'm sure it's just a misunderstanding, but I can get him to talk to you." He inserted the key in the door and turned the lock. "Dustin?" he called as he pushed open the door. "Maybe he's sleeping."

Or more likely he wasn't there. Jordan followed the man into the apartment, his hand close to his gun, but he didn't really expect to use it. Bob continued to call out as he entered the apartment, but when every room had been checked, he sighed. "I guess he's not here."

"Where would he go? Where would he take her?"

Bob scratched his head as the thought. "My sister has an old place a few miles outside of town. No one lives there now, but he could go there I suppose."

"Get me the address. Now."

Jordan placed the call for backup as he sped toward the address. He just hoped they arrived when he did. He wasn't sure he would be able to wait outside knowing Cassidy was so close and probably in danger.

Cassidy awoke with a start when she heard a bang. Had that been a gun shot? Something falling over? She put her ear to the door to try and hear the commotion outside. Had she been found? If it wasn't rescuers, she might jump from the frying pan into the fire if she banged on the door, and someone worse than Dustin found her. Although, right now she couldn't imagine someone worse than Dustin. However, if it was rescuers, she had no idea if they would find her if she didn't pound on the door. She had no reference on where this door was in relation to the rest of the house. There was the one window, so she wasn't completely underground, but it could still be the basement if this was a split-level house.

Deciding the benefits outweighed the drawbacks, Cassidy threw her fists against the metal. "In here. I'm in here. Somebody please help me." There was another crashing sound followed by shouting and then the clear sound of a gunshot. Cassidy's hand froze before banging the door again. She was no longer sure she wanted to be found. The gun could belong to her rescuers, especially if it was the police, but it could also belong to Dustin or someone worse.

Before she could decide, a creaking sound filled the room. The lock turning on the door. Cassidy tried to scan the dark room for anything she could use, but she had nothing. Nothing but a plastic plate and bowl somewhere on the dark floor covered in oatmeal. She backed away from the door and crouched ready to launch herself at whoever came through the door. It wouldn't last long, but maybe she could overpower them with the element of surprise long enough to bolt for the door.

Light flooded the room as the door opened, and with a primal scream, Cassidy threw herself at the body in the doorframe. Only as her eyes adjusted to the light did she realize that the body belonged to Jordan, and by then, she was powerless to stop her force. Her body slammed into his sending him stumbling backward. His arms wrapped around her and he pulled her to his chest as they fell to the floor.

A grunting noise escaped his lips as they landed and then his hands flew to her face. "Are you hurt, Cassidy?"

"Jordan, I'm so sorry. I heard the gunshot and thought Dustin was going to kill me. I figured the element of surprise was my only shot." She ran her hands up his chest where they had landed to his face as if trying to feel out any injured spot.

A small smile played across his lips amid his pained expression. "I'd say you did a good job with that. You might have broken a few of my ribs, but it's worth it to see you safe."

Cassidy knew this was no time for emotions, but she couldn't help placing her lips against his – in apology, in relief, in love.

"I thought you said a relationship that began after a dangerous situation never lasted," he said with a smile as she pulled back.

She returned the smile and resisted the urge to kiss him again. "I decided it was worth it, but I thought you needed more time?"

"My brother convinced me otherwise."

She'd have to thank his brother when she met him, but suddenly she remembered where they were and she looked around. "Where is Dustin?"

"Injured." A woman's voice spoke up. Cassidy glanced around and found a young-looking woman leaning over Dustin and applying pressure to his stomach. "We better get an ambulance here."

Jordan grunted again and pushed Cassidy's hair back. "Cassidy, as much as I love holding you in my arms and want to continue, I need to reach my phone to call for a bus."

Cassidy scrambled off Jordan allowing him to sit up, but her mind wasn't on his phone call. It was on the words he had just said. He loved holding her and wanted to continue.

"How did you find me?" she asked Jordan when he ended his call.

"It's a rather long story," he wheezed as he stood and pulled her to his chest once again. "I promise I'll tell you all about it after we all get checked out. Al, are you okay?"

Al? So, this was his partner?

Al looked up at them an expression of hurt and understanding in her eyes. "I'm fine, but Dustin's vitals are falling. How far out is the ambulance?"

Cassidy thought back to the conversation she had overheard. There had been tension in Jordan's voice when talking about her to Al and from the look in Al's eyes, it was clear she was hurt by their kiss. Did she have feelings for Jordan then? And a better question was did he return them?

"Two minutes."

"Can I help?" Cassidy asked deciding the issue between Al and Jordan could wait for a better time. Dustin might have abducted her and held her hostage, but she didn't want him to die.

"Come help me apply pressure. My arms are starting to shake."

Cassidy took in the room as she crossed to Al. Chairs and tables were overturned and though she hadn't seen what happened, she had a pretty good guess. Jordan and Al had probably surprised Dustin who then kicked over tables and chairs to get away from them, but how had he gotten shot? She couldn't wait to get the full story from Jordan.

## 16

"All right, Cassidy, you're all clear," Dr. Brody Cavanaugh said as he finished the exam. "You'll have that bump and a black eye for another few days, but I believe you'll make a full recovery."

"Thank you. Can I go see Jordan now?" Cassidy hadn't wanted to be separated from Jordan when they'd reached the hospital, but the doctors had insisted she get looked at as well even though she'd told them she was fine.

Dr. Cavanaugh smiled and shook his head. "Yes, you can. He's right down the hall in room four."

Cassidy bolted out of the room and down the hall. It seemed like days since she and Jordan had shared that earth-changing kiss, and she didn't want to wait any longer to experience it again.

Jordan sat on the bed trying to get his shirt on, his face twisted in pain.

"Here, let me help you," Cassidy said hurrying to his side and helping him pull the shirt over his head.

"Thank you." He pulled the shirt down over his chiseled abs and then paused as if to catch his breath. "I was hoping you'd come see me." His voice was quieter than normal, but Cassidy wasn't sure if that was the hospital or the broken ribs speaking.

"I couldn't not come visit the man who saved me," Cassidy said as she placed a soft kiss on his cheek. She wanted it to be more but not while his face wrinkled in pain. There would be plenty of time for soul-shattering kisses when his pain lessened.

She sat down beside him on the bed and grabbed his hand. Funny how it still felt rough and strong though he looked so weak in the midst of his pain. "Can I ask you something though?"

"One question first. Did Dustin make it?"

"He did. The bullet missed all his vital organs, and he's getting psychiatric help now."

Jordan nodded. "Good, now what's your question?"

Cassidy took a deep breath. She'd thought about how to ask this but even though she'd rehearsed it, the words still didn't seem right. "Is there something going on between you and Al?"

He narrowed his eyes at her and cocked his head. "Why do you ask?"

"I saw the way she looked at me in the house after we kissed. It's obvious she has feelings for you, but I need to know if you have feelings for her too."

Jordan took her face in his hands. "Al, is my partner, and she means the world to me, but no, I don't have feelings for her like that. Seeing us kiss was probably a shock for her, but she'll get over it. Things will be fine." He leaned forward and placed a soft kiss on her lips.

Cassidy let herself enjoy the taste of his lips, the feel of security, but the story still wasn't complete for her. "Okay, but I have to know. How did you find me?" she asked when he pulled back.

The corners of his mouth pulled into a tight smile, and he took a shallow breath. "Of course you do. Well, when I called you this morning and you didn't return the call, I figured something might be wrong. I drove toward your apartment and saw the light pole you hit, but they had already towed your car. When I found out where it was stored, I searched your car and found your phone. Thankfully, Ivy was able to unlock your screen and get me the information on Scott. I paid him a visit – he's no longer interested just so you know."

"What?" Cassidy placed her hand on her cheek and pretended to be shocked.

"Yeah, he's says you're too much drama now. Anyway, confident he wasn't your stalker, I spoke to your landlord who admitted he knew Dustin was stalking you. Evidently, he had been leaving gifts on your doorstep but Bob had been removing them before you saw them because he was afraid you would freak out."

Now it all made sense. "So, that's what Dustin meant. He told me he had left me letters and gifts, but I didn't remember receiving any. That's why he switched to sending them to my work."

"Remind me to give that landlord of yours a piece of my mind when these ribs heal," Jordan continued. "Anyway, he gave me the address of the house where Dustin had you and the rest is history."

"Thank you for coming for me." Cassidy traced the veins in his hand relishing the feel of his skin beneath hers.

His lips parted in a soft smile as he lifted her chin to meet her eyes. "I will always come for you, but when you meet my brother, you should thank him." He shook his head. "It might have taken me a lot longer to find you if it hadn't been for him."

"Did I hear you mention me?" Cassidy turned to see a man who resembled Jordan in the doorway. He was clean shaven, wore glasses, and was dressed in a suit – about the polar opposite of Jordan – but the two shared the same strong jaw line.

"Of course he would hear that," Jordan muttered under his breath as he pushed himself up from the bed. "Cassidy, this is my brother Graham. Graham, this is Cassidy."

Graham's eyebrow rose as he stepped forward and extended a hand. "The firefighter, right?"

But Cassidy had no intention of simply shaking his hand. She threw her arms around the man who froze in shock. "Thank you."

"Uh, you're welcome?" Graham said. "Wow, maybe you should get injured more often if it'll mean beautiful women throw themselves at me."

"Not on your life," Jordan said as he grabbed his wallet off the nearby table before returning to stand beside Cassidy.

Cassidy turned her face up to Jordan's, a teasing glint sparkling in her eyes. "So, I've met your brother. Are you hiding any other family members from me?"

Jordan raised an eyebrow at her as he put his arm around her and pulled her to his chest. "To be fair, I've been a little busy saving children and rescuing you from a stalker to ramble on about my family, but I'll be happy to tell you whatever you want to know."

Cassidy didn't think she had ever heard sweeter words. She wrapped her arm around his waist and smiled up at him. "I want to know everything."

# THE EPILOGUE

"A few months ago, our father left us this building in his will, and I thought Graham was crazy to want to fix it up." The crowd cheered and clapped as Jordan tossed his brother a teasing grin. "But after taking some time off to heal and having to spend a lot of that time with my brother, I think he might have been right after all." Another cheer erupted and Jordan scanned the crowd. Many were firefighters who worked with Cassidy, some were paramedics or hospital staff, and the rest were cops.

Al caught his eye and nodded at him as she clapped. He'd been worried when he'd started seeing Cassidy, but Al had made it a point to let him know she was happy for him. For them. Perhaps she'd also realized dating a partner was not a good idea, or maybe she'd seen how perfect he and Cassidy were together. Regardless, he was thankful. He didn't want to lose Al as his partner

Jordan grinned as he returned her nod and wrapped his arm around Cassidy. He had never wanted this restaurant or the responsibility that went with it, but after spending the last few weeks fixing it up with Cassidy and Graham, it felt more like a second home than a responsibility.

And maybe that's why his father had kept it. Maybe he had seen how Graham and Jordan had drifted apart and how this project might bring them back together. It certainly would explain the posters in the walls. Perhaps, in a lucid moment, his father had walled up the posters knowing he would sell them and drink the money away if he didn't. Maybe his father hadn't even known about the posters in the walls. Jordan still didn't know how his father had acquired this building, but he supposed that part might just have to remain a mystery. For now. And he was okay with that.

"Thanks, big brother," Graham said taking over the announcing duty. "Ladies and gentlemen, Fire Dreams is officially open for business."

Fire Dreams. It might be an odd name for a restaurant, but it fit Jordan and Graham. So much of their dreams growing up had gone up in smoke, but fire held a cleansing power, and somehow this place also felt like a new beginning.

"You okay?" Cassidy asked as she laid a hand on his chest.

"Yeah, I was just thinking how I never saw myself here. Owning a restaurant, surrounded by firefighters, and in love with the prettiest one of them all."

Cassidy threw back her head and laughed. "Well, that's not hard considering the rest of them are men."

"That is a true statement, but I still think you're the prettiest one in here." He turned her to face him and let his hands slide down to her waist. "In fact, we might have to whip out one of those hoses because I feel the heat blaze every time I'm around you."

She rolled her eyes and batted his chest. "That might be the corniest line I've ever heard."

"But you still like me," he said as he lowered his face to hers and touched her lips.

"Yeah, I still like you," she breathed as his lips moved to her neck, "but I'm definitely going to have to work on your moves."

He pulled back and feigned a hurt expression. "There is nothing wrong with my moves. In fact, I almost forgot something." He stepped over to the bar and grabbed the rectangular box he had placed there earlier. "I got something for you."

"What? It's your opening night. I should have gotten something for you."

"Yeah, you should have, but you didn't. Maybe I need to work on your moves," he teased with a smile. "Open it." He placed the box in her hands and watched as she unwrapped the paper. He hoped she would like it. Most people might think it was just a trinket, but he suspected it would hold some significance for her.

She pulled off the top of the box and gasped. "Jordan, how did you? Where did you?" Her words trailed off as she pulled out the small license plate he'd had custom made for her. In the middle was her name and across the bottom was a row of flames.

"One of the guys who did the interior design has a custom trinket shop. I thought it was time you actually had something with your name on it."

Her eyes glistened as she met his gaze. "This is….thank you."

"See? I have good moves," he said pulling her close again.

"Yes, Officer Graves, it appears you do." She lifted her head and he wasted no time in claiming her lips once again.

"Help! Is there a doctor in here?"

Jordan pulled back and turned to see who needed assistance. A man stood in the doorway, a frantic look on his face.

"There was an accident. A woman's been injured, but the guy who hit her took off. She looks bad though. Are any of you doctors?"

"I am." Brody Cavanaugh fought his way through the crowd

followed by two or three other people Jordan recognized from the hospital.

"We better go too," Jordan said grabbing the license plate and stashing it behind the bar once more before hurrying outside with Cassidy and the rest of the crowd.

The sun had set, but the streetlights illuminated the area and down the street they could see the car – a red sports car – folded in an accordion shape.

"Get the Jaws of Life," Bubba ordered as he sprinted towards the car. Around him, firemen spread out. Some ran toward the firehouse a block away to get the truck and ambulance and others followed Bubba including Cassidy.

Jordan looked around for the man who had entered the bar. He stood a few feet away wringing his hands together. "You." Jordan hurried over to the man. "I'm Detective Graves. Did you see the accident happen?"

"It happened so fast. I heard the crash and then it sounded like he gunned it. Why would he gun it if he knew he'd hurt someone?" The man was rambling, clearly in shock.

"Can you tell me what the vehicle looked like that hit her?"

The man turned to face Jordan and for a moment his eyes were clear. "It was a truck. A black Ford truck."

Want to know who was in the accident and who was the driver of the truck? Find out the rest of the story in the riveting second book of the Men of Fire Beach series, Lost Dreams and New Beginnings coming soon.

The End

# IT'S NOT QUITE THE END!

Thank you so much for reading *Fire Games*. This book was originally planned to be the third full length book in the Blushing Brides series, but as it lent itself more to suspense, I decided to make it a spin off series. As you can see, there is more planned for The Men of Fire Beach and I hope you'll take that journey with me.

I hope you enjoyed the story as I really enjoyed writing it. If you did, would you do me a favor? If you did, please leave a review. It really helps. It doesn't have to be long - just a few words to help other readers know what they're getting.

I'd love to hear from you, not only about this story, but about the characters or stories you'd like read in the future. I'm always looking for new ideas and if I use one of your characters or stories, I'll send you a free ebook and paperback of the book with a special dedication. Write to me at loranahoopes@gmail.com. And if you'd like to see what's coming next, be sure to stop by authorloranahoopes.com

I also have a weekly newsletter that contains many

wonderful things like pictures of my adorable children, chances to win awesome prizes, new releases and sales I might be holding, great books from other authors, and anything else that strikes my fancy and that I think you would enjoy. I'll even send you the first chapter of my newest (maybe not even released yet) book if you'd like to sign up.

Even better, I solemnly swear to only send out one newsletter a week (usually on Tuesday unless life gets in the way which with three kids it usually does). I will not spam you, sell your email address to solicitors or anyone else, or any of those other terrible things.

God Bless,
    Lorana

The Men of
**FIRE BEACH**

*Lost*
# MEMORIES
## AND NEW BEGINNINGS

Best-selling author
# LORANA HOOPES

*To my wonderful readers who inspire me to write everyday.*
*To my lovely BETA readers who helped me make this the best*
*book it could be - Deanna, Cassandra, Shari, Billie, Linda,*
*and Dan.*
*To Dan, my amazing proofreader, who wordsmiths with the best*
*of them.*
*To Linda who told me this character's story needed to be told.*
*To Molly who helped me with the hospital scenes to make them*
*more realistic.*

A t the sound of the angry voices, she clasped her hand over her mouth to keep from making a sound. She had to get out of here, but the men were still in the room. Was this why he had been so angry when she came back? What would they do if they found her?

She faintly heard the sliding glass door to the balcony patio open. Now was her shot, and it might be the only one she had. As quickly as she could, she pushed open the door. *Don't look at them. Just grab your purse and get out of here.* But her eyes shifted to the left anyway. As if drawn by force. For a moment she froze. Long enough for the man on the patio to turn and catch sight of her. His face was shrouded in darkness, but she could feel the frosty hatred in his gaze. Her feet regained their ability to move, and she bolted out of the bedroom and down the stairs.

A noise sounded behind her, but she didn't know if it was the patio door or her overactive imagination playing tricks on her. She burst out the front door and raced down the driveway knowing the men were just behind her. Her breath and the sound of her heartbeat thundered in her head. Would she make it? Frantically, she pushed the unlock button on her key fob. She wanted to turn around, but she knew looking behind her would cost precious time. When she reached the car, she yanked the door open and slid into the seat. Her fingers trembled so badly that she nearly dropped the keys as she jammed them into the ignition. As they finally slid in, she chanced a glance at the front door.

He stood there in the shadows looking as if he belonged in the darkness. As if he owned it. She jerked the car into drive and sped out of the driveway certain that he would jump in a vehicle and follow her.

Fear and anger took turns controlling her body as she drove. Tears blurred her vision, and she blinked against the dam determined to hold them in. She would not cry. She did not cry. But what was she going to do now? It was supposed to have been a simple meeting, a chance to land a new publisher for her books after the last company dropped her. Instead it had turned into something else, something nefarious feeling, and she was a witness. A witness who was never supposed to be there.

She glanced in the mirror to see if he was following her, but only darkness stared back at her. He hadn't seemed in a hurry as he stood in the front doorway, but now he knew what she drove. Would he hunt her down? Why hadn't she done better homework on him?

Disgust filled her as she thought of how she had come crawling to him. How she was willing to do nearly anything to get him to promote her. How could she have gotten involved with a man like that? Well, almost involved. Her momma sure wouldn't be proud. Heck, she wasn't proud. She had no idea how she had wandered so far down the wrong path.

Maybe it had been the move to California or the first award. After all, she'd been a poor girl growing up with only her big imagination to keep her company. Especially after her father left them. Maybe it had been the first time she saw her name on a cover. When she'd first begun writing, she'd been young and idealistic. She'd wanted to write clean romances that people could read anywhere and not be ashamed, but the publishing world was competitive. New authors were writing books every day, and her work wasn't selling the way it used to. Then, after her attempt to discredit Ava McDermott had backfired, her publisher had let her go. Now, she had a stack of bills that needed to be paid and no way to do it. That was why she had gone to him.

But he'd wanted more than her books. He'd lured her there with big promises and the right words that fed her ego, but he'd really just wanted to get her into his bed. That low down, dirty…. No, she would own this. She had reached out to him. She had been the one trying to further her career. She was the one who hadn't done her homework completely. His personal life should have been in her research. Maybe then she would have known about whatever he had going on the side. Well, that wouldn't happen again. She would just have to be more careful in the future - cross all the "t"s and dot all the "i"s. If there was a future.

She wiped her finger across her cheek. A tear had escaped her eye and was trying to snake down her cheek, but she wasn't going to let it succeed. Of course, what would smeared makeup matter if he went after her? Her makeup should be the least of her worries.

Suddenly headlights flared in her rear-view mirror. Bright and unforgiving, they blinded her, forcing her to throw up a hand. Oh no, had he pursued her after all? The lights grew closer and filled her mirror. Was he trying to run her off the road? Maybe it wasn't him. Maybe it was just teenagers out for a joy ride, but they were driving awfully close to her - dangerous on city streets.

She slowed down to let the vehicle pass, but it didn't. Instead, it matched her pace. These weren't teenagers then. They would have driven past her. Maybe yelled or flipped her off, but they would have passed her. Her tears dried up as fear overtook her anger and self-pity. How was she going to get out of this now? She was unfamiliar with this area and had no idea how to outrun them.

She twisted in her seat to try and get a better view of the vehicle behind her, but it was too dark and they were too close. She glanced around for her phone to call 911 but it was on her passenger seat. Just out of reach. Wait! Where was her purse? Oh no, she had left it there. Her heart sank. Now they would know for sure who she was and where she lived.

The fear grew icy talons and clawed up her insides. Were they going to run her off the road and then shoot her? Suddenly, lights flashed to her right. She had just enough time to register a large dark truck approaching and then her head was thrown into the window with the impact.

"Help! Is there a doctor in here?"

Dr. Brody Cavanaugh looked up from his sparkling water to the doorway to see what the commotion was. A man stood in the doorway wringing his hands. Frantic fear covered his face, and his eyes shifted from one face to another as he scanned the crowd.

"There was an accident. A woman's been injured, but the guy who hit her took off. She looks bad though. Are any of you doctors?"

"I am." Brody knew Hollywood thought this happened all the time, but he could honestly count on one hand the times someone had come running in calling for a doctor, and only one had happened since he'd been in Fire Beach. He caught fellow doctor Nick Pearson's attention and pushed back from the table. His drink could wait. As could his dinner. He and Pearson fought their way through the throng of patrons and spilled out onto the street with the rest of the crowd following behind them.

The sun had set, but the streetlights illuminated the area, and down the street he could see the car – a red sports car – folded in a "C" shape. For one moment, time appeared to freeze as people assessed the situation. And then everything happened at once.

"Get the Jaws of Life," one of the firemen ordered as he sprinted towards the car. Tall and muscular, Brody thought he was the one they called Bubba. Around Brody, firemen spread out. Some ran toward the firehouse a block away to get the truck and the ambulance, and others ran with the large fireman toward the car including Cassidy.

Brody had met Cassidy a few times at the hospital when she came in with paramedic Ivy Hopkins, but it was not until he had assessed her after her abduction a few months ago that the bond between the hospital, the fire department, and the police department had begun to grow. Even though he worked in the ICU now instead of the emergency department, he had been kept in the loop of events, such as tonight's opening of her boyfriend's, Detective Jordan Graves, restaurant, Fire Dreams. However, this was probably not the opening Cassidy and Jordan had planned on or hoped for.

The firetruck and ambulance roared in a moment later, and two more large men carried the bulky machinery over to the car. Brody approached and stood to the side watching as Bubba and one of the other firemen worked the Jaws of Life to cut away the driver's door. The groaning sound of the metal snapping not only overpowered the roaring of the hydraulic tool but reminded him of nails on chalkboards, and he resisted the urge to place his hands on his ears. The red sports car was twisted in such an awkward shape that he feared the driver had been crushed in the crash.

Ivy Hopkins appeared beside him having hopped down from the ambulance. Her wide eyes were fixed on the scene. "Do you think she'll make it?" Her slender fingers pulled on the ends of her blonde hair.

"I don't know, but we'll do everything we can." Brody exchanged a glance with Nick. They both knew this driver needed a miracle.

"Her legs are pinned under the dashboard," one of the men called out as the deafening sound of the hydraulic ceased momentarily. The sudden stillness was jarring. "We need the ram."

Two other firemen hurried forward with a different tool, and after a moment, the hydraulic sound filled the night again.

"Okay, we've got her free."

That was their cue. The firemen stepped aside as he, Nick, and Ivy stepped up to the car. Brody tried not to focus on the metallic scent of blood in the air or the mangled mess that was the woman's right leg as he surveyed the scene closer. The woman wore a red suit, designer from the looks of it, and red acrylic nails covered her fingertips. She was either a woman of means or one who took pride in her appearance. He leaned toward the former assumption based on the car she was driving. A Firebird wasn't the cheapest car to own or insure.

Ivy checked for a pulse and performed a quick assessment of the woman before strapping on a neck collar. "She's breathing, but her vitals are weak." Her eyes locked with his and said more than her words did. She unfastened the seat belt and moved it away from the woman, taking extra care to pull it away from her right side which had taken the brunt of the force. Then she stepped back allowing him to snake his arms under the woman's arms while Nick took the woman's legs.

The woman's face and hair were covered in blood, and Brody thought some of the cuts on her face might need stitches, but that was not his immediate concern. No, his immediate concern was her head. A large cut indicated she had hit her head against the window, and her lack of response pointed to a concussion if not a possible brain injury. Plus, there was the probability of internal bleeding.

Nick appeared to share his assessment as he glanced up with grave eyes as they placed the woman on the stretcher. "Her right foot is in bad shape too."

"I'm going to call ahead and tell them what's coming," Ivy said as she caught a full glimpse of the woman.

Brody nodded as he and Nick helped the other paramedic load the gurney into the ambulance. Ivy returned and climbed in the back with Brody as the other paramedic and Nick climbed into the cab. Brody's previous ER training kicked in, and he took a closer look at the woman's feet as Ivy set up an IV. Her shoes were expensive looking red heels and though he knew she might be angry, her feet were already beginning to swell, and he couldn't wiggle the shoes enough to get them off. "Do you have scissors in here?"

Ivy handed a pair back to him and he inserted them in the side, cutting away the shoes until he could remove them from her feet.

"Is she going to lose them?" Ivy asked.

"Probably not the left one. It might be broken or sprained, but the right? I don't know, but it doesn't look good." The skin was still intact which was a good sign, but purple bruising was already starting to appear. It had been mangled badly in the crash and was twisted in an awkward angle. He just hoped that it had not been crushed. Crush injuries generally resulted in amputations, and though he knew they weren't the end of the world, no doctor liked performing them especially on someone so young. If she didn't lose it, she would probably need some reconstructive surgery on it.

The ambulance pulled to a stop, and the back doors opened. Nick and the other paramedic pulled the gurney down as Ivy and Brody climbed out after. Together they sprinted into the hospital. A wave of nostalgia hit him as the doors whooshed open.

"Female: mid-thirties, motor vehicle crash with jaws of life extrication, BP is ninety over palp, pulse is tachy and thready, O2 sats low nineties with fifteen liters on a nonrebreather. We secured I.V. access in route - sixteen gauge in the left AC," Ivy rattled off as the doctors on shift swarmed in around them.

"She sustained a substantial head injury with loss of consciousness as well, and her legs and feet need to be addressed," Brody added. "Particularly the right side. There might be crushing involved."

"Thank you, Dr. Cavanaugh. We can take it from here," Dr. Williams said brusquely.

Brody opened his mouth to protest but then closed it. This was no longer his domain, and she was a competent doctor. In fact, she had been the one who had taken his position when he moved. He trusted her, but Brody didn't want to let her take the woman. He wanted to jump in and work on this woman himself, but he would get his chance. He'd be on shift in less than eight hours, and she would probably end up in the ICU. He could check on her then. If she made it through the night.

## 2

The woman tried to open her eyes and grimaced against the pain. "Where am I?" Her voice sounded groggy and far away, and her head throbbed. After a few tries, she managed to get her right eye open, but the left didn't seem to work.

"Fire Beach Hospital. I'm Dr. Cavanaugh. How are you feeling?"

She searched for the source of the voice and found a handsome man in a white coat at the foot of her bed. His coppery hair was combed back, and his face sported a neatly trimmed beard and mustache. He held a clipboard in his hands. A doctor? Was she in a hospital?

The woman groaned and closed her eyes as another wave of pain followed by a wave of nausea hit. When it passed and she was sure she wouldn't vomit when she opened her mouth, she answered his question. "Like I've been hit by a train." She attempted to raise her hand to touch her head but cords and pain made her lay it back down.

"Close." He nodded and gave her a small smile. "'We heard

it was a black Ford truck. The police are looking for them now, but can you remember anything else?"

She tried to focus. "I was in an accident?" She felt like she should remember that, and there was this tiny spot in her brain that felt like a memory, but it was fuzzy and far away.

"You were. Banged you up pretty badly. Your left eye is swollen shut which is why you can't open it right now. You have a pretty deep contusion on your head, and your right foot was broken, but it looked a lot worse initially. Thankfully, you have no internal bleeding, but you were unconscious for a while. Can you remember anything about the accident?"

Fear. A feeling of fear crackled in the air. She remembered fear coursing through her body and bright lights. "I think someone was after me."

He raised an eyebrow as he marked something on his clipboard. "What makes you think that?"

"I don't know." Her words sounded desperate and angry in her ears. "I just feel like I was running from something, and someone was chasing me."

"Okay, we'll come back to that later." She could tell from his voice that he didn't believe her, but she knew what she felt. She didn't remember the details but the lingering caress of fear didn't dissipate.

"Let's start with something easier. Can you tell me your name?"

What kind of stupid question was that? Certainly she knew her name. It was... Suddenly her right eye shot open, and her heart thundered harder in her chest. The caress of fear shifted into a full embrace that covered her body. She caught the doctor's gaze and forced the fearful words out. "I don't remember my name. Is that normal?"

His jaw tightened - just the slightest twitch near his chin - but the movement was brief, and she wondered if she had just imagined it. "It can happen in cases like this. You hit your head pretty hard, and you had a concussion which can cause some memory loss. The CT showed some swelling, so we'll continue to monitor it."

"It will come back though, won't it?" Anxiety joined the fear coursing through her body. She couldn't have lost her memory.

"I've seen patients regain some memory, depending on how severe the concussion was."

"Some memory? I can't lose any of my memory." A desperate fear ravaged her and colored her voice. What would she do if she couldn't remember her life? "You have to do something to get it back."

He chuckled softly and shook his head. "There's no trick I can do if that's what you're looking for, but it does help if you don't stress yourself out."

"Not stress myself out?" Her voice took on a sharp edge. "That's easy for you to say, but I don't even know who I am at the moment, and there are clearly people out to get me, so not stressing is not really an option."

His smile faded, and a cool expression covered his face. "I know you're scared, but I need you to stay calm."

"Wait, what about identification? Did I have a purse? I feel like I don't go anywhere without a purse." She was desperate, but maybe if she saw her name it would all come flooding back.

"I'll check with Detective Graves who is probably the one handling your case. If there was a purse, we'll get it to you. Now, why don't you relax and let me examine you?"

The woman tried to relax but her brain continued to spin. Surely someone was missing her. Was she married? Did she have kids? Her gaze traveled to her left hand, but there was no ring. Had they removed her jewelry? "Did I have anything when I came in? Any jewelry?"

"I'm not sure, but I'll check." He shined a light in her eyes. "How is the pain in your head?"

"Awful. It feels like someone's beating a gong inside my

brain." She paused for a minute. Those words felt familiar as if she'd heard them before.

Dr. Cavanaugh chuckled. "Well, that's a saying I haven't heard before, so I bet you're not from around here."

She wasn't even sure where here was at the moment, but before she could ask, he continued. "How about your feet?"

She closed her eyes and tried to focus on her feet, but there was so much pain coursing through her body that she couldn't be sure where it was coming from. "All I feel is pain. Can't you give me something for the pain?"

"I have you on an IV delivering pain medicine. I can't give you any more, but the pain will lessen as you heal. Now, can you feel this?"

She blew out a frustrated breath and concentrated on her foot. Perhaps she felt something, but she wasn't sure. "Um, maybe?" She glanced up at him. From the expression on his face, that wasn't the answer he wanted. "Is it bad?"

"It's not what I would like, but it might be that the pain you are feeling is still affecting your movement. We'll give it another few days." He continued the exam pressing gently on her stomach and her thighs before scanning both her arms. When he appeared satisfied, he stepped back.

"Do you feel up to eating? I can have Valerie bring you some food."

Eating? How could she think about eating? Her world had just been turned upside down, but he must have taken her lack of response as a yes as he continued his spiel.

"If you would like to watch TV, the remote is here." He picked it up and waved it before setting it back beside her, "and here on the side of the bed is the call button. If you need a nurse, you hit that button. This button here you can hit if you need more medicine, but it will max out at a certain level. I'm afraid we can't take all the pain away. I'll be back to check on you before I leave for the day."

Anxiety clutched at her heart, and she heard it in her voice. "You mean you aren't going to be monitoring me directly?"

"I'm afraid I have other patients that I also have to check on, but I will look back on you before I leave."

She watched him walk out the door and tried to keep her tears in check, but the silence of the room pressed in on her. Except for the beeping of some monitor, she was alone. With no idea of who she was or when she might remember.

Brody sighed as he exited the woman's room. He had expected her to be demanding from the persona he had created of her, but he hadn't expected the memory loss. While some patients did regain their memories, many didn't, and he certainly couldn't release her until at least some of her memory returned. Plus, the loss of sensation in her feet bothered him. He had seen no blackening of her skin which was hopeful - it meant her foot was still getting blood flow, but that didn't mean she would be able to walk on it again if she didn't get sensation back.

"I was hoping I would find you here."

Brody looked up to see Detective Jordan Graves and a young-looking woman striding his direction. Jordan held a mangled object in his hand. "Dr. Cavanaugh, this is my partner, Al Parker. The woman had a phone in the car," he said holding up the object, "but no wallet. Is she awake yet?"

"She is, but she doesn't remember much. Not even her name."

The woman, Al, blinked at him. "Is that normal? Will she get it back?"

Brody shrugged and picked up the next patient info sheet. "I don't know. She hit her head pretty hard and sustained a concussion, but the CT didn't show any lasting damage although it did show swelling. My guess is that she will get at least some back, but I can't give you a timeline."

"Is she able to talk? Can we ask her some questions?" Jordan pressed.

"She is capable of speaking but don't push her too hard. Rest is important for her right now, and again, I don't think she remembers much. Although she does think someone was after her."

"She does? What did she say?"

"Not much. Just that she remembered being afraid and thought someone was after her. I was about to refer her to psych for an examination."

Jordan's jaw clenched and he exchanged a glance with Al. "Hold off on that for a while, will you? She might be right. We found no brake marks on the road, and our witness said the truck didn't even try to stop. My gut says this might not have been an accident, and we are determined to find out who hit her and why. Which room is she in?"

"Room six." Brody pointed behind him and watched the two detectives walk away. He felt his view of the woman shifting. She might be a bit challenging, but why would someone be after her? He found himself curious about her.

Maybe it was because he had been one of the first responders on the scene and ridden with her in the ambulance. Maybe it was because she seemed so vulnerable both with her injuries and with her memory loss. Whatever the reason, he needed to think less about the Jane Doe in room six and more about his job before he made a mistake.

## 3

T he woman looked up at the knock. A man in blue jeans and a leather jacket and a younger woman in a button-down shirt stood in the doorway of her room.

"Pardon me, ma'am, but I'm Detective Graves and this is Detective Parker. Do you think we could ask you a few questions?"

The woman lifted her hand a few inches and motioned them inside. "You can try, but I don't remember much – not even my name. The doctor already asked."

A small smile pulled at the male detective's lips. "Well, no offense to Dr. Cavanaugh, but he's not a detective, so he might not have asked the right questions." He held out a broken phone. "Do you recognize this?"

The woman looked at it and an image flashed in her mind. She closed her eyes against the fear that accompanied the vision. "That's my phone, isn't it?"

"We pulled it from your car, so we believe it was your phone."

"I was going to use it, but it was on the passenger seat and I couldn't reach it, but I can't remember why I was going to use it."

"Unfortunately, it's destroyed and there was no purse or wallet inside the car that we could find. Do you know why you might have been driving without your license?"

She opened her mouth to reply but then paused. Driving without a license was illegal. Somehow, she knew that, so was he trying to trick her? "Am I in trouble, officers?"

He stared at her for a second before chuckling softly. "For driving without a license? No. You should always carry it and you can be fined for not having it, but we're not here to issue you a ticket. We're more concerned with the accident. Our witness says the black truck hit you, but we aren't sure if the accident was on purpose or not. Do you remember anything?"

*Just the fear.* "I don't think it was an accident. I can't remember why, but I think someone was after me. Did the witness help at all?"

The female detective stepped forward, "He wasn't able to supply us with much unfortunately, so we were hoping this phone might jog some memories."

"I wish it did, but I have nothing more."

"That's okay, it will probably come back," Detective Graves said before the ringing of his phone interrupted him. He pulled it out and turned away. "Detective Graves. Yes, sir, we are here now. Tia Sweetchild?" He glanced back at her. "Yes sir." He hung up the phone and returned to the side of her bed. "Does the name Tia Sweetchild ring a bell for you?"

"Is that me? Am I Tia?" she asked.

"The car you were driving was rented to a Tia Sweetchild so yes, we believe so. However, the address listed on the rental agreement is in California, so we're not sure what you would be doing here in Illinois."

She rolled the name around in her head. It didn't feel wrong, but she wished it zinged or something, so she could feel certain.

Still, it was better than having no name. "I have no idea what I was doing here, but now that we know my name, we should be able to find out some more about me, right?"

"We'll certainly do our best," Detective Parker said. "If you remember anything else, please call us." She handed Tia a white business card.

"We'll be in touch as soon as we have more information," Detective Graves said.

When they exited, Tia picked up the broken phone the detectives had left. She turned it over in her hands and noticed her nails. Long and acrylic. A sign she took care of her appearance, but the phone gave her nothing more. With a sigh, she set it beside her and turned on the television. The news came on and the story caught her attention.

"Last night the opening of the new local restaurant Fire Dreams was overshadowed by a terrible hit and run accident. The driver of this vehicle survived but remains in intensive care." Tia sucked in her breath as the camera showed the car she was in. The other vehicle must have hit the passenger side which was lucky because her car was a crushed disaster. Had she been in the passenger side, she would not have lived. "The police believe the other driver was in a black Ford truck. If you saw the accident or have any information, you are being asked to call the Fire Beach Police Department."

A red sports car? That must say something about her. She either had money or wanted to appear that she did. What had she been wearing? Tia glanced around the room, but saw no clothes. Had the hospital taken them? She would have to ask when a nurse came in.

Her gaze wandered back to the TV. Would anyone call the number? She hoped they did because right now all she had was a name and an uneasy feeling that someone was out to get her.

Brody stared down at the burger and fries he had ordered and sighed. Around him, the restaurant hummed with conversation but he heard none of it. He had hoped leaving the hospital and grabbing some dinner would lift his mood, but it didn't appear to be working so far.

Nick folded himself into the booth across from him and grabbed one of Brody's fries. "Long day?" he asked before shoving the fry in his mouth.

Brody shrugged. "The usual, I guess. I just can't get that woman off my mind."

"The one from the car wreck?" Nick asked when his mouth was clear of food.

"Yeah, she woke up today but has no memory of who she is or what happened to her. I know she's just a patient and she's a little abrasive, but there's something about her. I just feel this need to protect her."

Nick's brow shot up. "Is the self-proclaimed done-with-love Dr. Brody Cavanaugh contemplating giving love another shot?"

Brody rolled his eyes at the name. He had never claimed he was done with love. He had simply not dated since his wife died. Though his friends had tried to get him back out there, no woman had held his interest enough to attempt going out with her. "No, I don't think so. I told you my heart died with Rachel, but something bothers me about this. The accident, her memory loss, the fact that she had no ID with her. Why would someone drive without ID?"

Nick shrugged and grabbed another fry. "Maybe she was just going out for a quick drive and forgot it. I've done that so many times." Brody had no doubt he did. Nick was the epitome of a laid-back surfer dude with his chin length blond hair and blue eyes. His attire consisted mainly of cargo pants, sandals, and chambray shirts, and Brody had never seen him angry. Ever.

"Maybe." But that didn't feel right to Brody. Even when he went out for a quick drive, he always brought his wallet. Sure, there had been the few times he'd forgotten it and maybe that was what had happened to her, but he didn't think so. She'd been dressed for a meeting or a date with her high heeled shoes and designer outfit - not the kind of thing one wore when just out for a drive. Plus, the no ID coupled with the hit and run just seemed too coincidental. "Plus, she also thinks someone was after her."

"Why?"

Brody shook his head. "I don't know. She said she remembered bright lights and being afraid. I was going to call psych to come evaluate her, but then Jordan showed up and said they weren't sure it was an accident. No brake marks on the road. But if it wasn't an accident, then it means someone tried to kill her, and if they come looking to finish the job, we have no idea who we are looking for. Her story was on the news today I heard."

"We have security guards," Nick said with a shrug.

"Yeah, but not enough and they've never been tested." In fact, the security guards were staffed by an outside company, and Brody had never seen them do anything except sit at a desk by the exit.

Nick paused his devouring of Brody's fries and cocked his head. "Are you sure you aren't developing feelings for this woman?"

"No," Brody said with a firm shake of his head. "But she does remind me of Rachel. I wasn't able to help her once the cancer took hold, and now I feel the same way about this woman. I mean I can monitor her injuries, but I can't get her memory back. I became a doctor to help people, Nick."

Nick held his hands up in surrender. "All right, I hear you, man." He leaned back and folded his toned tan arms across his broad chest. "So, what do you want to do?"

Finally. Now, he was getting through to his friend. Brody splayed his hands on the table top as he leaned forward. "I want to find out everything we can about this woman. When I made my final check on her, she told me the detectives found out her name was Tia Sweetchild from the vehicle rental agreement."

"Tia Sweetchild?" Nick rubbed his chin as he said the words thoughtfully. "Why does that name seem familiar to me?" He pulled out his cell phone and began tapping the screen.

"I have no idea." Brody took a sip of his drink. Why hadn't he thought to do that? He could have googled the woman just as easily, but the truth was he rarely used his phone. Nick was about the only person he called anymore. "A previous patient?" His eyes raked over the dinner. He'd box the food up for later. His appetite had suddenly disappeared as his curiosity had taken over.

"Nope." Nick smiled and his eyes held a triumphant gleam. He turned his phone so Brody could see it. "Try romance author."

Brody grabbed the phone and stared closer at the picture. The woman in the hospital was beat up, but the resemblance was there. He looked back at Nick. "You read romance novels?"

Nick scoffed and shook his head. "No way, man, but Erica, that nurse I was trying to date a few months ago, does. She was always reading on her break. I only remember the name because it was different, you know? I thought maybe it was a made-up name. You know like a pen name."

Clearly it wasn't a pen name unless she took it to the point of creating an address in a fake name, but that didn't answer the immediate question. "Why would anyone want to hurt a romance writer?" Brody asked returning his focus to the screen to learn more about Tia.

"My guess is if you find that out, you'll find out who's after her. If someone's after her." Nick took another French fry, and Brody pushed the plate toward him. He could eat at home later. Right now, he needed to find out everything he could about Tia Sweetchild.

❄ 4 ❄

"**G**ood morning. Would you care for a pen and some paper?"

Tia opened her eyes to see Dr. Cavanaugh standing over her bed. His hands were behind his back, but his eyes twinkled. Flecks of green and gold danced in them, and she thought she could get used to seeing those eyes gazing at her every day. Well, that was if she wasn't married or already dating someone. "Why would I need pen and paper? I'm not sure I could move enough to use them." Her pain was less intense today, but even with that, a stiffness had settled in much like sore muscles after a hard workout. Hmm, was that just common knowledge or did she have first-hand experience? Did she work out?

"How about a computer then or a dictation machine?" He continued to smile at her as if he had a secret he was bursting to share with her.

While she would love a computer to look up information about herself, she didn't think that's what he was getting at. "Okay, you look like the cat who ate the canary. Why don't you just tell me what this is about?"

"I just thought a romance author might have a reason to write." He brought his hands forward and held out a book to her. The title *True Love* filled the top of the book and underneath was a couple who looked very much in love, but it was the bottom of the book that caught her eye. Tia Sweetchild.

"Is that... is that me? Is that my book?"

He turned the book around to show the back which held a description and an author's photo. The woman on the back was blonde and had a perfect smile, but though she looked happy, her eyes contained a sadness. Had she not been happy? "It sure looks like you," he said, "and I did some research on the author. She lives in California."

"Where the rental agreement said I lived," Tia said softly. She lifted her hand to touch the book hoping it would jog a piece of her memory, but when she touched the cover, she didn't see a happy couple. Instead, she saw angry eyes. "What are you doing here?" With a gasp, she removed her hand.

"What? What is it?" Dr. Cavanaugh asked. Concern replaced the twinkling in his eyes.

"I saw something. A man, and he was furious. He asked me what I was doing there." Tia shook her head slightly wishing she could pull more from her memory.

Dr. Cavanaugh set the book beside her and touched her arm. "Hey, that's a start. We'll start keeping track of what you remember. I'm sure it will all come back eventually. In the meantime, how about I take a look under the bandage and see how your head is healing."

Tia nodded and let him peel the dressing from her head wondering how bad it was. A vague feeling of vanity passed through her. It was obvious from her nails and the car she had been driving that her appearance had been important to her. She supposed as an author she needed to at least be presentable, but she felt there was more to it than that. "What happened to the clothes I was wearing when I came in?"

"What?"

"The clothes I was wearing. I know I wasn't wearing a hospital gown when I got in the wreck, so where are the clothes I was wearing?"

"Oh, um, I don't know, but I'll check for you. I was there though. At the accident. You were wearing a red designer suit and expensive-looking heels. I had to cut your shoes off. My guess is they cut your suit off when you arrived here."

Designer clothes? Expensive heels? So, she must have money. She wished she could see the clothing to see if it opened any other shut doors in her memory. "Do they throw them away when they cut them off?"

"Sometimes. I'll ask around for you and have Valerie bring them in if she finds them. The cut is looking better by the way. The stitches are holding."

"Stitches? Will I have a scar?" Her voice had taken on a slight shrill irrational edge, but he didn't seem to notice.

"Probably a small one, but don't worry about it. You do feel warm though." He ran the thermometer across her forehead, and his brow furrowed.

"Is it bad?"

"It's one hundred and two. Not great and a little worrisome especially after a concussion and your foot surgery. I'll have Valerie keep a closer eye on you, and I'll check in more often as well." He replaced the bandage and then moved to her foot. "Let's see if you're feeling your toes today."

Tia closed her eyes to focus on his touch. "There," she said when she thought he had touched her toes.

"Good, there's a little sensation today. That's progress. It looks like you'll be staying with us a little longer though."

"It's not like I have anywhere to be," Tia said. "At least I don't think so. Does the biography on the back say anything about a family?"

Dr. Cavanaugh picked up the book and turned it over. "Tia

Sweetchild is a clean romance writer who lives in California. When not writing, she enjoys yoga, candlelit dinners, and long walks on the beach."

Yoga. Well that explained the feeling of stiff muscles. Unless she had always been nimble, she was sure she had felt some stiffness when she first started yoga, but candlelit dinners and long walks on the beach? The rest of her biography sounded more like a dating ad than a life.

"It doesn't say anything about a family. I'm sorry." His eyes held her gaze, and something akin to sadness flickered in them.

"Thank you." Tia didn't enjoy hearing those words, but they somehow felt right. She didn't feel like she had any family waiting for her, and the thought saddened her. "What about you? Do you have family?"

His lips pulled into a thin line, and his hand scraped across his chin. "My parents are still alive, though they don't live here. I have an older brother and a younger sister, but as for the family I think you meant...no. I was married, but my wife died a year ago."

"I'm sorry," Tia said. She hadn't meant to open wounds especially with him being so nice to her. A strained silence fell between them. "How old do you think I am?"

"What?" The question had obviously caught Dr. Cavanaugh off guard, and the look on his face displayed his discomfort in trying to answer. "I don't know. Close to thirty maybe?"

Thirty? That meant she was past prime child bearing years and she didn't even have a husband. Did she even want kids? Maybe she had been so focused on her writing that she had decided to forgo a family. That thought saddened her even more.

"Maybe even younger," he said as if sensing her feelings. "I'm a terrible judge of age."

"Oh, it's not that," Tia said. "I just can't believe I'm close to thirty and don't have a family. No one to miss me. It makes me wonder what my priorities were."

"I'm sure your fans miss you," he said. "From the research I did on you, it seems like you have some die-hard fans."

"You researched me?" Tia didn't know why but that thought made her smile. How long had he spent digging into her? And did he do this for every patient with amnesia or was she special? She didn't think she would mind if he found her special. He was definitely easy on the eyes and had a kind air about him. She could see herself dating someone like him – that is if she wasn't seeing someone already.

A red tint colored his cheeks, and he cleared his throat as his eyes flicked to the side. "Well, I wanted to have some information to share with you about who you were. Unfortunately, I couldn't find much other than great reviews. You must be a talented writer."

"I hope I remember how to do it again one day." Tia didn't know what she would do if she didn't remember how to write. She had no idea if she possessed any other skills. Had she always been a writer? Was it a full-time job?

"I bet you will." His eyes softened as he gazed at her. "You look like the kind of person who has stories running around in their head."

Tia's heart warmed at his statement, and she felt the corners of her mouth twitch into a flirtatious grin. "I do? What exactly does 'having stories running around in your head' look like?"

She was pleased to see another blush color his face. Had he been flirting with her? "Um, well, there's a depth in your eyes even for someone who doesn't remember who they are. My guess is you've led an interesting life."

"An interesting though private life it seems," she said remembering the lack of information he was able to find out about her. While that might not normally be bad, it certainly didn't help her current situation.

"Maybe you just don't like the fame," he offered with a crooked smile. Their eyes locked for a moment before he cleared his throat and checked his watch. "Anyway, I've got to go check on a few other patients. I'll leave the book with you and if you feel up to it, maybe you can read some. Perhaps that might help jog your memory."

Tia returned his smile and felt a bud of warmth erupt in her heart. "Thank you. I certainly hope so."

Brody was still smiling as he exited Tia's room. It was nice to be able to help her even if only a little. He picked up the chart for the next patient and perused it.

"Don't you think you're spending too much time with her?"

Brody looked up to see Valerie Givens, one of the nurses, staring at him. Her arms were folded across her chest, and her brow arched halfway up her large forehead. Valerie was a stickler for rules and often interjected her opinion without asking which made her amazing at her job but not the easiest person to get along with. It probably didn't help that she had indicated an interest in him when she'd heard his friends were trying to set him up, but he had declined even an initial get together. Dating where he worked held little appeal and she was so stiff that he couldn't imagine spending time with her.

He took a moment to compose his words before he spoke. There was no need to ruffle Valerie's feathers more than he already had. "She has no one. She isn't even sure who she is. I think it's acceptable to try and help her remember a little about herself. Besides as an ICU doctor, that's part of my job description."

Valerie's lips pursed into a tight light. "I know you like to be hands on, especially since your wife died, but are you sure that's all it is? You do remember developing a relationship with a patient is frowned upon."

Brody sighed and rolled his eyes. So was dating coworkers,

but that hadn't stopped her from trying. He'd never had this issue when Rachel was alive, but ever since she passed, people had either been trying to set him up or assumed he was flirting with every single woman he came across. It was tiring and flat out wrong. Rachel had been the love of his life, and he wasn't looking to replace her. Not now and, more than likely, not in the future. Work was his life now, and he was okay with that. "Oh, and Tia has a fever, so keep a close eye on her. I've got other patients to see."

She narrowed her eyes at him but said nothing more, and he turned to enter the next room. Before he reached the door, the familiar voice of Edith Wilkerson reached him.

"Dr. Cavanaugh. Dr. Cavanaugh, can I have a word?"

Edith Wilkerson was seventy years of age, short, and possessed a feisty albeit sometimes abrasive attitude. A little over a year ago, she had begun volunteering to read to patients in the ICU especially those who had no one to visit them. While he appreciated the help, she was often a pain to deal with, but she had been there for Rachel during the days he couldn't.

Pasting on his best smile, he turned to Edith. "Yes, Edith, what can I do for you?"

She waddled over to him and jabbed her finger up at him. "Why is your nurse giving me such a hard time? I've been coming here and reading to patients for over a year." She patted the bag that hung from her shoulder proudly. "Nobody else sits with them that long. You all ought to be thanking me, not shooing me out."

Brody tried not to roll his eyes. "I'm sorry, Edith, I'll have a talk with Valerie." He turned to step back into the room, but she grabbed his arm.

"It wasn't Valerie. She's a pain that one, but she knows better than to talk like that to me. No, it was one I've never seen before. Must be a new one. Italian looking with dark hair."

Brody tried to visualize the women who worked on the floor,

but he didn't recognize the woman Edith described. However, it felt like they were always assigning new nurses to the floor or moving them around. "I'm sorry, I'm not familiar with her, but maybe you're right, she could be a new hire. Just tell her you belong here, and I said you're okay to visit the patients. If she has a problem, have her come to me."

"I'll do that. You'd think you all would lay out the carpet for volunteers like me, but no, it's constant scrutiny and questions."

"It is a hospital, Edith," Brody said with a sigh. "We have to make sure our patients are safe."

She threw her hands up and shook her head. "And I look so threatening. Half of the patients here could run faster than I could."

That wasn't true, of course, as most of the patients on this floor were in critical condition, but he understood her sentiment. With her white fluffy hair and short stature, she certainly didn't look menacing. At least, not unless she caught you with her angry gaze. A gaze he'd only seen once, but that reminded him of the look his father had flashed before taking off his belt and whipping Brody with it when he was young. "I'll remind the nurses again, Edith."

"You do that. Now, who should I read to first today?"

As much as Brody didn't want to overwhelm Tia with Edith, she might enjoy the visit since no one had come to see her yet. "Try the woman in six. She lost her memory though, so be nice."

She shot him a pointed stare. "I'm always nice, Dr. Cavanaugh. You of all people ought to know that."

Brody didn't argue with her. Nice was subjective, and it wasn't always the adjective he would apply to Edith, but he did remember how she sat with Rachel while Brody worked. How she kept Rachel company when the pain got bad. How she read to Rachel when her eyesight failed. "Her name is Tia."

"Wonderful. I'll go make her acquaintance."

Brody nodded as he turned to head into the next patient's

room, but before he could, a beeping sounded and Valerie popped out of one of the rooms. "Dr. Cavanaugh, we need you in room four."

He spared one final glance at Edith before hurrying to help the crashing patient.

## 5

Tia smiled as the sound of footsteps entered her room. Was Dr. Cavanaugh back so quickly? Perhaps he had enjoyed their conversation as much as she had and wanted to continue it. Of course, it could be Valerie, the nurse who came in to check her vitals every hour or so, but she hoped it was Dr. Cavanaugh. Valerie was much brusquer and less talkative and either had a permanent chip on her shoulder or just didn't like Tia.

But it was neither. Instead, a short elderly woman with a full head of white hair entered the room. A visitor? She certainly looked too old to be a nurse.

"Can I help you?" Tia asked.

"I'm Edith Wilkerson. I'm a volunteer at the hospital here, and I've come to read to you." The woman did not phrase this as a question but as a matter of fact statement.

"Oh, I didn't realize the hospital did that."

Edith waved her weathered hand as she pulled up a chair. "The hospital doesn't. The Good Lord called me to do this and they tolerate me. Some new nurse even tried to shoo me away today. People have forgotten what God says about caring for the sick and the elderly."

"I'm not sure I know much about that myself." Tia didn't know if she was a church goer or not, but she thought it might be nice to believe in a higher power looking out for her. "What *does* God say about caring for the sick and the elderly?"

"That we should do it. Yet most people nowadays are glued to their electronic devices and rarely bother to think about others." She pulled a book out of her bag and opened it. "Now, I'm in Psalms. Is that okay with you?"

"Um, sure, I suppose." Tia got the feeling that it wouldn't matter to Edith if it wasn't okay with her. The woman looked like she did what she wanted regardless of what others thought, and Tia wondered if she were like that. If not, she thought she might like to be. There was a refreshing honesty to Edith.

Edith pulled out a pair of reader glasses, but before she got very far, another woman entered the room. Tia glanced over but she didn't recognize this brunette woman in cream colored pants and a flowy blouse either. Another visitor? She'd had no one come to see her and now two in one day. What were the odds? Though the woman flashed a smile, her expression seemed more anxious than friendly.

"Oh, I'm sorry, I didn't know you had a visitor already." A slight tremble laced the woman's voice, and she gripped the two bags on her shoulder tighter. Tia wondered if the nervous air the woman exuded was always there or if this situation made her nervous for some reason. Perhaps the nurse had told her Tia might not remember her. That would have to be jarring for anyone.

"I'm not a visitor," Edith said turning shrewd eyes on the woman. "I'm a volunteer."

The woman glanced at Edith before dropping her gaze to the floor. "Oh, well, can I have a moment with Tia?"

"I'm not leaving because I haven't finished my duty, but I'll go sit over there." Edith closed her book and moved to a chair across the room, but her eyes stayed on Tia and the woman.

"Do I know you?" It was a dumb question as the woman had just said her name, but it slipped out before Tia could stop it. She tried to recall any memory of the woman with her mousy brown hair and hazel eyes, but nothing appeared.

"You mean you don't know me?" The woman said the words slowly and her voice held a hint of disbelief, but at that realization, her posture seemed to gain confidence. Her shoulders pulled back, and her gaze landed on Tia fully instead of skirting to the side as it had done before.

Something in her gaze bothered Tia, but she couldn't put her finger on what it was. "I don't. I hit my head in a car accident, and I don't remember much before waking up here."

"Is that right?" The woman's voice sounded wrong somehow.

Fear bubbled in Tia's stomach, and she narrowed her eyes at the woman. "Are we friends?"

The woman's lips pulled into something close to a smile. "What? Yeah. Friends. I'm Debra Rearden." She looked at Tia expectantly as if waiting for the name to mean something.

And it did. Slightly. The name triggered something at the back of Tia's mind, something that made her heart beat faster and her pulse speed up, but she couldn't bring the memory forward. "I'm sorry. I still don't know you."

At this, the woman appeared to brighten even more. "Oh, well, I heard about your accident, and I wanted to bring you this." She slid one bag off her shoulder and held it out to Tia.

A memory flashed in Tia's head. She had bought that bag at an upscale boutique in California. She remembered touching the different colorful bags and finally choosing the brown leather because it felt so soft beneath her fingers. "That's my bag."

The woman's smile faltered, and her eyes shifted again. "So, you remember this?"

"I have a vague memory of purchasing it, but nothing more. Why do you have it? The police said it wasn't in my car."

"You left it at my place." The smile returned but it seemed to stop short of Debra's eyes. Their hazel depths contained no fondness, and Tia wondered why. Had they had an argument? "I'm not sure how you forgot it, but I found it on my table. When I saw your accident on the news, I figured you might be missing it." She stepped closer and handed the bag to Tia. Her eyes traveled from Tia's head to her foot. "It appears you'll be here a while."

"Yeah, they haven't given me a release date yet, but I figure it will be another week at least. I guess that's fine since I wouldn't know where to go anyway." Though Debra's behavior struck her as odd, she was also the only outside person who appeared to know her, and Tia hoped she might have some answers. "Do I live here now? They said I'm from California."

Debra's lips pinched together and her eyes flicked away again. Her hand clutched the remaining strap on her shoulder. "I think you were just out here visiting me actually. We hadn't gotten to visit much. Yet," she added hastily as if sensing the oddity of her words. Her eyes flicked quickly to Edith and then back to the floor. "You really don't remember?"

A visit? The feeling she had come to see someone felt right, but she didn't think it was this woman. Why would Tia visit someone and not talk about where she was staying or for how long? Was Debra lying then? Or maybe Tia had been visiting someone in addition to Debra? Still, she had Tia's bag, so at least part of her story was true. "I don't, but thank you for bringing this by. Maybe it will jog some memories."

"Of course, I'm happy to help," Debra said, but her voice held that sappy fake-pleasant tone that people used when they said something they didn't mean. As Tia thought the words, she realized she had used that very tone herself. Often. She couldn't remember exact instances, but she knew she had that delivery down to a tee.

Debra glanced over at Edith and readjusted her bag. "I'll let you get back to whatever I interrupted as I have to run to a meeting, but I'll be back to see you. Soon."

Tia glanced up at Debra with her one good eye. Apprehension filled her as something in Debra's tone bothered her, but she didn't know what it was. "Thank you."

"I don't like her," Edith said when Debra left. "She seems off."

Tia had to agree with her. "She does, but she brought me my purse, so how bad could she be? Maybe this will hold some keys to who I am." She opened the bag and looked inside. Not much was in there: a maroon wallet, a black and gold makeup case, a hairbrush, and a crumpled piece of paper. Not much to go on. She pulled out the wallet first and opened it. The left side held rows of credit cards all in the name Tia Sweetchild. Behind them was a pocket that contained fifty dollars in cash. So, whoever Debra was, she hadn't wanted to steal from Tia. Maybe she really was a friend and hospitals simply made her nervous. On the right were cards for other businesses - a movie theater, a coffee shop, places she must frequent.

Tia pulled out the movie card and held it in her hand. An image of her and a handsome man standing in line to buy tickets flashed into her brain and then disappeared. A date? A relative? She truly had no idea.

She pulled out the coffee card next. A skinny caramel macchiato with no foam? Was that what she drank? Tia replaced the coffee card and pulled out the license. The same blonde woman from the back of the book stared up at her from the license, and when she read the address, she could picture a pool, but that was all.

With a sigh, she replaced the wallet and pulled out the makeup bag. It was stuffed with all sorts of makeup - eyeliners in three different colors, four different eyeshadows, two blushes, two mascaras, and four lipstick containers.

"That is a lot of makeup," Edith said as she watched Tia pull everything out. "I gave it up many years ago, but at my age, it isn't really necessary. Not like you young things. You must have liked it a lot."

"I suppose I did." Tia's fingers pulled out a gold plated compact and trembled as she held it. She hadn't asked to see her face, and she wasn't sure she wanted to, but the need to spurred her fingers. As the mirror lifted, Tia sucked in her breath. The face staring back at her didn't look much like the woman in the picture. Angry bruises and red raw scrapes covered most of her face. A large white bandage blazed out from the top of her left forehead, and her left eye was a black and purple mottled mess. She shut the mirror not wanting to see any more, but she couldn't stop the tear that trickled out of her right eye. "I'm so hideous."

Edith placed a wrinkled hand on her arm. "You are not hideous. You are a beautiful creature in God's eyes and whatever scars you may have from this accident, they don't have to define you."

Tia nodded, but Edith's words didn't replace the sickening feeling in her stomach. Everything she had learned about herself - from her nails to her makeup - was that image was important to her. What would she do if she was scarred for life? After replacing the makeup bag, she bypassed the hairbrush and pulled out the crumpled paper. Rico Rearden, six pm, 144 Palisade Drive. Rico Rearden? An image of a house exploded in her head, and she dropped the paper. She had been meeting Rico Rearden, not Debra, but the question was for what? And who was Rico Rearden?

"Are you okay?" Edith asked squeezing her arm.

"No, I don't think that I am," Tia said.

Brody opened his fridge and stared at the scant offerings. He really needed to get better about going to a store, or he should break down and hire an assistant like Nick had. Nick had a woman who bought for him, laid out ingredients for dinner, and straightened up. With as much as he worked, Brody should do the same, but having another woman in his house, even just to shop and do meal prep, felt like an affront to Rachel.

He still remembered coming home to her each night. The smell of whatever she was cooking would greet him as he walked in the door tantalizing his taste buds and sending his stomach growling. Rachel had been a fantastic cook.

He would drop his work gear by the front door; then he would wander into the kitchen and greet her by wrapping his arms around her waist and nuzzling her neck. She would pretend to bat him away with whatever cooking utensils she had in her hands, but he knew she loved the attention. After dinner, they would wash the dishes together trading secret smiles and glances when their fingers touched. Then they would retire to the bedroom where they would read or watch television before falling asleep in each other's arms.

Brody hadn't been able to sleep in the bed for a month after Rachel passed. It held too many memories. Many nights, he still crashed on the couch though recently that was due more to exhaustion from work than anything else.

With a sigh, he shut the fridge door. He would order pizza again and see if Nick wanted to swing by. Lately, it was how they spent most nights after work. Either his place or Nick's or out. Except on the nights when Nick had a date.

Brody wondered if he would ever date again. He'd thought about it once or twice after Rachel's death, but after having someone so amazing, he could tell just by meeting a woman that they would never measure up. But he was still young. And he knew Rachel would want him to find someone to spend his life with. His thoughts drifted to Tia.

What must it be like to wake up and have no memory of who you were? In his own case, he couldn't decide if that would be a good thing or a bad thing. On one hand, he would have no painful memory of Rachel's death, but on the other hand, he would have no loving memory of Rachel in his life either. It was better to have loved and lost than never to have loved at all. Wasn't that what the old saying was?

Brody shook his head to clear the fog. He was too philosophical tonight. He should skip the pizza and the conversation and just grab something quick. There was a restaurant just down the street that stayed open late. He would grab dinner and one drink and then return to bed. Before he could change his mind, he exited the house, locked the front door behind him, and headed down the street.

The restaurant was busy when he opened the door, but he managed to find an empty barstool.

"What'll you have?" the bartender asked as he sat down.

Brody surveyed the drink selection. He wasn't a big drinker, but he and Rachel had partaken on occasion. "A Sam Adams?"

With a nod, the bartender turned and grabbed a bottle, popped the lid, and handed it to Brody. "You want to open a tab?"

Brody pondered the question. He'd told himself he would just have one, but now that he was here, he wasn't sure. He was about to agree when a voice beside him said, "No need. It's on me." He looked up to see Detective Graves standing next to him. "Grab that and follow me."

Curious, he followed Jordan to an empty booth. "Were you following me, detective?"

"No, but I'm glad I ran into you. Did our patient remember anything more today?"

Brody shook his head. He had checked on Tia before his shift ended, but she hadn't said much. "No, but I didn't really ask today. I did find out she is an author though and I brought in one of her books hoping it would help."

Jordan's eyes narrowed. "How did you find out she was an author?"

"I had dinner with Nick last night and he recognized her name, so we googled her. Anyway, when I showed her the book, she said she remembered something when she touched it." He paused, trying to remember her words. "A man saying 'What are you doing here?' But that was all she could remember. She didn't even remember being an author. Should I be asking specific questions? Did you find something out?"

Jordan blew out an agitated breath. "Not much more than that, but it just isn't sitting well with me. Why would anyone want to harm an author? She's not a big name like Stephen King or J.K Rowling so I don't think it was about money, and she writes clean romance so I doubt she offended someone enough to want to kill her. All I have are questions - the biggest one being what was she doing here in the first place?"

"I don't know." Brody shook his head and took a sip of his beer. He had his own questions, but they were more about the woman herself than why she had come to Fire Beach in the first place. "She said a woman visited her today and claimed she was in town for that reason."

Jordan's head snapped forward. "What? She had a visitor?"

"Yes, she didn't remember the woman, but she hasn't remembered much. Why? Is that a bad thing?"

Agitation filled Jordan's face. "It could be. We asked her to call us if anything else happened. We need to know everything if we are going to figure this out. I can't believe she didn't tell us she had a visitor. Did you get the woman's name?"

Brody shook his head. "No, sorry, I was a little busy, but I can ask tomorrow."

"I'll go over myself tomorrow to ask, but please, Brody, we can't help if we don't know everything. Even if it seems trivial."

Brody gave a curt nod. He was glad Jordan was helping, but he didn't like someone telling him how to do his job. "I understand. It seems she gets a few pieces of her memory back every day. Maybe we'll know more in a day or two."

"Let's hope that's soon enough, but please keep an eye on her and call me if you learn anything. I just have a bad feeling about all of this."

## 6

T ia couldn't wait to see Dr. Cavanaugh today. She was bursting at the seams to tell him she had remembered a little bit more about her past. Specifically, that she was from Texas and her mother had a strong southern drawl. The memory had come to her as she was watching Sweet Home Alabama on the TV the night before, and while an Alabama accent wasn't the same as a Texas drawl, there were similarities.

"Well, don't you look chipper today," Dr. Cavanaugh said as he entered her room.

Her lips split in a wide smile. "I am. I remembered a little more of my past. I'm originally from Texas." She said the words proudly as if they were a star achievement, which in her case, they sort of were.

"Is that right?" His eyes did that twinkly thing that set her heart fluttering as he returned her grin. "So, a girl from Texas, living in California, but out in Illinois. Maybe you like to travel?" He raised a brow at her as he checked her chart.

"Maybe or maybe not." She watched him move to the IV to check the levels.

"Detective Graves wasn't too happy that you didn't call him about your visitor."

Tia dropped her gaze. "I know. He's already been here this morning. Reamed me pretty good, but I honestly didn't think about it. She said she was a friend and I was in town visiting her. It's not like I would know differently. Detective Graves also took my purse and the note."

Dr. Cavanaugh's head snapped toward her. "Note? What note?"

Oh right, she hadn't told him about the note either. "I went through my purse when she brought it back and I found a note in my purse with a man's name on it. I feel like I was visiting him, but I don't know why."

"Perhaps he's someone you're seeing?" Was she imagining his smile looking a little more forced as he asked those words? Was he upset at the thought of her seeing someone? "Regardless, I bet you'll remember soon, and I'm sure Detective Graves will look into him. You did tell him about your feeling, right?"

"Yes, I told him." Tia felt like a child being scolded. First Detective Graves had jumped on her case and now Dr. Cavanaugh.

"Good. I'm going to change the bandage on your head now."

As he removed the bandage from her head, Tia tried not to focus on the strong angle of his chin or how his touch sent her heart skidding in her chest. She wondered what his beard would feel like under her fingertips? Would it be rough and bristly or softer? And if she touched it, would he lean into her hand or bat it away? He'd told her of his wife's death, but she hadn't asked if he were still single.

"You know what? The stitches are healing nicely. I think it's time they got some air."

His voice brought her back to reality, and she struggled to keep her voice from betraying her thoughts. "That's good, right?"

"It's excellent." His eyes caught hers and Tia's breath stilled. There was something in his gaze. Something more than a doctor caring for a patient. She was sure of it. Should she say something? Ask him if he was single? "Look at that, your left eye is open a little too."

Her breath tumbled out in a sigh, and a tinge of sadness filled her. Of course, he was looking at her eye. He was her doctor, nothing more. She would do good to remember that.

"The cuts on your arms appear to be healing nicely too."

"How much longer until I'm released, do you think?" She didn't really want the answer, but felt like she should ask it. With still so much of her life unknown, she felt more comfortable just staying at the hospital and seeing Dr. Cavanaugh every day. When she left, would she have a reason to see him again?

"I'm not sure," he said as he ran the thermometer across her forehead. "While you are healing nicely on the outside, I am still concerned about your memory, and though the fever has gone down, it is still slightly above normal. Plus, Dr. North will probably want to look at your foot again before she releases you. Speaking of which, we should check your foot." He finished examining her legs and touched her toes. "Can you feel that?"

Tia smiled as she felt his fingers. This time she didn't have to guess. "I can. Just barely, but I can."

"Excellent. That is what I like to hear." He made a few notes in the chart and then turned his full attention back to her. "Did you read your book yesterday?"

Tia glanced at the book on the table next to her bed. "A little, but reading with only one eye was giving me a headache. I probably should have asked Edith to read that to me instead of the Bible. Maybe I'll try again today though and see if it helps me remember any more."

Dr. Cavanaugh smiled and touched her arm. "I think that is a great idea. I'll be back to check on you later." His fingertips pressed just slightly on her arm. Only the slightest hint of pressure, but Tia felt there was more there than a simple touch.

As he walked out of her room, she rolled her eyes. She was seeing romance where there was none. Perhaps she could write again. Maybe this was why she had become a romance author in the first place.

She grabbed the book off the table and opened it to try reading some more, but she had only gotten through a few pages when footsteps in her doorway grabbed her attention. Tia looked up to see Debra in her room again, but this time the smile was gone and a cold gleam shone from her eyes.

"What's wrong, Debra?" Tia inched her finger up toward the call button. Perhaps it was nothing, but Debra's expression was setting off alarm bells in her body.

"Wrong? Nothing's wrong. I've just come here to finish business." Her voice was as cold and soulless as her eyes.

Fear raced through Tia's veins, and she placed her finger on the button. She would press it, but she needed answers first. "Business? What are you talking about? I thought you said we were friends."

Debra's expression turned into a snarl. "Friends?" she spat before issuing a derisive laugh. "Friends don't sleep with their friend's husband."

"What?" Tia's body froze. She hated that she had little memory, but she couldn't imagine herself doing that. "I would never..."

Debra cut her off with biting words that carried their own weapons. "How do you know what you would never do? You told me yesterday you had no memory."

"I may not remember much, but I don't think I would do that." The thought of that sent such revulsion through her that Tia couldn't believe it was true.

"You don't think...." Condescension dripped from Debra's

voice like venom. "Do you want to know where I found the purse that I returned to you yesterday?"

Tia fought to remain calm. "You told me I left it on a table in your house."

Debra's predatory smile widened, creating an effect much like The Joker's signature smile on her face. "Yes. On the table in *my* bedroom. So, if you weren't sleeping with my husband, how do you propose it got there?"

"I have no idea, obviously."

"Well, then I guess my version is the only one that matters, but I'm done being the cheated-on wife." From within the bag, she withdrew a gun, and with shaky hands, she pointed it at Tia.

Tia pressed the call button hoping someone would see or hear it before Debra shot her. She had no idea if the woman was a good shot or if the obvious nervousness would allow her to miss, but Tia couldn't move, so rescue was her only option.

"Why did you say we were friends?" Tia asked hoping to buy a little time.

"I needed an excuse to see what room you were in and check out the security at the hospital. I had planned to kill you yesterday, but then you had that busybody old woman in here, so I had to adjust my plan. We'd never officially met, so I didn't think you would recognize me unless you paid attention to the pictures of me all over the house, but you were probably too busy with my husband to do that, weren't you?"

Another image flashed into Tia's mind, and she saw herself picking up a picture of Debra and Rico. "You're married? Why did you invite me up here if you were married?"

"You never said it bothered you," he said stepping closer to her.

"Put the gun down, ma'am." Dr. Cavanaugh's voice brought both relief and frustration as the flashback she had been seeing vanished from her mind.

Debra turned to look at him briefly before returning her

attention to Tia. "No. She slept with my husband, and now she's going to pay."

"I know how distressing that can be, but is it worth spending the rest of your life in prison?" Dr. Cavanaugh's voice was calm, and he inched toward Debra slowly.

"She deserves to die."

"If she did what you claim, then she deserves punishment, yes, but retribution is not ours to dole out." Tia looked at him. She hoped he didn't really believe Debra's words; she couldn't stand the thought of him thinking so poorly of her.

"She did," Debra screeched shrilly and the hand holding the gun began to shake. "I found her purse in my bedroom. I've known he was having an affair for a while. Always off on his 'business meetings' but I never knew who it was until I found her purse."

"Debra, is your husband's name Rico?" Tia asked. She knew without asking the question that it was, but she hoped to draw Debra's attention long enough for Dr. Cavanaugh to overpower her.

"You know it is." She glanced quickly at Tia before returning her gaze to Dr. Cavanaugh. "You see? She admits it."

"I don't remember him," Tia said though that was a tiny lie. She had remembered talking to him just now, but there was no need to share that, "and I definitely don't recall sleeping with him, but I found a crumpled piece of paper in my purse with his name and a time on it."

Hesitation flickered in Debra's eyes, but she didn't lower the gun. "That proves it then. You were meeting with him."

"That only proves a meeting," Dr. Cavanaugh said. "Perhaps they were meeting about something else."

"In my bedroom?" A hysterical edge colored her voice, and she took a deep breath. "No, she was sleeping with him, and if I don't punish her, who will?" Her hand wavered as she turned to look at Tia again. It wasn't long, but it was long enough for Dr.

Cavanaugh to knock the gun out of her hands and tackle her to the ground.

"What are you doing?" Debra screamed as she writhed on the ground. "She's the criminal, not me."

A moment later, security rushed in and handcuffed Debra before leading her out of the room. Her screams carried down the hall and echoed in Tia's ears long after she was gone.

"Are you okay?" Dr. Cavanaugh asked coming to Tia's side.

Tia ignored his question - he could see that she hadn't been physically injured - and posed her own in return. "What's going to happen to her?"

"I don't know. They'll take her to the police, and I'm sure Detective Graves will see if she owns a black Ford truck or knows someone who does. It certainly sounds as if she had a vendetta for you."

Her eyes found his, and she stared into the depths that had once held kindness and now held questions. "Do you think I really did that? What she said?" She needed him not to believe it. Tia still didn't feel that behavior was like her, but the purse was hers and the crumpled paper proved she'd scheduled a meeting with the woman's husband. Plus, there had been that tidbit she'd remembered. She thought she'd sounded angry and confused at finding out he was married, but she couldn't explain why her purse would have been in the woman's bedroom if something illicit wasn't going on.

"I... don't know. It's not my place to judge anyway." The question clearly made Dr. Cavanaugh uncomfortable, and he steered his gaze away from her face. "Did she say anything else to you?"

Tia closed her eyes and tried to remember the words. "Just that she came yesterday to see what the security in the hospital was like and to see if I would recognize her name. She planned to kill me yesterday, but Edith was in here." Tia couldn't keep the intense sadness and disgust out of her voice. "What kind of a person was I?"

Dr. Cavanaugh cleared his throat and ran the back of his fingers down his cheek. "Maybe it's not what it seems. You said you had a paper with meeting details?"

"Yeah, his name, address, and a time."

"Well, I'm no expert, but I don't know many people who schedule trysts like that, so maybe he was an associate or something."

He was guessing, making up options to make her feel better, but Tia appreciated the effort. "Even if he was an associate, I don't know why I'd be in his bedroom which is where she claimed she found my purse."

Dr. Cavanaugh opened his mouth as if to speak, but no words came out.

"It's okay," Tia continued. "You should get back to your other patients. I'm fine now."

"Of course. Call if you need anything." Though they were the same words he often said before leaving, they sounded different this time and Tia couldn't help feeling saddened by the fact she had disappointed him.

Brody stood outside the police station gathering his courage to go in. He didn't even know why he was here especially if Debra's words were true, but the need to help Tia still burned strong within him. Rachel had often accused him of having a 'knight in shining armor complex' and perhaps she had been right because here he was trying to defend a woman who might have been in an affair. He supposed she could have had a different personality before the accident – it certainly happened with traumatic brain injuries - but he just didn't believe the woman in his hospital could have done what Debra claimed.

Before he could grasp the handle, the door swung open and Jordan stared at him from the other side. "Brody? What are you doing here?"

"I was hoping I could talk to you about Tia and the woman from the hospital earlier."

Jordan looked over his shoulder and then back at Brody. "Not here. I'm headed over to Fire Dreams. Meet me there and I'll tell you what I know, but it isn't much."

Brody nodded and returned to his car. Not much was better than what he knew now which consisted of more questions than answers.

Ten minutes later he sat in a booth with Jordan, a glass of water in front of each of them and a basket of chips in the middle. The place was hopping, having recovered nicely from the spoiled opening a few days before, and Jordan kept glancing around as if realizing he should be helping rather than sitting and talking.

"So, the lady from the hospital is indeed Debra Rearden. If you or Tia had told us about her yesterday, we could have looked into her sooner. She's clean, but her husband, Rico, has a few questionable connections."

"What kind of questionable connections?" Brody asked.

"On paper, he's the head of a publishing company which might explain the connection to Tia, but we've found some unusual activity with some known drug dealers. Nothing that points to him being directly involved, and Narcotics has never been able to pin anything on him, but we're widening our search to be sure."

Brody nodded and snagged a chip. "Drugs? Really?" This image just didn't jive with the woman he'd gotten to know the last few days. "Tia said she had a meeting with Rico, but she doesn't seem like the type to be into drug deals."

Jordan took a sip of his water. "Maybe she isn't, but I did a little more research on her today. It appears she stayed under the radar. At least recently. Evidently a few months ago, she kind of lost it after trying to damage the reputation of a fellow romance author, Ava McDermott. She sent photos to tabloids and appeared on a few talk shows claiming the relationship Ava was in was a fake one. I don't know why anyone would fake a relationship, but maybe if you are a public figure, it's more important."

"What?" Brody knew he didn't know Tia well, and she could have been awful before the accident, but he couldn't fathom the sweet Texas girl doing such a thing. Oh dear, did he just call her sweet? Maybe he *was* becoming attached to her.

Jordan shrugged. "Well, maybe the head injury changed her or maybe she changed after the incident. She failed to do much except soil her own reputation. Regardless, it's clear Tia did know Rico. There's no other reason Debra would have come after her. Perhaps she was talking to him about new publishing opportunities. We just don't know any more than that."

"Is there a chance she was having an affair with him as his wife claimed?" Brody asked before taking a drink of his water. He didn't want this to be true. He knew Tia was just a patient. And she lived in California. *And* he shouldn't care about her personal life, but he did.

"That I can't speak to. Yet. But we'll be looking into Rico more." Jordan shook some salt on a chip before stuffing it into his mouth.

"And what about the black truck. Did it belong to Debra?"

Jordan shook his head as he finished chewing. "No, neither she nor her husband appear to own one."

"So, someone might still be after Tia."

"It's possible or it could just be that the accident was just that. An accident."

"But you don't believe that, do you?" Brody asked.

"No, I don't. It's just a gut feeling, but I don't. I've talked with the hospital about posting a security guard outside her door as well." Jordan looked around again and waved at someone across the room. "I have to help out here, but I promise to keep you in the loop of what we find."

"Thank you." Brody stayed and ate a late dinner alone, but his thoughts weren't on the food. They were on the blonde woman whose present didn't seem to match her past.

## 7

"You know he's not interested in you romantically, right?"

Tia glanced over at Valerie who held a vase of flowers in her hand. "I'm sorry, what?"

She set the vase down, plucked the card, and handed it to Tia before leaning back and folding her arms across her chest. "Dr. Cavanaugh. He's not interested in you. He doesn't date. Not since his wife died, and he certainly doesn't get involved with patients."

"I never said he was," Tia said. She picked up the card wondering who the flowers were from and why Valerie was bringing this up. The woman had never been overly friendly, but she'd always been professional. This wasn't.

"Maybe not, but you have the look in your eye. That moony starry-eyed look when you talk about him or when you look to the doorway. I'm just warning you those feelings will only end in heartbreak."

Ah, now it made sense. Somehow Dr. Cavanaugh had broken her heart. Had they dated? Or had Valerie simply wished they had? Was it before his wife? Or had he gone on a few dates after her death? "Well, thank you for the information, but Dr. Cavanaugh is my doctor. Nothing more." Though Tia could not deny she imagined something more. She had imagined what it would feel like to touch his face, to run her fingers through his hair, to kiss his lips.

"Mmmhmm." Valerie said nothing more as she ran the thermometer over Tia's forehead and wrote the information down, but her eyes spoke volumes. "I'll send Sophie in later to do another sponge bath."

Relief that Valerie would not be doing her sponge bath filled Tia along with the sudden urge to request another nurse. She was the patient here, and she didn't need a nurse casting a critical eye on her. Tia had enough on her plate trying to remember who she was and why someone might want to hurt her. She opened the card and stared at the writing inside. Or perhaps the lack of writing inside because all that was on the card was the picture of a face with its eyes and mouth stitched shut.

"Good morning. How about we try to get you moving some today?" Dr. Cavanaugh asked as he entered Tia's room. At the sight of her face, his smile faltered and concern filled his voice. "What's the matter?"

Tia held the card out to him. "This came on the flowers Valerie brought in this morning."

Dr. Cavanaugh took the card and opened it. His face paled and his eyes widened as he took in the image. "Where are the flowers?"

Tia pointed over to the table where Valerie had set them. He picked them up, sniffed them, and poked through them as if looking for any other clues. "I'm going to call Detective Graves. He needs to know about this." He pulled a phone from his pocket. "I'll have Valerie come in and take you for a walk."

"No, please not Valerie. Anyone but Valerie." Not only was panic coursing through her veins at the note, but she didn't think she could handle any more time with Valerie.

He paused and caught her eye. "What's wrong with Valerie?"

"She abrasive and she just..." Tia paused. She wasn't sure she wanted to tell Brody what Valerie had said.

"She just what?"

"She just rubbed me the wrong way. In fact, I was going to ask if I could get a new nurse." She didn't know why she didn't tell him the whole truth. Except that she was afraid her attraction would be evident in her words. And she wasn't sure she could take it if he didn't feel the same."

"I'll see what I can do. I know Valerie can be brusque at times, but she is an efficient nurse."

Tia watched his face as he spoke. Did he care about Valerie? Or was he just being professional? Before she could ponder the issue much longer, he stepped toward her.

"I'll tell you what. Let me call Jordan, and then I'll take you for a quick walk today, and we'll figure tomorrow out when it comes."

"Can you do that?" He normally only entered her room twice during the day – once in the morning and once in the evening.

"I'm your doctor. I can take you for a walk if I desire." His jaw tightened and she wondered if there was more to it. Was he worried about her safety as well? "Just give me a second."

He stepped back and then punched numbers into his cell phone, turning slightly away from her as he put it to his ear. "Jordan? It's Brody. Tia received some flowers this morning, and I think you need to come and see the card." He glanced back at her. "Yes, I'm going to take her for a short walk, and then we'll be back.... Got it." He pocketed the phone and then smiled at her. "Ready to go then?"

Though Tia was excited to get out of the bed and move a little, she also worried about her safety and her appearance. She hadn't showered in days though Sophie had given her a sponge bath yesterday. Still, her hair was a greasy mess, and she probably smelled. Sponge baths were like trying to clean an entire house with one wet wipe. "I must look a fright."

"You look…. fine." He paused, and she glanced at him. Did he feel an attraction to her? Though Valerie claimed he wasn't interested, there had been many moments like these. Moments where she caught his eyes and unsaid words passed between them. "Especially for someone who had to be rescued with the Jaws of Life," he continued.

Though not entirely a compliment, Tia decided to take it as one. "What about my leg though? Can I walk on it?"

"Uh no." He chuckled and shook his head. "Today we are just going to try getting you into a wheelchair and out of this room. Then we'll talk about crutches."

"But I don't see a wheelchair," Tia said, and she wondered how she was supposed to get into it without exposing herself with her open-backed gown.

Dr. Cavanaugh flashed her a charming smile. "Ah, just you wait. I have one on order." He walked over to the cabinet in the room and pulled out a robe. "And I think this one is just your size."

She realized he was giving it to her as a way to cover up her bare back, and relief flooded her.

"Let me help you sit up, and then we'll get this robe on you. It will pull on your IV a little, so please tell me if it bothers you. Your transportation should arrive about the time we're finished."

Tia couldn't help the smile that crossed her lips, but it was short lived as Dr. Cavanaugh pulled her to a sitting position. Her hand squeezed his arm, her fingers digging into his flesh, as the room began to spin from lying down for too long and the injury to her head.

"It's okay. We'll go slow," he said. His mouth was close to her ear, and his breath sent a shudder down her back that she hoped he interpreted as her being cold.

She nodded and when the room stayed still, she continued

the process of sitting up. Tia was sure she had done this a thousand times in her life, but today it took all of her energy and concentration. When she was fully upright, he helped guide her arms into the robe, and she saw for the first time the damage she had received to them. Cuts and bruises discolored her right arm, and again she briefly wondered if she would have scars.

The aide with the wheelchair showed up as she tied the robe in front of her, and Dr. Cavanaugh grinned. "See, what did I tell you? I'll take it from here, Eric. Can you let Valerie know I'm taking my break?"

"Sure, Dr. Cavanaugh."

His break? He was using his break time to take her out? What would Valerie think of that? Had he ever spent his break time with her? Tia blinked the thoughts away. She needed to focus less on Dr. Cavanaugh and more on her recovery.

He wheeled the chair as close to the bed as possible and then helped her stand. Again, she had to take a moment and clutch onto his shoulder before she could lower herself into the chair. Then he grabbed her IV pole and brought it around to her. "Can you hang onto this?"

She grabbed the pole and pulled it beside her as he wheeled her out of the room. Her eyes glanced around for Valerie and she was glad not to see her in the immediate vicinity, but she was surprised to see the security guard outside her room. He stood as they passed.

"Excuse me, sir, but where are you going?"

"I'm taking Ms. Sweetchild out for some air. Don't worry, I've already cleared it with Detective Graves. You can call him and check for yourself."

The security guard looked as if he were about to argue, but after a moment of exchanging stares with Dr. Cavanaugh, he nodded and then took out his phone.

Brody didn't know what he was doing taking her out in the middle of the day. It wasn't technically against policy, but it certainly wasn't necessary. Yes, he wanted to share what he had learned last night from Jordan and see if it helped jog her memory at all, but he could have done that in her room. Maybe it was his complex kicking in again. Maybe it was the note she had received. Maybe it was her reaction to Valerie. Maybe it was just the fact that for the first time since Rachel's death, he felt something for a woman. He wasn't sure it was attraction. Perhaps it was just concern, but it *was* something.

As he wheeled her down the hall, he could feel the eyes of the nurses on him. There would be retribution for this in the form of their gossip and curious gazes for a few days, but he could handle that.

"Where are we going," she asked as he took a detour from the hallway.

"To get some fresh air. I think you could use some." He pushed open the door to a little covered patio on the south side of the hospital and wheeled her toward the lone bench that sat in the concrete area just outside the door.

The air was warm but a light breeze floated through stirring the crunchy leaves on the concrete and creating a rustling sound. He wondered if she would be warm enough. He should have asked if she wanted a blanket.

They kept some in a warmer by the door. He would remember that next time. Next time? Why was he already thinking about next time with Tia? What was it about her that kept her on his mind? Was it just her memory loss? Was it his need to protect her? Or was there more?

After making sure the brakes were locked on her wheelchair, he sat down on the bench and faced her. "I spoke with Detective Graves last night, and I thought you might want to know what he told me."

Her lips parted in a slight smile before sadness crossed her face. "Why are you doing this for me? If what that woman said is true, I'm not a very nice person."

Brody understood why she would feel that way but it bothered him that she did. Everyone made mistakes, and he couldn't imagine the woman before him doing anything like that now. He also knew the information he was about to share wouldn't make her feel any better, but if he were in her position, he would want to know all of it. The good and the bad. Knowing it all was the only way to make a change going forward. "Does the name Ava McDermott ring a bell for you?"

"Ava McDermott?" Tia turned the name over in her mouth like a fine wine, and her eyes stared into space as if searching for images to apply to the name. Then suddenly her eyes lit up. "I do remember an Ava McDermott. She's a..." She paused for a moment as if having to coax the memory forward. "She's a romance writer like me, isn't she?"

Brody nodded. "She is."

"I remember..." Tia's face fell, and her gaze dropped to her hands. "Oh no, I remember being condescending to her at a ceremony for coming without a date. In fact, I think I was rather haughty quite often, but I feel like Ava and I might have been friends at one point."

Brody doubted they were friends now, but he didn't tell her that. Her remembering Ava was a step in the right direction, and he didn't want to push her too hard. "Do you remember anything else about her? Anything more recently?"

Tia pursed her lips together. "I don't, but I'm guessing I'm not going to like the sound of what I did."

"Probably not, but it might explain what you're doing here." Brody took a deep breath as he thought about how best to tell her. "Evidently, you tried to ruin her reputation by outing her to tabloids for what you thought was a fake relationship."

Tia closed her eyes and sighed. "Maybe I don't want to remember my past. I don't sound very nice."

Brody had had the same thoughts when Jordan told him the story. Even now, he was having a hard time imagining the woman in front of him running to the tabloids. "Maybe the accident is God's way of giving you another chance. I have to say that even though I've only known you a few days, I can't see you doing those things now."

"Is that because of the brain injury?" Tia asked.

"It could be. Brain injuries can often change the personality of the patient." He watched her face fall. "But it could also be that you are changing."

"Do you really believe in God?" The simple question held none of the condescension he usually felt when people posed that question.

Brody hadn't been to church in a while, not since Rachel's death, but they had gone regularly when she was alive, and he did still believe. "I do though I can't say I've been a great Christian since my wife died. We used to attend every Sunday, but that stopped when she got sick. And though I know the importance of community in the church, I haven't been back much." He ran a hand across his chin. "Still, as a doctor, I have seen too many things I can't explain, so to answer your question, yes I do believe in God."

"I feel like I did at one time too. Do you think He forgives even people like me?"

"Hey." Brody grabbed her hands. "First of all, you don't know everything. And everyone has parts of their past they wish they could redo or forget. That's normal. What we do about it is ask for forgiveness and strive to be better. You have this amazing opportunity before you to completely change your direction in life."

He paused as he realized he was still holding her hands, and the warmth from them was taming the gnawing ache in his soul. Her eyes locked on his, and so much emotion flashed in them. Fear, longing, hope, desire. Though a solid blue color, the emotions they conveyed were like a quilt of many different fabrics sewn together. He should let go of her hands; he had no business falling for her, but he found he didn't want to. Still, if someone came outside and saw them…. With great effort, he cleared his throat and dropped her hands, moving his to his pants leg. "How about Rico Rearden? Did you remember any more about him?"

She tilted her head at him, and her gaze tore through him. Could she see the effect she was having on him? Finally, she shook her head. "Nothing more than I was meeting with him about something, but I can't remember what."

Brody supplied her with the little information he knew in hopes it would help her. "He owns a publishing company, so perhaps you were meeting with him about that?"

A pained expression covered Tia's face. "I don't know. I remember calling him and asking for an appointment, but I don't remember what happened after."

Brody could tell she was getting frustrated, and his break was over anyway. It was time to return her to her room and finish his rounds. "Well, Detective Graves is still looking into both Rico and Debra. Neither appear to have a black truck, so even though you are fearful of what you will remember, getting your memory back is vitally important. Someone might still be after you."

## 8

D etective Graves was in the room when they returned. "Where do these flowers come from?" he asked.

"From the gift shop downstairs usually or from outside sources," Dr. Cavanaugh said as he wheeled Tia back to the bed.

"And how do they get delivered?"

Dr. Cavanaugh held out his hand and helped Tia stand and get situated back in the bed. "An orderly generally brings them to the floor and then either delivers them or gives them to the nurses to deliver."

"Valerie brought mine in," Tia supplied.

Detective Graves glanced over at her before turning his attention back to Dr. Cavanaugh. "I'm going to need to speak with her as well."

"Fine, I'll introduce you." Dr. Cavanaugh turned back to Tia. "I'll check on you before I leave for the night."

Tia nodded, but she didn't really feel like being alone. Even the security guard outside her door didn't make her feel much safer. The flowers had still gotten to her, and what if they put anthrax or some kind of air borne poison on them next time? She supposed that was unlikely, but it could happen, right?

Plus, she had the information Dr. Cavanaugh had shared with her rattling around in her head. She'd had enough glimpses of her past to know that she had turned from a sweet Texas girl into a haughty nightmare of a woman, but she couldn't believe she had tried to damage someone's reputation. And while she agreed with Brody that it was important to remember her past for her current safety, she didn't want to think about what an awful person she might have been. Was he right? Was this why this accident had happened to her? Was she being given a second chance? If she was, maybe it would be better if she didn't remember her past.

"Hello, dear, would you like me to read to you some more today?"

Tia looked up to see Edith in the doorway. She held the Bible in her hands and a kind smile graced her face. "Do you come read to patients every day?"

Edith waddled into the room. "Not every day. I have Bridge on Mondays and square dancing on Thursdays, but I try to come on Tuesdays and Wednesdays and some Fridays if my health allows and I don't miss the bus."

Square dancing? This woman certainly seemed spry for someone so old.

"But you didn't answer my question. Would you like me to read to you?"

Tia glanced at the book Brody had brought her yesterday. "Yes, but can you read me that?" She pointed to the book on the table beside her.

Edith picked up the book and raised an eyebrow. "True Love? Is this some sappy romance?"

"Maybe." Tia shrugged. "I don't know. It appears I wrote it, but I don't remember it."

"Well, I don't normally read romances, but since you wrote

it, I'll give it a shot. If there are any heaving chests or panting of breaths in here, I stop though. Is that understood?" Edith flashed her a look that Tia imagined was the one she used when she reprimanded her children growing up. If she had any.

Tia nodded and smiled. "I don't think I wrote those kind of romances, but agreed." Having Edith read a scene like that out loud sounded just as mortifying to Tia as it must to Edith.

"Gayle climbed under her desk as the sound of her father's angry footsteps carried down the hall..."

Suddenly, another piece of her past opened up. Tia saw herself curled under a desk where the chair normally sat. A blanket, held in place by the middle drawer, blocked the outside world and allowed her to believe she couldn't be seen. A book lay open on her knees and she held a flashlight in one hand. She was reading. Reading under her desk to hide from her father.

Her father who had never wanted her. Who had told her she should have been a boy. Who had left when she was ten years old because he didn't feel like being a dad any longer. Then her mother appeared. A woman with shoulders rolled forward from heavy work but kind eyes. A woman who had worked two jobs to provide for her and never complained. Tia saw the times her mother cried in her room when she thought Tia wasn't watching. Cried because she didn't have enough money to purchase groceries to feed Tia.

Tia sucked in a breath. That's why she had started writing. She had hoped it would earn enough income that she could take care of her mother. Her teachers had always told her in school that she was creative - probably because she'd had to invent worlds to escape from her father's angry words. So, when had she changed? When had she gone from wanting to write to help her mother to obsessing about her career so much that she was willing to ruin the reputations of other writers and throw herself at men in power just to boost her career?

But that's where the memories stopped. She didn't know. She

couldn't recall what had triggered her to become a woman she was now ashamed of. She couldn't remember much after she had started writing except that, evidently, she wanted to be the most successful romance writer in the business, and the easiest way to accomplish that goal was to persuade herself to do despicable things.

Edith stopped reading and glanced up at Tia. "What is it?"

"I remember. I remember my past. At least most of it. My father hated me and left when I was young, and my mother worked hard to keep us fed. I remember wanting to write to make money to pay her back, but something changed. Somewhere along the way, I stopped caring about my mother and began only caring about myself." Shame filled her. Even though she couldn't remember every event, she knew there would be many she would regret when they surfaced in her memory.

"Fame can do that to people," Edith said.

"But I don't want to be that person any more. I want to go back to the girl who wanted to help her mother."

"Then do it. You control what you do, and it appears you've been given a second chance at your life."

"Oh, I'm sorry. I didn't know you had a guest. I can come back later."

Tia looked up to see an unfamiliar nurse in her doorway. She was slim with olive skin and dark hair. Had Brody reassigned Valerie then?

"It's no bother. You come do what you have to do. I can read around your examination," Edith said as she glanced briefly at the nurse before dropping her gaze back to her book.

"Um, okay. How is your pain today?" the nurse asked.

"It's better," Tia said, "but shouldn't you be writing that down?" She found it odd that this woman didn't have the clipboard that Valerie and Brody usually walked in with.

The woman's eyes widened, and her gaze flitted around the

room. "You're right. I must have forgotten it. It's my first week. I'll go get it and return later."

Tia watched the woman walk out of the room and wondered about her. Was she really new? Forgetting to bring in the clipboard seemed like a ridiculous error even for someone who was new. Perhaps she was affiliated with the people after Tia. Maybe she was disguising herself as a nurse, so she could take Tia out without suspicion. Tia shook her head. Her imagination was running away with her. Things like that only happened in movies or television, but perhaps if she couldn't remember how to write romances, she could write thrillers.

"They really need to train these nurses better," Edith said when the woman was gone. "She's the same one who tried to run me out yesterday. I told Dr. Cavanaugh he needed to talk to her. Guess I need to remind him again."

The topic of Dr. Cavanaugh distracted Tia from her runaway thoughts of killers in disguise and she found herself asking a question she didn't dare ask anyone else. "Do you know Dr. Cavanaugh well?"

"As well as you can know a doctor I guess," Edith said as her eyes returned to the book. "I read a lot to his wife during her last days."

"What was she like?" Tia had an image of Dr. Cavanaugh's wife in her head, and she wanted to know if the woman was as saintly as she pictured her.

Edith looked up at Tia with a scrutinizing gaze. "She was lovely. A real woman of God. Even when the cancer took hold of her, she always remained positive and friendly to everyone. Now, should I continue reading?"

Tia nodded, but her mind no longer listened as Edith continued reading. She had wandered through the past long enough for today. Now, she needed to figure out how to change her future.

"I hear you took your patient outside," Nick said as he came up behind Brody in the locker room.

Brody shrugged, but he was curious who had ratted him out. "It's not against the rules."

Nick opened his locker and pulled out his bag. "No, it's not, but it's not something doctors normally do. It's also very unlike Brody Cavanaugh who never dates and rarely looks at women. And it has the nurses in a fit. You know how they like to gossip."

Brody hung his coat up in the locker. "They gossip about everything. I doubt I'll be the topic of their gossip much longer. Some episode of a tv drama will have replaced me by tomorrow."

"Mmmhmm, but I thought you said you weren't falling for this girl."

Brody sighed and sank down on the bench seat that filled the wall on the other side of the small locker room. He dropped his head into his hands. "I wasn't, but I have to be honest that I am having a hard time getting her off my mind. Every moment I spend with her is….calming, if that makes any sense."

"It makes perfect sense," Nick said as he sat beside Brody. "Look man, I didn't know Rachel well, but I have to think that she wouldn't want this life for you. This throwing yourself into work and never having a social life. From what I did know of her, she would have wanted you to keep living, and part of living is not being alone. So, if you're not pursuing this woman simply because of Rachel…." he shrugged, "I think you're wrong."

"Maybe." Brody shook his head. "But she's also a patient who doesn't remember who she is. And someone is clearly after her. *And* the little I have found out about her past doesn't paint her in the best light."

"Maybe, she just needs something or someone," Nick looked at him pointedly, "to have a reason to change."

Brody smiled up at his friend. "I'll take that into considera-
tion, and I'll think about it. Right now, I better get to the store
though. My refrigerator is going to sue me for lack of support."
He grabbed his bag and headed for the door.

"That's why you need a Berta," Nick hollered after him. "I'll
send you her number."

Brody was still chuckling as he pushed the back door open
and found Jordan Graves leaning against his car. "Detective, did
you find out anything more about the flowers?"

Jordan pushed himself upright and glanced around the empty
lot. "Unfortunately not. They were purchased at the gift shop
here, but paid for in cash. The clerk couldn't remember who
purchased them and there's no camera that points that direction.
We do have some new intel though. It appears Rico Rearden may
be involved in drug trafficking over in Chicago. He didn't come
up on our initial radar because he doesn't deal here, but it looks
like he might hold meetings here and use his publishing business
as a front."

"Do you think Tia was helping him move drugs?" Just when
Brody thought maybe he could fall for this girl, another piece of
information rocked his heart. He had a hard-enough time imagining her sleeping with another woman's husband, but moving
drugs?

"We don't know what to think. It's possible she was involved
though nothing in her background suggests it. It's more probable
she was there for the meeting she had scheduled and may have
stumbled across a secret meeting. Either way, we need to keep a
close eye on her. She may not be as innocent as we think."

Brody shook his head. He'd had no idea one patient would
turn his life upside down so fast. "Okay, thanks Jordan, I'll do
my best." He shook Jordan's hand and then unlocked the car and
slid into the driver's seat. But he didn't start the car right away.
His thoughts were a tangled web and he wanted to clear them
before he started driving.

Tia Sweetchild certainly was a conundrum. His first assumption of her had been a snobby rich girl, but that image had softened as he'd spent time with her. Her past showed that she had deliberately tried to ruin someone's career, but she had acted appalled when he'd told her about it. Was she a good con or had the brain injury changed her personality? Now there was the possibility of drugs? He didn't want it to believe it. He felt an attraction to Tia. A connection he couldn't explain, but how could he be attracted to a woman with such a shady past?

Rachel had been nothing like that. She'd grown up in a Christian home, and he was pretty sure the champagne they had on their wedding night had been her first taste of alcohol. Curse words never crossed her lips, and she always scolded Brody when he let one slip. And she'd been a genuine, generous, faithful woman. She would never have pursued men to get ahead no matter the circumstances. So, why would he feel an attraction to someone so unlike the love of his life? Or was there more to Tia than he knew?

He had no answers, and with a sigh, he turned the key and pointed the car towards home. Maybe some time in the word and a decent night's sleep would give him some clarity.

## 9

Tia glanced with dread at the doorway every time she heard footsteps. She wasn't looking forward to seeing Dr. Cavanaugh this morning. What she had remembered of her past was too shameful, and she was sure she wouldn't be able to hide the shame from him. Maybe it was his day off, and she wouldn't have to face him today.

"Good morning, Tia. Did Detective Graves stop in to see you yesterday?" And there he was.

Tia nodded. "He did though he said the flowers were a dead end. No way to trace who bought them. The security guard is supposed to intercept any from now on."

"Probably a good idea. I'm sorry he wasn't able to obtain more information about the flowers, but how are you feeling today?"

She forced her lips into a smile she didn't feel and hoped he wouldn't notice the difference. "Physically? Not too bad. The ache in my head is down to a dull roar, and the throbbing in my foot has intensified which I guess is good because it means I'm feeling it more."

Dr. Cavanaugh nodded and made some notes in the chart.

"Pain is rarely fun, but it does sometimes serve a good purpose. And as much as I don't want you in pain, I am glad to hear you have more feeling. I'll schedule a follow up with Dr. North." He lowered the clipboard and regarded her. "Now, how about emotionally?"

Tia scoffed softly and bit the inside of her lip. "Okay, I guess. Edith read some more of this book you brought me, and I remembered a little more of my past."

"That's great," Dr. Cavanaugh said with a smile and what sounded to Tia like a false cheeriness in his voice.

Tia wished it were. Yes, she had remembered some good things about her past, but she also knew somewhere along the way she had changed into an unlikeable person, and she still didn't know exactly why. Nor did she want to share that detail with Dr. Cavanaugh.

He started his daily assessment of her by checking her IV and the monitor that beeped constantly next to her bed. Then his fingers were on her forehead as he checked her stitches. "This is healing nicely. I bet the scar won't be too noticeable."

Tia was fairly certain that a scar of any kind would have sent her over the edge at one point, but now she felt as if she deserved it. And maybe more.

"Your fever appears to be gone as well. We might be able to get you out of here sooner than I thought."

Tia wasn't sure how she felt about that. She certainly hadn't planned on living in this hospital, but she still had no idea where she was staying or who was after her. What would she do when she was released? And would she ever see Dr. Cavanaugh again? Maybe he would be glad to get her out of the hospital.

He had just moved the blanket from her feet when the intercom sounded. "Attention personnel. This is a code silver. I repeat we have a code silver in the ICU."

Dr. Cavanaugh's hands froze, and Tia felt a string of fear grip her heart. "What's a code silver?" she asked in a frightened whisper.

"It means someone has a weapon. Stay calm. I'm going to lock the door." He shut her door, locked it, and then began scooting a chair up against the door. When that was in place, he returned to Tia's side.

"This isn't going to feel good, but I need to move you."

"What? Why? What's happening out there?" Panic filled Tia's voice.

"I don't know, but Detective Graves told me yesterday that Rico Rearden is involved with drug trafficking. Now, it's possible you were helping or you stumbled into a meeting you weren't supposed to. Or maybe that weapon has nothing to do with you, but I don't want to take the chance. I've locked the door which will hold them for a bit, and I'm certain the security guard will defend the room, but you're a sitting duck in the bed. If I can get you into the bathroom, it buys us a little more time and hopefully it will be enough."

"And if it's not?" It was not a question she needed an answer to, but he gave one anyway.

"Then I hope you're prepared to meet your maker." He held her gaze for just a moment before snapping back to the task at hand. "If you can grab that pole, I can leave the IV in, but I'm going to have to pick you up."

A million thoughts raced through Tia's head. She hadn't had her sponge bath today, he would touch her bare back, if she didn't allow him to pick her up then they could die. "Okay."

As he snaked his arms under her head and knees, she reached for the pole. "Not yet," he said grunting with the effort of lifting her. "I need to get around the bed first."

Tia wrapped a free arm around his neck in hopes it might lessen his load and grimaced against the pain as her foot fell below her heart. The throbbing intensified, but she pressed her lips together to keep from complaining. He was doing the hard work here, and she would not whine.

When they cleared the bed, he took a step toward the IV drip and she grabbed the pole. The wheels squeaked softly as they made their way across the floor, and Tia hoped the sound wasn't carrying outside the room. An eerie silence filled the air.

When they reached the bathroom, he set her down in the tub as gingerly as he could. The pain from her foot made the world go black for a moment, but then he was propping her foot up with towels from the shelf. Once it was above her heart again, the pain lessened and the blackness receded.

"I hope you aren't afraid of the dark," he said as he pulled the door shut and locked it.

Tia wasn't normally afraid of the darkness, but she'd long hated darkness if mirrors were involved. A silly childhood game had planted an absurd fear of nightmarish things coming out of mirrors in the dark, and though she'd realized as she grew older that the game was just that, her fear hadn't diminished. Though she couldn't see him, she was glad Dr. Cavanaugh was in the room with her.

Brody tried to calm his breath as he pulled his phone out of his pocket. He punched in Jordan's number and hoped he would get bars. The reception in the hospital was spotty enough in the break room, but he'd never tried it in a bathroom. He pressed the call button and watched as the phone searched for a connection. "Please God," he whispered. A moment later, two bars appeared. It wasn't much, but he hoped it would be enough. He held his breath as he waited.

"Detective Graves," the voice on the other end said as his call went through.

"Jordan? It's Brody Cavanaugh at Fire Beach Hospital. We

are in lockdown. A code silver was reported a few moments ago in the ICU. I am locked in the bathroom in room six with Tia." Brody was surprised at how calm his voice sounded as his heart pounded in his chest.

"I'm on my way. Do you know what the weapon is?"

"No, I haven't seen anything. I locked the door per protocol as soon as the announcement was made."

"Understood. I'm going to transfer you to a dispatch operator and I want you to stay on the line until I get there."

"I'll try, but we're in the bathroom and I only had two bars. I don't know if they'll hold….. Hello?" He pulled the phone away from his ear and sighed as he saw it searching for connection again. At least the bars had been there long enough for him to place the call. The rest was in God's hands now.

He turned toward the bathtub. "Tia, how are you holding up?"

"Okay, I think. The throbbing has subsided in my foot."

Brody reached out a hand, hoping it would land on her arm and not some other body part. He felt the flesh of her bare skin and a moment later, her hand covered his.

"Are you scared?" she asked in a timid voice.

He interlocked his fingers with hers. "A little. You?"

"Yeah. A lot. Do you think the police will make it in time Dr. Cavanaugh?"

Brody shook his head though he knew she couldn't see it in the darkness. "I hope so. Tia?"

"Yeah?"

"I think considering the circumstances that you can call me Brody."

He could hear the smile in her voice even though it was laced by fear. "Okay, Brody." She squeezed his hand, and he liked how his name sounded on her lips. "Can I ask you something?"

Brody didn't think their voices would carry out of the bathroom, especially in the hushed whispers they were using, and talking sounded a lot better than sitting in silence and worrying if someone would bust in and end their lives. "Sure, ask away."

Her deep breath sounded nearly deafening in the dark silence. "How did you know you wanted to be a doctor?"

"Oh, um." No one had asked him that question in a long time. He thought back over the years and smiled as he recalled his childhood. "My mother said I always enjoyed pretending to heal animals and people when I was young, but I think the first time I knew I wanted to become a doctor was in high school. There was a student with epilepsy and one day she had a grand mal seizure in class. I remember everyone being so scared, even the teacher, and I wished I knew what to do to help her. After that, I began researching what it would take to become a doctor and never turned back. What about you? Do you remember why you became a writer?"

Her voice was barely above a whisper as it came back to him. "I do. I remembered yesterday that my father left us. He never wanted me. He said he wanted a boy, but I'm not sure he really wanted a kid at all. Before I could write, I used to make up stories to escape his anger, but after he left, I began writing stories of the family I wished I had. I wanted it to be a career, so I could support my mother and repay her for all she did."

Brody's heart broke with her words. Fathers were so important, and in this age where families broke apart and men encouraged their wives and girlfriends to have abortions, good father figures were harder and harder to find. He'd been lucky. Not only were his parents still together, but his father had always been there for him.

"I'm so sorry, Tia. I can't imagine how hard that must have been." Though he didn't condone some of her past behavior, this admission could explain why she had done some of the things she had. If she had become so focused on making enough money to help her mother, greed might have taken control of the once sweet girl and changed her into the woman who would throw another person under the bus to further her career.

"Me too." Another long sigh. "Can I ask you something else?"

"Go ahead." Talking broke the heavy silence, and he didn't think she could ask him anything he might not want to answer.

"Do you think you'll ever marry again, Brody?"

Except that! He bit the inside of his lip as he thought of how to answer.

## 10

B rody. The name felt like candy on her tongue. How she would have enjoyed this moment of holding his hand and saying his name if it weren't clouded with the darkness and fear around them.

Darkness and fear.... Suddenly, the events of a few nights ago came back to her. She saw herself entering Rico's house and following him to his bedroom. While sleeping with him hadn't been her plan, she had been prepared to use flirtation and her good looks on him to try and get her book promoted. At least until she saw the picture of his wife on the nightstand. "Oh my gosh, Brody, I remember." She squeezed his hand tighter as excitement joined the fear coursing through her.

"What?" he asked.

"I went to Rico's to try and convince him to promote my latest book, but I didn't know about his wife. When I realized he was married, I told him I wouldn't cross that line. I've been pretty awful the last few years, but that was too much for even me. But as we were talking, his phone rang. His demeanor shifted immediately, and he ushered me out of the room. I was almost to my car when I remembered my purse. I ran back up to his room, but he freaked out when he saw me and shoved me in a closet." She shivered as she remembered sitting in the unfamiliar dark closet.

"I thought he was hiding me from his wife, but then I heard other masculine voices join his. They were angry and yelling about something, but the words were muffled inside the closet. Anyway, I heard the balcony glass door open, and I took the chance they had stepped outside. I bolted, forgetting my purse in the process. I just wanted to get out of there."

"Do you think they were in the black truck that hit you?" Brody asked.

"It's possible. I never saw the driver, but I remember one car blinding me from behind and then the truck hitting me. If it was them, I don't think they'll stop until I'm dead."

Her words hung in the air, a fatal prophecy. Neither of them had a word to say in response. Suddenly, there was a pounding on the door of her hospital room. Tia squeezed Brody's hand tighter. "Brody? If we don't make it out of here alive, I want you to know that I'm glad you were my doctor. You're a good man, and you've made me want to be a better woman."

"Shh, don't talk like that," Brody said, but the fear was evident in his voice.

Suddenly, there was pounding on the bathroom door. Tia squeezed Brody's hand tighter with one hand and clapped the other over her mouth to keep from screaming.

"Dr. Cavanaugh? Open up. It's Detective Graves."

Relief flooded Tia and her breath escaped in one giant sigh. Even when Brody let go of her hand to stand and open the door, she had never felt so blissful. The bright light blinded her for a moment, and she blinked rapidly to readjust her eyes.

"Is it safe to come out then?" Brody asked.

"It is," Detective Graves said, "Evidently, it was a patient who suffered a psychiatric break and grabbed a scalpel off a tray."

Tia might have laughed at the situation if her heartbeat wasn't still thundering in her chest.

"I'm sorry," Brody said, "after our conversation-"

"You were right to do what you did," Detective Graves assured him. "We still haven't found the driver of the black truck or who sent her those flowers, and what you did made perfect sense. However, unless you need further assistance, we'll get back to work on finding the suspects."

"Wait, Detective Graves?" Though Tia didn't want to recount her story again, she didn't want another reprimand from Detective Graves either. He turned back to her and waited for her to continue. "I remembered more. I was there to see Rico about a publishing opportunity, but I turned it down when I found out he was married and looking for an affair. He kicked me out, but I had forgotten my purse. When I returned, he shoved me in a closet. I heard men's voices arguing, and I thought perhaps they were reporters out for a story on me which is why I ran when I did."

"Did you see any of the men? Do you remember anything about them?"

"Not their faces. When I stepped out of the closet, I looked left. They were on the balcony, but it was dark outside. I couldn't see their faces, but I felt the icy hatred in their gaze when they saw me. I didn't think they had followed me at first, but then lights blinded me on the road. I slowed down thinking maybe it was just teenagers out for a joy ride, but when they didn't pass me, I figured they had followed me after all. Then the truck hit me."

Jordan's face hardened and he exchanged a glance with Brody. "Okay, thank you, Tia. We'll look into all of this and let you know what we find. Do the two of you need anything else?"

"I think we'll be fine." Brody turned to Tia as the detectives left. "Well, that was some excitement for the day. How about we get you back in bed?"

"Could we take a walk instead?" Tia asked. "My heart is still pounding, and I feel like I could use some fresh air after this."

His lips pulled into a smile. "I think that's a great idea."

Brody tried to ignore the sensations that flooded his body when he picked Tia up again. He'd been sure there was no emotional attachment or he'd at least been trying to convince himself there was no attachment, but the near-death experience had blown that out of the water. Holding hands with her in the dark had sent emotions careening through his body that he hadn't felt since Rachel's death.

But he still didn't know her. Was she the overly ambitious, conniving person of her past? She said she hadn't had an affair or involvement with drug trafficking. But was that true? Or was she the sweet, kind person that he knew her to be? He had to admit that even though he didn't completely know her, the things in her past seemed to matter less now. She seemed sincere.

"Let me get you a robe," he said as soon as he got her situated back on the bed. He grabbed one from the wardrobe in the room and helped her shrug into it before paging for a wheelchair. Then he looked at her, a million things running through his mind – none of which he could say. "I'll check your IV."

"You've taken very good care of me, Brody. Thank you," Tia said holding his gaze.

He liked how his name sounded when she said it. And he liked taking care of her. Egad, was he falling for her?

"Dr. Cavanaugh? Your wheelchair."

The sound of the orderly snapped Brody out of his daydream and he flashed Eric a smile. "Thank you. Can you let Valerie know I'm taking a walk?"

Eric paled. "I will, sir, but you should know they are talking about you. About how much time you're spending..." he glanced over at Tia, "with patients."

"That's all right, Eric. I can handle it, but thank you for the information." Brody didn't like being the subject of gossip, but he hadn't been exaggerating when he told Nick they gossiped about everything. He wasn't about to change his behavior just to avoid being their topic.

"Can we go without the pole?" Tia asked. She had either not caught Eric's implication or she was simply ignoring it.

"If you think you can handle no pain meds for a bit, I can cap your plug."

"I think I'll be okay. Honestly, the pain is getting better. Of course, that could be the medicine talking." She flashed him a crooked smile, "or maybe the adrenaline. But really, I think I'll be fine for the walk."

He pushed up the sleeve of her robe and unhooked the IV, being careful to leave the plug in her arm. Then he wheeled the chair closer to the bed and helped her sit down. Moments later, they were outside breathing in the sunlight and fresh air.

"You know for a minute, I thought that might be the end," Tia said as he pushed her down the path. She had suggested they walk this time instead of just sitting, and after the scare, Brody was in need of some exercise to settle his nerves as well. "I real-ized I don't want this to be the end of my life. Whether this personality change is because of me or the brain injury, I want to do something with it. I want to apologize to Ava and the other people I have hurt and start walking a different path."

"I think that's a great plan," Brody said with a smile as he imagined helping her accomplish that goal. But then he remem-bered she lived in California and he lived here. "Will you go back to California then?"

"I don't know," she said. "I mean I guess I will have to go back to check the details of my life there, but I might like it here. Or I might when people aren't trying to kill me."

"Yeah, that could prevent someone from liking a place," Brody chuckled.

"You know, you never answered my question."

"What question?" In all the commotion of her memory coming back and the rescue, he had forgotten what she had asked.

"Do you think you'll ever marry again?"

Brody was glad he was behind her and she couldn't see his facial expressions because he had no idea what emotion might be playing on his face right now. "I don't know. When Rachel died, I was pretty sure that was it. I threw myself into work and convinced myself it would be enough, but now I'm not so sure. I suppose I'd like a companion again. If I could find the right woman."

She smiled up at him, and Brody felt the ice around his heart melt a little more. Though he hadn't expected it to happen, she had managed to capture a piece of his heart. "Well, I hope you do then. You seem like you would make a great husband."

Brody didn't know what to say to that, so they continued on in silence. They walked around the entire hospital enjoying the sun and fresh air.

"Oh, I never thanked you," she said as they reached the entrance again.

"For what?" he asked.

"For reassigning Valerie. The new nurse is much nicer though I feel like she might need more training. She forgot the clipboard when she came in to check me."

Brody felt a tendril of fear reach around his heart and begin to squeeze. "Tia, I didn't assign a new nurse to your room."

She turned to face him, panic in her eyes. "Then who is the nurse who was in my room yesterday?"

"I don't know, but we better find out." Brody's shoulders, having just relaxed, tensed again, and he pulled out his cell phone to dial Jordan once more as he wheeled Tia back inside.

Tia flipped on the television to pass the time before Brody's return. Her heart still thudded faster than normal in her chest. When they had returned to the room, Brody and Jordan had gone in search of the nurse she had seen yesterday. Jordan had left strict instructions with the security guard outside that no one was allowed in her room except Sophie, but that thought didn't make her feel much safer. What if the security guard fell asleep or was overpowered or went to the bathroom for goodness sake?

She wished Brody had stayed with her. It wasn't even evening yet, but the day had been more eventful than most. More eventful than she thought her life back home ever was. In fact, though she still didn't remember everything, when she thought of her life back home, she only felt loneliness. Did she really want to go back to that?

"Reflecting on your poor choices?"

Tia's eyes flicked to the doorway and she sucked in her breath. A man she did not recognize stood in the doorway dressed in an orderly uniform. Except for the ice flowing out of his gaze and the hard lines of his face, he might have been any orderly in the hospital, but she knew he was not. Fear raced through her. "How did you get in here?" she asked as she inched her finger toward the call button.

"I wouldn't do that if I were you." He let go of the door and lunged toward her with a vicious scowl. The door shut behind him, and the movement caused Tia to jump and her hand slipped away from the call button. "You want to know how I got past your security guard?"

Tia nodded, fear constricting her voice.

He flashed a cold, predatory smile. "I just gave him a little something to help him sleep. The same thing I'm going to do to you. See, Rico's wife came in guns blazing, the idiot, but I'm smarter than that. I think things through. I gather all the information, and I don't make mistakes."

"Who are you and why are you doing this?" Tia asked hoping to stall him. "I didn't hear the conversation and wouldn't have remembered it if I had. And I never saw your face. Until now. You could have just let it go. Let me go."

He shook his head as his lips pulled into a chilling smile. "Who I am is unimportant. At least to you. But you? You're a loose end. I don't like loose ends." He pulled a syringe from his pocket. "Do you know what this is?"

"No, but I bet you're going to tell me." Tia's eyes darted to the door hoping for someone, anyone to walk in. Brody had no reason to return so soon, but maybe Valerie? As much as she didn't like the nurse, she would welcome her presence right now.

"It's insulin." He took another step toward her. "Do you know what happens when you get injected with insulin too quickly and you're not diabetic?"

"I'm sure nothing good." Tia's heart pounded in her chest. Should she scream? Would anyone hear her through the closed door? Maybe she could try for the button again, but she wasn't sure this man didn't have another weapon. Would he just pull out a gun and shoot her if she tried?

"First, it will make you groggy and confused before you pass out completely. The damage to your organs will be done before they even know what happened, and the best part is that insulin is already in the body, so nobody will think twice if they find it. They'll probably assume you just had a delayed traumatic reaction to today's events."

Panic squeezed on her heart, but she forced herself to keep him talking. "Did you have something to do with the code silver?"

Something akin to pride filled his face. "I may have helped a patient secure a scalpel and then prodded them in the right direction. It would have been the perfect time to silence you, especially since your security guard was tasked to help, but I wasn't counting on your doctor being in the room." Anger replaced the pride for a moment and transformed his face into an expression of rage.

"I thought you didn't make mistakes." What was wrong with her? Why was she goading him on? Did she really think she was buying enough time for someone to come to her rescue?

"Hmm," he chuckled, but it was a cold, calculating laugh. "See? I knew you listened, and now it's time to rectify that mistake."

As he lunged toward her, Tia did the only thing she could. She opened her mouth and screamed.

As the dark-haired nurse caught sight of them, she ran. Jordan bolted after her, turning his head just long enough to order Brody back to Tia's room. Then, he disappeared around the corner as well.

Brody hurried back to the ICU floor. He had just reached the center desk when he heard the noise. He wasn't sure it was a scream, but the sound of it sent the hairs on the back of his neck standing at attention. He glanced around at the few nurses who were in the ICU with him. "What was that?" Then his eyes darted to Tia's room. Her door was shut which was unusual, and the security guard was slumped in the chair outside. "Call security," he hollered as he raced across the floor to her room.

He checked the pulse of the security guard first. Weak, but still there. He didn't know for how long. "Someone get this man some help," he ordered, and then, without a second thought to his own safety, he burst through the door in time to see an orderly inject something into her IV. "What are you doing?"

The man looked up at him, and the expression chilled Brody to the bone. His eyes were hard and cruel as if chiseled from stone, and there was not a shred of remorse or decency in them. "You don't work here. Get away from her." Brody glanced to Tia whose eyes were beginning to close. What had he injected her with? He had to find out soon or he might not be able to counter it.

"Gladly," the man said, "my job here is done anyway." He began to skirt around the bed, but Brody had no intentions of letting him get out of the room. For every step he made, Brody countered. "Out of my way," the man snarled.

Brody had taken some self-defense classes in college and he had done some kickboxing. But fighting someone was an experience he had never had before. "I don't think so. The police are on their way. I think you'll be staying here until they arrive." He stepped into the fighter's stance his muscles remembered - left foot forward, hands at the ready by his chin.

The man chuckled. "You want to fight me?"

"If that's what it takes to see you arrested, I will."

"You're no match for me." He reached into his pocket and pulled out a knife.

Brody had never fought anyone with a knife and images of previous stab victims bleeding out on his ER tables flashed through his mind, but he wasn't going to give up. Surely, he could last until security or Jordan arrived.

The man lunged for him and Brody stepped to the side and threw a left hook. He missed the man's chin, but his fist hit the man's face with enough force to cause him to stumble forward. Brody took the opportunity to deliver a low kick to the back of the man's knee and he went sprawling. The knife skidded away. With an angry roar, the man lunged at Brody and threw him into the wall. Brody hit the sharp corner where the bathroom jutted out and felt the pain race down his left side, but he didn't have time to dwell on it long before the man was on top of him. His powerful hands closed on Brody's throat, and the world began to go dark.

And then there was air. Brody opened his eyes to see security hauling the man out of the room, but his head was still spinning from the momentary lack of oxygen.

"Are you okay?" Valerie's face appeared above him.

"Tia," he croaked and coughed. "He injected her with some-thing. Probably insulin. Get her some Glycogen. The security guard outside too."

Valerie looked as if she wanted to argue, but she nodded and raced over to the bed. Brody reached a hand up to massage his neck. He'd been lucky, and he knew it. When he could take a solid breath, he pushed himself to a sitting position and then stood, pausing only long enough to make sure the world wasn't spinning before racing to Tia's side.

Valerie stepped back from the IV and then hurried out of the room to administer one to the security guard. Brody stared down at Tia. Suddenly, her eyes fluttered open and she blinked. Then her gaze locked on Brody, and she gripped his arm. "Did he escape?" Fear threaded Tia's voice and her eyes shifted to the doorway.

"No, security got him."

"But not before he got Dr. Cavanaugh," Valerie said pointedly as she re-entered the room. "You need to get checked out yourself."

"I will," Brody said. In addition to a pounding in his head, he could feel the left side of his body stiffening. "But not until I talk to Detective Graves."

## 12

Tia found it nearly impossible to relax even with Brody sitting beside her. Every sound made her jump and look to the doorway.

"It's going to be all right," Brody said as he held out a hand. She was grateful for his touch, but even that didn't calm her racing heart. In just a few days, she'd been in an automobile accident, had a gun pulled on her, been locked in a bathroom due to a code silver, and been injected with Insulin. She wasn't sure her heart would ever return to its normal rhythm.

"How are you two doing?"

Tia looked up to see Detective Graves in the doorway.

"Did you get the guy?" Brody asked. "Who was he?"

Detective Graves nodded. "We did. His name is Adrian Petrov. He's the leader of one of the bigger gangs out of Chicago and the head of a drug organization. He isn't saying much right now, but Stone will take care of that. We did manage to ascertain his address." He turned to Tia and a slight smile pulled at his lips, "Where we found a black Ford truck, and though he tried to have it fixed, we are almost certain it was the same truck that hit you. It's over, Tia."

"That's wonderful." Brody turned to Tia, and a broad grin graced his features.

Tia forced a smile in return, but her worry wasn't entirely eased. She didn't know why, but the situation still bothered her. "Wait, what about the nurse?"

"We got her too. Susanna Petrov, his wife. She's not talking either, but from what we can gather, they obtained uniforms when they saw on the news that you were in ICU. We're not sure whether she was merely keeping him informed or if she was a backup plan, but we do know that she's the one who bought the flowers. We showed pictures to the clerk at the gift shop, and he was able to ID her."

So that was it. It was over, except…. "What about Rico?" Where did he fit into all of this? Why hadn't he come after her?

Jordan's jaw clenched and his eyes shifted just slightly. "He's in the wind. We think he's in Chicago hiding out and trying to clean up this mess, but I promise you we're still looking for him."

It should make her feel better, but it didn't. "Thank you, Detective Graves."

"Call me Jordan," he said as he held her gaze.

"Yes, thank you, Jordan," Brody said clapping a hand on Jordan's shoulder before turning back to Tia. "We need to monitor you to be sure the insulin didn't damage anything, but if all goes well, and as long as your fever is still gone, you might be able to leave the hospital tomorrow."

She should be glad. No one wanted to live in a hospital, but Tia didn't know what life held for her now. Did she go back to writing? She wasn't sure her stories would be the same after everything that had happened, and she didn't want to chance falling into the person she had been before. But, if she didn't write, what would she do?

As if sensing her unease, Detective Graves stepped forward. "I know this is a lot to deal with, Tia. If you'd like to stay in town a little longer, I can find you a temporary place and set you up with a counselor who might be able to work through some of the trauma with you."

Tia smiled up at him. "Thank you, I might take you up on that."

"And I don't know how your recovery will be, but I own a restaurant. I have a need for a good hostess if your doctor says it's okay."

Brody nodded. "I'd be okay with it as long as she can stay off her leg. It would be great if you stayed in town, and I was able to check up on you as well."

Check up on her? Was that all he wanted? She had thought after their two near death experiences that he might want more, but perhaps that had just been adrenaline acting and not any real affection for her.

"Thank you, Jordan. I think I'll spend tonight thinking about where I see my life going from here, and I'll let you know."

"You do that." He pulled a card from his pocket and handed it to her. "I know Al gave you a card the first day we were here, but this one has my personal cell. You call me if you want some help. I'm sorry this happened to you, but you are strong. You will be okay."

Tia nodded and hoped her lips formed a smile though she didn't feel much like smiling. After Jordan left, Brody went to check on other patients, promising to check in on her before he left for the night.

As she lay in the quiet room, Tia wondered what the rest of her life held for her. If Brody didn't have feelings for her, would she stay in Fire Beach? There wouldn't really be a need, but could she readjust to her life back in California? It already felt a lifetime ago. Though she couldn't remember the last time she had, Tia turned her eyes to the ceiling and whispered a prayer.

"God? I don't know if I used to do this. I'm not even sure I'm doing it right, but if I am, please help me know what to do. I don't want to go back to the person I was before, but I have no idea how to go forward."

She hadn't expected a booming answer, but Tia sighed when all she received was the stillness of her room broken only by the beeping of her monitor.

"Whew, you took quite a pounding," Nick said as he helped Brody get his arm out of the shirt. Though he didn't think anything was broken, Brody wanted to get a second opinion before heading home for the night. Besides worker's compensation required he receive medical attention for his claim.

Brody tried not to grimace as the pain shot through him. His arm was already turning an ugly collection of blues and purples. "I know, but it was either take the guy down or let him get away."

"In that case, I think you chose wisely, but you should remember that you're not Superman. You're going to have a sizable bruise on this shoulder. I'd ice it tonight and think about taking a few days off to recover. You certainly have enough saved up."

"Yeah, maybe after Tia gets released," Brody said with a nod. He tried to lift his arm to replace his shirt, but the pain made him stop.

Nick stepped back and narrowed his eyes at Brody. "Tia, huh? You've saved this woman twice now, and you don't want to take time off while she's here. Are you really going to tell me you don't have feelings for this woman?"

Brody sighed. "I don't know what I have - whether it's feelings or some crazy case of needing to protect her, but I want to be here until she's released."

"You don't even know how bad you have it, man," Nick said

with a shake of his head as he helped Brody place his arm back in his sleeve. "Okay, let me see the hip."

Brody took a deep breath, stood, and lowered his pants. His hip was definitely sore and would probably be just as colorful, but his shoulder actually ached more.

"Yep, you're going to have fun walking the next few days. Ice and rest, man. Ice and rest. And no more fist fights or wall slams."

"I'll do my best," Brody said with a smirk. "It's not like I practice them on a regular basis." He zipped his pants back up and grabbed his bag. "Thanks, Nick. I'll see you tomorrow."

"You too. Oh, and Brody?" Brody turned back to his friend. "She won't be your patient much longer."

Brody smiled and flashed his friend a wave as he stepped out of the door. Was that his hang-up? Was he worried about how it would look if he were seeing a patient? He supposed it was possible. There was no denying he had feelings for Tia now, but were they worth pursuing? Would she return to California when she was released? He had so many questions and no real answers. Perhaps tomorrow would bring more clarity.

## 13

Tia's eyes snapped open at the sound of footsteps. Her room was dark, too dark. It was night, so it had to have just been a nurse, but why wouldn't they identify themselves? She blinked trying to adjust to the light level and held her breath to hear any sounds better. But there was nothing. Had it all been a dream then? It had seemed so real.

As she exhaled, she wondered if she would face this the rest of her life. Would she always be jumping at shadows and feeling like she was being watched? Jordan had said it was over, but what if it wasn't? What if someone was still out there? What if Rico came after her? What if there were more people involved in the meeting than who Jordan arrested? Would she ever be safe?

She was still tired when the sun woke her the next morning. That certainly hadn't been her best night of sleep, and the responsibilities of the upcoming day wore heavy on her. If she got released, she needed to find a place to stay at least until her foot healed. Though Brody had said she could fly, trying to maneuver travel with a cast didn't sound appealing at all. Besides, she was in no hurry to get back to her life. Plus, she would need to contact Jordan about his job offer.

Tia hoped to return to writing one day, but until she got back on her feet, she needed a job that provided consistent income.

"Are you ready for your final evaluation?" Brody asked entering the room.

"I should say yes, right?"

"Most people can't wait to leave though I think it's mostly to get better food," he said with a smile.

"Well most people don't have people trying to kill them either."

"Did something happen?" Brody's voice oozed with concern, and his eyes raked over her as if looking for injuries. "Jordan said it was over."

Tia shook her head. "Just a dream. I know he said it was over, but I don't feel like it is, and I feel it will be worse out there. I certainly won't have you to protect me." She had meant for the words to sound light - an attempt at humor - but they hung heavy in the air.

Brody set his clipboard down on the table and approached her side. His eyes grew serious as he picked up her hand. "About that, Tia. I'm kind of a mess, and I've probably forgotten how to date, but I can't stand here and say I don't care about you. And as much as I don't know what the future holds, I'd like to see if there's a future for us."

Tia's mouth opened, but she couldn't form the words she wanted to say. She had hoped he felt the same as she did, but he'd been impossible to read accurately.

"I can't promise any more Superman stunts, but I'll try my best to protect you."

"Did you hurt yourself badly?" she finally managed.

"I'll have some good bruising on my left side where I hit that corner," he pointed to the area that jutted out due to the bathroom, "but nothing that won't heal with time. Now, what do you say we get you looked at and get you out of here?"

Tia nodded and chuckled. "I don't think I've ever wanted anything more."

Brody decided to start at the top and checked Tia's head first. As his fingers touched near her stitches, he couldn't help but wonder how touching the rest of her face would feel. He let his eyes wander down her slender cheek bones and to the curve in her neck before clearing his throat and forcing his focus back to her wound. "This looks good. You ready for the stitches to come out?"

"I suppose." Her eyes flicked up to meet his gaze. "Does it hurt? I don't think I've ever had stitches before."

"Not generally. Most people say it tickles, but I did have a patient once who healed rather quickly and her skin grew over her stitches a little."

"Oh great, thanks for sharing that."

He smiled down at her and squeezed her arm for reassurance. "I'm sure that won't be your case. You've had enough issues to deal with." He crossed to the medical cabinet and pulled out a pair of scissors before returning to her side. With a quick snip, he popped the first string holding it all together and then tugged on it until the rest came out. "All done. Did it hurt?"

Tia's face scrunched as if she were deciding. "I guess not, but it didn't tickle either. Is the scar bad?"

Brody pressed around the red puckering to make sure it was holding before answering her. "It's a little red right now, but that's to be expected. It will fade and eventually you'll just have a tiny white line. Besides, scars build character."

"I guess I'll have a lot of character then," she said with a chuckle.

He checked her eye next. The colors had faded to an ugly yellow brown, but she could open it fully, and nothing else appeared to be damaged. The cuts on her face and arms were almost healed as well, so he moved down to check her foot. "Can you feel this?" he asked touching her toes.

Her smile was wide as she nodded. "I can."

"Good, and how about the pain today?"

"Not bad although I assume I don't get to take the good stuff with me when I leave?"

He chuckled as he checked off her progress on the chart. "No, but I'll get you a prescription for some stronger ibuprofen than you can get over-the-counter just in case. I want Dr. North to check your foot as well, but it looks like you're cleared to go unless she says otherwise. You won't be able to drive though. Do you have anyone who can pick you up?"

Her face fell and understanding filled her eyes. "I don't. I don't have a car or a place to live yet."

"Hey, it's okay. I'll call Jordan and see if he can help you out. If he's busy, you can stay here until I get off and I'll drive you wherever he sets up for you."

"Thank you. I promise I won't always be so needy."

He picked up her hand and squeezed it. "We all need people, and I'm happy to help. You just relax and enjoy your last day. I'll take care of the rest."

## 14

Jordan showed up shortly after Dr. North finished her assessment and announced she was cleared to go as well.

"Brody said you could use a lift," he said with a grin. He held a bag in his hands, and she wondered what it contained.

"Yeah, I could. Plus, I thought I'd take you up on your offer for a place to stay and a job. I'd like to stay in town a little longer."

His eyes danced and the corners of his lips twitched as he set the bag beside her on the bed. "Would that have anything to do with a handsome doctor by chance?"

"It might," she said, "but I also don't know if there's much to go back to in California. I feel like I can start over here except...." Her voice trailed off as she remembered her dream from the previous night.

"Except what?"

Tia sighed and shook her head. "I had a dream last night that someone is still after me. I'm sure it was due to the activity yesterday, but do you think there's any chance that it might be true?"

Jordan ran a hand across his chin. "I'd be lying if I said no. I do think we got the main people involved, but there's always the chance that someone else decides to seek retribution. If it makes you feel better, the lady who runs the house I'm taking you to is former military. She'll keep an eye on you."

"Did you get any news on Rico?"

He shook his head. "Sorry, we're checking with the PD in Chicago, but it's going to take some time."

"Thanks Jordan." She wished that made her feel better, but at least she felt like she had friends looking out for her. Something she didn't think she'd had the last few years.

"You're welcome. Now, in that bag are some clothes and shoes. My girlfriend Cassidy deduced that you had none here. She picked them out, but I had to guess on your size, so don't blame her if they're off. She did bring some things with draw-strings, so the size shouldn't matter too much."

Tia's fingers touched the bag. Brody was so thoughtful. She hadn't even realized she had no clothes with which to leave the hospital. "Thank you, Jordan, and tell Cassidy thank you."

He nodded, clearly embarrassed and took a step back. "I'll give you a chance to change and see about getting a wheelchair so we can get you out of here."

As he ducked out of the room, Tia opened the bag. Not only did it contain socks and underwear in a few sizes, but there were also stretchy pants and sweats along with a few shirts. As she pulled out a simple green shirt, another piece of her past opened. Back home, she had a large closet full of designer clothes, and she would never have been caught dead in a shirt like this, one that looked as if it came from a bargain store, but Tia found she didn't mind now. Designer clothes seemed insignificant compared to everything she had faced recently.

She pulled on the green shirt and a pair of wide-leg navy

stretchy pants, gritting through the pain and stiffness of her body. Then she attempted to put a sock on her left foot, but no matter how hard she tried, she couldn't reach it. She finally decided just to use the sandals Cassidy had provided and forgo the socks altogether.

A knock sounded at the door a few minutes after she finished. "It's Jordan. Can I come in?"

"Yes, come on in."

"Hey, looking good," he said as he wheeled a chair in. Tia wasn't sure she would go that far, but she was thankful for all he had done. "You about ready? I just got called back to work, so I'm afraid I'll have to drop you and run."

"That's fine, Jordan. Really, you've done so much for me."

"So, I took your advice," Brody said as he set his food down across from Nick.

"Oh yeah, about what?" Nick picked up his burger and took a huge bite sending a blob of ketchup down his hand.

Brody rolled his eyes. He loved his friend but sometimes he had the manners of a pig and the memory of a gnat. "About Tia. I've decided to date her and see what happens."

Nick licked the ketchup off his arm. "That's great man. You take my advice about the other stuff too? The icing and time off from work?"

"Yes. Today is my last shift for a week. I'm not sure exactly what I'll do, but I imagine helping Tia get settled will take some of that time." Brody took a bite of his own burger, making sure to hold it over the plate in case he had a similar experience with his ketchup.

"Take her out, man. Fancy dinners, movies, anything that has a ton of people and will keep you both safe. Dancing is probably out for the moment though." Nick chuckled at his own joke before wolfing down another large bite of hamburger.

"You think?" Dancing would probably be out of the question for another few months as would anything requiring both legs, but fancy dinners and movies he could do. He just hoped he remembered how to date. He had met Rachel in college, and he'd known from the first date that he was going to marry her. They'd been married for ten years, so his knowledge of dating protocol was definitely rusty.

"It hasn't changed much if that's what you're worried about," Nick said as if reading his mind.

"What?"

"Dating. You had this look on your face - the one you get when you're really thinking about something or about to throw up - so I thought I'd clarify. Just ask the girl to go places with you and have fun. It's still the same."

Brody chuckled and shook his head. "I don't know how you know me so well, Nick. It's kind of creepy."

Nick shrugged and shoved the last of his burger in his mouth. "I'm just that good," he said around his mouthful of food.

Brody smiled as he finished his own lunch. He might not miss this hospital for the next week, but he would miss seeing Nick every day.

## 15

J ordan parked the car in front of a weathered-looking rambler close to the beach. The yellow paint was faded but still cheery. "Sorry, it's not much to look at on the outside, but Cara takes good care of the inside."

"It's fine," Tia said. "Hopefully, I don't have to inconvenience her too long."

Jordan touched her arm. "It's no inconvenience. We take care of each other here."

Tia smiled and thanked him. She couldn't remember a time she'd had friends like this - friends willing to help her out even though she had brought trouble to town and had a checkered past.

"Come on, I'll introduce you and help you get settled before I jet back to work."

He turned the engine off and walked around to Tia's side. Before helping her out, he grabbed her crutches out of the back seat, handed them to her, and made sure she was stable. Only then did he grab her bag. Tia smiled at his thoughtfulness. She didn't know Cassidy, but she believed the woman had been lucky finding a man like Jordan.

Jordan led the way up the short walk and pushed open the door without knocking. He must know this Cara well. "Cara? It's Jordan and Tia, the woman I told you about."

A woman with short spiky hair appeared in the doorway. Trim and athletic, the woman looked as if she could tangle with the boys any day with her broad shoulders and bold arm definition. "Jordan, good to see you again." She extended a hand in greeting.

Jordan shook the woman's hand and then turned to Tia. "This is Tia. She's recovering from memory loss and a few attempts on her life. She's going to need some help getting back on her feet."

Cara extended her hand to Tia. "It's a pleasure to meet you, and any friend of Jordan's is welcome here as long as needed."

Tia shook the woman's hand and returned the smile. "Thank you. I appreciate it."

"I hate to run, but I have to get to work. Cara will take good care of you, but please call me if you need anything." Jordan squeezed her shoulder before dropping her bag and exiting out the front door.

"Okay, want to follow me and I'll show you to your room?" Cara asked picking up the bag.

Tia nodded and followed her down the hall, her crutches tapping on the wooden floor. Cara stopped in front of a door and opened it to a small room decorated in tan and beige. It held only a bed, nightstand, and dresser, but it was better than the hospital room.

"There's a bathroom right next door. Sorry you'll have to walk a bit to get there, and the dining room is down the hall there. I serve breakfast at seven, lunch at noon, and dinner at seven. If you want a snack during the day, you're welcome to the kitchen."

"Thank you. This is more than I expected," Tia said surprised at the hitch in her voice.

"We've all been there," Cara said and though she didn't put a hand on Tia's shoulder, she felt the sentiment all the same.

After Cara left, Tia sat on the bed for a moment and looked around. It wasn't home, but it would do. For now.

Brody pulled up in front of the house and turned off the car. It appeared weathered and in need of repair on the outside, but Jordan had assured him that Tia would be well taken care of. He planned to help out as much as possible as well.

A blonde woman he had never met before opened the door at his knock. Her features were stern, but kind. "You must be Brody," she said, extending her hand. "I'm Cara."

"I am." He shook her hand surprised at her grip strength. Jordan had said she was ex-military, but if her physique was any indication, she still worked out as if she were active. "Did Tia get settled all right?"

"I suppose. I haven't checked on her since I showed her to her room, but you're welcome to now. She's in room three down that hallway." Cara turned and pointed behind her. "I've got a dinner to prepare for."

"Thank you." Brody headed the direction she had pointed and paused when he reached room three. He felt like a high schooler again, showing up for a first date. It was an odd feeling considering he was over thirty years old, but it didn't change the fact that his heart thundered loudly in his chest and his palms had collected a wet sheen. He ran them down his pants leg and then curled his right hand into a fist to knock.

"Come on in. It's open," came Tia's voice from inside the room. He pushed the door open to find her sitting on the bed. "I didn't have much to unpack and nothing else to do," she said with a shrug as if answering his unspoken question. "Cara said I could watch TV in the living room, but I didn't feel like it. Do you think while we're out, we can stop by an electronics store so I can get a new phone and computer?"

A grin tugged at Brody's lips. "We can stop wherever you would like. I figured we could get dinner and then possibly hit a clothing store, but we can add an electronics store in as well."

She pushed herself off the bed and grabbed her crutches. "You would go to a clothing store with me?"

"Yes?" he asked hesitantly, not knowing if this was a trick question or not. He hadn't gone to many clothing stores with Rachel but only because he never really thought about it.

She laughed at him. "It's just that most men don't like waiting around for women to try on clothes."

Ah, now that made sense. He supposed that would get boring if she spent too long there, but he also knew she had spent the last week in a hospital gown and had nothing except what Jordan had brought her. He would wait all night if it meant she was able to find some clothes to make her feel more comfortable. "Well, I think you'll find I'm not most men."

She had reached his side by the time he spoke, and she turned her blue eyes up at him. A slight smile sent the corners of her mouth twitching in an adorable manner, but her voice was low and sultry when she spoke. "I think I've already realized that."

He felt the pull between them, the desire to kiss her, but it was too soon. He hadn't kissed a woman since Rachel, and he wanted to do it right. So, instead he cleared his throat and motioned to the door. "Shall we go?"

Confusion flashed in her eyes for a moment, but then she put on a smile and nodded. He followed her out, mentally berating himself for confusing her. She'd been through enough bad experiences to last a lifetime; she didn't need him adding to her confusion.

When they reached the car, he held the door open for her and helped her in before loading her crutches in the back. As he walked to his side, the hairs on the back of his neck rose. He felt as if someone was watching them. With a surreptitious glance, he scanned the area, but he saw no one. Perhaps it was just a nosy neighbor watching out a window. He would scan the windows as they drove off. No need worrying Tia if it was nothing. He drove past the other houses slowly glad for the low speed limit, but there was no one in any of the windows. Probably just his over-active imagination then.

Though he rarely went out anymore, Brody had scheduled a dinner at an upscale Italian restaurant. "I hope you don't mind Italian," he said as he pulled the car into a space. "I suppose I should have asked."

She flashed him a wide grin. "I love Italian. In fact, I love cheese and bread and pasta of all kinds which is why I do yoga."

"Well good," he said with a chuckle, "we are in the right place then."

16

Tia followed Brody out of the restaurant feeling a little like Cinderella, underdressed and out of her element. Though she'd enjoyed dinner immensely, she'd felt people's eyes on them. The rest of the diners wore button down shirts and dresses while she was in the pants Jordan had brought her. She couldn't wait to get to the clothing store and pick up some new clothes for occasions like these. Assuming there were more occasions.

When Brody had picked her up from Cara's, there had been a moment. A moment where she thought he was going to kiss her, where she wanted him to kiss her, but then he hadn't. She knew it probably had more to do with the loss of his wife, but it had still sent the insecurity fluttering in her stomach. What if he decided she wasn't interesting enough now that she was out of the hospital? What if what he thought was attraction was more what they called 'Rescue Romance' and now that she didn't need to be saved, the attraction had faded?

"Did you get enough to eat?" Brody asked as they stepped into the cool evening air. The sun hadn't set completely, but the last orange, pink, and red rays were low on the horizon.

"I did," Tia said with a laugh. "It's probably a good thing I'm wearing stretchy pants or I might have popped a button, but I promise I'll dress nicer next time."

"I think you look beautiful," Brody said as he opened the car door.

Their gazes locked again, and Tia felt the pull once more. His eyes peered into her soul, and she opened every door to him, willing him to kiss her. A light breeze traipsed across her arms sending goosebumps erupting on her skin. Her breath stilled as her lips parted and his face lowered to hers. When his lips touched hers, sparks darted through her body and though it was crazy, she felt as if she were experiencing her last 'first kiss.' Even more, she felt the last of the locks on her memory fall away. She gasped and pulled away from him.

"What? Was it awful?" he asked. "I know I'm out of practice."

She placed a finger against his lips to stop his ramblings and smiled. "I remember, Brody. Everything."

Light radiated from his face as he threw his arms around her. "That's wonderful." And then he kissed her again, slow and deliberate. Her body trembled with emotion. "So, do we still head to a store or do we head to your place?" he asked when he pulled back.

Her face fell and the joyful emotions she had just experienced vanished. "I didn't have a place here. I'd expected the meeting with Rico to go quickly. I thought I could use my good looks to persuade him." She dropped her eyes to the ground, embarrassed by her choices. "Oh gosh, I was an awful person."

"Hey," he said putting a finger under her chin and tilting it up. "You might not have made the best decisions in your past, but we are all guilty of that. You have a Savior who forgives you, and you have the opportunity to make new choices from here on out."

"Do you think it's really that easy? Can I just forget my

past?" She wanted him to say yes, but that old insecurity that had driven her to do horrible things whispered that he wouldn't want her now that he knew what she was really like. How could anyone want her?

He brushed her hair behind her ear, his fingertips lighting up the nerves in her face. "No, you may never forget it, but you can apologize for what you need to and learn from the rest. Your past doesn't have to define your future."

"Hmm, that is sound advice," she said breathlessly. Did he realize his words could also apply to him though in a slightly different way? He'd lost someone he loved, but he didn't have to let that be the end of his story either.

"Yeah, I guess it is." His eyes stared into hers again before closing as he leaned down. Before his lips touched hers, the sound of an engine revving grabbed Tia's attention.

She turned her head to see a vehicle heading their direction. It was going fast, too fast, and the night of the accident came flooding back. Her body froze as she saw the headlights in her mirror again, blinding her.

"Tia? You okay?" Brody's voice seemed far away as she watched the vehicle come toward them, helpless to do anything. "Tia."

The vehicle roared past them, and Tia blinked. "I'm sorry," she said. "That car - I heard the engine rev - and the lights reminded me of the accident. I couldn't move."

"Hey, it's okay," he said running his hands down her arms. "You're going to be okay. It's going to take some time to heal completely. How about we hit that department store and then I take you home? I think you could use some rest."

"Yeah, thanks." Tia's head was still spinning, and her heart was still pounding though as she buckled her seatbelt. She'd been so sure that vehicle was out to get them. Would she ever relax again?

Brody sighed as he walked back to his car after dropping Tia off at Cara's place. She'd been so relaxed at dinner and then the car revving its engine had sent her back into her shell. Even the trip to the department store and an hour of trying on clothing hadn't brought her back entirely. He wondered if she would always be chasing shadows.

As he unlocked the car, a movement out of the corner of his eye caught his attention. He turned to see what it was, but only darkness stared back at him. Probably a raccoon or some other night animal out scrounging for garbage. Here he was worried about Tia relaxing and he couldn't even calm himself down. He thought he'd seen something when he picked her up and now again when he dropped her off. Perhaps he needed a good night's sleep as well. He certainly had been on edge all week. In fact, he didn't think he'd had a decent night's sleep since Tia's car accident. He would remedy that tonight.

As he turned back around, he got only a glimpse of the man before pain shot through his head, and the world went dark.

## 17

"How was your date?" Cara asked as Tia sat down in one of the chairs in the living room. She hadn't meant to disturb Cara's reading, but she also didn't feel like going to her room alone yet.

"It was…." she hesitated as she set her crutches on the floor beside her, "good."

"That's not very convincing," Cara said sticking a bookmark in her book and shutting the cover to get Tia her full attention. "What happened?"

Tia sighed. She wished she had a better answer for that question. "Brody is great. He opened the doors for me, and we had a wonderful dinner at a little Italian place. Then he kissed me, and the rest of my memory came back."

Cara tilted her head and tiny wrinkles appeared on her forehead as she furrowed her brow. "That all sounds better than good - I mean the man kissed you. And that was good right?"

Heat crept up Tia's face. "Yeah, that part was perfect. No complaints for sure."

Cara grinned and pulled her feet up under her. "So, I'm guessing there's more to it."

Tia nodded. "There's two more pieces. The first one is my past. I was not a nice person, and I think I went down that road because of my father, but still... How do I date this amazing man who is practically a saint while I have this checkered past?" Her gaze dropped to her hands and she picked at a rogue cuticle. "I mean I'm only here because I flew out to try and convince a man to promote my book. And I was willing to use almost any means necessary."

Cara's head bobbed as she let out a long breath. "Yeah, I can see why you feel that way. Does Brody know?"

"A little," Tia said with a shrug. "I haven't told him everything yet. I'm afraid he'll run away."

"He might." Cara's matter-of-fact tone caused Tia to raise her head. "But if he does, then he's not the man for you."

Tia's mouth fell open. That was certainly not the advice she had been looking for.

"Look, that's a hard lesson for a woman to learn at any point. I haven't dated a lot, but I gave my heart to this guy once who said all the right things until it came time for the rubber to meet the road. Then he was nowhere to be found - wouldn't return my texts or calls. I spent a few days wondering what I had done wrong, analyzing the relationship, agonizing over it really. But then I realized, it wasn't me. It was him. He wasn't ready for a real relationship with me. If Brody runs from your past, then it's just a sign you aren't meant to be together, and it would be better to find out now than to date for months and find out then."

"I suppose you're right." Tia wished she had Cara's confidence, but growing up feeling unloved by her father had fertilized this insecurity in her that she wasn't good enough until it had taken root and overrun her life.

"You said there were two reasons. What is the second one that is keeping you from smiling and walking on cloud nine?"

Tia dropped her eyes back to her fingers. She pulled off the rogue cuticle, grimacing slightly at the pain that shot through her finger momentarily. "When we left the restaurant, I heard this car rev its engine, and I thought it was coming right toward us. I froze and couldn't move until the car passed us. It reminded me so much of the accident, and I thought someone out there was still after me." She lifted her eyes. "I don't know how to stop being afraid."

Sympathy and understanding flooded Cara's eyes and she leaned forward. "That will come with time too. You've been through a traumatic experience. You can't expect it's going to be unicorns and rainbows right away. I still have nightmares about my deployments sometimes. I'll see bombs exploding or injured civilians in my dreams." She chuffed out a breath and ran her hand through her spiky hair. "And don't get me started on loud noises. I still jump. Fourth of July is no longer my favorite holiday, but it gets easier. Every day will get a little…"

Her words stopped abruptly as the lights in the house went out and darkness filled the room. The mood in the room shifted and Tia could feel the fear pressing against her. She didn't believe this was a simple case of the electricity going out. There had been no storm, no reason. No reason except her.

"Tia, do you have Jordan's number on you?" Cara asked in a forceful whisper.

"I do, but I don't have a phone." Why had they forgotten to stop at the electronics store on the way home? "And I don't know this place well enough to go stumbling around in the dark." There was no way she could navigate her own home in the dark on crutches. She certainly couldn't do it in this house she didn't know.

"I'm going to hand you my cell phone. There's a hall closet about fifteen feet to your left and nothing is blocking your way. I want you to crawl that direction as quietly and quickly as possible. Get inside, shut the door, and call Jordan."

"What are you going to do?" Tia's voice trembled with the fear racing through her.

"I'm going to do what I said I'd do. I'm going to protect you. Now go."

Tia didn't need a second urging. As soon as she felt the phone hit her palm, she lowered herself to the floor and began crawling the direction Tia had said. Her cast made a soft scratching sound as it dragged across the floor, and her breath sounded like a freight train in her head. Surely, she was giving her location away as silence filled the rest of the house.

When she had gone approximately fifteen feet, she began to feel around for the door of the closet. With every second her hand didn't find it, her anxiety increased until she nearly screamed for joy when her fingers finally found the knob.

She opened the door and crawled inside, shutting it after her. Only then did she turn on Cara's cell phone, grab the card Jordan had given her from her pocket, and dial the number.

"Jordan?" she asked in a hoarse whisper when he picked up.

"Tia? What's wrong?"

"I'm at Cara's, but someone's here. The electricity just went off. Cara sent me to the closet to call you." Just then the door swung open and the light from a flashlight blinded her.

"Hello, Tia, I've been looking for you."

At the sound of the man's voice, Tia screamed and dropped the phone.

"Tia? Tia?"

The sound of a scream stirred Brody. He struggled to open his eyes, but the pain in his head was severe. He reached a hand up and was not surprised to find it come away sticky with blood. What had the man hit him with? More importantly, was Tia okay?

Another scream carried out of the house. Groaning with effort, he pushed himself up. He wanted to rush into the house, but the spinning of the world around him forced him to wait. Rushing in without all his faculties wouldn't help anyone. He pulled his phone out and dialed 911 while the world slowed down.

"911, what's your emergency?"

"My name is Dr. Brody Cavanaugh. I'm at 212 Whistler Avenue. I've been attacked and I think the attacker is in the house with hostages."

"I'm sending help. Please stay on the line until they arrive."

Brody knew that's what he should do. He was certainly in no shape to help Tia much, but he couldn't sit out here and do nothing. He couldn't let another woman he cared for die. "I'm sorry; I have to see if I can help," he said before ending the call.

He pocketed the phone and then stood testing his vision and balance. Another deep breath and he felt okay to move. The only problem was he had no weapon. Nothing but his hands and with the blow to his head, he didn't trust their power or their efficiency.

He scanned the area for anything he could use, and then he remembered the tire iron in his car. Popping the trunk, he grabbed it and headed for the house. Brody had never wielded a weapon at anyone, but if it meant saving Tia's life, he would.

The dark house was silent as he approached. Fear that he was too late raced through his body as he pushed open the door. He wished he had a flashlight as he didn't know the layout of Cara's house, but with the front door open, a little light spilled in from the outside. Enough for him to see a few feet in front of him. The immediate area was deserted. He had two choices; he could turn left toward the bedrooms or right toward the kitchen and living room area.

A scuffling sound to his right sent him that direction, and a moment later, the soft light of a flashlight illuminated the room. Tia sat on a chair, tears streaming down her face as she stared into the barrel of a gun.

"Don't come any farther or I'll shoot," the man said as if sensing Brody's approach. As he glanced Brody's direction, Brody saw Cara out of the corner of his eye. She was trying to get the jump on the man, but she couldn't get in the right position unless the man was facing Brody.

"Who are you and what do you want with Tia?"

The man smiled and turned his attention back to Tia. Cara ducked down in just the nick of time. "Why don't you ask Tia that?"

Brody looked to Tia trying desperately to come up with a plan to get the man focused on him.

"This is Rico," Tia said, her voice cracking with emotion. "It was you on the patio and in the doorway, wasn't it? I thought it was the other man, Adrian, but it was you."

Rico nodded and waved his hands out for a minute as if bowing. "So, it was. You could have left – should have left when I told you, and all of this could have been avoided, but you didn't. You had to come back and become a loose end."

"But I didn't hear anything," Tia said. "I had no idea what you were discussing."

"Maybe not, but you were seen leaving and you left evidence. I couldn't let you live after that. It would have jeopardized my authority."

Realization dawned on Brody. "You're the head of the drug ring, aren't you? Not Adrian."

Rico's head shot his direction. "Adrian was too rash to be head of the organization. He planned better than my wife, but he still got caught. Him and his wife. Besides, he was known. I managed to keep my cover in place and lead a profitable life here in Fire Beach on the side."

"Except they know about you now," Brody said hoping to keep Rico's attention on him long enough for Cara to strike. "The police know all about your connections in Chicago. Your publishing company will fold, your wife is going to jail, and

the Chicago police won't rest until they destroy your organization."

"The only one who will be destroyed tonight is you....." Cara
was in position and Brody held his breath hoping Rico wouldn't
turn her direction. "And her." His gun swung back toward Tia,
and his face was just a moment behind, but it was long enough
for Cara to spring up and ram her head directly into Rico's chest.
The gun went flying as he crashed to the floor, and the sound of
the gunshot filled the air, leaving a ringing in Brody's ears.

He glanced first toward Tia, but though shaken, she appeared
uninjured, so he turned his attention to Cara who lay on the floor,
her arms wrapped tightly around Rico's neck, and her muscular
legs pinning his arms to his body even though he writhed against
her.

"What do you have to secure him with?" Brody asked
looking around the room.

"Zip ties," Cara grunted. "Over in the desk drawer."

Brody followed the motion of her head and could just make
out the form of a desk. He hurried over and rifled through the
drawers until he found the zip ties. Grabbing them, he returned
to Cara and secured the man's hands together. Only then did she
let up her grip on him.

"Thanks," she said shaking out her arms. "He's a strong
one."

Rico said nothing as he watched them with his icy stare.
"How did you manage to secure him so quickly?" Brody asked.

She ran a hand down her thighs as if to loosen those muscles
as well. "MMA training in college. It wasn't as big for women
back then, so I used to wrestle with all the guys. There's a reason
they called me Leech. Once I grab on, I don't let go."

Somehow Brody didn't doubt that. "Good work," he said
before turning to Tia. "Are you okay?"

"Shaken up, but okay," she said, but her eyes stayed focused
on the man on the floor. "Will this ever stop?"

"Hey." He placed his hands on either side of her face and tilted it up until she was looking at him. "We'll figure this out. Together."

Her eyes widened when she saw his head. "You're hurt!"

"Yeah, I'll need to get checked out, but I'll be okay too."

A moment later, Jordan, Al, and two other men Brody vaguely recognized filed into the room. The two men grabbed Rico while Al attended to Tia and Jordan sauntered over to Cara.

"Thank you. I knew you were the right woman for the job."

She shot him a glare as she massaged her forearms. "Next time, a little warning of what I might be facing would be nice."

"I would have warned you except we didn't know what to expect. We thought it was over after the attempt at the hospital, but we didn't realize Rico was not just the front for the organization - he was the head."

"Yeah, we know," Cara said, "He had a hard time keeping his mouth shut."

"Does that mean it's really over now?" Tia asked.

"It does. Rico's going away for a long time along with his wife and the Petrovs. You may have to testify, but we all owe you a debt of gratitude. I know it wasn't your intent, but through your actions, you've managed to help us take down a pretty large drug organization."

Brody smiled and squeezed Tia's shoulder. "See? I told you everything happens for a reason. I think you've just made up for a lot of the mistakes in your past."

"Thank you," she said and when she smiled up at him, Brody knew she was going to be okay.

## 18

Tia woke more rested the next morning than she had in a long time. Some of it was probably not sleeping in a hospital room, but she knew some of it was finally feeling as if she were home and safe. Even in her old life, she'd had no friends like Brody, Cara, and Jordan - people willing to risk their lives to keep her safe. It was nice. And humbling. And today Brody was going to take her to lunch before she started her first shift at Fire Dreams.

She couldn't remember the last time she had worked in a restaurant, but she was looking forward to it today. Actually, she was just looking forward to not being in a hospital, being shot at, poisoned, or run over. It had been a long week, and one she would probably never forget.

Pushing back the covers, she rolled out of bed and hobbled over to the bag of clothes she had bought the night before. She hadn't even managed to unpack with all the craziness of Rico, and she definitely wanted to take a bath before she fully dressed. That was another thing she hadn't done properly in the last week. She'd have preferred a shower but supposed it was out of the question. Surely, she wouldn't have to only do baths until the cast came off though. She'd have to ask Brody when she saw him for lunch.

After grabbing clothes to change into, Tia grabbed her crutches and made her way the few feet to the bathroom. The bath proved to be challenging since she couldn't get her cast wet, but after a few tries, she managed to get her foot positioned in just the right way so that it was out of the water while most of the rest of her was in. Though she normally didn't like baths, this one held just the right remedy to wash her fears and anxiety away.

When she was dry and dressed - another adventure she would not miss when this cast came off - she crutched down the hall to the dining area. Cara had a display of food laid out - eggs, waffles, fruit, coffee, juice.

"Good morning, Tia. How did you sleep?" Cara asked as she placed a large plate of pancakes down as well.

"Actually, pretty well. How long have you been up cooking this breakfast?"

Cara laughed. "I know, it's overkill, but I cooked a lot in my unit. Got used to feeding a dozen hungry soldiers. Guess old habits die hard, but don't worry the guy in room one will eat half of this when he gets up."

Tia shook her head as she imagined the stomachache she would have if she ate even half of this. "I'll just get some eggs and fruit."

"You sit," Cara said pointing to a chair, "and I'll get what you want and bring it to you. Jordan and Brody would have my hide if you tripped trying to carry food and injured yourself at my house."

Tia laughed but she could see it. "Okay, okay. Eggs, oranges, and coffee please. With cream if you have it."

"Of course I have it." Cara loaded up a plate and set it before Tia before filling a cup and returning with it and the creamer carafe. "So, what's on your agenda for today?" she asked as she grabbed her own coffee mug and sat across from Tia.

"Brody is coming by in an hour or so. I think he planned an early movie and then lunch before my shift at Fire Dreams." She smiled as she speared a little egg and shoveled it in her mouth. Her day sounded so ordinary - a welcome sound after the last week.

"Jordan roped you into working for him, did he?" Cara picked up her cup and took a sip.

"He did, but only until I get back on my feet. Now that I remember everything, I want to get back to writing soon, but I need to do a few things first. Make some apologies, buy a new computer, move my stuff here."

Cara raised a brow as she leaned back in her chair. "You plan to stay then?"

Tia grinned as she peeled the orange. "I do. I think there's definitely some things worth staying here for."

"Good. I'm glad to hear it. This town could use a little excitement."

Tia laughed so hard she nearly spat her food out. "You don't think the last week counted as excitement?"

"Nah," Cara said with a flick of her wrist. "That's not what I mean. We need some excitement people can get behind, and I think a romance author writing about our town might be just the ticket. Be good for business."

"Well, I'll do what I can," Tia said with a smile.

Brody smiled as he spied Tia behind the counter. She not only looked lighter without the weight of fear on her shoulders, but she looked at home greeting guests as they entered the restaurant.

"Brody." Her mouth broke into a wide grin when she spied him. "Let me clock out and I'll be ready to go."

"Take your time," he said as he watched her crutch off to the back room.

"She's kind of a natural," Jordan said coming up beside him. "I hope she decides to stick around a while."

Brody smiled at the man he now considered a friend. "She is. Told me this morning when I picked her up. She wants to go to California and make amends and get her affairs in order, but then she plans to find a place to rent locally."

"Glad to hear it. She seems like a completely different person here."

Brody shook his head. "No, she seems like the sweet woman I believe she was until greed corrupted her. I just hope she stays that way."

Jordan put a hand on his shoulder. "With a good man like you by her side, I can't see her taking that path again."

"Are you two talking about me?" Tia asked with a smile as she approached them.

"Just telling Brody what a good job you're doing," Jordan said.

"Good, then I hope you won't mind if I ask for a week off? I want to close the chapter on my life in California, so I can start fresh here."

"I think that's a great idea, and I'm fairly certain I can convince the owner to give you a week even though you just started." He gave her a friendly smile before excusing himself to take care of a customer.

"Will you come with me?" she asked Brody as he held the restaurant door open. "To California? I don't think I can do it alone."

Brody wanted to say yes, but a trip with her? That was a big step. And it would require more time off work. However, he hadn't taken a day since Rachel died. He had enough days saved up, and he hadn't taken a vacation in years. Besides, if he really wanted Tia to make a change, then he needed to support her in any way possible. If that meant a trip to California, then he guessed he could take a little more time off. "I'll be with you every step of the way."

She leaned up and placed a kiss on his lips. "I don't deserve you Brody Cavanaugh, but I'm going to thank God every day for sending you into my life."

Brody returned her smile and thought he might do exactly the same thing.

## 19

Tia stood outside the door of Ava's office and took a deep breath. She wanted to apologize, but actually being here was another thing entirely. What if Ava slammed the door in her face? What if Justin kicked her out? They had both agreed to meet her here when Tia called, but what if it was just to tease her about how far she'd fallen?

"You have to knock," Brody said beside her.

She looked up at him, a pained smile on her face. "I know, but what if they slam the door in my face? I was so awful to them."

He laced his fingers through hers and squeezed. "They won't. Besides, you aren't the same person anymore."

Right. She wasn't the same person anymore. She no longer cared solely for money. Not after four attempts on her life. Her priorities had definitely shifted, and while she did want to make enough money to take care of herself and her mother as she'd promised herself so long ago, she no longer needed to be the best. Just being Tia seemed like enough.

She raised her hand and knocked on the door. A moment later, it swung open and Ava McDermott stared back at her.

"Hello, Tia," she said with a slight smile. She stepped back and held the door open. "Won't you come in?"

Tia squeezed Brody's hand one more time before letting go of it to crutch into the waiting area of Ava's office. Justin sat in one of the chairs there and rose as they approached. For a moment, no one said anything and the silence sat heavy in the room.

Tia cleared her throat, forcing her nerves to stop fluttering. "Thank you for agreeing to see me."

"You said it was important," Ava said as she sat down and motioned for everyone else to do the same.

"It is." Tia glanced over at Brody who smiled and motioned for her to continue. "I came to apologize to you. To you both. A few weeks ago, I landed in the wrong place at the wrong time, and it almost killed me, but as I healed, I realized how awful I'd been. I'm working to change, but before I could, I needed to apologize to those I've wronged." She chuckled ruefully. "It's been an awfully long list."

Justin glanced over at Ava and then back at Tia. "We're sorry for whatever you've been through, Tia. It appears like a lot, but we forgave you a long time ago."

Tia's eyes widened and she blinked at them. "You did?"

"Of course we did," Ava said. "None of us are perfect, and we both know that we've made poor decisions in our past as well, but God has forgiven us. However, we couldn't gain that forgiveness from Him if we didn't also forgive those who wronged us."

Tears filled Tia's eyes, blinding her vision for a moment. "You two are both so amazing. I hope that I can learn from your compassion."

Ava smiled at her. "I think you already have."

Brody stared at the woman next to him as they drove to their final destination before returning home. Though her fingers still sported acrylic nails, nothing else about her appearance looked like the rich woman he had first seen when he pulled her from the wrecked sports car.

Her long blonde hair was pulled back in a simple loose pony, and her outfit was a t-shirt and shorts with no designer tag in sight. He'd wondered if she might revert when she saw her old things and outfits in her apartment, but instead, she'd decided to hire someone to sell it all and send her the money. "That way I don't have to pay to have it shipped," she'd said, but he thought it was because those things no longer suited her.

She still was very different from Rachel, more extroverted than she'd been and able to spit words out faster than he could listen half the time, especially when she was excited, but despite her differences, she had one vital thing in common – the ability to make him feel like he was the only man in the room and that he could do anything. He'd certainly proved that to himself over the last few weeks as his healing hand and head proved.

"You ready?" he asked as he pulled up in front of the run-down trailer. He had a hard time believing that this was where she had grown up, but recognition mingled with fear covered her face, and he knew it was true.

Her shoulders pulled back with her breath. "Yeah, I guess I am," but her eyes stared out the window and he wondered if she really were. It was one thing to apologize to people you once considered friends. It was another thing entirely to apologize to the woman you promised to provide for and then failed.

Brody turned off the ignition and walked around to Tia's side to help her out. He handed her the crutches from the back seat and followed her up the overgrown pathway to the front door. She paused, took another deep breath, and then knocked on the door.

A moment later, the door swung open, and a woman who

looked like a much older version of Tia opened the door. Her blonde hair was streaked with gray, and from the wrinkles and age spots dotting her face, it appeared life had not been easy on her. Beside him, Tia sniffed and covered her mouth with her hand.

But the woman's face transformed as recognition dawned in her eyes, and a smile lit her face. "Tia?"

"Hi, Momma. I know I'm a little late, but I came to fulfill my promise."

Tears filled the woman's eyes and she pulled Tia in for a hug. "I never gave up hope, Tia. Even when you stopped calling and coming by, I prayed God would send you home one day, and He has." She pulled back, holding Tia by the upper arms, and then her eyes flicked to the side. "And you've brought a friend. Who is this?"

"Dr. Brody Cavanaugh, ma'am. It's a pleasure to meet you." He held out his hand and the woman smiled as she shook it.

"A doctor? Well, I have missed a lot. How about you come inside and we can catch up?" She stepped back and held the door open, and Brody followed Tia into the home she had grown up in.

The inside, though sparse, was neat and tidy. Her mother led them to the living room and a well-worn couch where they sat and stared at one another for an uncomfortable moment. "Can I get you something to drink?" the woman asked.

"No Momma, we aren't staying long."

The woman's face fell. "Oh, well, I'm glad you stopped by for as long as you could."

"Momma, I want you to come back to Fire Beach with me."

The woman blinked at her. "I don't... what do you mean?"

Tia leaned forward and took her mother's hands. "I've missed too much the last few years, Mom. I don't want to miss any more time with you. I've sold my home in California, and

I'm moving to Fire Beach to start over. I'd like you to come with me."

"But...but I have a job here."

"And you can have one there if you want. I know a great restaurant that's going to need a hostess when I return to writing, but you've worked your entire life for me, so I could have a better life. Now, I'd like to give back to you. I've already found the perfect place. All it's missing is you."

Brody held his breath as he watched emotions flutter across Tia's mother's face. If she said no, Tia would be crushed, but she had prepared herself for the possibility as they drove here. However, he hoped she said yes. Family was important, and he knew being able to provide for her mother would be the final block in Tia's healing process.

"What do I need to bring?" her mother finally said as she smiled widely at Tia.

"Nothing, Momma, just you." Forgetting her crutches, Tia launched herself out of the couch and into her mother's arms. Brody smiled at the touching scene. Somehow, he felt that no matter what life threw at her now, Tia would be all right.

# THE EPILOGUE
## TWO MONTHS LATER

Tia smiled at the group of people around the table. She'd met so many wonderful friends over the last few weeks. Cassidy, Jordan's girlfriend, had quickly become one of her closest friends along with Cara, and because of that she'd met many of the other firemen sitting around the table – Bubba, Luca, Deacon, and Ivy, the paramedic.

There was also her mother, Brody and his friend Nick, Jordan's brother Graham, and some of the other police officers on Jordan's unit. She'd never had such a great group of friends in her life, and she couldn't believe they had all wanted to celebrate her book release. She had decided not to pursue another publisher but to self-publish this book because she hadn't wanted a company to demand changes. This was her story, and it needed to be told exactly the way she had written it.

"Thank you all for coming," Jordan said as he banged his water glass with a spoon to quiet the chatter. "As you all know, we have a resident celebrity in our midst."

Tia ducked her eyes as heat flared up her cheeks. This was way too much.

"And she has finally finished her masterpiece. Tia get up here and show off your beautiful book."

Tia shook her head as she pushed back her chair. She loved that they cared enough about her to want to celebrate her accomplishment, but she would have been just as happy to do a small get together instead of this large party Jordan had thrown for her. However, he was still her boss, and it appeared to make him happy, so she had agreed.

She grabbed the bag which held her book and walked to the front of the table. Her cast was gone, and her injuries had healed except for the scar that still ran across her forehead, but Tia didn't mind. She now considered it a badge of honor – her second chance at life.

"Thank you all for wanting to celebrate this with me. This wasn't an easy book to write, but your support helped me get past all the hard parts, and while I've loved a lot of books I've written, I think this might be my best."

"Hear hear," Brody said lifting his glass and flashing her a large smile. "What?" he asked as he looked around the table. "I already read it, so I know that it's good. She got the doctor spot on."

She shook her head and smiled at him. "Anyway, I think it is because of all of you that it turned out so well, and that's why I'm pleased to present to you…" she paused for dramatic effect as she pulled the book out of the bag, "The Key to Remember."

Cheers and clapping sounded as Tia passed the book around the table.

"Hey, this might even be a book you could read, Luca," Bubba teased as he flipped through the pages.

"Only if it's on audiobook," Luca shot back. "I can't sit still long enough to read a paper book. Sorry, Tia."

She laughed and shook her head as the teasing comments continued to flow around the table. Brody caught her eye and flashed her a wink, and Tia didn't think she'd ever felt more loved than she did right now.

"Excuse me?"

The conversation stilled at the unfamiliar voice, and they all turned to see a petite woman in the doorway.

"I'm sorry to interrupt, but do any of you know where I can find Matt Fisher?"

Confused glances shot around the room, and Jordan stood to address her. "I'm sorry, ma'am, there's no Matt Fisher here."

"Actually, there is."

Time seemed to freeze as every eye turned to Bubba as he pushed back his chair and stood. "I'm Matt Fisher."

If you want to know what Bubba's story is, be sure to order your copy of *Never Forget the Past* today!

# IT'S NOT QUITE THE END!

Thank you so much for reading *Lost Memories*. This book was inspired by one of my readers who reached out to me after reading The Producer's Unlikely Bride and told me Tia needed her own story. I had never planned a story for Tia, but I was so touched by her connection to the character that I had to do it. As I've always wanted to attempt an amnesia book, I figured Tia's story was the perfect opportunity, but boy was it harder than I thought.

I hope you enjoyed the story as I really enjoyed writing it. If you did, would you do me a favor? If you did, please leave a review. It really helps. It doesn't have to be long - just a few words to help other readers know what they're getting.

I'd love to hear from you, not only about this story, but about the characters or stories you'd like read in the future. I'm always looking for new ideas and if I use one of your characters or stories, I'll send you a free ebook and paperback of the book with a special dedication. Write to me at loranahoopes@gmail.com. And if you'd like to see what's coming next, be sure to stop by authorloranahoopes.com

I also have a weekly newsletter that contains many wonderful things like pictures of my adorable children, chances to win awesome prizes, new releases and sales I might be holding, great books from other authors, and anything else that strikes my fancy and that I think you would enjoy. I'll even send you the first chapter of my newest (maybe not even released yet) book if you'd like to sign up.

Even better, I solemnly swear to only send out one newsletter a week (usually on Tuesday unless life gets in the way which with three kids it usually does). I will not spam you, sell your email address to solicitors or anyone else, or any of those other terrible things.

God Bless,
    Lorana

# *When*
# QUESTIONS
## ABOUND
### A LOST MEMORIES COMPANION SHORT STORY

Best-selling author
## LORANA HOOPES

# NOTE FROM THE AUTHOR

Thank you so much for picking up this book. When I wrote Lost Memories, I never intended to write Jordan's point of view, but I had so many readers ask for it that I knew it had to be done. While you don't have to read Lost Memories and New Beginnings or Fire Dreams for this book to make sense, reading them will help you get to know the characters better.

I hope you like this book. If you do, please leave a review at your retailer. It really does make a difference because it lets people make an informed decision about books.

Sign up for Lorana Hoopes's newsletter and get her book, The Billionaire's Impromptu Bet, as a welcome gift. Get Started Now!

"Help! Is there a doctor in here?"

Detective Jordan Graves pulled his attention from his girlfriend Cassidy to see who needed assistance. A man stood in the doorway of the restaurant, a frantic look on his face. "There was an accident. A woman's been injured, but the guy who hit her took off. She looks bad though. Are any of you doctors?"

"I am." Dr. Brody Cavanaugh fought his way through the crowd followed by two or three other people Jordan recognized from the hospital.

"We better go too," Jordan said to Cassidy. He flashed an apologetic look at Graham, his brother and co-owner of Fire Dreams, before hurrying outside with the rest of the crowd. The sun had set, but the streetlights illuminated the area, and down the street Jordan could see the car – a red sports car – folded in a "C" shape.

"Get the Jaws of Life," Bubba, one of the firemen, ordered as he sprinted towards the car. Around him, the rest of the firemen spread out. Some ran toward the firehouse a block away to get the truck and ambulance, and others followed Bubba including Cassidy.

Jordan glanced around for the man who had entered the restaurant. He stood a few feet away wringing his hands together. "You." Jordan hurried over to the man. "I'm Detective Graves. Did you see the accident happen?" He pulled out his notepad to write down the details.

"It happened so fast. I heard the crash and then it sounded like he gunned it. Why would he gun it if he knew he'd hurt someone?" The man was rambling, clearly in shock.

"Can you tell me what the vehicle looked like that hit her?" The man turned to face Jordan and for a moment his eyes were clear. "It was a truck. A black Ford truck."

"Did you see anything else? A license number by chance?" Jordan asked.

"It just drove off. Why would anyone do that?" Clearly this man wasn't going to be of any more help. His state of shock was simply too great. At least for now.

"Can I get your name?" Jordan asked. Perhaps the man would remember more when the shock wore off.

"It's Ethan. Ethan Bower."

Jordan took down the name and number of the man though he doubted they would contact him again. He appeared to have supplied as much as he could.

Having finished his interview of the witness, Jordan walked over to the wrecked car. The firemen had succeeded in getting the woman out, and the ambulance had driven off a few minutes ago. That left the car as his domain. His and Al's, his female partner.

"Find anything yet?"

Al was already poking around inside the car. She popped her head out and held up a mangled phone. "Found this, but there's no purse, no wallet. I haven't checked the trunk yet, but I can't find anything to let us know who this woman was. Did you get anything from the witness?"

"Not much. He said he heard the wreck while he was closing shop. When he looked, the black truck was speeding off. He didn't get a license plate number."

Al sighed and crossed her arms. "We better hope the driver makes it then because all I have right now is a lot of questions."

Jordan agreed. "Can you pop the trunk?"

Al leaned back inside but though he could see her tugging on the lever, nothing was happening. "Is it working?"

"No, it must have gotten damaged in the accident." He scanned the area. Bubba and Luca were just putting the Jaws of Life back on the truck. "Bubba, can you guys use that on the trunk? We can't get it to open."

"Wish you'd said something earlier," Bubba said with a teasing smile. "This thing isn't exactly light, but Luca could use the extra workout."

"Speak for yourself," Luca retorted.

Jordan stepped back as the two large men approached. The hum of machinery filled the air again until they were able to cut a hole allowing access to the trunk. Jordan joined Al at the back as Bubba and Luca headed back to the truck. With her flashlight, they examined the trunk, but there was nothing there either.

"Guess that's it," Al said.

"Yeah, I'll write down the license plate number and we can run it tomorrow. Perhaps that will give us something to go on."

"Sounds good. Sorry the opening of your restaurant was interrupted, but it looks like it will be a great place."

Jordan looked back at the restaurant he and Graham had worked so hard to open. It certainly wasn't the opening night they had planned for, but he hoped this night wouldn't keep people from coming back. "Thanks, Al. I hope so. Guess I'll see you tomorrow."

## 2

"Sir, I'd like permission to investigate this hit and run further," Jordan said as he looked at his notes from the night before.

"You have reason to believe it was more than an accident?" Jack Stone, head of the unit, asked as he looked at the board of their current cases. It was rather quiet at the moment for which Jordan was glad.

"Just a feeling sir. The witness said the truck didn't even bother to slow down which was supported by the lack of brake marks at the scene. Plus, we found no wallet, no purse, nothing in the car besides the woman's cell phone. It just feels wrong." Jordan had no concrete evidence that it was anything but an accident, but he had long ago learned to trust his gut. And his gut was telling him there was more to this case.

Stone turned from the board and fixed Jordan with his classic stony stare. "Two days. If something hasn't come up that proves this wasn't an accident, you let it go. Understood?"

"Crystal. Thank you, sir." He looked over at Al who was working on something at her desk. "Al, you want to come with me to the hospital? I'd like to see if our victim made it through the night and if she remembers anything."

Al nodded and grabbed the mangled phone. "Yep, let's go. I was looking for traffic cams, but there was nothing pointed at that intersection."

Figured. Even with all the traffic cameras in the city, they rarely seemed to catch a break from them on any case they worked. "Hopefully, our victim will have some information."

A few minutes later, they pulled into the hospital parking lot. After a brief stop at the desk to sign in and declare their weapons, they headed toward the ICU.

"I was hoping we would find you here," Jordan said as he spied Dr. Brody Cavanaugh near the main ICU desk studying a clipboard. "Brody, this is my partner, Al Parker. The woman had a phone in the car," he said holding up the object, "but no wallet. Is she awake yet?"

Brody glanced up at them. "She is, but she doesn't remember anything. Not even her name."

Al blinked at him. "Is that normal? Will she get it back?"

Brody shrugged as he replaced one clipboard and picked up another. "I don't know. She hit her head pretty hard and sustained a concussion, but the CT didn't show any lasting damage although it did show swelling. My guess is that she will, but I can't give you a timeline."

Memory loss was certainly not what Jordan had been hoping for, but perhaps with the right questions they could jog her memory. "Is she able to talk? Can we ask her some questions?"

Brody regarded Jordan and flashed a concerned stare. "She is capable of speaking, but don't push her too hard. Rest is important for her right now, and again, I don't think she remembers much. Although she does think someone was after her."

Jordan's ears perked up at that. "She does? What did she say?"

"Not much," Brody said with a shrug. "Just that she remembered being afraid and thought someone was after her. I was about to refer her to psych for an examination."

Jordan's jaw clenched, and he exchanged a glance with Al. "Hold off on that for a while, will you? She might be right. We found no brake marks on the road and our witness said the truck didn't even try to stop. My gut says this might not have been an accident, and we are determined to find out who hit her and why. Which room is she in?"

"Room six." Brody pointed behind him.

Jordan motioned to Al, and the two of them headed toward the room Brody indicated. The door was open, and Jordan knocked softly on the jam so as not to startle the woman.

"Pardon me, ma'am, but I'm Detective Graves and this is Detective Parker. Do you think we could ask you a few questions?"

The woman lifted her hand a few inches and motioned them inside. "You can try, but I don't remember anything. The doctor already asked."

A small smile pulled at Jordan's lips. "Well, no offense to Dr. Cavanaugh, but he's not a detective, so he might not have asked the right questions." He held out the broken phone. "Do you recognize this?" As the woman looked at it, he assessed her injuries. Her right foot was in a makeshift cast, cuts and bruises covered her right leg and arm, and a bandage wrapped around her head. Though she stared at them with her right eye, the left was purple, blue, and swollen shut. She had definitely taken a beating. It was a miracle she was alive.

A spark of recognition flared in the woman's eye before she shut it again. "That's my phone, isn't it?"

"We pulled it from your car, so we believe it was your phone."

"I was going to use it," she said slowly as if coaxing the words from memory, "but it was on the passenger seat and I couldn't reach it, but I can't remember why I was going to use it."

"Unfortunately, it's destroyed, and there was no purse or wallet inside the car that we could find. Do you know why you might have been driving without your license?"

She opened her mouth to reply but then paused. Her eye opened again and looked from him to Al and back again. "Am I in trouble, officers?"

He stared at her for a second before the realization of her hesitation made sense. Then he chuckled softly. "For driving without a license? No. You should always carry it and you can be fined for not having it, but we're not here to issue you a ticket. We're more concerned with the accident. Our witness says the black truck hit you, but we aren't sure if the accident was on purpose or not. Do you remember anything?"

"I don't think it was an accident. I can't remember why, but I think someone was after me. Did the witness help at all?"

Al stepped forward, "He wasn't able to supply us with much unfortunately, so we were hoping this phone might jog some memories."

"I wish it did, but I have nothing more."

"That's okay, it will probably come back." Jordan was about to thank her when his phone rang. He pulled it from his pocket and turned away slightly when he recognized Stone's number. "Detective Graves."

"Jordan, are you with the hit and run victim?"

"Yes, sir, we are here now." Did Stone have information?

"Ask her about the name Tia Sweetchild."

Jordan glanced back at the woman. "Tia Sweetchild?"

"Yes, the license plate you ran just came back as a rental car. I called the company and they said a Tia Sweetchild rented the car. The funny thing is, her address is in California, so she's not from here."

Interesting. If she wasn't from Illinois, what was she doing here? "Okay, sir." Jordan hung up the phone and returned to the side of the woman's bed. "Does the name Tia Sweetchild ring a bell for you?"

"Is that me? Am I Tia?" she asked.

"The car you were driving was rented to a Tia Sweetchild so yes, we believe so. However, the address listed on the rental agreement is in California, so we're not sure what you would be doing here in Illinois."

The woman paused, and he wondered what she was thinking. Did the name sound familiar to her? Was she simply pretending not to know? "I have no idea what I was doing here, but now that we know my name, we should be able to find out some more about me, right?"

"We'll certainly do our best," Al said. "If you remember anything else, please call us." She handed Tia a white business card.

"We'll be in touch as soon as we have more information," Jordan said. As they exited the room, he turned to Al. "What do you think?"

"I think she's beat up pretty badly."

"Yeah, but do you think she's telling the truth?"

Al's lips formed a tight line. "I don't know, but something about this case bothers me. I think we better have a look into Tia Sweetchild."

Jordan couldn't agree more.

## 3

J ordan sighed as he shut down his computer for the night. He had been hoping to find out more about Tia Sweetwater, but other than discovering she was an author of clean romance books, he had come up empty handed. Maybe dinner would help.

He pulled out his cell phone and dialed Cassidy's number. He hadn't had a chance to catch up with her since the accident, and he was missing her company.

"Hey Jordan," she said when the call went through.

"Hey Cassidy. You feel like dinner tonight?"

"I'd love to," she said sighing softly, "but I'm on shift tonight. Tomorrow though, okay?"

"Sure thing." Jordan shouldn't be upset that Cassidy had work especially since his own job wreaked havoc on their plans a lot of the time as well, but he missed her. The opening of Fire Dreams had kept him busy in the evenings the last few weeks, and now there was this hit and run case. Hopefully, things would slow down again soon.

With a sigh, he headed out of the office and to his car. There was a restaurant down the street from his house. He could pick up a dinner and ponder the case as he ate.

The unintelligible hum of conversation assaulted him as Jordan stepped into the dim atmosphere. He scanned the area - a habit he'd had even before becoming a cop - and was surprised to find Brody at the bar. Jordan didn't drink, but he was curious if Tia had remembered anything more.

"You want to open a tab?" the bartender asked Brody.

"No need," Jordan said, pulling out a five and placing it on the counter. Brody looked up at him in surprise. "It's on me. Grab that and follow me."

"Were you following me, detective?" Brody asked as he sat in the booth.

"No, but I'm glad I ran into you. Did our patient remember anything more today?"

Brody shook his head. "No, but I didn't really ask today. I did find out she was an author though, and I brought in one of her books hoping it would help."

Jordan's eyes narrowed. He hadn't shared the information with Brody yet. "How did you find out she was an author?"

"I had dinner with Nick last night and he recognized her name, so we googled her. Anyway, when I showed her the book, she said she remembered something when she touched it." He paused, as if trying to remember her words. "A man saying 'What are you doing here?' But that was all she could remember. She didn't even remember being an author. Should I be asking specific questions? Did you find something out?"

Jordan blew out an agitated breath. "Not much more than that, but it just isn't sitting well with me. Why would anyone want to harm an author? She's not a big name like Stephen King or J.K Rowling so I don't think it was about money, and she writes clean romance, so I doubt she offended someone enough to want to kill her. All I have are questions - the biggest one being what was she doing here in the first place?"

"I don't know." Brody shook his head and took a sip of his beer. "She said a woman visited her today and claimed she was in town for that reason."

Jordan's head snapped forward. "What? She had a visitor?" Why did neither of them tell him about this?

"Yes, she didn't remember the woman, but she hasn't remembered much. Why? Is that a bad thing?"

Agitation filled Jordan. He would never solve this case if they didn't give him all the information. "It could be. We asked her to call us if anything else happened. We need to know everything if we are going to figure this out. I can't believe she didn't tell us she had a visitor. Did you get the woman's name?"

Brody shook his head. "No, sorry, I was a little busy, but I can ask tomorrow."

"I'll go over myself tomorrow to ask, but please, Brody, we can't help if we don't know everything. Even if it seems trivial."

Brody gave a curt nod. "I understand. It seems she gets a few pieces of her memory back every day. Maybe we'll know more in a day or two."

Jordan ran a hand across his chin. "Let's hope that's soon enough, but please keep an eye on her and call me if you learn anything. I just have a bad feeling about all of this."

## 4

"So, I hear you had a visitor yesterday," Jordan said as he entered Tia's room.

She looked up at him in surprise. "I did. How did you...?"

"I ran into Dr. Cavanaugh last night. I thought we told you to call us."

"You asked me to call you if I remembered anything else. I didn't remember Debra. She said we were friends and brought me my purse."

Jordan sighed as he realized she was right. Next time they would have to be more specific. "Wait, did you say she brought you your purse?"

Tia pointed to the nearby table. "I didn't remember much from it either before you ask. I remember buying it at a shop, and I remembered attending a movie and what kind of coffee I drink. Nothing that would change the world."

"I'm going to need to examine your purse and its contents," Jordan said, plucking the purse from the table.

Tia took a deep breath, and her eye shifted. "I did remember one more thing. Well, at least I think I did."

"What's that?"

"There's a note in the purse with the name Rico Rearden and a time on it. I think I was visiting him and not Debra."

Interesting. "Why would Debra lie about that?"

"I don't know. Maybe I was visiting them both and just remember him?"

Jordan doubted that. More likely Debra was lying about something. The question was what? "Tia, I really need you to call me or have Dr. Cavanaugh contact me if anything else happens. We can't protect you if we don't know everything."

"I understand."

Jordan wasn't sure she did, but he hoped so. There were already enough questions in this case. He didn't need anymore. "I'll bring this back after we process it," he said holding up the purse. "Remember, anything else."

"I promise."

He shook his head as he walked out of her room and back to his car. He loved his job but dealing with a woman who remembered nothing was definitely proving challenging especially if someone was out to get her.

"Nice purse," Al said as he set the bag down on his desk.

He shot her a smirk. "Very funny. It's not mine. It's Tia's. Evidently, a visitor dropped it off to her yesterday. A visitor she neglected to tell us about."

"We better get to work on that name before Stone finds out."

She didn't have to tell Jordan twice. "Okay, you take the name Debra and Rico Rearden. I'm going to go through the bag and see if I can get any fingerprints." While he suspected the only fingerprints he would find would belong to Tia and Debra, he wanted to make sure nothing else slipped past him.

"Wait, what? Yeah, I'll be right there." Jordan shook his head as he ended the call.

"What was that about?" Al asked.

Jordan sighed and ran his hand across his chin. "Evidently Debra came back to the hospital today. With a gun."

Al's eyes widened. "What?"

"Yeah, she tried to kill Tia. She's claiming Tia was having an affair with Rico, her husband." Jordan shook his head, not sure how this had gone south so quickly. "Stone is going to lose it. Keep digging while I go pick her up. Maybe that will at least help."

Jordan grabbed his keys. He felt like he had just left the hospital and here he was going back once again.

He pulled into the lot and hurried into the hospital, heading directly for the security office. Debra Rearden sat with her hands cuffed and resting in her lap. A blank expression lay on her face.

"Has she said anything?" Jordan asked as he signed the paperwork to take custody of Debra.

The security guard shook his head. "Not since we dragged her from the room. She said plenty in the room though. Dr. Cavanaugh wrote up a statement already." He handed it across the table.

Jordan scanned it before folding it and placing it in his pocket. "Thank you. Can you get a security guard posted outside Tia Sweetchild's room?"

"That might be challenging," the security guard said with an apologetic grin, "we're short staffed as it is."

"Look, station someone there, and I'll see if the police department can help with the cost." He hoped Stone would okay the cost but figured with the attempt on Tia's life that he would find it somehow. Jordan turned to the woman. "Let's go, Debra."

She stared at him with cool eyes, but didn't budge, forcing him to haul her up. "You want to tell me why you tried to kill Tia Sweetchild?"

Her answer was a tilt of her chin into the air. Well, Jordan wouldn't push her - Stone would get the information he needed when he took a turn at questioning her.

Debra said nothing on the ride to the station. Nor did she say a word as Jordan processed her and led her toward the holding cell.

"What the heck happened this morning, Jordan?" Stone's angry voice filled the room after Jordan returned from placing Debra in the holding cell.

Jordan shook his head. It wasn't his fault, but Stone didn't often care about fault, he cared about results. "Tia didn't call us when the woman visited yesterday. I found out about her late last night from Brody and went in this morning to talk to her, but we were still running her background."

"Our job is to stay on top of this, not clean up messes."

Jordan nodded and shot a look at Al. She had briefed him on his way back with Debra. "I understand, sir. We've been working since I returned this morning, and we do have some information. Debra Rearden is clean, but she is married to Rico Rearden."

Stone's eyes narrowed. "Rico Rearden? Why does his name sound familiar?"

"Because his name has appeared on a few narcotics searches. So far, they haven't been able to pin anything on him, but they think he might be involved in a drug trafficking ring."

"A drug dealer? What was our amnesic author doing with a drug dealer?"

"We're still working on that," Al said, "but Rico also owns a publishing company – PressBooks, LLC. It's possible Tia didn't know he was a dealer and was meeting with him about a publishing opportunity."

Stone stalked around the board perusing the evidence. "And what about the black truck?"

Jordan shook his head. "No luck on that so far. Rico owns a

Mercedes and a Mustang and Debra drives a Firebird. No black truck registered in either of their names."

"So, we have nothing?" Frustration flooded Stone's voice and his eyes as he turned back to them.

"We'll keep digging."

"You do that. I'll talk to Debra," he said as he turned on his heel and stalked out of the room.

## 5

J ordan sighed as he headed out of the office for the night. He still didn't have as much information as he would like, but he had promised Graham to help out at Fire Dreams tonight. He didn't really feel like a shift, but a promise was a promise. Surprise flooded him as he pushed open the door and found himself face to face with Brody. "Brody? What are you doing here?"

"I was hoping I could talk to you about Tia and the woman from the hospital earlier."

Jordan looked over his shoulder and then back at Brody. Stone wouldn't care that he filled the doctor in, but there was no need to share where other ears could hear. "Not here. I'm headed over to Fire Dreams. Meet me there and I'll tell you what I know, but it isn't much."

Ten minutes later they sat in a booth. Jordan had procured a glass of water for each of them along with a basket of chips and persuaded Graham he would only be a minute. Still, the place was hopping, having recovered nicely from the spoiled opening a few days before; and Jordan kept glancing around, realizing he should be helping rather than sitting and talking.

"So, the lady from the hospital is indeed Debra Rearden. If you or Tia had told us about her yesterday, we could have looked into her sooner and possibly avoided the murder attempt. She's clean, but her husband, Rico, has a few questionable connections."

"What kind of questionable connections?" Brody asked.

"On paper, he's the head of a publishing company which might explain the connection to Tia, but we've found some unusual activity with some known drug dealers. Nothing that points to him being directly involved, and Narcotics has never been able to pin anything on him, but we're widening our search to be sure."

Brody nodded and snagged a chip. "Drugs? Really? Tia said she had a meeting with Rico, but she doesn't seem like the type to be into drug deals."

Jordan took a sip of his water. "Maybe she isn't, but I did a little more research on her today. It appears she stayed under the radar. At least recently. Evidently a few months ago, she kind of lost it after trying to damage the reputation of a fellow romance author, Ava McDermott. She sent photos to tabloids and appeared on a few talk shows claiming the relationship Ava was in was a fake one. I don't know why anyone would fake a relationship, but maybe if you are a public figure, it's more important."

Brody nearly choked on his chip. "What? I can't see her doing that."

Jordan shrugged. "Well, maybe the head injury changed her, or maybe she changed after the incident. She failed to do much except soil her own reputation. Regardless, it's clear Tia did know Rico. There's no other reason Debra would have come after her. Perhaps she was talking to him about new publishing opportunities. We just don't know any more than that."

"Is there a chance she was having an affair with him as his wife claimed?" Brody asked before taking a drink of his water.

Jordan hadn't found anything pointing to an affair, but there was still so much they didn't know. "That I can't speak to. Yet. But we'll be looking into Rico more." He shook some salt on a chip before stuffing it into his mouth.

"And what about the black truck. Did it belong to Debra?"

Jordan shook his head as he finished chewing. "No, neither she nor her husband appear to own one."

"So, someone might still be after Tia."

"It's possible or it could just be that the accident was just that. An accident."

"But you don't believe that, do you?" Brody asked.

"No, I don't. It's just a gut feeling, but I don't. I've talked with the hospital about posting a security guard outside her door as well." Jordan looked around again and waved at Graham behind the counter area who was shooting him a glare. "I have to help out here, but I promise to keep you in the loop of what we find."

"Thank you," Brody said as Jordan stood.

Jordan nodded and hurried over to Graham. "Sorry, it was about the case."

"It always is," Graham said with a sigh, "but Jordan if we are going to make this restaurant work, I need your help. I need you here mentally as well as physically."

"Got it." This was exactly why Jordan hadn't wanted to open a restaurant. Maybe if the restaurant continued to do well, they could hire more help, giving him more time off. Between work and Cassidy, he just didn't have a lot of time to spare.

## 6

J ordan leaned back and rubbed his eyes. He had been staring at the computer screen for hours trying to find out more about Tia and the Reardens, but nothing was popping up. No other connection beside the publishing company, and even that was a guess.

"Coming up empty over there?" Al asked from across the desk.

"Yeah, crickets." Thankfully, Stone had forgotten about the deadline after the attempt on Tia's life, but Jordan was starting to wonder if his gut was wrong, and the accident was really just an accident.

Beside him, his cell phone rang. He glanced down surprised to see a number he didn't recognize. "Detective Graves," he said after punching the answer button.

"Jordan? It's Brody. Tia received some flowers this morning, and I think you need to come and see the card."

"The card is suspicious?"

"Yes, I'm going to take her for a short walk, and then we'll be back." Brody's voice remained calm as if he was trying not to scare Tia any more than she already had been.

"I'll be right there."

"Back to the hospital?" Al asked glancing up at him.

"Yes, Brody said Tia received suspicious flowers. I shouldn't be long."

When Jordan arrived at the hospital, he once again declared himself before heading to Tia's room. The flowers were on the table, but an examination of them revealed nothing out of the ordinary. However, the note left by her bed was another matter entirely. There were no words on the card, only a human face with its eyes and mouth sewed shut. It was creepy to say the very least.

"Where do these flowers come from?" he asked when Brody and Tia returned to the room a moment later.

"From the gift shop downstairs usually or from outside sources," Brody said as he wheeled Tia back to the bed.

"And how do they get delivered?"

Brody held out his hand and helped Tia stand and get situated back in the bed. "An orderly generally brings them to the floor and then either delivers them or gives them to the nurses to deliver."

"Valerie brought mine in," Tia supplied.

Jordan glanced over at her before turning his attention back to Brody. "I'm going to need to speak with her as well."

"Fine, I'll introduce you." Brody turned back to Tia. "I'll check on you before I leave for the night."

Jordan followed Brody out of the room and into the main ICU area. "That's Valerie there, the one with the dark hair," Brody said pointing. "Valerie? Can we have a moment?"

Valerie looked up at them, questions in her eyes, but she made her way over to them.

"The flowers you delivered to Tia Sweetchild this morning. How did they get here?" Jordan asked.

"An orderly brought them up as they do every day. I

distributed them to the correct rooms. Why?" Her gaze fluttered from Brody to Jordan and back again.

Jordan shot Brody a silencing look. It would be better to keep the information on the card to as few people as possible. "I just need to investigate the situation a little more. Where is the gift shop?"

"Downstairs," Brody said. "I would show you myself, but I do need to check on the other patients."

"I'm sure I can find it," Jordan said. "Thank you for your help, Valerie."

Jordan left the ICU and headed down to the gift shop. It was a small office-sized room stuffed full of baskets, animals, and balloons.

"Can I help you?"

Jordan looked over to see a young man, probably in his early twenties stand up from behind the small counter. He quickly stashed something in his pocket which Jordan assumed was a cell phone.

"Yes, can you tell me who bought flowers for the woman in ICU room six today?" He pulled back his jacket so the clerk could see the badge on his jeans.

"Um, I'm not sure, but let me look." He tapped the screen on the tablet in front of him and scrolled with his finger. "Sorry, the person paid in cash. We only take names if they pay with cards."

Jordan was not surprised. He hadn't expected the person to leave a paper trail. "Do you happen to remember them?"

The young man had the decency to look chagrined. "I'm sorry; I don't. This is a part-time gig for me, just helping to pay for college."

"Is there a camera that looks into the shop?" Jordan tried to keep his patience with the young man.

He shrugged and dropped his eyes to his lap. "You could check with security, but I just don't know."

"Thank you." Jordan was fairly certain that security would be a dead end as well, but he would be remiss if he didn't at least ask.

The security guard in the office today was not the same one from yesterday, and Jordan wondered briefly how many security guards the hospital employed.

"Can I help you?" the man asked when Jordan entered.

"Detective Jordan Graves. I was hoping to see camera footage that points to the gift shop."

"There is no camera on the gift shop," the security guard said. "We don't have a large enough budget to cover a lot of the areas, so the cameras are only in the high traffic areas - entrances and the like."

Jordan figured as much. After thanking the guard, he returned to the police station to see what progress Al had made.

"Dead end on the flowers?" she asked.

"Yeah, creepy card though." He showed her the image nodding as she grimaced. "I'm going to send it to the lab for prints, but I doubt we'll find any. Whoever this is, they've taken care to not be noticed. Paid cash too. Did you find anything else about Rico and Debra?"

"A little." Her eyes dropped to her computer screen. "Evidently Rico is quite the playboy. He's had a string of women he's paraded around places which explains why his wife was so angry. She probably thought Tia was one of those women. Narcotics said the Chicago office thinks he's involved with some deals there, but they can't prove any yet. They think this publishing company might be a front."

"If we can get this Rico, the Chicago chief would be very grateful," Stone said joining the conversation.

"We'll keep doing our best," Jordan said.

## 7

J ordan stopped by the hospital on his way home in hopes of catching Brody on his way out. Until he was sure Tia was innocent, he felt safer sharing his intel with Brody and letting him decide how much to pass on. He obviously had a better idea of who Tia was since he saw her every day.

"Detective, did you find out anything more about the flowers?" Brody asked as he approached.

Jordan pushed himself off Brody's car and glanced around the empty lot. "Unfortunately not. They *were* purchased at the gift shop here, but paid for in cash. The clerk couldn't remember who purchased them, and there's no camera that points that direction. We do have some new intel though. It appears Rico Rearden may be involved in drug trafficking over in Chicago. He didn't come up on our initial radar because he doesn't deal here, but it looks like he might hold meetings here and use his publishing business as a front."

"Do you think Tia was helping him move drugs?" Emotions struggled across Brody's face as if he didn't want to believe Tia could be involved in criminal behavior.

While Jordan didn't believe Tia was a criminal, he had worked on the force long enough to know that sometimes people weren't as they seemed. "We don't know what to think. It's possible she was involved though nothing in her background suggests it. It's more probable she was there for the meeting she had scheduled and may have stumbled across a secret meeting. Either way, we need to keep a close eye on her. She may not be as innocent as we think."

Brody shook his head. "Okay, thanks Jordan, I'll do my best."

Jordan nodded and returned to his car. He had another late shift tonight at Fire Dreams, but Cassidy had promised to stop by after her shift and he was looking forward to seeing her. He felt like he hadn't seen her in days.

"Well, I didn't think I'd beat you in here," she said with a smile as he stepped behind the counter area. The restaurant didn't serve alcohol, but he and Graham had wanted a counter area where people could sit and be served quickly.

He leaned in and placed a quick kiss on her lips. "I'm sure glad you did. How was work?"

"Slow thankfully," she said. As a firefighter, her job was a lot like his, nicer when it was slow. "I cleaned the truck today, broke up a bickering argument between Luca and Deacon, and avoided kitchen duty, so all in all, a good day."

"That's good. I'm glad to hear it. When this case gets settled, how about we plan a movie night?"

She smiled at him. "That sounds delicious, Detective Graves. So, how is your case coming along? How is the woman?"

Jordan glanced around to make sure no one else was listening to their conversation, but thankfully tonight the counter area was slow. Most of the patrons had chosen booths or tables out in the main restaurant, and Cassidy was the sole patron at the counter.

"She is recovering though she has memory loss. Someone's already tried to kill her, and I don't think the accident was an accident. I just worry something worse is going to happen, but I can't be at the hospital all day to protect her either. I asked for a security guard for her, but I worry that it still isn't enough."

Cassidy laid a hand on his arm. "I am sure you are doing all that you can."

He hoped so, but if he was, why did it still seem as if it wasn't enough?

## 8

J ordan sighed as the fingerprint report came across his computer. Nothing. Just as he'd expected. This case was a plethora of questions with no answers.

"Nothing?" Al asked.

"No fingerprints," Jordan said as his phone rang. He pulled it out and punched the answer call button. "Detective Graves."

"Jordan? It's Brody Cavanaugh at Fire Beach Hospital. We are in lockdown. A code silver was reported a few moments ago in the ICU. I am locked in the bathroom in room six with Tia."

Jordan sucked in his breath surprised at how calm Brody sounded. "I'm on my way. Do you know what the weapon is?"

"No, I haven't seen anything. I locked the door per protocol as soon as the announcement was made."

"Understood. I'm going to transfer you to a dispatch operator, and I want you to stay on the line until I get there."

"I'll try, but we're in the bathroom and I only had two bars. I don't know if they'll hold....."

"Brody? Brody?" Jordan held the phone out and looked at the screen. "Grab your stuff, Al. We need to get to the hospital."

"What's going on?" Stone asked entering the room.

"Brody just called. There's a cold silver at the hospital."

"Go," he said with a wave of his hand.

Jordan rushed out of the room with Al close on his heels.

"Do we even know what we're getting into?" Al asked as they climbed into his car.

"I'm not sure. Brody couldn't see the weapon or the perpetrator, so we go in carefully, and we check with security first. Hopefully, they put someone outside her room." He flicked the button to turn on the lights and siren and pressed his foot on the accelerator.

The parking lot looked no different when they arrived, and Jordan wondered how they handled Code Silvers. Did everyone lock down in individual rooms as Brody did? Or was there another procedure for other areas? He realized he had no idea, and he probably should. After this case, he would familiarize himself with the hospital's procedures.

The main hospital entrance opened for them, but the security guard there accosted them before they got very far. "Are you here about the Code Silver?"

"We are. Do we need to do anything special?"

The security guard shook his head. "Tom is covering the door from inside. I'll radio him when we get there to let you in."

Jordan and Al followed the security guard, whose nametag read Roger, down the hall to the ICU. The doors were indeed locked, but after a quick conversation with the guard inside, the door opened and the security guard ushered them in. Jordan scanned the area as he stepped in.

Most of the patient room doors were closed. A doctor, a nurse, and another security guard hovered around a patient who held a scalpel in his hands. Was this the code silver?

Cautiously, he and Al approached the small group. "Is there anything we can do to help?" Jordan asked.

At the sound of his voice, the patient turned to look at

Jordan, and the nurse jammed a syringe in his arm. The patient cried out in surprise or pain, Jordan wasn't sure which, but he dropped the scalpel and folded to the floor.

"Looks like you already did," the doctor said. "Thank you."

"Was that it? That was the Code Silver?" Al asked.

The doctor turned confused eyes on her. "Did you want it to be worse?"

"No," Jordan said jumping in, "It's just we received a call from Dr. Cavanaugh. Since there had already been an attempt on his patient's life, we assumed it was another one."

"Thankfully not. We'll make the announcement that the Code Silver is lifted, but you can go rescue Dr. Cavanaugh now," the nurse said.

Jordan wasted no time. He hurried over to Tia's room, but the door was locked. "Dr. Cavanaugh," he hollered pounding on the door, "you can open up."

Al tapped him on the shoulder to grab his attention. "Hold on there, Hulk. Let me get the key."

Jordan watched her walk over to the nurse and return with the woman a moment later. The nurse produced a master key from her pocket and opened the room for him. Silence greeted them, and Jordan wondered if there had been more to the Code Silver that maybe the doctor and nurse didn't know about.

Then he remembered Brody stating they were hiding in the bathroom. He crossed the room in three strides and pounded on the bathroom door. "Dr. Cavanaugh? Open up. It's Detective Graves."

A moment later, the lock clicked and the door opened. Tia lay in the bathtub with her injured ankle propped up on the side, and both she and Brody blinked against the bright lights.

"Is it safe to come out then?" Brody asked.

"It is," Jordan said, "Evidently, it was a patient who suffered a psychiatric break and grabbed a scalpel off a tray."

"I'm sorry," Brody said, "after our conversation-"

"You were right to do what you did," Jordan assured him. "We still haven't found the driver of the black truck or who sent Tia those flowers, and what you did made perfect sense. However, unless you need further assistance, we'll get back to work on finding the suspects."

"Wait, Detective Graves?" Jordan turned to Tia and waited. "I remembered more. I was there to see Rico about a publishing opportunity, but I turned it down when I found out he was married and looking for an affair. He kicked me out, but I had forgotten my purse. When I returned, he shoved me in a closet. I heard men's voices arguing, and I thought perhaps they were reporters out for a story on me which is why I ran when I did."

"Did you see any of the men? Do you remember anything about them?"

"Not their faces. When I stepped out of the closet, I looked left. They were on the balcony, but it was dark outside. I couldn't see their faces, but I felt the icy hatred in their gaze when they saw me. I didn't think they had followed me at first, but then lights blinded me on the road. I slowed down thinking maybe it was just teenagers out for a joy ride, but when they didn't pass me, I figured they had followed me after all. Then the truck hit me."

Jordan's face hardened and he exchanged a glance with Brody. "Okay, thank you, Tia. We'll look into all of this and let you know what we find. Do the two of you need anything else?"

"I think we'll be fine," Brody said. The look he flashed Tia held more than concern, and Jordan wondered if a relationship might bloom between the two of them.

"Do you think we're looking for two cars then?" Al asked as they exited the room.

Jordan shook his head. "I have no idea, but I suppose we have to assume so. Everything we learn about this case just brings more questions."

"That's true, but we haven't even found the black truck yet. How do we find a second vehicle when we have no idea what it was?"

Jordan didn't know. He just didn't know.

## 9

J ordan had just pulled into the parking lot of the police
station when his phone rang again. His eyes widened as
he looked at the number. "It's Brody. Again."

"What? We just left."

Jordan nodded at her and then answered the phone. "Brody?
What's going on?"

"Sorry to bother you, Jordan, but Tia just informed me she
had a new nurse yesterday."

"Okay, I'm not following," Jordan said.

"I didn't assign a new nurse. Maybe it's nothing, but it's the
second time I've heard about this new nurse. One of our volunteers told me a new nurse tried to keep her from reading to the
patients the other day, and Tia confirmed it was the same woman."

With any other case, Jordan might consider this information
innocuous, but he wasn't going to count anything out in this
case. "I'll be right there."

He ended the call and turned to Al. "Go tell Stone what
we've found. Brody says there's a woman I need to check into –
might be nothing but definitely suspicious."

"Be sure and watch your back," Al said as she stepped out of the car.

"Always do," Jordan said before she shut the door. Then he pointed the car back to the hospital.

"So, tell me about this woman," Jordan said when he was back in Tia's room.

"She's got shoulder length dark hair, olive skin, and brown eyes. She wasn't wearing a name tag when she came in, so I don't know what name she is going by, but she looks young. Under thirty probably," Tia said.

"All right, we'll inform the guard to let no one in," Jordan began.

"We need to allow one nurse," Brody said, "to check on Tia if necessary."

"Okay, one nurse, but no one else," Jordan agreed though it didn't sit well with him. "Not until we find this woman and get her story."

"Agreed. Sit tight, Tia. We'll be back soon."

Even Brody's words didn't erase the apprehensive look from Tia's face, but she agreed.

After a quick stop to inform the security guard not to allow anyone but Sophie into the room, Jordan and Brody set off in search of the mystery woman. Jordan wished they had a picture of the woman, but Tia couldn't travel quickly enough and the volunteer wasn't at the hospital.

They started in the ICU first, but after a glance into every patient room and the break room, no dark-haired unknown nurse appeared.

"Where to next?" Jordan asked. Brody was much more familiar with the hospital than he was.

"Let's check the surrounding areas and their break rooms. If she's after Tia, I doubt she will wander too far from ICU."

They moved to the department closest to ICU, but it did not reveal the woman in question either. However, as they turned the corner to the break room, a dark-haired woman exited and headed away from them.

"Stop," Jordan called.

The woman glanced back at them, and her eyes widened before she took off running down the hall. Jordan bolted after her, turning his head just long enough to holler back to Brody, "Go check on Tia."

As he ran, he grabbed his phone and punched the number to reach Al. "Al, get over to the hospital and bring backup." He hung up before she could ask questions and shoved the phone back in his pocket. The woman was fast, and she had just burst through the stairwell door. He pushed it open behind her, hoping the woman wasn't carrying a gun. She looked up as the door opened, and it caused her to miss a step. She stumbled down the last two, falling into the wall and allowing Jordan to catch up with her.

"You're under arrest," he said pulling her hands behind her back and slapping on a pair of handcuffs. "Want to tell me why you ran?"

She shot him an icy glare but pulled her mouth into a tight line.

"Fine. You'll talk to us soon, although anything you say can and will be used against you in a court of law. You have the right to an attorney. If you cannot afford an attorney, one will be appointed for you." He continued spouting the Miranda rights as he led her back toward ICU.

"Detective Graves, we have another one for you," the security guard said as Jordan entered the ICU.

"Another one?"

"Yes, a man tried to take out Tia's security guard and then

her with a syringe full of insulin. Thankfully Dr. Cavanaugh arrived in time. They are both recovering."

Jordan shook his head. How had this gotten so crazy so fast? "Where is he?"

"In the security office," the man said, "waiting for you."

Al and Stone appeared before Jordan could head that direction, and he filled them in.

"Let's pick him up and get them processed," Stone said taking charge of the unknown woman.

Jordan pulled out his phone when they reached the security office and snapped a picture of both the man and the woman. "I'll meet you guys back at the station. I'm going to see if our clerk can identify either of these two."

Stone nodded and Jordan headed back toward the gift shop. Relief filled him when he found the same young man from earlier still behind the counter. He wasn't sure what the hours of the gift shop were or how long his shift was, but God was on his side today.

"Hey, remember me?" he asked as he approached the counter.

He looked up, stashing his phone under some papers. "Yeah, sure, what can I do for you?"

"I want to show you two photos and see if either of these people might be the ones who bought flowers for room six."

"Okay, I can try."

Jordan pulled up the picture of the man and then turned his phone toward the clerk. He scrunched his eyes at it but shook his head.

"Sorry, he doesn't look familiar."

"All right, how about her?" He flicked to the picture of the woman and repeated the process.

The clerk nodded. "Yeah, she looks familiar. Only she wasn't wearing a nurse's uniform. I would have remembered that."

"Thank you. You've been very helpful," Jordan said before

exiting the gift shop. Whoever the woman was, she was involved in this case somehow.

"I've got names," Al said, a note of triumph in her voice. She stood and walked over to the white board. "Meet Adrian and Susanna Petrov." Al scribbled the names quickly above the pictures. "Adrian Petrov is the leader of a large gang in Chicago, and Narcotics believes he is the head of a drug organization."

"I've got an address too," Jordan added as his computer pulled up the information. "233 Palisades Drive. Oh, and guess what Adrian drives?"

"I'm going to go out on a limb and say a black truck," Stone supplied. "Okay, you two go check out the place. Take Albright and Givens with you. I'll stay here and see what I can get from the Petrovs."

The four cops nodded at each other and headed out. Jordan was beginning to feel as if he spent more time on the road than at his desk lately.

233 Palisades Drive was a large two-story house on the outskirts of town. Jordan doubted they would meet resistance, but they went out with guns drawn anyway. They didn't have a search warrant yet, but the garage had windows and the view inside revealed a black Ford truck. Enough probable cause for a closer look.

Albright got the side door opened and they stepped inside. "I'd say this is your vehicle."

Jordan stared at the dented front end and smiled. Adrian had obviously tried to have it fixed, but there was enough damage and a few conspicuous flecks of red paint remaining that he was sure this was the vehicle they were looking for. He'd finally be able to tell Tia it was over.

"How are you two doing?" Jordan asked as he entered Tia's room an hour later.

They turned fear-filled eyes on him. "Did you get the guy?" Brody asked. "Who was he?"

Jordan nodded. "We did. His name is Adrian Petrov. He's the leader of one of the bigger gangs out of Chicago and the head of a drug organization. He isn't saying much right now, but Stone will take care of that. We did manage to ascertain his address." He turned to Tia and a slight smile pulled at his lips, "Where we found a black Ford truck, and though he tried to have it fixed, we are almost certain it was the same truck that hit you. It's over, Tia."

"That's wonderful." Brody turned to Tia, and a broad grin graced his features.

Tia forced a smile in return, but it was still riddled with worry. "Wait, what about the nurse?"

"We got her too. Susanna Petrov, his wife. She's not talking either, but from what we can gather, they obtained uniforms when they saw on the news that you were in ICU. We're not sure whether she was merely keeping him informed or if she was a backup plan, but we do know that she's the one who bought the flowers. I showed pictures to the clerk at the gift shop, and he was able to ID her."

"What about Rico?"

Jordan's jaw clenched and his eyes shifted just slightly. Rico was the one missing link. "He's in the wind. We think he's in Chicago hiding out and trying to clean up this mess, but I promise you, we're still looking for him."

"Thank you, Detective Graves."

"Call me Jordan," he said as he held her gaze.

"Yes, thank you, Jordan," Brody said clapping a hand on Jordan's shoulder before turning back to Tia. "We need to monitor you to be sure the insulin didn't damage anything, but if all goes well, and as long as your fever is still gone, you might be able to leave the hospital tomorrow."

She should be glad, but the expression on her face looked anything but. Jordan stepped forward hoping to ease her unease. "I know this is a lot to deal with, Tia. If you'd like to stay in town a little longer, I can find you a temporary place and set you up with a counselor who might be able to work through some of the trauma with you."

Tia smiled up at him. "Thank you, I might take you up on that."

"And I don't know how your recovery will be, but I own a restaurant. I have a need for a good hostess if your doctor says it's okay."

Brody nodded. "I'd be okay with it as long as she can stay off her leg. It would be great if you stayed in town, and I was able to check up on you as well."

"Thank you, Jordan. I think I'll spend tonight thinking about where I see my life going from here, and I'll let you know."

"You do that." He pulled a card from his pocket and handed it to her. "I know Al gave you a card the first day we were here, but this one has my personal cell. You call me if you want some help. I'm sorry this happened to you, but you are strong. You will be okay."

## 10

"Hey, I thought you were going to focus on a movie night with me now that the case is over," Cassidy said laying a hand on his arm. They were sitting on the couch, but Jordan had no idea what the movie on the television was about. His mind was still on Tia.

"Almost over," Jordan said. "Rico Rearden is still out there somewhere."

"And you'll find him," Cassidy said. "You always do."

Jordan smiled at his girlfriend and opened his arm for her to curl into. "What did I do to deserve you?"

"Well, saved me from a stalker for one," she said before placing a kiss on his lips, "but you're an amazing man and probably would have won me regardless."

"I just wish there was more I could do for Tia. She's going to be released tomorrow, and I can still see the fear in her eyes. I just wish I could give her more assurance."

"She's being released tomorrow?" Cassidy asked.

Jordan heard the tone in her voice and glanced down at her. "Yeah, why? What's going on in that pretty head of yours?"

"Well, I can't help with easing her fear, but I do know something that would be good to do."

"What's that?"

"She hasn't had any visitors, right? Not friends anyway."

"No." What was Cassidy getting at?

"So, she's been in the hospital gown the whole time, right?"

Jordan shrugged. "I guess so."

"Well, she can't go home in a hospital gown, so how about we get her some clothes?"

As her words sunk in, Jordan's lips pulled into a wide smile, and he kissed Cassidy again. "You're amazing. Why didn't I think of that?"

"Probably because you're not a girl," Cassidy said swatting his chest playfully. "Now, we just need her size."

Jordan's face fell. He had no idea what her size was or how to tell. "How do we do that?"

Cassidy chuckled and moved out of his arms to stand before him. "Is she about my size? Larger? Smaller?"

Jordan had never seen Tia standing, but he guessed she was a few inches shorter and a little smaller. "Smaller but not by much and a little shorter."

"See? Was that so hard? We'll pick up some outfits with elastic waists one and two sizes smaller than me. Something is bound to fit. At least until she can purchase more herself."

Jordan stood and wrapped his arms around Cassidy. "You, Cassidy Marcel, are one in a million, you know that?"

She smiled up at him as her arms moved to his neck. "I do, but I certainly don't mind hearing it again."

Jordan chuckled as he leaned down to place his lips on hers. He still couldn't believe his luck in finding Cassidy, and he would tell her every day if that's what it took to keep her in his life.

## 11

J ordan knocked on Tia's doorframe before entering the next morning. "Brody said you could use a lift."

"Yeah, I could. Plus, I thought I'd take you up on your offer for a place to stay and a job. I'd like to stay in town a little longer."

Jordan was glad to hear that, and the corners of his lips twitched as he entered and set the bag beside her on the bed. "Would that have anything to do with a handsome doctor by chance?"

"It might," she said, "but I also don't know if there's much to go back to in California. I feel like I can start over here except...."

"Except what?"

Tia sighed and shook her head. "I had a dream last night that someone is still after me. I'm sure it was due to the activity yesterday, but do you think there's any chance that it might be true?"

Jordan ran a hand across his chin, wishing he could allay her fears. "I'd be lying if I said no. I do think we got the main people involved, but there's always the chance that someone else decides to seek retribution. If it makes you feel better, the lady who runs the house I'm taking you to is former military. She'll keep an eye on you."

"Did you get any news on Rico?"

He shook his head. "Sorry, we're checking with the PD in Chicago, but it's going to take some time."

"Thanks Jordan."

"You're welcome. Now, in that bag are some clothes and shoes. My girlfriend Cassidy deduced that you had none here. She picked them out, but I had to guess on your size so don't blame her if they're off. She did grab some things with draw-strings so the size shouldn't matter too much."

Tia's fingers touched the bag, and her voice was quiet and full of emotion when she spoke again. "Thank you, Jordan, and tell Cassidy thank you."

He nodded, embarrassed, and took a step back. "I'll give you a chance to change and see about getting a wheelchair so we can get you out of here."

He shut the door behind him and turned to the main ICU desk. "How can I get a wheelchair for Tia Sweetchild? She's checking out."

"I'll order you one right away sir," the nurse said as she picked up a phone. "Can I get a wheelchair to ICU? Thank you." She smiled at Jordan as she replaced the phone. "It will be just a minute."

Jordan nodded and waited for the orderly to arrive with the chair. When he finally came around the corner, Jordan took the chair and returned to Tia's door. He knocked lightly. "It's Jordan. Can I come in?"

"Yes, come on in."

"Hey, looking good," he said as he wheeled a chair in. She had managed to get on a stretchy pair of pants and a shirt, and neither appeared to be swimming on her. He'd have to tell Cassidy she did a wonderful job in choosing the outfits. "You about ready? I just got called back to work, so I'm afraid I'll have to drop you and run."

"That's fine, Jordan. Really, you've done so much for me."

Jordan could hear the emotion in her voice, and he wished he could do more. He wished he could assure her she was safe, but while he couldn't do that, he was going to do the next best thing.

He was taking Tia to Cara Hunter's house. Though technically a bed and breakfast, Cara specialized in helping people who needed to get back on their feet or needed extra protection. Former military, Cara had never completely adjusted to civilian life and was always willing to help out. Cara was as close as Jordan could get to having someone protect Tia twenty-four seven.

Jordan parked the car in front of a weathered-looking rambler close to the beach. The yellow paint was faded but still cheery. "Sorry, it's not much to look at on the outside, but Cara takes good care of the inside."

"It's fine," Tia said. "Hopefully, I don't have to inconvenience her too long."

Jordan touched her arm. "It's no inconvenience. We take care of each other here."

Tia smiled and thanked him, but it was a small smile. Jordan hoped one day he would see a genuine smile on her face.

"Come on, I'll introduce you and help you get settled before I jet back to work."

He turned the engine off and walked around to Tia's side. Before helping her out, he grabbed her crutches out of the back seat, handed them to her, and made sure she was stable. Only then did he grab her bag.

Jordan led the way up the short walk and pushed open the door without knocking. Cara had told him long ago he was welcome anytime. "Cara? It's Jordan and Tia, the woman I told you about."

A woman with short, spiky hair appeared in the doorway.

Trim and athletic, Cara looked as if she could tangle with the boys any day with her broad shoulders and bold arm definition. "Jordan, good to see you again." She extended a hand in greeting.

Jordan shook her hand and then turned to Tia. "This is Tia. She's recovering from memory loss and a few attempts on her life. She's going to need some help getting back on her feet."

Cara extended her hand to Tia. "It's a pleasure to meet you, and any friend of Jordan's is welcome here as long as needed."

Tia shook the woman's hand and returned the smile. "Thank you. I appreciate it."

Jordan wished he could stay until he made sure Tia was situated, but duty called. "I hate to run, but I have to get to work. Cara will take good care of you, but please call me if you need anything." Jordan squeezed her shoulder before dropping her bag and exiting out the front door.

J
ordan's phone rang as he sat down for dinner across from Cassidy. It was Cara's number, but she rarely called him. A feeling of dread spread through him as he answered the phone.

"Cara? Is everything okay?" Across from him, Cassidy set down her fork and fixed questioning eyes on him.

"Jordan?" The woman's voice was a hoarse whisper, but even so he could tell this was Tia on the other end and not Cara.

"Tia? What's wrong?"

"I'm at Cara's, but someone's here. The electricity just went off. Cara sent me to the closet to call you."

Jordan heard an intake of breath and then the muffled sounds of a man's voice followed by a scream and then silence.

"Tia? Tia?"

"What is it?" Cassidy asked.

"Trouble. Sorry, I have to run." He placed a quick kiss on her lips before grabbing his keys and gun. "I promise I'll make it up to you."

"I know you will. Be safe," she called after him.

Jordan flashed her a wink, but he was already dialing Stone's number as he stepped into the cool night air. "Sir, there's trouble over at Cara's. Can you send everyone?"

Jordan put the lights on but left the siren off as he drove through the city streets. When he reached Cara's street, he turned the lights off as well and coasted to a stop a few doors down. Stone, Al, and Albright pulled up just after him. Jordan wondered briefly where Givens was, but he knew the man lived farther away.

"What do we have?" Stone asked as they consulted together.

"At least one unknown assailant in the house," Jordan said. "I have to assume from the phone call he has Tia. I'm not sure where Cara is, but she'll be an asset if she's uninjured."

"All right. We go in with signals only. We don't want to give away our position in case there's more than one."

The group nodded, and Jordan led the way into the darkened house. No sound came from the front entrance way, but he could hear voices down the hall toward the living room. He motioned to the officers behind him before continuing down the hall.

When they reached the living room, he stopped short. Even in the dim light, he could see that Cara had already taken care of things. Rico Rearden lay on the ground, his hands zip tied together. Brody sat a few feet away next to Tia. Blood ran from his head, and Jordan assumed Rico had jumped him either before continuing into the house or before he found Tia. Tia appeared scared but otherwise unharmed.

"I'll call for a bus," Al said as she made her way to Brody and Tia.

Stone and Albright hauled Rico up and led him out of the house as Jordan crossed to Cara who was rubbing her arms. Jordan knew her well enough to know she must have overpowered Rico somehow, possibly a choke hold. He was aware of her college nickname 'The Leech.' "Thank you. I knew you were the right woman for the job."

She shot him a glare as she massaged her forearms. "Next time, a little warning of what I might be facing would be nice."

"I would have warned you except we didn't know what to expect. We thought it was over after the attempt at the hospital, but we didn't realize Rico was not just the front for the organization - he was the head."

"Yeah, we know," Cara said, "He had a hard time keeping his mouth shut. At least while he had the gun on Tia."

"Does that mean it's really over now?" Tia asked.

"It does. Rico's going away for a long time along with his wife and the Petrovs. You may have to testify, but we all owe you a debt of gratitude. I know it wasn't your intent, but through your actions, you've managed to help us take down a pretty large drug organization."

Brody smiled and squeezed Tia's shoulder. "See? I told you everything happens for a reason. I think you've just made up for a lot of the mistakes in your past."

Jordan smiled at the couple. He had a feeling this would bond them together, allowing them to survive anything thrown at them in the future. As for himself, he was glad to mark this case complete. With Rico in custody, all the known players were accounted for, and Jordan believed they could finally call this one done.

If you'd like to know the rest of Tia and Brody's story, be sure to read Lost Memories and New Beginnings to hear this story from their point of view. And if you'd like to read more about Jordan and Cassidy, pick up Fire Games, the first book in The Men of Fire Beach series!

# IT'S NOT QUITE THE END!

Thank you so much for reading *When Questions Abound*. This short story was meant to be a companion story to Lost Memories to give the police procedural side. As you can see, there is more planned for The Men of Fire Beach and I hope you'll take that journey with me.

I hope you enjoyed the story as I really enjoyed writing it. If you did, would you do me a favor? If you did, please leave a review. It really helps. It doesn't have to be long - just a few words to help other readers know what they're getting.

I'd love to hear from you, not only about this story, but about the characters or stories you'd like read in the future. I'm always looking for new ideas and if I use one of your characters or stories, I'll send you a free ebook and paperback of the book with a special dedication. Write to me at lorana-hoopes@gmail.com. And if you'd like to see what's coming next, be sure to stop by authorloranahoopes.com

I also have a weekly newsletter that contains many wonderful things like pictures of my adorable children, chances

to win awesome prizes, new releases and sales I might be holding, great books from other authors, and anything else that
strikes my fancy and that I think you would enjoy. I'll even send
you the first chapter of my newest (maybe not even released yet)
book if you'd like to sign up.

Even better, I solemnly swear to only send out one newsletter
a week (usually on Tuesday unless life gets in the way which
with three kids it usually does). I will not spam you, sell your
email address to solicitors or anyone else, or any of those other
terrible things.

God Bless,
    Lorana

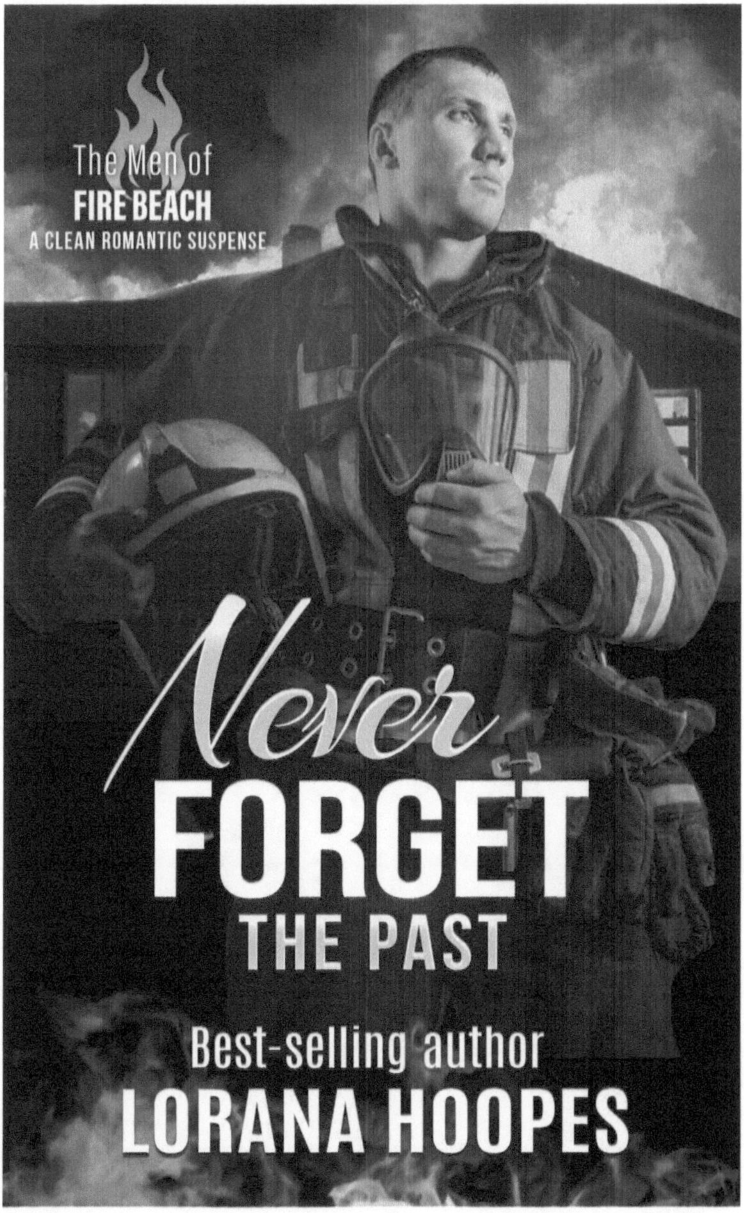
The Men of
FIRE BEACH
A CLEAN ROMANTIC SUSPENSE
Never
FORGET
THE PAST
Best-selling author
LORANA HOOPES

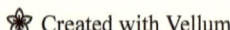

*To my wonderful readers who inspire me to write everyday.*
*To Shari who helped me make this the novel it needed to be.*
*To my writing students who read my first chapter and inspired*
*me to keep going.*

She loved to watch things burn. Fire meant renewal. It allowed the old and useless items to be destroyed so new and worthwhile things could take their places. It was also cleansing. Sins could be erased in fire. The hot, searing heat held perfection and no mercy. No one could escape the fire's wrath. Which was why it had to be done.

Some people believed that God doled out judgement, but the truth was that God was often too merciful. Too full of grace. He forgave people who didn't deserve it. Therein lay the need for His angels. People who could witness the depravity of man or woman and take the necessary steps to cleanse the world. People like her.

She let the match burn to her fingertips, enjoying the heat that pulsed through her hand. Some angels preferred fancier ways to fulfill their duties. The news was littered with stories of shootings, drownings, some even used drugs, but she had always enjoyed the simplest way. A little gasoline and a match. All it took was an open window, a splash of gas, one strike, and the fire would lick the gas up in giant gulps. Flames would race each other to the top of the house and snake their way along the walls.

She never had to be inside this way, but she always made sure they were. And she always struck at night when the blanket of deep sleep would keep them from escaping. So far, no one had escaped.

The match, a charred remnant of wood now, floated to the ground. When it landed, she placed the toe of her shoe over it and twisted, burying it into the dirt. She only ever left one. To leave any more would be tempting fate. Even the one she left was always a way back from the scene, but it was her homage, her thanks for being bestowed with this honor. Not everyone could do what she did, and she willingly bore the weight of her title.

As the flames licked higher, she stepped back into the comforting dark of the forest. The limbs of the trees reached out for her like arms of a mother, and the leaves hid her form so she could watch undisturbed. Watching was her favorite part. She thrived on the fear that graced each face that saw the fire, the terror that colored each voice as they yelled out orders or cried. Even the nervous bustling activity brought a smile to her face. But the best part by far was when the coroner arrived, and the body left the house in its black bag.

A finality existed just in the word black - its heavy feeling on the tongue and its abundance of thick blended consonants - but even more in the form of it. Zipped from head to toe, no more light poked into the bag. No more grace. Only darkness. A shiver of delight ran down her spine at the thought. Yes, that was her favorite part.

She settled against the tree and waited. It had been a long time, but finally, she was back.

Captain Makenna Drake ran a slender hand through her chin-length brown hair as she stared at the charred remains of a house - her crime scene - and sighed. It had been so quiet the last few years. Why did this have to start again now?

"Do you think it's the same guy?" Tad asked from behind her shoulder.

She glanced up at her lieutenant, the only other cop still on the force who had worked the murder case five years ago. He'd been young then, fresh out of the academy and eager to learn even though he had spent more time typing reports and fetching coffee than he had processing evidence. He was older now, but his face still boasted his youth. It was not yet marred with the wrinkles the stress of this job brought, but it would be if he stayed a cop much longer.

It happened to them all, she supposed. Death would come across their paths and leave his mark - a graying of the hair here, a few wrinkles there, the inability to process emotions or maintain healthy relationships sprinkled in for good measure. She had seen it before with her first captain. Fierce and stoic, he had been a force to reckon with - hard to please and even harder to earn praise from. But he'd been unhappy. After two divorces and little contact with the children who had written him out of their lives years ago, drinking had become his companion. First, a little nip here and there when an especially tough case crossed their desks - the death of a child, physical abuse, or the like. But then she'd noticed it more often - the frequent trips to his office, the darker mood, the sallow complexion.

And so she had transferred to a smaller department. Convinced that the crime of the bigger city had been his down-fall, she'd chosen a smaller town with a lower crime rate, but she found the same markers here. Sure, it took longer, but the aging still happened. Her superiors both looked a decade older than they were. The captain had recently filed for divorce and the sergeant's relationship was hanging on by a thread, but she would be different. She'd promised herself she would find time to date, that she would leave her work at work and fully engage at home, but she hadn't.

And then one day, she'd seen the toll in her own mirror - the bags under her eyes where there had previously been none and the coarse gray hairs that contrasted with her dark hair - both in color and in manageability.

Tad's hair held no traces of that gray yet, and his eyes glistened with curiosity and wonder - something she had lost long ago. But he hadn't been entrenched in the previous case the way she had. And life had returned to normal after the last death - traffic stops and bar brawls, but nothing serious. She wondered if he would still look so young when this was over, or if, like her, his face would bear the brunt of the weight of cases like this.

"I don't know if it's the same guy," she said, returning her gaze to the blackened structure. "The MO is the same. House fire at night, open or broken window where the fire starts, but all the victims last time were women."

"Except for Matt Fisher," he said.

Right, Matt Fisher. The final victim. The man everyone thought was dead. Everyone except Makenna who knew better. Everyone except Makenna who sent him away when he came to her after the attempt on his life. "Yes, except for him." She forced her face to remain impassive. Tad didn't know what she had done, and she wasn't sure she was ready to tell him yet. "But if our killer changed his victim MO with Matt, why the long break?"

Confusion clouded Tad's face, dimming the brightness of his eyes momentarily, and he shook his head. "Something must have triggered him."

"Yes, but what?" Makenna hated that this guy was killing again. She hated the fear that would blanket the small town as it had five years ago. She hated the fact that she hadn't caught the guy last time. Even more, she hated the fact that she had told Matt Fisher to leave, had let his family believe he was dead, for nothing. She'd thought she was saving him, had thought the killer was after him, but now he was striking again even though Matt Fisher was long gone. How much of Matt Fisher's life had she destroyed with her wrong choice?

She supposed it could be a copycat. The fires always started at night when the victims were asleep. They always started inside an open window, and the only accelerant they could ever determine was gasoline. Sometimes the window was broken, but they never found fingerprints or what he used to break it which meant he took the item with him and probably wore gloves. It wasn't much to go on, but it was possible someone had read about the old cases and decided to try his hand. It certainly wouldn't be hard to copy.

Makenna didn't think so though. Woodville was a smaller town - not tiny but small enough that violent crimes were few and far between. Most of her time was spent ticketing speeders or the occasional red light runners. Besides those murders five years ago, the only other big case they'd had was when Tommy

Granger went missing for a few hours and his parents believed he'd been kidnapped. Turned out, he had fallen asleep in the dog house with their new puppy and just didn't hear all the shouts.

So, the chances of a copycat choosing their town again just didn't sit right with her. It made much more sense that something had appeased the killer last time and something had triggered him again this time. Of course, the only thing that could have appeased him last time was the death of Matt Fisher, but then why start killing again? As far as Makenna knew, she was the only one who knew Matt was alive, who knew where he was. Had there been more to it last time? Something she had missed?

"What are we going to do, Captain?" Tad asked.

Makenna took another deep breath and uttered the words she'd both hoped and dreaded to say. "I guess I'm going to bring someone back from the dead."

Billy "Bubba" Campbell glanced around his apartment as he locked up. Though he enjoyed his alone time, he wished he had someone to share the evenings with, but his job as a firefighter kept him busy. And then there was the issue with his past. No one in Fire Beach knew his real past, and though he had fully embraced his current life, that reality made it hard to let people in - really in - enough to form a relationship with. Besides, what if it happened again? He couldn't stand any woman he cared about getting hurt again. No, it was better this way. He would just be content with good friends and the good Lord.

Speaking of good friends, he better hurry up. Tonight, Detective Jordan Graves, was throwing a party for Tia Sweetchild, the author who had ended up in their town after a car accident the opening night of Jordan's restaurant. They had all worked to save her, and though she'd had a long recovery, she'd done it with the help of her now-boyfriend, Dr. Brody Cavanaugh.

Bubba still marveled at how the members of the different departments had bonded.

The rest of the crew was already at the restaurant when Bubba entered, but thankfully, his friend and fellow firefighter Luca had saved him a seat. Luca was a Southerner like Bubba, but Bubba had quickly learned after meeting Luca that there were two types of Southerners. There were southerners from Texas like he was - people who said ya'll, loved okra, and called every drink a coke. And then there were the people from the deep south, like Luca who was from Georgia. The differences were few, but they came out occasionally, usually around food. Bubba still remembered the time Luca had called him a Yankee for not knowing what a ham hock was. Weird that they now both lived up North in Illinois.

He slid into the seat next to Luca just as Jordan tapped his water glass with a spoon. Though he would never have opted for the title, Jordan had become their representative, their glue. His commanding presence was a large part of that - he had a natural ability to draw the attention when he walked into a room. Couple that with his occupation as a cop as well as the co-owner of the restaurant, and he was in the forefront quite often.

The conversation quieted, allowing him to speak. "Thank you all for coming. As you know, we have a resident celebrity in our midst." He smiled at Tia, and she dropped her eyes as a soft pink color crawled up her cheeks. "And she has finally finished her masterpiece. Tia get up here and show off your beautiful book." Tia had been an author before her accident, but after it, she had taken some time to work in the restaurant while she healed. Somehow, she had managed to write a book at the same time.

Tia shook her head as she pushed back her chair. Bubba didn't know all of Tia's story, but he'd heard a little through the grapevine and he'd been there when she had first been rescued with the Jaws of Life. It would be hard to tell she had ever been in a serious accident except for the large red scar that still arced across her forehead.

She grabbed a bag and walked to the front of the table. "Thank you all for wanting to celebrate this with me. This wasn't an easy book to write, but your support helped me get past all the hard parts. Now, I've loved a lot of books I've written, but I think this might be my best."

"Hear, hear," Brody, her boyfriend and ICU doctor, said lifting his glass and flashing her a large smile. "What?" he asked as he looked around the table. "I already read it, so I know that it's good. She got the doctor spot on."

Tia shook her head and smiled at him. "Anyway, I think it is because of all of you that it turned out so well, and that's why I'm pleased to present to you..." she paused before pulling the book out of the bag, "The Key to Remember."

Bubba joined in the cheers and clapping as Tia passed the book around the table. He hadn't read it yet, but if it chronicled her narrow escape from the men who had been after her when she lost her memory, he had no doubt it would be interesting. When the book reached his hands, he flipped through the pages before turning to Luca Sanders. "Hey, this might even be a book you could read, Luca."

"Only if it's on audiobook," Luca shot back. "I can't sit still long enough to read a paper book. Sorry, Tia."

"You probably couldn't focus long enough to listen to an audiobook either," Bubba said with a deep chuckle. "Unless maybe it was a Dr. Seuss book."

"Hey, there is nothing wrong with Dr. Seuss," Luca said, punching Bubba in the arm. "I still remember Green Eggs and Ham. Of course, maybe that's because our teacher actually made us eat green eggs." A grimace contorted his face and Bubba laughed out loud.

"Excuse me?"

The conversation stilled at the unfamiliar voice, and Bubba's blood ran cold. It couldn't be. She'd promised not to come find him unless the murders started again. He turned toward the doorway where a petite woman stood. She was thinner and her hair held a few more silver strands, but Bubba would have wagered a year's wage that the woman was Makenna Drake.

"I'm sorry to interrupt, but do any of you know where I can find Matt Fisher?" Her eyes scanned the room, and Bubba knew when they reached him, she would recognize him. He hadn't changed that much in five years. They hadn't thought a change of appearance would be necessary. Moving him a few hours away and giving him a whole new name and past had seemed like enough, especially since Makenna hadn't known the name he'd chosen. She had set him up with a hacker she knew who could arrange a new identity complete with documents. She'd agreed to know the town he moved to in case she needed to find him again, but she hadn't wanted any more knowledge in case the killer ever realized they had faked Matt's death and went after Makenna for information.

Confused glances shot around the room and Jordan stood to address her. "I'm sorry, ma'am, there's no Matt Fisher here."

"Actually, there is." Bubba took a deep breath and let it out in a sigh. Time seemed to freeze as every eye turned his direction, and he pushed back his chair and stood. "I'm Matt Fisher."

"What? What are you talking about, Bubba? Who is this woman?" The questions fired at him from all across the table and Bubba held up his hands to quiet them down.

"I'll answer all your questions, but let me start with the last one first." He turned to Makenna and motioned her to join them. "This is Lieutenant Makenna Drake."

"Actually, it's Captain now."

Bubba raised a brow and shot her a glance riddled with questions. She was a good cop, but captain already?

She smiled and shrugged as if reading his mind. "It's a small town."

He chuckled at that. "It is, but somehow I doubt that's the only reason you're a captain now. I should have expected nothing less." He looked away from Makenna and back to his friends to continue his story. "Captain," he emphasized the word, "Drake is from Woodville where I used to live."

"Woodville? I thought you were from Texas," Luca said.

"I am originally from Texas, but I moved to Woodville in high school. I graduated there and trained to become a firefighter."

"You? Or Matt Fisher?" Jordan asked, and Bubba did not miss the note of suspicion threading his voice.

"Matt Fisher. That is the name I was born with. Anyway, for a couple of years, it was great. I loved the area and my job, but then about five years ago, people began dying."

"Women, specifically," Makenna said, joining in. "Women who happened to die in fires and all had some connection to Matt."

"You didn't honestly think he was responsible, did you?" Cassidy asked. Daggers flew from her eyes and laced her voice.

Bubba had to smile at Cassidy. She was the only female fire-fighter in their unit, and she was like his little sister. He was fiercely protective of her, and it appeared she was of him as well.

"We didn't have much to go on," Makenna said sadly. "Nothing is ever left at the scene, and the only link seemed to be Matt."

"So, what changed your mind?" Officer Alayna "Al" Parker asked.

"When I became a victim," Bubba said. "Maybe it was because I'm always around fires, but the smell woke me up, and I escaped. Makenna decided then that I wasn't the perpetrator and that it would be safer if I left town and changed my name. She helped me set up this new identity. I didn't mean to lie to you all." Bubba meant every word, but he also couldn't deny feeling lighter finally sharing his past with his friends.

"That all makes sense," Jordan said, "but why are you back now?"

Makenna bit her lip and then sighed as she caught Bubba's eye. "Because the murders have started again."

Bubba's heart sank at the words, and a seed of anger sprouted in his chest. Makenna had told him that whoever was behind the killings held a vendetta against him for some reason and would stop with the news of his death. He had believed her. He had let his family believe he was dead and broken all communication with them. And for what? Nothing, it appeared now.

"I know you have no reason to come back, but I'm hoping that you will. You were the only victim who survived, though the killer doesn't know that. I'm hoping that seeing that you survived might fluster him enough to mess up and give us some clue as to who he is."

Bubba leaned back as he thought about her request. He owed her nothing. He'd spent the last five years trying to put Woodville out of his mind, to pretend he didn't miss his family. And he was happy here in Fire Beach, mostly. But there had always been that nagging thought in his head. The thought that wondered if he would really ever forget Matt Fisher and truly be Billy Campbell. The thought that the killer had some connection to him and by running, he had put more people in danger.

"I'll do it," he said finally. The thought of going back to Woodville held a sense of relief along with a feeling of terror, but it also felt right.

"Are you sure, Bubba?" Cassidy asked. "It sounds danger-ous. Maybe Jordan should go with you." She looked to her boyfriend, but his face was impassive.

"I'm about out of leave, but I'll check with Stone and see if he'll give me some more leave."

"I could go," Al said. "I'm pretty certain I have some leave saved up."

"Guys, I'll be fine," Bubba said, though inside he wondered

if that were true. He'd gone through a lot of counseling after leaving Woodville. He'd spent an abundant amount of time trying to forget the women who were killed, trying to forget his family. Could he really go back and relive it all again? What would his parents say?

"Thank you, Matt. I guess it's settled then," Makenna said.

But it didn't feel settled to Bubba. Could he really face his old demons? What if he didn't make it back this time? No, that was out of his hands. God had protected him last time, and He would do it again this time if it was His will. Bubba shook his head to clear the voices and turned to Makenna. "When do we leave?"

＃ 3 ＃

Makenna felt like a trespasser as she stood in Matt's apartment waiting for him to gather some items. She had told him to pack for a week, but what if it turned out to be longer? What if Matt wasn't the link and seeing him did nothing? What if it really was a copycat who would have little knowledge of Matt Fisher at all? Then she would have disrupted his life for nothing.

Trust. She had to trust God that this was the right move. She'd learned to trust her instincts when she became a cop, and they had rarely proved her wrong. But, she knew that trusting God was even more important, and she felt sure He'd led her back to Matt Fisher.

She'd begun looking to God after the case from five years ago. She'd needed a way to deal with her anger and frustration at not finding the killer. Then, the promotions had happened and stress had consumed her life. Church and her time with God had been the only sanity-saving times for a while.

"Almost ready," he called from the bedroom.

His place was small - a one bedroom apartment, but he had decorated it tastefully. The furniture matched, and the pictures on the wall complemented them. She wondered if he had decorated the place himself or if a woman had?

There had been several women at the restaurant where she'd found him, but none of them appeared to be more than a friend, and she saw no sign of a woman living in the apartment. Of course, it was none of her business if he did have a woman, but for some reason the thought that he didn't... affected her. She told herself it was simply because she too was single and she liked the validation that it was okay to be in your thirties and still single, but if she were honest with herself, she would acknowledge that Matt had a place in her heart.

She had truly believed sending him away was saving not only his life but the lives of his family and friends, but she had never forgotten him. She'd thought often of checking up on him to see how he was doing, but she hadn't wanted to chance the killer finding out he was still alive and coming after him. Now, here he was back in her life. As strong and handsome as he had been five years ago.

"You ready?" he asked.

His voice shook her back to reality, and she nodded. "Do you have anyone to look after the place while you're gone?" It was a cowardly way to ask, but his answer would tell her if he was seeing someone or not.

"Cassidy and Luca both offered to check in on the place."

Makenna nodded and stepped out the front door. "They seem nice. Your friends."

"They are. And protective. They're all I've had for the last five years." She heard no condemnation in his voice, but she felt it all the same - a tiny tug on the invisible chain she wore around her neck.

"I'm sorry, Matt." She hated those words. They sounded trite and empty, but what could she say? There was no manual for situations like this, no course taught at the academy. Even the previous cases she had handled had never forced her to fake a death and destroy a family.

He held up a hand and shook his head. "Let's not rehash the past. You did what you thought was right, and I went along with it. Let's just hope it ends differently this time."

Makenna nodded. What could she say to that? He locked the front door and followed her to her car, but the tension lay heavy between them. Like an unseen barrier. She hoped she hadn't made a mistake coming back here and upending his life. Again.

She turned the key and let the hum of the engine break the silence for a moment. Then she shifted the gear into drive and pulled away. Her fingers tapped against the steering wheel - her nervous gesture - and she searched her mind for anything to say.

"There's a radio," she said, tapping the button on the console. "You can turn it to whatever you want. The country station comes in super clear, but the other ones are a little finicky." She was rambling, but she couldn't seem to keep the words from falling out of her mouth.

"I don't need music, Makenna."

"Right. Sorry." What was she thinking? Of course he didn't need music. He probably needed to process, but why did he seem so comfortable with the silence while it ate her alive?

Although maybe he wasn't comfortable. His posture was so stiff that it looked as if a metal rod had replaced his spine, and his eyes stared vacantly out the window. She wished that she could see what was going on in his head. Was he scared? Nervous? He certainly had every right to be. She sure was. It had been a nightmare working this case five years ago, but she'd still been learning then. Now, she was running the department which meant that more responsibility lay on her shoulders. She had to catch this guy.

"Why Bubba?" she asked. The sound of her voice surprised her. She had been wondering about the nickname from the moment she heard it, but she hadn't meant to ask the question aloud. At least, not yet.

Matt shrugged and turned his head slowly in her direction. "Bubba seemed to fit the Southern personality I had created. Once I said it out loud, it just sort of stuck."

"Should I call you that?" Makenna wasn't sure what to call him. She knew him as Matt, but she also knew he'd been living under a different name for the last few years. How odd must that be? She didn't even like nicknames though her old captain had called her Mac. He was the only one though.

Matt appeared to think for a minute as the knuckles of his right hand ran down the side of his square jaw. She'd forgotten how solid he was, but now that he was in her car, it was hard not to notice how his broad shoulders filled every inch of the passenger seat and how the seatbelt accentuated his muscular chest.

"Yeah, Bubba would be nice. It's the only name that's felt right since I quit being Matt."

"Was it hard to adjust?"

The seatbelt groaned as it stretched with his deep breath. "It was at first. Especially leaving my life behind. How is my family anyway?"

"They're fine," Makenna said, careful to keep her voice even, but she knew that was far from the truth. His parents had been devastated by Matt's "death," and the grief had aged them faster than they might have without it. She knew he probably had other siblings, but the only one she had ever met was Felicity, his sister who worked for a local doctor. She had grieved briefly, but then she had seemed to continue on as if nothing had happened. Perhaps, it was because of her job. Maybe her boss had given her counseling, but it had still given Makenna pause. His parents, however, would probably be overjoyed to see him now and know he was alive, but Makenna knew they would rain fire down on her for the lie, even if it had been a lie to keep him safe.

"That was the hardest part," he continued. Makenna breathed a sigh of relief that he hadn't pressed about his family any further. "Not seeing my family and learning to respond to a different name. It's not something I ever thought I would have to do, and I wouldn't wish it on anyone. I often felt like I was developing multiple personalities."

Makenna could understand that. Even though she knew he was the same person, the man sitting next to her was different from the one who had left five years ago. His voice was softer. His eyes carried a little more sadness. Even some of his mannerisms seemed different.

"I'm sorry. I thought it was the best way to keep you safe." She hated that she kept apologizing - it made the words sound trite - but what else could she say?

He shrugged again and turned his face back to the window. "It probably was."

Silence filled the car, and Makenna forced her mouth shut. She wanted to ask him more questions. About the last few years, about what he remembered from the previous case, about how he was feeling, but she could tell he wasn't ready to throw that door wide open yet.

"Why do you think he started again?" Matt asked as he turned to her suddenly. No, not Matt. Bubba. He wanted her to call him Bubba, and she would try and honor that. The name felt weird in her head and she imagined it would on her tongue as well, but she would bury her discomfort for him. She owed him that much.

Makenna shook her head but kept her gaze focused on the road in front of her. "I'm not sure. Something definitely triggered him. Maybe a death." She paused, unsure if she should tell him the rest of the issue now or when they could look over the evidence.

"What aren't you saying?"

Her eyes flicked from the road to meet his steely gaze. Now, it was. If he hadn't become a firefighter, he would have made a great cop. "Something in the MO changed."

"A copycat?" Bubba asked.

Makenna shook her head. "No, we're pretty sure it's the same guy. Same details. Fire started at an open window, gas for accelerant, single match found at the scene. Details we never released to the public."

"So, what's changed?"

"The victim. When he struck five years ago, all the victims were women. Except for you. Our current victim is another man."

"What does that mean?" Bubba asked as he shook his head.

"We don't know. We're hoping maybe you can help us figure that out."

Bubba swallowed the lump that clogged his throat as they passed the small green "Welcome to Woodville" sign. Conflicting emotions raged within him. On one hand, he was excited to see his parents and his sister, who still lived in the town, but coming back here also brought back a flood of memories.

*Bubba's eyes snapped open. For a second, he wasn't sure what had woken him, but then the odor hit his nose - the acrid smell of smoke. Light but definitely there. Once you've been in a burning building, the smell of the smoke never leaves you, and he had been in enough buildings to never mistake the scent no matter how faint it was. Then the soft crackle of the fire met his ears. He threw his covers back and could already feel the gentle tease of the approaching heat. Out! He had to get out.*

*He touched the handle of his door and quickly pulled his hand back. An intense heat coated the metal. The fire was right outside of the door then. No opening the door to make it to an exit. No using his fire extinguisher to tame the fire. The idea of losing his house and belongings was sobering. Pictures of his family had been hung around the living room, and his favorite Toby Mac CD was probably melted into the coffee table his parents had bought for him when he first moved out. Even his computer, the Mac he had saved the last few paychecks to get, would be a puddle of melted plastic and metal, but they were just things. As much as he would miss them, things could be replaced, but he hadn't started this fire. Someone else had. Someone who could be the same arsonist who had killed three women in fires recently. Someone who could still be around - watching, waiting to see if Bubba escaped. From his years in the department, Bubba knew many arsonists liked to stay and watch the fires.*

*Bubba turned from the door and scanned his room. There wasn't time to take much, but he could grab his cell phone and a pair of shoes. No need to destroy his feet as he climbed out of the window or ran to safety. Safety. Could the killer be out there? Waiting for him to open the window? He crossed to the window and peered into the darkness but saw no one waiting in the immediate vicinity. Still, what if the killer was waiting outside? He could be lurking in the shadows of the large oak tree. Just waiting and watching to make sure Bubba didn't escape. He should have trimmed the tree or better yet removed it altogether, but how could he have known?*

*It didn't matter if the killer was out there. It was a chance he had to take. At least outside, he had a possibility of escape. If he stayed in this room, the smoke would choke him, and the fire would eat him alive. And he had no desire to become the fire's victim.*

*He grabbed his cell phone and threw on a pair of shoes, and then he opened the window and knocked out the screen. It would be a tight squeeze for his large frame, but he thought he would just fit.*

*The cool night air sent a shiver down his back as it dispelled the heat he had felt just moments before. He should have grabbed a shirt too or a jacket. His feet hit the ground, and he stepped back. The fire had already claimed half of his house, and the flames licked closer to where he stood. With a final glance around him, Bubba shot off in the direction farthest from the fire's origin. Only when he felt he was far enough away not to be seen or heard did he pull his cell phone out and dial 911.*

Bubba squeezed his eyes shut to dispel the images of the past and then took a deep breath. He could do this.

"You okay?" Makenna asked beside him.

"Yeah, just dealing with a few old demons."

She didn't press the issue for which Bubba was glad. He didn't want to relive the nightmare out loud. He'd done enough of that in counseling when he'd first moved to Fire Beach. The therapist had been cleared and sworn to secrecy, but Bubba had still been relieved when the sessions ended.

"I know you want to see your family, but I have a feeling it might be a long and emotional reunion, so do you mind if we hit the station first? I want to see what we've found out about our victim."

"Fine." Bubba did want to see his parents and his sister, but he was nervous about it as well. He wouldn't mind the extra time to prepare himself mentally. "Is anybody else from the old case still here?" An unspoken code existed among departments, and so even when he had been a suspect, most of the cops had treated him with respect, but there'd been one, an older, gruff man who had glared at Bubba every time he'd come around.

"Just Tad Brewer. You might not even remember him because he was so new back then, but he's my lieutenant now. Everyone else either retired or took a position in another town."

"Couldn't handle the pressure of the investigation?" Bubba asked.

She glanced at him as she pulled into the parking lot. "I'm sure that was the issue for a few of them - the ones who have always tied everything up with a nice bow. For the others," she shrugged, "I think they thought a small town would be less work."

Bubba chuckled at that, but he bet she was right. Fire Beach couldn't really be classified as a small town, but he had known a few people who had joined the fire department thinking it would be easy money only to find out they stayed relatively busy. Not Chicago busy, but not slow either.

"You ready?" she asked as she turned off the engine.

"As I'll ever be, I guess." Could one ever be ready for something like this? To step back into the fire after narrowly escaping with his life? What if the killer found out he was still alive and went after him again? No. Trust. He had to trust. He whispered a silent prayer as he put his hand on the door.

"Okay, let's go."

## 4

Makenna pulled open the door and stepped inside the small station first, but she could feel the hulking presence of Bubba behind her. Had he always been such a presence? She remembered him being handsome back then, but she'd been too focused on her career to notice many men. Plus, he'd been a suspect at first, making him unsuitable to date, but now she was settled and he was cleared. And she couldn't deny that he was attractive.

"Hey, Captain," Clark, her newest recruit, said from the front desk. He had just graduated from the academy and was greener than she would have liked, but he seemed like a good kid. Eagerness and a willingness to learn were his best traits, and she would take those over a knowledgeable curmudgeon any day.

"Clark." She nodded at him before continuing through to the evidence room. Tad, Kelsey, and Brayden sat at their respective desks, but all looked up as they entered.

"Guys, this is Matt Fisher, er Bubba, the guy I was telling you about. He's the only one to escape the arsonist, and he's offered to lend whatever help he can. Bubba, you might remember Tad Brewer." She pointed to the dark haired lieutenant before turning to her other two officers. "This is Kelsey Knight and Brayden Cook."

Tad stood first and extended a hand. "Good to see you again, man." The two men shook and then Kelsey stood and threw out her hand as well.

Kelsey had been the first one hired after Makenna's predecessor, Stillman, had made captain. She was good, thorough, and though her thinner frame mislead people, she was tough as nails. Her blond hair was pulled back in its customary ponytail, and her face was nearly devoid of makeup. Still young, she could pull it off, and there were days when Makenna envied that fresh face.

"Nice to meet you, Bubba. Wish it was under better circumstances."

"As do I."

Brayden was the last to stand. He'd sent his application in right after the arsonist story made the news. Makenna hadn't been sure whether he was simply chasing the story or if he was hoping to be the one to break the case. He was tall and lanky, and he had an ego the size of Texas. Had it been her decision, she might not have hired him, but he had turned out to be a decent cop.

"Welcome, Bubba."

"Okay, now that introductions are made, let's catch Bubba up on the case. As you remember, there were three women killed the first time." Makenna moved over to the board where pictures were hanging. She pointed first to the young, perky blond. "Daisy Johnson who worked at the coffee shop you stopped at regularly." Her hand moved to the stunning brunette. "Alexis Gibbons who worked out at the same gym you did, and," her finger moved one more time to the final picture, a pretty redhead with a dusting of freckles across her nose, "Clarissa Wiggins who was a massage therapist and whom you dated briefly, am I right?"

Bubba nodded, but his eyes were wide as he looked from one

woman to the next. "When you lay it out like that, I can see why you thought I was a suspect."

Makenna nodded. "You were the only link we could find between these three women. Clarissa and Daisy didn't attend the same gym Alexis did. Neither Alexis nor Clarissa drank much coffee, and we found no record that Daisy or Alexis were ever clients of Clarissa."

"So, if the killer was after me, why go after these women? I barely knew Daisy. I mean I spoke to her the mornings I ordered coffee, but I'd never seen her outside of the coffee shop, and Alexis led the aerobics classes at my gym which I didn't take. The only one I had a true connection with was Clarissa, and we broke up months before she was killed. And it was amicable."

"That's what we've been trying to figure out," Tad spoke up and joined Makenna at the board. "At first we thought the killer was a spurned interest or something. All of these women are beautiful, so perhaps he tried to ask them out and was rejected. That made sense until the attempt on your life."

"When you were brought into the equation, we were left with two scenarios," Makenna continued. "Either the killer wanted to hurt you and he chose these women because he thought they meant something to you or you represented what he would never be."

"But if it were the latter, wouldn't he have kept killing even after me?" Bubba's eyes flicked from Tad to Makenna. "You said the killings stopped after the attempt on my life."

"They did. Until the other night. Now, we have another victim." She motioned to Kelsey who stood and took her place at the board.

"This is Peter Smith," Kelsey said pointing to a picture of a young looking man. "Single though we believe he had a girlfriend. He owned a repair shop on Fifth that he opened a few years ago. There's only one other employee, and we're still working on his friends, but his parents live here as well."

Bubba's brow creased as he gazed at the man. "I don't understand. I don't know that man, and he isn't in the same occupation that I am. Does the killer want to be both of us?"

Makenna exchanged glances with her team. Bubba not knowing Peter did blow a hole in the first theory, and he was right - the other man didn't look like him. He was smaller, more average looking, and his job didn't hold the clout that a firefighter's did. "We don't know."

She hated saying those words. She was supposed to be in control here, but this guy - if it was the same guy and not a copycat - just made no sense. Why the shift in victims? Why the long break? Why did he start killing again? There had to be some connection, some trigger, but she had no idea what it was.

Before she could say more, the door to the room opened and Natasha Kingston, head reporter for the Woodville Gazette and a pure pain in Makenna's backside, burst into the room. "Oh, my word, it is true."

Clark entered behind her, chagrined and apologetic. "Sorry, Captain, she blew right past me."

"It's fine, Clark." Makenna had dealt with Natasha enough to know the woman took pushy to a whole new level. Clark would have been no match for her. "What can I do for you, Natasha?"

Her bright red lips pursed as her eyes shifted from one person to the next until they finally landed on Bubba. "I thought Old Henry was yanking my chain when he burst into my office stating he had just seen a ghost. I almost wrote him off. I am in the middle of a big story, you know, but my back was aching, and I figured I could use a break. So, I decided I would see if there was any truth to the ghost of Matt Fisher getting out of your squad car and entering the building. Boy, am I glad I did."

Makenna rolled her eyes and stifled a sigh as Natasha pulled a portable recorder out of her purse and stepped toward Bubba. "Matt, do you want to tell me your story? I'd be delighted to write an exclusive on you."

Disgust erupted in Makenna's throat at the words that sounded more like a seductive purr than an actual question. While she wanted word to get out about Matt's return, Natasha would not have been her choice.

"Natasha, Matt just got to town. He hasn't even gotten the chance to see his family. Perhaps your exclusive could wait until tomorrow?"

Natasha turned to Makenna, a fake smile plastered on her face. "Captain Drake, it is my job to deliver the news to the good people of Woodville, and this is definitely news. Now, I could run yet another story on how the police department has yet to find the killer who is terrorizing our town after a five year hiatus, or," she turned back to Bubba, "you could give me a few minutes with our former hero here, and I could put out a much nicer piece."

Makenna forced herself to remain calm. Natasha was a dislikeable person, but she was just doing her job. Still, she didn't like the thought of Bubba being subjected to her, especially on his first day back before he'd even had the chance to reunite with his family. She looked to Bubba and shrugged. "I'll leave the decision up to him. We're done here for the day anyway."

Natasha's lips morphed into a sultry pout, and she placed a hand on Bubba's arm. "What do you say, Matt? Can I have a few minutes of your time?"

Though the desire to say no was written all over his face and evident in his posture, Bubba nodded. "Sure, I can give you a few minutes. On one condition."

"What's that?"

"You don't run the story until tomorrow. I want to talk to my folks before they read it in the paper."

Her lips pursed as she appeared to think over the offer. It was early afternoon, and Makenna thought Natasha could get a paper out tonight if she busted her butt, but did she want to work that hard? Besides, evening papers were a rarity in Woodville and most people wouldn't read it until the following morning anyway.

"Fine. I promise not to print it until tomorrow."

"Then you have yourself a deal."

Makenna wanted to apologize for putting Bubba on the spot, but there was no chance to get him alone during the short walk down the hall to one of the conference rooms. She waited in the door frame for an invitation to sit in, but when he didn't offer one, she took the hint and closed the door. He was an adult, and he could take care of himself. So, why did she hate the thought of leaving him alone with Natasha?

Bubba settled in his seat and leaned back. He was familiar with Natasha and knew that for the next few minutes, he would need to choose his words carefully. She was a good journalist, but like most, she tended to focus on the words that would make her story pop and bury the rest, even if it ended up twisting the meaning of the interviewee. Thankfully, he had avoided most situations with her when he worked at the firehouse, but he'd heard his captain complain more than once when what she printed took his words out of context.

"So, Matt, why did you let everyone here think you were dead five years ago? Were you hiding something?"

"On the contrary. After the attempt on my life, Captain Drake and I thought my "death" might keep the killer from going after my family."

"Really? You left your job as a fireman, deserted basically, and you want us to believe you did it to save your family? You were a suspect originally, am I right?"

Bubba didn't like where this was going, and he knew the spin on it would do nothing for his image. He didn't care so much about that as he did about the backlash that would fall on his parents. They'd probably already had to deal with questions and pitying looks and apologies for the last five years, he didn't want any more grief put on them.

He leaned forward and stared into Natasha's eyes. She was tough, but he was tougher, bigger, and had much more at stake. "I know you want a sensational story, Natasha, but that is the truth."

"Perhaps it is." Confidence flowed out of her voice, and her steely eyes never wavered. "But I find it odd that you were the main suspect until your house caught fire. And then after your "death," the fires stopped. Don't you find that a little coincidental?"

"I might. If I were you, and if they hadn't started back up again. What's your spin on that, Natasha? I was hundreds of miles away when this latest one happened."

She smiled, but it was not a warm, friendly smile, more the smile of a predator searching for her next meal. "I think there are two possibilities. Either, you came back early and wanted us to think you were still wherever you've been hiding, so that you would have an alibi. Or you have someone here you've been in contact with doing your dirty work."

Bubba shook his head and leaned away from her. "You have quite the imagination, Natasha, but why don't you try this one on. Imagine that you were the subject of a murder investigation even though you had dedicated your life to saving people. Imagine waking up to the smell of smoke and knowing that everything you own will soon be a pile of black ash. Imagine that you are told the only way to save the ones you love is to leave them forever, never communicate with them, and try to pretend they never existed. Imagine having to move to a new town with a name you've never been called, with a past not your own and try to fit in."

He pushed back his chair and stood up. "And if you finish

that and still think you should write the story in your head, then I want you to think about your parents. Think about them mourning you for five years and having to deal with questions and stares from the neighbors and people they once called friends. Imagine their joy when they realize you're alive and then their utter destruction when someone fabricates a story about you and calls it news simply because they can."

Her mouth opened, but Bubba had no intention of letting her have the last word. "You can write whatever story you want, Natasha, but God help your soul if you write the trash you can't back up with facts and pretend it's truth."

With that he walked out of the room and found himself face to face with an embarrassed Makenna.

"I'm sorry, I didn't mean to listen." The corners of her lips twitched as if fighting a smile. "But that was great. You don't know how many times I wanted to tell that woman off, but in my position-"

"Makenna," he said, cutting her off, "can you take me to see my parents?" He wasn't mad at Makenna, but frustration raged through him.

Her smile faltered as she shifted back into her profession. "Right. Of course. I'll take you right away."

"Makenna." He grabbed her arm as she stepped away from him. "I'm sorry. I didn't mean to snap at you. It's just been a long day, and I have no idea what that woman is going to write. I'd just like to spend some time with my parents before," he shrugged, "you know."

She offered a small smile. "I do, so let's get you home."

## 5

B ubba stared at the single level house that belonged to his parents. He had only spent a few years in this house as they had moved to Woodville when he was in high school, but for a time, at least, it had been home. Now, it felt like someone else's life. He hadn't been in this house for nearly five years, and he'd had no contact with his family since then either. What would they say? Would they hate him? His nerves twisted and knotted in his stomach, creating the feeling of having swallowed a lead weight.

"Should I come in with you?" Makenna asked, touching his arm.

The gentle feel of her hand focused Bubba, and he nodded. "That would be nice. There are parts I can't explain, but will your family mind you being out so late?"

A look of regret passed briefly over Makenna's face. "No one is waiting up for me except my cat, Tabitha."

Bubba knew that feeling. He'd tried dating a few women when he'd first moved to Fire Beach, but he could never completely relax. A sense of guilt about the women who had been murdered still plagued him even though he knew it wasn't his fault. Still, they had been killed simply because they knew him. That was hard to get over. Plus, deep down inside, a part of him feared it would happen again if he found someone and opened up about his past. It had just been easier to keep a distance and pretend he didn't need the company or the companionship, even though he did.

Perhaps Makenna was the same way. She'd definitely been devoted and eager when he'd met her five years ago. Maybe she too dealt with the guilt of never catching the arsonist or maybe her job was her life. To make captain as quickly as she had meant she was dedicated to her work. Perhaps, there was no time for a man in her life. He didn't know why that thought pulled at his heart.

"Okay, let's do this then." With a final deep breath, Bubba opened his door and stepped out of the police cruiser.

Makenna fell into step beside him as they walked up the concrete path to the front door. His finger was almost on the bell when Makenna's hand stilled his arm.

"Wait, Bubba, I should tell you that your "death" hit your parents hard. They've aged faster than they might have otherwise, I think." Her eyes brimmed with apologies. "I just thought you should be prepared."

Her words broke his heart, but Bubba had known the ruse would be hard on his parents. He was the oldest, their first born, and no parent should ever have to bury their child, no matter how old. He had argued about it with Makenna on the night of his escape.

*"I think we need to pretend you were killed, and you need to leave town,"* Makenna said as she paced her living room.

*Matt shot up from the couch and threw his hands in the air. "Are you kidding me? I have a life here. My family is here."*

*"That's exactly my point." She turned and closed the distance between them. "I thought you were the arsonist because all the women were connected to you, but now I think you may have been*

*the target all along. I think the arsonist was choosing women he thought you cared about, and when that didn't faze you, he targeted you. If we let him believe you're dead, then maybe this will end, but if he knows you're still alive, who will he target next? Felicity? Your mother? Your father? Do you really want their lives on your head?"*

*Matt stared into her eyes. Of course he didn't want to see his parents hurt or his foster sister, but was this really the only way? "You really think the killings will stop if he thinks I'm dead?" She was asking him to give up everything - his life, his family, his job. Everything he had worked so hard for, but if it meant the killings stopped, he had to do it, didn't he?*

*"I don't know, but my gut says yes. Look, let's get you out of town and continue the charade. If the killings continue, I'll bring you back and explain to your family. But if they don't continue, if they end-"*

*"Then you'll know it was about hurting me all along," Bubba finished. Why anyone would want to hurt him was beyond comprehension. He was a fireman. He saved lives. He attended church and volunteered. He donated to charities. Why would anyone want to hurt him? He searched his memory for any alter-cation, any event that might have been misconstrued enough to set someone off, but he came up with nothing.*

*"I'm sorry, Matt. I know this is a lot to ask, but I think it's the only way."*

And she'd been right. The killings had stopped. For five years. For five years, the people of Woodville had been safe. His family had been safe. But now that safety was crumbling yet again, and every bone in his body wanted to catch this guy. To stop him. To make him pay for the five years he had stolen from him.

He took a deep breath and then pressed the bell. The familiar melody echoed through the house, and a moment later, a soft shuffling sound carried forth. The lock clicked followed by a creak as the door opened, and then Bubba saw his mother's face for the first time in five years.

She did appear older. New lines had sprouted near her eyes and across her forehead, and her hair - once streaked with gray - was now completely devoid of color. But her eyes were the same deep pools of chocolate that he'd grown up seeing - the ones that oozed concern with every skinned knee and exuded love every time she kissed his forehead. They were filled with a resigned sadness now, but the light he remembered emerged as she recognized his face.

"Matt?" One hand flew to her mouth as the other gripped the door more tightly to keep her steady.

"Hi, Mom," he said, hoping she wouldn't pass out. He wasn't sure he'd make it through the door in time to catch her.

"Matt?" She let go of the door and then her hands were on his chest, his arms, his face, patting him as if to make sure he was real and not an apparition. "It's really you?"

"It's really me, Mom." Emotion choked his voice and tears stung his eyes, but it didn't matter. His mother threw her arms around him, and he returned the hug, relishing the warmth of family for the first time in half a decade.

"Margaret, who is it?" His father's voice carried in from the living room, and the familiar tone sent a flood of memories washing over Bubba.

"You better come see for yourself." His mother's voice was quiet, but it held a note of authority and moments later, his father appeared in the doorway. He too had aged, but the effects were not quite as dramatic. His hair was grayer, but he still stood straight and displayed the confidence in his posture that the military had taught him so long ago.

"Hi, Dad." His mother still clung to him, but he stood taller than she did and could see over her head.

"Matt? Is that you?" His father's eyes roamed his face as if he couldn't believe it, and then they turned to Makenna. "What is this? Is this your idea of some sick game?"

Bubba flinched at the sharp edge in his father's voice.

"If you'll let us come inside, I'll explain everything," Makenna said beside him. Though her exterior appeared brave, Bubba could see that his father's words had shaken her normal stoic face. A slight tremble hovered in her voice.

"Let's let them in, Patrick," his mother said, and though she did not let go of Bubba entirely, she shifted so that her arm remained firmly around him, but she could see his father. His father hesitated, but then he stepped back, and Makenna and Bubba entered the living room.

Waves of nostalgia washed over him as he took in the faded couch and the well-worn recliner where his father always drank his morning coffee. A painting his brother had made in high school still sat over the couch, and even the color of the walls was the same. It was like time had stood still in this living room, and Bubba wondered if they might be able to pick up where they left off.

"I'm going to call Felicity and see if she wants to come over," Margaret said as she motioned everyone to sit down. "She'll be so happy. She's had a rough week, but this might be just the thing to cheer her up."

"What do you mean a rough week?" Makenna asked. Though it was rare for an arsonist to be a woman, she was counting no one out, and as the murders had just started, anyone who'd had anything upsetting in the last month was a suspect in her book.

"She and her boyfriend broke up. They'd been together for years. She's pretty torn up about it, but she'll be so glad to know you're not dead." For a moment, she paused as if afraid Bubba might disappear if she wasn't touching him, but then she pulled out her cell phone and dialed.

Makenna sized up her options as everyone sat down. Patrick sat on the couch and Bubba took the recliner which left standing or sitting in the other chair. She didn't want to stay long and interrupt their family reunion, but standing seemed rude.

"Felicity, Matt is alive. He's here right now. You must come over and see him." She paused while she listened to the voice on the other end, and then her smile faltered. "But can't that wait until later?"

Makenna watched Margaret's reaction. Had his sister really declined coming to see the brother she thought was dead? That seemed odd to her. Had it been her brother, she would have dropped everything to come see him.

"Okay, I'll tell him. See you later." Margaret hung up the phone and stared at it a moment. "Um, she said she had some work she couldn't leave tonight, but she'll come see you tomorrow, Matt."

He flashed her a sympathetic smile. "It's fine, Mom."

She nodded, but she didn't appear convinced. "I'll call Jacob and Rachel. I know they don't live here anymore, but they'll want to know."

Bubba stood and placed a hand on her shoulder. "Mom, why don't you let Makenna explain first and then we can call anyone you want, okay?"

She nodded and allowed herself to be led to the couch. Bubba squeezed her shoulder and then returned to the recliner.

Makenna took a deep breath as she stared at Patrick and Margaret staring back at her. Flashbacks of the night she had come to tell them Matt was dead filled her mind, and she had to blink to dispel them.

"Five years ago, I sat here and told you that Matt had been killed in a house fire," she began, "but that wasn't the truth."

"You lied to us?" Patrick exploded, jumping up from the couch. "I'll have your badge for this."

"Please, Dad, hear her out." Bubba motioned for his father to sit back down.

She shot him a grateful look and then continued. "When the fires first started, the only clues we had pointed to Matt being involved. He knew all the women, and he had knowledge of how to start fires. But, then the killer went after Matt. He escaped that night and came to me. I realized then that Matt might have been the target all along. The killer chose the women he did in order to hurt Matt, and when that wasn't working, he went after Matt himself. I asked Matt to continue the charade that he had died. I knew that if the killings stopped, my assumption would be right. It meant Matt would have to stay "dead" to all of us, but it would keep you safe. If the killings had continued, I would have told you his death was a lie, and he could have returned home."

"I hated not being able to say goodbye," Bubba said, "but if it meant keeping you both safe, it was worth it."

A tear escaped Margaret's face, and she crossed the room to where Bubba was sitting. "Oh, my baby! That must have been so hard on you."

Makenna looked away from the touching scene. This was her fault. Her decision had torn this family apart five years ago, and those were years they would never get back. She'd have to live with the consequences of that decision for the rest of her life.

"I assume you've brought him back because of the recent murder." Patrick said from the couch. His crossed arms and passive face hid his emotions, and Makenna wondered what he was thinking.

"Yes, sir. The other night, a man was killed in a house fire. I believe it is the same guy even though we aren't sure why he is attacking men now instead of women. My hope is that when the killer finds out he didn't kill Matt after all that he'll mess up and give us some clue."

"So, you're using my son as a pawn once again."

"Dad," Bubba cut in, "she's not using me. She asked and I agreed. Besides, it allowed me to see you guys again."

"I don't like it," his father said. "She was wrong the first time. What if she's wrong this time too, but you really do get hurt?"

"Dad, you know I can't just sit around knowing people are being killed. I have to at least try to help."

"You always were like that," Margaret said, stroking Bubba's hair. "I remember you used to always bring home stray animals to save them. Do you remember that?"

"I do, Mother."

Bubba appeared embarrassed by the hint of his childhood, and Makenna took that as her cue to let them catch up. "Well, it's getting late, and I have a feeling you'd all like to catch up." She turned to Bubba. "How about I swing by around nine in the morning and pick you up? I'd like you to go with me to interview some of the friends and employees of our victim."

"That sounds great. I'll see you then, Captain Drake."

Makenna stood and walked through the uncomfortable fog that filled the room. She might have reunited the family, but she'd also been the one who tore them apart. Nothing could change that, and she knew it would be a choice that would haunt her forever.

Was this why she had avoided having a family of her own? Was she so jaded from watching families grieve that she unconsciously pushed men away? Or was it simply her job? Even though they didn't have a lot of crime, her work load had increased dramatically with each promotion, and now as captain, she spent most of her time at work. Yes, that was probably it. There was no time for a family or even a man in her life as long as she stayed in her current position which left the question, was it time for a change?

## 6

Makenna showed up at nine a.m. on the dot the next morning, and though Bubba wasn't sure what help he would be able to provide, he was glad for the excuse to get out of the house for a few hours. He loved his parents, and he loved catching up with them, but the emotional intensity had been a little much for him to handle. He hadn't been that close to anyone in the last five years.

"You ready?" Makenna asked him as he slid into the passenger seat of her cruiser.

"As I'll ever be, I guess."

"How was the reunion?" Her eyes glanced his way for only a moment, but he could tell his answer was important to her. He couldn't imagine the weight she must be carrying.

"It was good. I'd almost forgotten how much I missed having a family. I think I spent half the time just staring at them to prove to myself it was real."

Her jaw tightened, and he knew he had just made her feel worse even though that wasn't his intention. "Makenna, I don't blame you. You did what you thought was right." His words probably wouldn't relieve the guilt she was placing on herself, but he had to try.

"Thank you, Bubba, but I can't get back the time you lost, and that's a little hard to come to grips with."

There was nothing he could say at this point to change her mind, so he decided to change the subject instead. "Where are we going?"

"First stop is coffee and then we'll hit Peter's repair shop."

"Sounds good." Bubba stared out the window as Makenna drove through town. Not much had changed. The post office looked the same, and the parking lot still held the flagpole where the faded American flag waved gently in the breeze. Bubba was glad to see it still flying - there had been a debate over whether to take it down shortly before he'd left town. Evidently some new residents found it offensive, something Bubba would never understand.

A frozen yogurt store with a large neon sign was new as was some sort of gaming center. At least that's what he assumed it was from the name Creative Consoles. And then there were the new hotels. He had never understood why the town had so many hotels. They had no claim to fame - no big sports team, no prestigious university, not even a famous statue like some of the towns near them. So, what brought people to Woodville? Was it the feeling of peace and tranquility the surrounding woods provided? Was it its location away from big cities? Was it the promise of a simpler life that the downtown buildings seemed to boast with their faded paint and weathered signage?

The coffee shop she pulled into was not the same one Bubba had frequented when he lived here as they were on the other side of town from the firehouse, but it was bustling nonetheless. He could remember a time when there was only one coffee shop in town, and it was never busy. Now, patrons filled every table, and a line of at least five more stood waiting to order.

"Busy place," Bubba remarked as he took in the interior which appeared much like most other coffee shops he had been in. The walls were a soft tan color which was brought out in the tile flooring. Tables capable of sitting four filled the room with a few smaller tables made for two by the windows, and one small couch sat nestled in the corner surrounded by a reading lamp and a glass table. A man immersed in his laptop took up most of the couch, and his books filled the other side. He lifted his mug to sip every few seconds but never seemed to look away from his screen.

"I know," Makenna said with a frown as she checked her watch, "but it's the best coffee in town, I think, so it's worth the wait."

The line moved quickly, and they reached the front in under ten minutes. "Welcome to Love a Latte," the employee said as she placed the previous payment in the register. "How can I-" Her words cut off as she raised her eyes and met Bubba's gaze. The color drained from her face as if she'd seen a ghost, which in his case, he guessed she sort of had. "Oh mylanta, as I live and breathe. Matt Fisher, is that you?"

"It is," Bubba said quietly, hoping she would do the same, but he should have known better. Daphne Rodgers had been a cheerleader and a prominent thespian in high school. Two things that rarely seemed to go together, but worked for Daphne. Outgoing and bubbly, temerity was not her strong suit.

"I thought you were dead. Everyone said you died in the house fire five years ago."

Heads turned their direction as her words floated over the hum of conversation. "Matt Fisher? I thought he died." "Who's Matt Fisher?"

Bubba felt the eyes of the customers on his back, and he turned and offered a small smile and a wave. Most simply stared at him in confusion, but one pair of eyes seemed to burn with an angry intensity. He stared back at the woman, curious as to why she might have so much hatred toward him, but he didn't recognize her. At least he didn't think he did. Perhaps, she was just angry that his entrance had disintegrated her silence. The laptop in front of her might hold her work as it did for the man on the couch or a book.

"It's a long story," Makenna spoke up beside him. "Can we just get our coffees to go?" Her authoritative voice dragged his attention back to Daphne who still stared at him with wide, disbelieving eyes.

"Sure. Sorry, I didn't mean to blow your cover. I'm just so glad to know you're not dead." She gazed at Bubba a little longer than necessary before taking their orders and payment.

Bubba still felt as if every eye was on him and every whisper discussed him as they waited at the end of the counter for the drinks. "It's going to be like this everywhere, isn't it?"

"It's what I was hoping for honestly," Makenna whispered back. "Word will spread like wildfire, and hopefully the killer will tip his hand."

"And if he doesn't?"

Makenna's lips pinched together, and she shook her head. Evidently she didn't want to think about that possibility either. They stood in silence for a minute, until their drinks were placed on the counter. Then, drinks in hand, they made their way out of the shop.

Bubba sighed with relief as he slid into the passenger seat. He was not used to being the focus of attention, and it would only get worse when Natasha's article came out.

"So, how do you know Daphne Rodgers?" Makenna asked as she pulled her door shut, closing the two of them off from prying eyes and ears. "She seemed mighty interested in you."

He took a sip of his coffee as he debated his answer. It was good; the hazelnut just strong enough to add flavor. "We went to high school together. She was the head cheerleader, and I was the captain of the football team, so everyone expected us to be together. I think she wanted to date me, but I was looking for a woman with a little more substance to her."

Daphne had been pretty with her auburn hair and bright green eyes, and she certainly was adored by everyone at the school, but Bubba had tried having a few conversations with her, and every time he had left feeling as if a few intelligence points had trickled out of his brain. So, he'd never been able to date her.

"Vapid?" Makenna asked as she pulled out of the parking lot.

Bubba smiled at her. "To say the least. She hounded me all through school, and she would try to stop by the firehouse when she knew I was working."

"Do you think she felt slighted by you?"

"Enough to kill people?" Bubba couldn't believe they were having this conversation about Daphne Rodgers of all people. She hadn't even dissected the frog in biology because of her aversion to blood and all things disgusting - her exact words if he remembered correctly.

Makenna shrugged and, after sipping her own coffee, placed it in the middle cup holder. "Sometimes the visage we see is not the real person underneath."

"Visage? I don't think I've heard that word since high school English class."

A soft pink colored Makenna's cheeks, and she averted her gaze from his as she inserted the key into the ignition. "I may be guilty of reading a few classic novels in my free time."

Bubba chuckled. He was guilty of the same thing. At the firehouse, he hid his books under the mattress so as not to get razzed by Luca. He'd seen Bubba reading *A Tale of Two Cities* once and teased him mercilessly for the next week. "I'm guilty too, but I think you're wrong about Daphne. What you see is pretty much what you get, and I can't imagine her starting fires."

"You're probably right." Makenna sighed. "I'm just so

focused on finding this guy that I'm seeing connections where there might be nothing."

"We'll find him." But as Bubba leaned back in the seat, he wasn't sure if he was trying to reassure Makenna or himself more.

"Was this always here?" Bubba asked as they pulled into Peter's repair shop. "I don't remember an auto repair shop here before."

Makenna turned off the engine and stared out the windshield at the large black tire atop a metal pole that sat to the right of the building. Above the door, the sign read: Peter's Parts. "No, you wouldn't. It used to be a butcher shop until Peter converted it a few years ago. Seemed like a nice enough guy. A little rough on the exterior but good at his job."

"So, what are you hoping to find here?"

She turned to face him and shrugged. "I honestly don't know. A disgruntled employee, a jealous ex, a secret smuggling operation. Some reason for someone to want him dead." One corner of her mouth twitched up into a half smile. "I'm reaching at this point, but what have I got to lose?"

"I'll follow your lead then," Bubba said and then opened his door.

Makenna was actually a little surprised to see the open sign on the door. It was a small business, and she only knew of one other employee besides Peter. Was he trying to run it on his own? She supposed there could have been more than just the one guy she knew of. She'd only been here a couple of times when the check engine light came on in her cruiser. Though usually nothing, she could never ignore warning signs in her official vehicle like she could in her own car. They always had to be in perfect working order. Just in case.

The soft tinkling of an overhead bell announced their

entrance, and a blonde popped up from behind the counter. Sparkly was the best word Makenna could come up with to describe her. Her tightly curled hair - most likely from a perm - fell to her shoulders. Glittery eyeshadow covered her lids, and her mouth glistened with some shade of pink. In addition, her top sported sequins that caught the light and appeared to shimmer. She looked anachronistic, like she belonged on a bad eighties sitcom instead of current time. Makenna had heard of previous fashions coming back in style, but even if that was the case, and she certainly hoped it wasn't, this was quite the odd outfit choice for someone working in a repair shop.

"Who are you?" Makenna asked. She'd never seen this woman before. She rarely forgot faces, and this getup was one that would regrettably be burned into her retinas for some time.

The girl placed her hands akimbo on her hips, and Makenna expected her to smack gum loudly in her mouth as she spoke. "I'm Skye. Who are you?"

No gum, but the effect was still there. "I'm Captain Makenna Drake. Do you work here, Skye?"

"Do I look like I work here?" she asked rolling her eyes. "No. I'm Peter's ex-girlfriend. He owed me money, and I came to collect what I was owed."

"You can't steal money from his shop." Makenna hoped she wasn't going to have to arrest this woman and book her for theft. That hadn't been on her plans for the day and would mean paperwork to fill out, sucking her time from the more important matter at hand of finding a killer.

"I'm not stealing. I'm taking what's mine. He owed me a hundred dollars." She raised one manicured hand to flick her blond hair off her shoulder.

Makenna's eyes narrowed as her intuition perked into gear. As the saying went, money was the root of all evil, and she'd seen men killed for less. An ex-girlfriend with a monetary vendetta certainly had motive, and Skye had just made herself a suspect. "What for?"

"For spilling beer on my purse. I had to throw it away because I couldn't get the smell out," she wrinkled her nose and shivered, "but he promised he'd buy me a new one. Course then I saw him schmoozing with my ex-best friend a few days later. That's when we broke up, but he still owes me the money for the purse he ruined."

Makenna's head spun, and she glanced at Bubba to see if he found this as preposterous as she did. He shrugged and shook his head, clearly agreeing with her unspoken question. Did this woman have any idea how much motive she had just laid out before Makenna? Somehow, she doubted it. "Let me get this straight. Your boyfriend ruined your purse and cheated on you with your best friend?"

Skye's eyes widened as she nodded. "See? You get it. He wasn't a great boyfriend anyway, but cheaters get what they deserve."

"Uh huh. Skye, where were you two nights ago?" Makenna asked. This woman hardly looked capable of killing a spider should it run across her path, let alone a man, but not only did she have motive, she had also just stated that Peter had gotten what he deserved. Makenna would be remiss if she didn't at least ask.

"You mean when Peter was killed?" Skye's tone stayed completely even as if the thought of his death didn't affect her at all. "I was with Nick. Nick, come here and tell this fine police officer about our second date."

Nick stepped out of the work bay area, a complete opposite of Skye. As he was covered in grease and at least one tattoo that Makenna could see peeking from his collar, she assumed the bulging muscles protruding from his sleeves was what attracted Skye to him.

"You're dating Peter's employee?" Makenna asked. Now, she suddenly had two suspects. "Did Peter know?"

"He saw us together the night before he was killed," Skye said with a shrug as if this sort of thing happened every day. "Made a big scene about it and everything. I don't know why since he was still with my ex-best friend."

Makenna felt like slapping her forehead or pinching herself to make sure this was real. This situation was more like a "B" horror movie than actual life. "I'm afraid I'm going to have to bring you both in for questioning."

"What for?" Skye's wide eyes appeared clueless. Did she really not understand what she had just admitted?

"For saying too much," Nick hissed under his breath. Clearly he was the brains in the relationship which Makenna wasn't sure was saying much. "You just made us both suspects in Peter's death."

"What? But we didn't kill Peter. I can't be arrested. I can't have mug shots."

"I'm not arresting you." Makenna couldn't believe this woman was more worried about mug shots than a possible murder rap. "Not yet. But I do need to ask you a few questions. If you come with me, I won't have to pull out the handcuffs."

"I'll answer whatever you need as long as there are no mugshots."

"I can't believe you got me into this," Nick grumbled as he glared at Skye. "Now, I have to close the shop and lose money."

Makenna rolled her eyes at Bubba as she opened the back door for Nick and Skye. She'd quit her job on the spot if either of these two turned out to be the arsonist. Still, with so few leads, she couldn't let any possibility slip through her fingers.

"Looks like we'll be making a slight detour before talking to family. Do you mind?"

Bubba shrugged his broad shoulders. "I've got nothing else to do today."

Makenna flashed him a grateful smile. She felt taxed and overburdened by this case, but just having Bubba around calmed her a little though she didn't know why. Maybe it was the sheer masculinity he exuded. Maybe it was that he had been involved in the original case. Maybe it was the simple fact that she hadn't really conversed with a man not employed by her in ages, and it felt nice. She really needed to look into taking some time off when this case was wrapped up.

## 7

Surprise shot through Bubba as they pulled up to the station and he noticed Felicity standing against the wall. His mother had said Felicity would try to see him today, but he had expected she would come to the house tonight, not show up at the police station. Though she hadn't appeared to change as much as his parents, the tight ponytail holding back her dark hair made her facial features appear more severe than normal.

Felicity was not his biological sister. After he and his siblings graduated high school, his parents felt the desire to help more kids, and they began fostering. Felicity was one of those foster kids. She joined their family when she was seventeen and Bubba was twenty-one, so he was not as close with her as he was with his biological brother and sister. But when Jacob and Rachel had moved away, he and Felicity had spent more time together, and they had grown closer the last year before he left.

Almost too close from Bubba's point of view though. There had been a few times when he'd heard her mumble snide remarks once or twice when he brought a woman home to meet his parents. As if she had any say. Still, she was family, and she'd had a rough childhood, so Bubba had always dismissed it.

"Why don't you take a few minutes to reconnect, and I'll come back for you when you're through?" Makenna asked as if reading his mind.

Bubba nodded and opened his door.

"Matt Fisher, I can't believe you let me think you were dead for five years."

He was unsure if the anger in her voice was real or forced, but before he could decide, she threw her arms around him in a giant hug.

"I've been so lonely without you here. How could you just leave without a word?" she asked when the hug ended and she stepped back.

"It was important to the case, Felicity. When the arsonist made an attack on me, Captain Drake figured we would all be safer if he thought I was dead."

A dark expression took over Felicity's face for a moment as she watched Makenna walk inside, and then as quickly as it came, it was gone. "Turns out she was wrong though, wasn't she? Since the murders have started again? So, you lost five years of your life and put us through the ringer for nothing."

Bubba didn't appreciate the tone in Felicity's voice even though that very thought had crossed his mind when Makenna first reappeared in his life. "She couldn't have known that though, and I was worried the killer would go after you or Mom and Dad. Plus, they didn't start again for five years, so for awhile, at least, Makenna was right."

"Hmph. Well, anyway, it's good to see you again, big brother." She placed a hand on his arm and squeezed. "I've missed you."

The last three words felt wrong as they landed on Bubba's ears, and his body stiffened. He didn't even know why, but something in the tone of them had been off. Perhaps he was making

too much out of it though. Coming back to a town where
everyone believed you were dead and stared and whispered about
you was much harder than it had sounded initially, and it could be
that he was the one off. He was definitely out of his comfort zone.

"It's good to see you again too, Felicity." He patted her hand
before removing it from his arm. "You couldn't have missed me
that much though since you didn't come over last night."

Another cloud crossed her face for a moment and then she
smiled. "Yeah, sorry, I wasn't feeling well, and I had some work
to catch up on, but you should come over for dinner tonight.
Now that Roger and I are no longer together, I suddenly have a
lot of free time on my hands."

The idea of a dinner alone with Felicity sent the hairs on the
back of Bubba's neck up, but it would be rude not to accept,
especially since she was family. "Sure, that sounds good. I'm
staying with Mom and Dad, so maybe we should all do dinner
together there."

Her lips pulled into a tight smile. "Yeah, that would be great.
I'll see you tonight."

The door behind him opened as Felicity walked away.
"Everything okay?" Makenna asked.

He watched his sister walk away and tried to put a finger on
what was bothering him, but it was still too ambiguous. "Yeah,
fine, it's just weird being back here. Everyone feels different or
maybe I'm just different."

She placed a hand on his arm, and Bubba's gaze dropped to
the heat creeping up his arm from her touch. How different her
touch felt from Felicity's "I know it's hard, but it will get easier."

"I certainly hope so," he said as he followed her toward the
station door, but as he grasped the handle, he wondered if that
was true. Did one really ever get used to being the focus of town
gossip? As the door swung open, a movement to the right caught
his eye. He peered closer, but nothing appeared different.

"You okay?" Makenna asked.

"Yeah, I thought I saw something, but I must just be tired. I'm good." Still, he gave the surrounding area one more perusal before he followed Makenna inside.

"I can't take you in the interrogation room, but you can watch the whole thing from here," Makenna said, showing Bubba into a small room with a few chairs. On either side were large windows that looked into the interrogation rooms. Skye sat in the room on the left and Nick in the room on the right. She hadn't had many people watch interrogations, but the thought of Bubba on the other side of the glass sent her nerves coiling in her stomach. Was she afraid of messing up in front of him? Afraid of what he might think?

She shouldn't care what he thought. He lived in Fire Beach and her life was here. Besides, their schedules would probably never work, but she couldn't deny that there was something about Bubba. Growing up with two older brothers and learning to shoot rifles at the age of twelve, Makenna was used to defending and taking care of herself. She'd always felt tough and maybe a little too masculine, but Bubba made her feel feminine again. His six foot two frame dwarfed her five feet seven inches, and he exuded a protective vibe. She could imagine a life with someone like him, a life where she didn't feel like she always had to be the one calling the shots.

"I'm going to talk to Skye first and then Nick, though I doubt I'll get much," Makenna said, forcing her mind away from thoughts of curling up on a couch in Bubba's arms and to the task at hand. She turned up the knob to Skye's room. "This way you can hear us. When the interview is over, you can turn this down and turn the one on the other side up."

"Sounds good. I've never been on this side before," Bubba said with a playful smile. "I bet I'll enjoy it more."

Makenna swallowed the sting of embarrassment. Now that she knew him better, she couldn't believe she had ever thought he could be a killer, but she'd been greener then and the evidence had pointed to him - what little they'd had. Still, as much as she wished she could erase that experience, it had made her a better cop. She didn't jump to conclusions as quickly, and she challenged herself to consider other options.

"I'm sure you will," she said as she exited the room. She grabbed the folder with the case files from a hanging compartment outside of Skye's room and then pushed open the door.

"Do I get to go home soon?" Skye asked as Makenna entered the interrogation room. "I thought this was going to just be a few quick questions."

"I'll get you out as soon as I can," Makenna said pulling out the chair across from Skye and sitting down. Her eyes wandered to the two-way mirror, but she forced them back to the folder in her hand. "Now, tell me again where you were on the night of the sixteenth."

Skye sighed and rolled her eyes. "I told you. I was out with Nick."

"Right, your second date. Did he pick you up?"

"No way," Skye said with a shake of her head. "I don't let a guy know where I live until the fifth date. Have to make sure he's not crazy, you know?"

Makenna bit her lip to keep from laughing. This woman exemplified crazy but didn't seem to recognize it. "Okay, so where did you meet?"

"At Darby's over on Sixth Avenue. I wanted to go dancing, but he wanted dinner first, so we decided to meet up there." Skye ran her hand through her blonde mane, fluffing the hair as she did.

"And what time was that?" Makenna asked as she made a note in the file.

"Seven. I remember because we were only able to get one drink before their happy hour ended at seven-thirty. Who ends a happy hour that early?"

"I don't know." Makenna didn't drink, so she had no answer to the question. She'd only ever tried alcohol once, and it had been disgusting enough to turn her off of it after that. She still remembered leaning against the tractor on a hot, sunny day and watching her father pop the beer can open. The sound of the fizz had fascinated her, and she'd asked him for a drink. He'd paused and then, evidently deciding it wouldn't hurt, he'd held the can out to her. The smell had hit her first, that weird yeasty odor, but being the fearless child she was, she had tipped back the can and filled her mouth only to spit most of it out again when it hit her taste buds. That had been her first and last drink, so she had no idea what restaurants even had happy hours. "What time did you leave?"

"Eight thirty. I wanted to get into The Hop before they raised the price at nine."

The Hop was the closest thing to a club that Woodville offered. A couple had purchased the old warehouse a few years ago and fixed it up. Makenna had broken up many fights in that place.

"And how long were you two there?"

Skye placed her hands on the table and leaned forward. "Only till midnight. I had to work the next morning, and if I don't get a full eight hours, this is a puffy mess the next day." She made a circle around her face.

Midnight would be cutting it close. The fire was reported at one a.m., so she supposed Skye could have had time to get home, grab supplies, and get over to Peter's house, but every bone in Makenna's body was telling her that this woman was not a killer. "I'm assuming you left The Hop alone?"

"No, I left with Nick. We had taken one car from Darby's, so he drove me back there, but I left Darby's alone and so did Nick. Are we done now? I really have to get my nail fixed." She held out her hand and wiggled her ring finger. That nail didn't look any different than the others to Makenna, but she didn't say that.

"Almost. I have a few more questions, and I need to talk to Nick, but then I'll get you processed." Unless Skye said something revealing with the next few questions, Makenna didn't have enough to hold her even if she wanted to.

"Do you know any of these women?" Makenna pulled the photos of the three women out of the folder and spread them on the table.

"Her," Skye said, pointing to the fitness instructor. "I took a few classes with her, but I don't know the rest."

"Okay, thank you, Skye. I'll be back in a minute." Makenna slid the photos back into the folder and exited the room. She had to question Nick, but she was certain his answers would be the same.

## ❦ 8 ❦

**B**ubba found the whole interrogation process fascinating, but a part of him felt they were wasting time interviewing these two. Skye had seemed to have nothing more than a weak motive to kill Peter, and if her alibi checked out, there would be no need to question her further. Plus, she didn't seem to know any of the other victims. Which begged the question of who would? Even though Woodville was a smaller town, what sort of person would know all five people from very different jobs and social statuses?

He turned the knob up on Nick's room, but before Makenna began the process, his phone rang. Cassidy's number flashed across the screen, and Bubba smiled as he clicked the talk button. It had only been two days, but he missed his friends back home.

"Hey, Cassidy, how are you?"

"I'm fine, Bubba. How are you doing there? Have you found any leads?"

"Not much yet. Makenna is interrogating a couple who knew the victim, but I don't think they did it." He glanced over at Nick and Makenna, but Nick leaned back in his chair, laid back and relaxed, as if he had nothing to hide.

"How's it been coming back from the dead?"

Bubba couldn't stop the sigh that escaped his lips. "That part has been harder for sure. You know me. I'm not one for the lime-light, and it is on me everywhere I go here. How is everything back there?"

"Oh, you know, the same. A lot of sitting, a little bickering, and a few fires to put out. Thankfully, it's been a little quieter."

"Are Deacon and Luca still at it?"

Cassidy laughed on the other end. "When aren't they?"

"Yeah." Bubba missed the camaraderie of his friends. After he'd had to leave his family behind, Luca, Deacon, Cassidy, and the rest of the firefighters had become his surrogate family. As much as he was enjoying seeing his Mom and Dad again and even spending time with Makenna, he couldn't wait to get back. "Hopefully, we'll figure this out soon, and I'll be able to help you buffer them."

"We're all praying for you," Cassidy said.

Praying. That was something he hadn't done enough of since he arrived here. He should do that. If life had shown him anything, it was that he couldn't do much on his own, but with God, all things were possible.

"Thanks for the reminder, Cassidy. I need to do some more of that myself."

Before she could reply, he heard the sound of the alarm going off behind her. "Gotta run, Bubba, but we'll talk again soon."

The line went dead before he could say goodbye, but he took no offense to it. A fire took precedence over everything, and he'd been guilty of the same behavior more than once. He put the phone back in his pocket and decided now would be the perfect time to do what he should have done so much sooner.

"Lord, I'm not sure how to progress from here. Please give

Makenna and me the knowledge on where to go and what to do next. And please keep the people of this town safe."

He let the words repeat in his mind as he turned his attention back to Nick and Makenna in the interrogation room.

Makenna thanked Nick and Skye for their time as she led them to the front door. "Please make sure you stay in town in case we have any more questions."

"We aren't going anywhere," Nick said. "I have a shop to run now at least until I find out if Peter left it to anyone else in his will."

Skye said nothing, but she nodded in agreement as she followed him out the front door.

"Well, that wasn't much of a help," Makenna said as she turned to Bubba. "Not that I expected it to be, but I was hoping we might gain some new knowledge."

"Maybe we will with his family?" Bubba asked.

"Yeah." Makenna checked her watch. It was nearly lunch time, but Kelsey had said Peter's parents were retired. Hopefully, they were the kind who stayed home and not the kind who filled their hours with traveling or shopping. "We better get going then."

As she reached for the door handle, the door flew open and Natasha Kingston entered, the glare on her face darker than a tornadic cloud. She shoved a paper at Bubba. "Here. I wrote your feel good resurrection story, but this isn't over yet. I'll be watching you, Matt Fisher." She narrowed her eyes at him before turning her vitriol on Makenna. "You too, Captain Drake. You better hope you find the killer this time or I'll strongly be advocating that we find a new captain." Before Makenna could utter a reply, Natasha spun around and left in the same whirlwind manner she had entered.

"Well, that's always fun," Makenna remarked, but Bubba's focus was on the paper in his hands. "Is it bad?" Natasha had stated it was a feel good piece, but Makenna knew that Natasha's definition of things wasn't always the same as her own.

"No, surprisingly, it's not, and it's probably exactly the publicity you were hoping for. I just hope it doesn't put my family in danger."

Makenna hadn't even considered how Matt's return might endanger his family, and she mentally kicked herself for not thinking it all the way through before acting. She'd thought she had gotten better at that but evidently not. She touched his arm and waited until he met her gaze. "We'll keep them safe, Bubba. I promise."

He nodded, but she knew he was thinking the same thing she was. How? They still had no idea who this killer was or how he chose his victims, and other than not sleeping at night, no way to stop him. But she was determined that she would not let his family be harmed any more than it already had been.

She led the way out of the station, and a few minutes later, they were on the road. Peter's parents' house was a small rambler on the outskirts of town that looked as if it had seen better days. Large curls of paint flaked from the house, and the grass appeared brown and crunchy. It hadn't rained much, so most people's grass was more brown than green, but this lawn was the epitome of neglect.

"I guess Peter didn't help out much around the house," Bubba said as his eyes scanned the yard.

"Yeah, it doesn't appear so." Makenna wondered how a son could do that. She didn't live near her parents, but if she did, she would definitely come help them out and she had little free time. Surely Peter had more time. She doubted he'd taken his work home with him like she did most days.

The porch creaked under their feet, and Makenna hoped it

wouldn't crumble beneath their combined weight. There was no bell, so she rapped on the door and pulled out her badge. She'd worked with enough older people to know most of them wanted to see a badge before they would open their doors.

"Who is it?" a woman's voice called from the other side.

"Captain Makenna Drake with the police department," she said, holding her badge up to the peephole.

There was a moment of silence and then the door opened. A crack. Enough for a pair of eyes to peer out and observe them but not enough to see the woman's face. "Who's that with you?" The eyes flicked to Bubba.

"This is my friend Bubba. He's a firefighter who is helping me with a case. We need to ask you some questions about Peter."

The door opened a little farther to reveal a petite, weathered woman. Time had shown her little mercy. Age spots marred her face, and her hair, while still brown, was so thin in places that her scalp shown through. "I'm not sure what I can tell you. Peter stopped coming around about a year ago."

"Was there a reason?"

The woman shrugged and dropped her gaze to the floor. "He wanted money for his business. I guess it wasn't doing too well, but we didn't have any. We suggested he come work for his dad - he's an electrician - but Peter wanted nothing to do with that. Said if we didn't have money to help him, we weren't good parents. He never came over after that."

Makenna couldn't imagine someone disowning their parents simply because they couldn't afford to help, and she wondered if that was what had affected this woman so profoundly. "Was that his normal behavior?"

"No." His mother's eyes glistened with unshed tears. "He was the sweetest boy in high school. I don't know what made him change except maybe money. We never had much when he was growing up, but he always had food, clothes, and a roof over his head." She said this as if reassuring Makenna, or maybe herself, that she hadn't been a bad parent.

"When he first started his business, it was to help people. He'd always been good with cars - tinkered on ours from about the age of twelve - and he decided he would use that skill to help people. Lord knows we'd have been out more money than we could afford plenty of times if we hadn't had Peter to fix our cars, but then I guess he got greedy. Began raising his prices and complaining when people couldn't pay their bills."

Makenna's heart went out to the woman. She couldn't imagine how hard it would be to see your son behave so uncharacteristically and then cut you out of his life. "I'm so sorry for that and for your loss, but can I ask you just a few more questions?"

The woman sniffed, wiped a hand under her eyes, and nodded. "Sure, go ahead."

Makenna pulled the pictures out of the folder tucked under her arm. "Do you recognize any of these women? Ever see Peter with them or hear him talk about them?"

The woman took the photos and flipped them slowly. "No, I don't recognize any of them. Do you think they had something to do with his death?"

"I'm not sure, ma'am, but if I find out, I'll let you know."

"I know we hadn't spoken in a year, but I still loved him." Her hand snaked out and grasped Makenna's arm. "Please tell me you'll find who killed my son."

"We'll do our best," Bubba said from behind her, speaking up for the first time.

"Thank you." The woman let go of Makenna and held Bubba's gaze for a moment before stepping back into the house and closing the door.

"We can't disappoint her, Makenna. She's lost so much already," Bubba said as they made their way back to the car.

Makenna knew that. She wanted to catch this guy as much as Bubba did. She wanted justice for the victims and families, and she didn't want any more lives lost, but the pressure was already high. She wasn't sure she could take much more.

## 9

S he stared at the picture of Matt Fisher in the newspaper as the fire raged within her. How had he escaped? No one ever escaped.

Her mind raced back to the night she had started his fire. She had broken the window with her rock. Being a firefighter, Matt was too careful to leave his window open or unlocked even on a hot summer evening. She had poured the gasoline and struck the match. Just like she always did. And the house had caught fire. She had watched it burn herself. So, what had she missed? How had he gotten away?

She closed her eyes to picture the house in more detail and that's when she knew. She had watched the front of his house, expecting he would try and escape through the front door if he woke up, but he must have gone out his window. His bedroom had been on the opposite end of the house. How could she have been so careless? He was a fireman, trained to deal with fires. She should have had every exit covered, but how could she have? She was just one person. One angel on a mission.

So, what did she do now? Did she continue ridding the town

of its blemishes or did she go after Matt Fisher and complete her mission from five years ago?

"You don't have to do either," a voice whispered in her ear. "You could stop now and leave this all behind. Find someone and settle down. Be happy."

"No, I can't," she yelled, shaking her head. "If I don't stop them, who will?"

No, she couldn't stop now. The face of the next victim flashed again in her mind. She'd been given a mission, and she would fulfill it. Then, she would go after Matt Fisher again.

She slipped on her gloves and grabbed the small gas can she always took. A pat of her pockets reassured her that her matches were still there, and she slipped out of her house and into the darkness.

She could have driven, but she enjoyed the feel of the night air. The moon guided her, granting her light from above, and the chill of the cool air honed her senses. She passed no one on her way which was not unusual. This town seemed to fall asleep as soon as the sun set. Stores closed by nine p.m., and people shuttered themselves inside to watch their television shows or curl up with a book. No one seemed to suspect the evil that moved outside their windows.

All the lights were out in the house when she arrived. It was not a large house, but that simply meant he was squirreling his money away for now. She'd been told all about his scams and how much he was taking from innocent people, but after tonight that would no longer be an issue.

She walked the perimeter of the house, making sure to keep to the shadows. His neighbors weren't that close, but it wouldn't do to be seen.

No lights shone from inside the house, and she heard no noise either. Unfortunately, due to the chill in the air from the approaching fall, there also weren't any open windows. But that was okay. She had her rock.

Her hand found it in her pocket as she circled back to the living room window. These windows were her favorite. Partly because she didn't always know which rooms were bedrooms and in which bedroom the victim might be, but also because they almost always had curtains. And curtains loved fire.

When she reached the living room window, she scanned the area one more time to make sure no eyes were out, but it was silent. The night was her friend like always, and tonight, it shielded her. She withdrew the rock and smashed it against the window. Glass shards tinkled like tiny bells as they fell, and she held her breath to listen for any movement from within.

When there was nothing, she placed the rock back in her pocket and unscrewed the cap of the gas can. The spout fit perfectly in the hole, and she poured the contents in. Then she replaced the cap and set it on the ground beside her.

A tingle raced down her back as she pulled the book of matches from her other pocket. This was the part she waited for, the part that haunted her dreams until she fulfilled her mission. She struck the match and stared at the flame for a moment. Fire. Cleansing renewal. If only it could renew her, change her past, but perhaps that day was coming. Today was his day.

She dropped the match before it could burn her gloves and smiled as the flame caught the gasoline. A burst of heat flowed out of the window and then the greedy flames began their destruction. She picked up the gas can and stepped back. Now, she would wait. Wait until the black bag left the house and her mission was complete.

## 10

M akenna slapped at her nightstand, trying to find the ringing phone in the dark. Her fingers touched the solid form and she brought it to her ear, clicking the call button as she did. "Captain Drake." Her voice sounded heavy with sleep.

"Sorry to wake you, Captain, but I thought you might want to know there's been another fire."

At the sound of the fire chief's deep voice, her eyes snapped open. "Another one? Are you sure?" She glanced at her watch. It was two a.m., but there would be no more sleep tonight.

"Yes Ma'am. I'm here now with my crew putting it out, but we were too late."

Makenna sighed as she flipped back the covers and stepped out of bed. "Another victim?"

"Afraid so. The address is listed as Dustin Cox."

"Okay, I'll grab my team and be there shortly. Can you try to keep the crowd back until we get there?"

"Already have a man on it."

"Thank you." She hung up the phone and changed into her

uniform before she sent out the call to her team. It would be another long day for all of them.

Makenna was the first to arrive on the scene. Black smoke still wafted in the sky, but the flames had been doused. All that remained of the house was charred bricks and partial walls. She was getting tired of seeing this in her town.

The fire department had a spot light set up to see in the dark night, but she pulled her flashlight as she approached anyway. She didn't want to miss anything.

"Same as the last one?" she asked Chief Frye when she reached him. Frye had been the chief for ten years, so he'd been at all the previous fires as well.

He nodded and glared out at the scene. "Smashed window, gas, nothing left. It sure looks the same."

She understood his anger. They were supposed to be protecting the town, the citizens, but because she was failing, he was as well. "Thank you, Chief." She clicked her flashlight on and scanned the ground as she walked the perimeter of the house. Unfortunately, the hard ground didn't help. Her own steps left no prints, so she doubted the killer's had either.

"Hey, Captain," Tad said as he jogged up to her. Kelsey and Braydon were a few steps behind. "Any luck yet?"

"No, and I doubt we're going to find anything, but we gotta look. Kelsey, you and Braydon take a circle farther out. Scan for anything. Footprints, weapons, and don't forget to scan the crowd. This guy probably sticks around to watch. Maybe he's still here. Detain anyone who looks sketchy."

"You got it," Kelsey said as she and Brayden flicked on their own flashlights and began walking the perimeter she had assigned.

"I don't get it, Tad. How can this guy leave nothing? No prints, no weapon, nothing." Frustration colored her voice, but she couldn't help it. She had hoped bringing Matt back would disrupt the killer. Instead, she had another body on her hands and still nothing to go on.

Bubba woke to the sound of bacon sizzling and coffee dripping. He'd forgotten how noise carried in his parents' house. When he'd been in high school, he'd hated it. Not only could his mother hear his phone conversations no matter how quiet he was, but sneaking out, or in for that matter, had never been an option. Not that he was the type of kid who sneaked around, but he'd wanted the option. The one time he had tried though, his father had been there to meet him as he climbed in the window and nearly scared the daylights out of him. This morning though, he didn't mind. His stomach rumbled as he kicked back the covers and padded over to his suitcase to get dressed.

Across the room, his cell phone buzzed. It had to be Makenna. No one else he knew would text him at seven in the morning. He picked it up and sighed when he read the message. Another fire. Another life taken. Who was this guy?

"Good morning, Matt," his mother said as he entered the kitchen. "Did you sleep well?"

Matt. The name still caught him off guard, but he hadn't had the heart to ask his parents to call him Bubba. After all, he'd let them believe he was dead for five years. "I did, but unfortunately, Makenna will be here soon. There was another fire last night."

Fear clouded his mother's eyes as she set a plate of bacon and eggs in front of him. "Do you think it's safe for you here? Won't he go after you again?"

"I don't know, Mom. If I even had an idea of who this guy was, maybe I could tell you, but I've got nothing. Still, I can't go back to Fire Beach knowing this is happening. Now that I'm here, I have to stay until it's over." He speared an egg and shoved it into his mouth, but his mind wasn't on the taste. It was on his past life here. Who had he known who would want to kill him?

The answer was no one. He hadn't been mean to people in high school, and while there were women he hadn't dated, he had always been as nice as he could when turning them down. Then he'd gone to the fire academy and been a firefighter. His job was to help people. Had there been someone he saved who hadn't wanted to be saved? He'd heard stories about people like that going after the people who saved them, but no one had ever blamed him that he knew of.

The knock on the front door came just as he finished break-fast. "Gotta run, Mom. That will be Captain Drake."

"Please be safe," his mother said. "I don't want to lose you again."

"I promise." The words were easy to say, but he just hoped they were the truth.

"Sorry for the early text this morning," Makenna said as he opened the door. Dark circles ringed her eyes, and his heart went out to her. A part of him wanted to take her in his arms and ease her stress, and the other part of him wondered what he was thinking. He didn't have feelings for Makenna, did he? No, it was probably just seeing his family again and realizing his parents had something he might never have, but he couldn't deny there was something appealing about Makenna. She held herself with an air of confidence that he found attractive.

"It's no problem," he said shutting the front door behind him. "It's what I'm here for."

"Right," she said. Was that disappointment he heard in her voice? Was she feeling something too?

"So, what's the plan for today?"

"A quick stop at the station to gather information about our victim and then we'll go to his place of employment and inter-view friends and family just like yesterday."

"Sounds like a plan," Bubba said as he slid into the passenger seat and buckled the seat belt.

Ten minutes later, they were in the station and staring at another photo on the board. Another young man, probably in his late twenties. Bubba hated the loss of lives so young.

"This is Dustin Cox," Kelsey said. "Twenty-eight and single. He worked for Harrison Insurance where he was a claims agent. No family in town and no apparent connection to Peter, the first victim."

Makenna sighed. "Okay, Bubba and I will go to his job and see what we can find. You guys keep digging. There has to be some connection we're missing."

What were they missing? Two men from different backgrounds who worked different jobs. Why were they being targeted? Bubba shook his head in frustration sure that the answer was right in front of their faces.

## 11

Makenna expected the stop at the insurance company to be routine, but as she parked the cruiser, a call came through on her radio from dispatch.

"Captain Drake, we have a report of a woman acting erratic in the Harrington Insurance building."

Makenna exchanged a startled glance with Bubba. "Harrington Insurance? Are you sure?"

"Yes, ma'am, the call just came in. Should I send Lieutenant Brewer or Officer Cook?"

"No need. I'm here at the building with Matt Fisher. We'll check it out." She clicked the radio off and glanced at Bubba again. Though he wasn't a cop, firefighters were also trained to deal with situations like this, and his hulking presence certainly wouldn't hurt in de-escalating the situation. "Feel up to this?"

"Whatever I can do."

Makenna nodded and opened her door. As she stepped out of the car, she could hear what sounded like screaming coming from inside the building. She shot Bubba a concerned glance as her hand touched the butt of her gun.

She led the way up the walkway and pulled the door open. A

harried-looking receptionist glanced up at them and motioned them to continue. A glass door separated the reception area from the office area, but the screaming was audible even before Makenna opened the door.

"Where is it? I just want what he owed me." An edge of hysteria filled the shrill voice.

As Makenna opened the door, a blonde woman came into view. She held a knife in her hand and was whirling around with it whenever anyone came too close to her.

"Ma'am, I need you to drop the knife," Makenna said as she stepped closer.

The woman turned wide, frantic eyes on her. "Not until I get what he owed me. They know where it is, but they won't tell me."

"Okay, so how about you tell me? Who owes you and what does he owe you?" Makenna scanned the area as she stepped closer to the woman. Most of the employees were cowering in fear but she never knew when one might decide to be a hero and send the situation careening downhill.

"Money. He owes me money. I filed a claim when my house was broken into a month ago, and he's been sitting on my claim. I need that money to fix my house." Her hand trembled sending the knife wavering like a shiny, floating ripple.

"All right. I hear you. Why don't you put the knife down and tell me who your agent was?" Makenna held her hand out as she took another step closer to the woman. From the corner of her eye, she saw Bubba move off to her right, and she knew he was placing himself behind the woman.

"Dustin Cox was my agent, and I know he has my check somewhere in his desk, but they won't let me look." She pointed the knife at a balding man in a suit who Makenna deduced to be the boss. "I just want my money."

"Ma'am, I'm sorry you didn't get the money owed to you,

but I'm here now. I'm Captain Makenna Drake, and I can get them to help you if you just put your knife down."

The woman's eyes twitched as if she wasn't sure she believed Makenna's words. But after a moment, her hand opened, and the knife clattered to the floor. Makenna rushed in and snapped the cuffs on the woman.

"What are you doing?" the woman asked. "I thought you were going to help me."

"I am, but I also need to ask you a few questions, and I need to make sure you aren't going to harm anyone until I can do that, okay?" Makenna motioned Bubba to come forward and take the woman's arms. At the sight of him, the woman stopped struggling and dropped her eyes to the floor, but not before Makenna saw the sheen of unshed tears.

Makenna picked up the knife and turned to the balding man. "Is there truth to her words? Did Dustin Cox have her check?"

"I don't know," the man said. "I'll have to look into it, but I can tell you that Dustin was on our radar for insurance fraud. She's not the first one to claim that money owed was never received."

"Okay, I'm going to need you to investigate as quickly as you can, and then I want all the cases he was working on." Makenna felt her suspect pool growing. If this woman was angry enough to come in with a knife, could she have been angry enough to light his house on fire? Could any of his other victims?

The man nodded. "I'll compile them myself and send them over this afternoon."

"Great, thank you." She glanced over at the sniffling woman who no longer appeared a threat to anyone. "Do you want to press charges?"

The man's lips pinched together for a moment. "Not if she's right. If it turns out Dustin was stealing her money, then let her go."

Makenna nodded and picked up the knife. She handed it, handle first, to Bubba as she took the woman's arm. "What's your name, Ma'am?"

The woman lifted a splotchy, tear-stained, and defeated face. "Chloe. I wasn't really going to hurt anyone. I just need the money."

"Okay, Chloe. I understand that, but brandishing a knife is not the best way to go about getting what you want. I'm going to take you to the station and ask you some questions, but we'll figure it all out."

Chloe nodded, but she said nothing more as Makenna led her out to the car. A sigh escaped Makenna's lips as she closed the door after securing Chloe in the back seat.

"Do you always see this much action?" Bubba asked with a teasing smile. He was obviously trying to ease the tension of the situation.

She smiled and shook her head. "No, it's usually pretty sleepy around here, but these murders have everyone acting crazy. And this admission just opens up a whole new bunch of suspects."

"Well, I don't know what I can do to help, but I'm here. Whatever you need."

His last three words stirred something in Makenna's heart and she sneaked a glance at him. She knew he was talking about helping with the case, so why did it feel as if some other innuendo existed in those words?

As he held her gaze, she felt something between them shift. She cleared her throat and tore her eyes away from his penetrating stare. "Thank you. I'll question her if you want to grab some lunch and then maybe we can begin looking into other victims of Dustin Cox's."

"I'd be happy to. Would you like me to pick up something for you?"

"A sandwich would be great," she said as her stomach rumbled at the thought.

"You got it." The smile he sent her direction caused her heart to skip a beat, and she shook her head to bring it out of the clouds and back to the case at hand. She could daydream later when her town was safe again.

## 12

Bubba opened the door to Charlie's, the small family run sandwich shop just a few blocks from the police station. Charlie's had been one of his go to restaurants when he had worked at the fire station, and he was glad to see they were still in business.

The traditional lunch crowd packed the interior, and Bubba scanned the area as he waited. He wished they had more information on the arsonist. With so much ambiguity, he couldn't help wondering if anyone in this room could be the suspect. Would he know it if he spoke to them? Would the killer give off some creepy vibe or feel?

"Can I help you?"

Bubba glanced up and realized the line had moved without him and the cashier was waiting for him to order. He didn't recognize the woman, and he wondered if Charlie and Darla still owned the place. They had been the sweetest couple always making time to circle the room and ask about the food or life in general. Charlie would sometimes even pull out a chair and sit with patrons until Darla good-naturedly ushered him back to work. He would hate to hear they no longer ran the place.

Stepping up, he placed his order and handed over the money. She took it and handed him a receipt as if it were the most normal thing in the world. He had almost forgotten that feeling. The stares and whispers as he passed had become so common that when they didn't happen, it felt odd.

When his name was called, he grabbed the food and made his way toward the front door, but before he reached it, a hand landed on his arm. He whirled to see who had touched him and found himself face to face with Daphne.

"Hey, Matt," she said in her soft, flirty voice. "I was hoping I would run into you again. I know we never got a chance in high school, but I thought maybe we could do dinner or lunch?"

Bubba forced his face to remain impassive, but the thought of having dinner with Daphne ranked about as high as watching paint dry in his book. He had a feeling it might be about as intellectually stimulating as well. "I don't know if I'll have time as I'm helping Captain Drake out, but if I do, I'll let you know."

Her smile faltered for a moment, and a cloud passed over her eyes, but then she brightened again. "Sure, sounds good. You know where to find me."

"That I do. Good to see you again, Daphne."

"You too. Be careful out there," she called to him as he opened the door.

He turned back to her, the choice of her words stopping him in his tracks, but she had already turned away and was stepping up to the counter. What had she meant by that? Did she know something about these murders? Or was that just something she said?

As quickly as it was gone, the unease returned, and Bubba returned to the prayer he'd uttered the day before. He hoped they found the killer soon. This constant state of uncertainty was wearing on him.

He opened the door and nearly collided with Davis Redman.

Davis had been a fellow firefighter, but Bubba had never been close to him. There always appeared to be a current of anger brimming just under his surface.

"Well, if it isn't Matt Fisher back from the dead."

Bubba flinched slightly at the hatred that assaulted him with Davis's words. "Davis, good to see you again."

"Is it?" He folded his beefy arms across his chest and leaned back. "We had a funeral for you, you know? Dress uniforms and all. Your picture hangs on the wall with the other firefighters who actually lost their lives in a fire. Guess we can take that down now, huh?"

Bubba could feel his own temper rising. Normally cool headed, this guy was pushing all the right buttons. "Look, Davis, I didn't ask to be targeted, and if I hadn't thought my family was in danger, I wouldn't have left. I'm sure if you had been in my position, you would have done the same thing." Bubba had no idea if the man even had family or if he was close to them, but he had to assume there was decency in Davis somewhere even though something had clearly happened to make him fixate on the negative so much.

"That's where you're wrong." Davis leaned forward and for a moment, Bubba thought he was going to poke him in the chest. "I would have stayed and found the person responsible. Stopping them is the only real way to protect your family."

"Then I guess we'll have to agree to disagree, Davis." Bubba was careful to keep his voice even. Clearly, Davis was agitated at him, but getting in a fight was not something he wanted to do. He hadn't seen Natasha, the dogmatic reporter, today, but if she truly were watching his every move, the last thing he needed to do was hit anyone - even someone who might deserve it.

"Now, if you'll excuse me, I have to get back to the police station. Captain Drake and I are working hard to find the killer so that no one else has to go through what I or my family did."

Before Davis could say another word, Bubba stepped around him and continued to the police station. He couldn't help wondering if his other firefighter brothers felt the same way as Davis though. A part of him wanted to go to the firehouse and apologize, and the other part of him felt that might just make the situation worse.

"I don't know why you brought me back here, Lord, but I sure hope something good comes out of it," Bubba said under his breath as he pulled open the door to the police station.

"Hey, you okay?" Makenna asked as he entered her office with the food.

"Yeah." He set the bag down on her desk. "I just had a run in with a guy from my past. He was pretty angry that I faked my death. I guess I never realized people might be mad; I just thought they would understand the reasoning."

She rose from her chair and crossed to the space in front of him. "Bubba, I wish I had the words to make everything better. I know that everything you are going through right now is my fault, and I just…" She shook her head as if her words had run out mid sentence. Her bottom lip folded under her top teeth, and for the first time since he'd known her, a sense of vulnerability floated around her.

He placed a hand on her arm and forced it to stay there and not wander up to her dark hair which fell to her shoulders today. "It's no use living in the past, Makenna. We have to focus on today and finding the killer."

Her eyes met his, and every nerve in his body tingled. He wanted to kiss her, to take her in his arms and forget their current predicament for just a moment, but before he could, Natasha's voice carried across the room.

"Now this will make a great headline. Captain Drake fails to find the killer because she's too busy canoodling with the victim who got away." She lowered her iPhone and flashed her predatory smile at them.

Bubba dropped his hand from Makenna's arm but not before he felt her tense.

"What are you doing here, Natasha?" Makenna's voice was cool but professional.

"I came to see if you had a comment about the most recent death but clearly you're too busy to be doing your actual job."

"That's enough," Bubba said. "Makenna has been working tirelessly to find this killer-"

"Bubba, please," Makenna said, cutting him off. She shot him a look that said she appreciated his help but could defend herself, at least in this situation. Then she turned back to Natasha. "I appreciate your doggedness on this case, Natasha, but you know I can't discuss details of the case with you. What you can tell your readers is that we are doing everything we can to catch this guy and that if the public wants to help, they can be vigilant watchers and report anything suspicious."

"Hmph, I'll be sure to do that, Captain Drake, but you should remember that a picture's worth a thousand words." She waved her phone as a reminder. "I'll see myself out."

"That woman is a piece of work," Bubba said when he was sure Natasha was gone.

"She is," Makenna said with a sigh, "but she's also right. Perception is everything, and I need to make sure that the town believes we are doing everything we can. The last thing I need is a vigilante on my hands trying to take matters into his own hands because he thinks we aren't doing enough."

"Of course," Bubba said, but he caught her unsaid words. They couldn't be seen in a compromised position like that again. Even though nothing had happened, they needed to be careful to keep their relationship strictly professional. "I take it you had no luck then?"

Makenna ran a hand through her hair as she walked back to the other side of her desk. "None. She's clean. I don't know what I'm missing, Bubba."

"I don't either, but I know when I get stuck that praying often helps." He took her sandwich out and set it in front of her.

"You're a believer too?" she asked, looking up at him.

"I am. I think I always believed in God - my parents took us to church every Sunday - but I don't think I had a relationship with Him until I left here. When I ended up in Fire Beach and had to start over, that's when He really took ahold of me. How about you?"

"Kind of the same," she said as she unwrapped her sandwich. "I learned to lean on Him when I couldn't solve the case five years ago. Sometimes, He's all that keeps me going."

"You never wanted a family?" Bubba hoped he wasn't being too personal as he pulled up a chair and sat across from her.

"Never had time for one, I guess, but I think about it."

The look she gave him as she spoke sent his heart thumping in his chest. His brain understood they had agreed to remain professional, but he hadn't felt his heart move like this in a long time. Was he falling for Makenna?

Makenna stared at the information in the report and tried not to think about the almost kiss with Bubba. He had been about to kiss her. She knew it, could see it in his eyes. And she'd wanted him to. At least until Natasha had shown up and ruined every-thing. She had a knack for that, but Makenna couldn't blame Natasha this time. She was asking what everyone else wanted to know. When was she going to find this killer and put a stop to him?

Besides, it wasn't Natasha's fault that Makenna was sitting here with a stomach full of conflicting emotions. No, that was completely her fault. She shouldn't have told Bubba they needed to stay strictly professional. They did, at least until this case was over, but now she was afraid he'd taken her words to mean she had no interest in him and that was about as far from the truth as one could get. Since she'd driven to Fire Beach to get him, her mind had warred between thoughts of the killer and thoughts of Bubba.

She had tried convincing herself that the thoughts of him were just feelings of remorse for his lost years, but she knew that wasn't true. Thoughts of remorse wouldn't have her imagining what his hands would feel like on her neck, in her hair. And they certainly wouldn't have her imagining what his lips might feel like pressed against her own. But she'd had to go and ruin it. Now, she had her feelings for him along with feelings of guilt for making him think she didn't care along with her feelings of failure at not catching the killer. To put it mildly, she was a hot mess.

She chanced a glance at him from the corner of her eye as she chewed on the sandwich he had brought her. She hadn't told him how much she enjoyed salami, so she was surprised he had returned with an Italian sandwich for her. He was definitely surprising. And dedicated. His eyes were focused on the paper in front of him as well. He'd offered to help her go through the list of Dustin's clients as they ate, and though she could have had Tad or Kelsey do it, she'd agreed. She enjoyed spending time with him, even if it was searching for a killer, and she knew she would miss it when he was gone.

Gone. She needed to keep reminding herself of that fact too. When this case ended, he would probably return to Fire Beach and then where would she be? Alone. Again.

Makenna hadn't meant to marry her work, but it had sort of happened. In the beginning, she had thrown herself into the job in order to learn and prove herself, but then the case five years ago had happened. When everyone else had left, she quickly climbed the ladder, and once she made captain, she rarely had time for anything else. Or anyone else.

Still, she couldn't deny the feelings. She hoped one day to

find someone she could share evenings and weekends with, someone she could take to church, and someone who could listen when she needed to process cases. She could see Bubba filling that role in her life, but she knew that wasn't reality. When this case ended, he would return to his life, and her life would continue here.

"What?" he asked, catching her staring at him.

Heat filled her face. "Nothing, I was just thinking it's been nice having you here."

He smiled at her. "It's been nice being here with you. I'm certainly glad I'll get to be in my family's life again, and maybe..." he trailed off and looked away as if unsure how to finish that sentence.

"Maybe what?" she asked. Was he going to tell her she'd been wrong? That they could have a relationship and still solve this case?

"Maybe I'll come back more often and stop in and see you."

"I'd like that," she said, but that wasn't what she had been hoping to hear. She didn't know if a long-distance relationship would last, but she might be willing to try it with him.

"Hey, look at this," he said, pushing his paper her direction. "This looks like a lot of denied claims doesn't it?"

Makenna stared down at the paper, but she was no insurance agent. She had no idea if these were legitimate denials or Dustin's denials that he had then pocketed. It appeared they would need more information. "Yeah, it does. We should definitely look into that."

And the moment was gone. It was back to work. She shouldn't be sad; this was the life she'd chosen, but she couldn't help wondering if maybe she had made the wrong choice. Her mind wandered back to the night she had sent Bubba away.

*Makenna's eyes snapped open at the ringing of her phone. The clock beside her read two in the morning. Who would be calling her at two in the morning? There was only one answer to that question. Work. Snapping awake, she grabbed her phone and pressed the call button.*

*"Sergeant Drake here."*

*"Makenna, we've had another fire. I need you to get over to 232 Overside Street." The voice of her captain was firm, so even though she knew someone else had to be working the night shift, she didn't argue.*

*"232 Overside?" The address felt familiar in her head. "Wait! Isn't that Matt Fisher's address?" Matt Fisher was a local fireman, but he was also her number one suspect right now. He knew all of the previous victims, even if only slightly, and he understood fire. She just hadn't figured out a motive yet, but now her captain was telling her he was not the arsonist, but a victim.*

*"Yes, it is. Get over there and see if you can help determine if he set this fire himself to divert suspicion."*

*"Yes, sir. I'll be right there." She ended the call and grabbed her uniform. She had just holstered her gun when the pounding began on her front door.*

*She peeked through the spy-hole surprised to see Matt Fisher standing on her front porch. He was clad only in shorts and a pair of tennis shoes, and he appeared out of breath.*

*"He got my house, Drake," he said when she opened the door. "Now, do you believe I'm not your suspect?"*

*For a moment she wasn't sure what to believe. Was this part of his elaborate plan? It seemed crazy, but then he would have to be crazy to be starting fires like this. However, when she looked in his eyes, something in her knew that he was innocent. She stepped back and opened the door for him. "Come inside and tell me what happened."*

*As he stepped past her, she scanned the area for anyone who might have followed him, but the neighborhood seemed to sleep on around them. She shut the door and turned to Matt.*

What if instead of telling him to run that night she had worked with him then? Would they have ended up together? She didn't know, but the one thing she did know was that she couldn't live in the past. Those decisions were made and done. She could only move forward from here.

## 13

S he approached the police station as she made her way
home that evening. It was not her normal route, but some
unseen force seemed to guide her in that direction. She
wanted to see if Matt was still there. Matt, the man who should
be dead. The one who had gotten away. The one she needed to
take care of, but not yet. She'd been given another name, and he
would have to come first.

As she reached the corner where the station sat, voices
carried on the air. She flattened herself against the corner and
peeked around. Matt and Captain Drake were talking as they
walked to her car.

Their words were too soft to make out, but she could read the
attraction that sizzled between them. What did Makenna Drake
see in him? Didn't she know what he had done? A renewed
anger washed through her.

"I should take him now," she whispered. She didn't have her
gas can, but the matches were in her pocket. They were always
in her pocket, a tactile device she could touch and draw comfort
from when necessary. Would a car catch fire with just a match?
She doubted it, and it would be stupid to attack them in front of

the station. Someone was probably still inside, and if she were caught now, she couldn't finish her mission.

"His time will come." She felt the voice more than heard it, but it calmed her seething nerves nonetheless. The voice was never wrong. If it said Matt's time would come, then it would. And she would watch him take his last breath when it did. This time she would be sure.

An engine hummed to life, and a moment later, she watched the car drive away. She waited until the car turned the corner before she continued toward her house. She still had hours to kill. Hours before she could fulfill her mission and rid the town of one more monster.

The large house appeared before her, and she paused momentarily. What if he had an alarm system? He was wealthy enough to afford one. Not only was he the prominent doctor in town, but she had it on good authority that he was overcharging patients and pocketing the extra.

It almost always came down to money, didn't it? Money ate at men's hearts and fueled greed and jealousy. The gospels had been correct when they stated that it was "easier for a camel to pass through the eye of a needle than for a rich man to enter the kingdom of God." Just another reason, she had been called to rid the town of these men. They would never enter the kingdom of God, so there was no reason for them to continue life on Earth.

"Leave it alone," the voice whispered. "It's too dangerous."

"No," she hissed. She hated that voice. That weak voice. The weak voice had controlled her for too long. Until she had broken free five years ago. Until she had been shown what she had to do.

The first kill had been the hardest because the voice kept trying to dissuade her. She had hesitated when she struck the first match and burned her finger through her gloves, but she knew her mission had to be completed. Her first mission had been simple - to hurt Matt Fisher. He needed to pay, but he couldn't be first. He needed to feel the pain she had felt, so she'd been shown women in his life.

After Matt's death, the visions had stopped. She had missed them, but without them there was no sense of purpose, so she had let the weak voice take over again. Until the visions returned. But this time they had been different. They told her she had proved herself, that she had earned a more important mission - to rid the town of those who cheated and stole. And Dr. Hayworth was one of the worst.

She walked around the perimeter of the house looking for any signs of a security system but saw none. No cameras, no motion sensors, no lights of any kind shining from within. Probably too confident in the safety of this small town to spend the money. She returned to the living room window.

She tried lifting the window, but it was locked just like the one last night. She cursed the changing weather. Winter was coming, and the need for open windows had diminished. She withdrew the rock from her pocket. It was the perfect size really, small enough to fit in her hand but large enough to make the necessary hole in a window. She drew her hand back and slammed the rock into the side of the window nearest the curtain. Her body froze as the glass shattered, and she waited for any indication it had woken the occupant. But the silence pressed on.

Unscrewing the cap, she poured the contents of the gasoline into the window and then set the container on the ground to pull out the matches. The moon had disappeared behind a cloud offering the perfect shadow of obscurity. She struck the match, enjoying the heat and the light of the dancing flame for a moment before she dropped it inside the window. It only took an instant to find the gasoline, and then the blaze climbed to the roof.

She stepped back to admire her work, but suddenly a light flicked on in the house. She hissed under her breath and turned to run. There would be no sticking around to enjoy this one.

"I told you so," the voice whispered as she fled the scene. Too late she realized she had forgotten her gas can, but no matter, she always wore her gloves. There would be no finger-prints on it, and she could easily pick up another one. No, the focus now was getting away unseen. She was almost off his property when her foot slipped in a soft piece of ground, and she tumbled to the ground. Pain tore through her hand and she lifted it to see a jagged cut. She looked around for the rock she must have landed on, but the moon had slipped behind the clouds again. It was too dark.

"Run," the voice whispered again. "Get out now."

"Shut up," she hissed at the voice, but a trickle of fear pressed in on her. Had she left a footprint when she slipped? Had she bled on the rock? Surely, she was far enough away that it wouldn't matter. Would they search this far? She should stay and search, but then the faint sound of sirens in the distance reached her ears. Would they have been alerted so quickly? He must have called. That was the only explanation.

Two failed missions. The failure pressed down on her like a smothering blanket. She was losing her touch. No, it was Matt's fault. Seeing him alive again had thrown her for a loop. She would have to put this mission on hold and take care of him. Him and the female cop.

## 14

"You look tired," Bubba said as he slid into the passenger seat of Makenna's cruiser. Dark red lines stood out in her bloodshot eyes, and the circles from yesterday were even darker.

"It was an interesting night last night." She put the car into reverse and backed out of the driveway. "There was another fire, but thankfully Dr. Hayworth was awake. He managed to call the fire department and get out before the fire reached his bedroom."

"Did he see anything?" Bubba asked.

"No, it was after midnight and dark. He said he would normally have been asleep, but a case was bothering him. We processed what we could last night, but it's hard to find evidence in the dark, so we're headed back out there this morning."

"Sounds good," Bubba said, but his eyes were on a woman across the street. It was the same woman from the coffee shop the other day. "Makenna, do you know her?" he asked, pointing at the woman.

Makenna followed his finger and nodded. "Yeah, that's Rachel Hanes. She's a bit of an odd duck but harmless. Keeps to herself mostly. Why?"

Rachel Hanes. Why did that name seem familiar to him? He could feel it, how he knew her, circling in his brain, but he couldn't place her yet. "I saw her at the coffee shop too, and she looked angry at the sight of me. Now, she's here near my parents' house. It just seems odd."

"Hmm." Makenna's eyes were back on the road. "She wanders the city a lot, but that is a little odd. We'll look into it when we get done this morning."

Bubba nodded and tried to dislodge the unease from his stomach. Could she be important? Was he missing something by not remembering who she was?

Fifteen minutes later, they pulled up to the charred house. Another police cruiser sat in the street and yellow crime scene tape surrounded the area.

"Stay close to me so you don't accidentally contaminate the scene," Makenna said as she parked the car.

Bubba fell into step beside her, but as he approached the charred house, visions of his own narrow escape filled his mind. He could hear the crackling flames and feel the heat seeping in through his bedroom door. He shook his head to clear the past and focused on the house in front of him.

Though Makenna had said the fire department arrived quickly, most of the house was still blackened and charred. The far end, which must have housed the bedroom the doctor escaped from, was still intact though Bubba knew smoke damage would have ruined the interior of it as well.

"Captain, I think you're going to want to see this," Tad called from the left.

Bubba followed Makenna to where Tad and Kelsey stood staring down at the ground. A yellow evidence flag stuck up out of the ground marking something.

"Is that a shoe print?" Makenna asked.

"It is. It's not clear because it looks like maybe the person slipped, but that's not the weird part."

Bubba stared down at the footprint trying to discern what Tad was talking about, but he didn't see anything out of the ordinary. It looked just like a-

"Is that a woman's shoe print?" Makenna asked.

And then Bubba realized. The print did look too thin and too short to belong to a man which meant that if this print did belong to the arsonist, they were looking not for a man, but for a woman.

"It sure looks that way to me, Captain."

"Well, this changes everything," Makenna said.

"There's more," Kelsey said and pointed to another flag sticking up a few feet away. "We found a rock with blood on it."

"Is it enough to process?" Makenna asked.

"I don't know, but we'll sure try. Regardless, if these belong to the arsonist, she'll probably have a cut somewhere on her. Judging by the distance, I'd say her hand or arm. Maybe even her face if she's shorter."

A woman. She had definitely not been expecting that. Female serial killers were rare. Female arsonists even rarer. "We need to go back and look at the last victims again. And Dr. Hayworth. I want everything on him you can find."

"What are you thinking?" Bubba asked as he followed her back to the car.

She stopped and faced him. "Statistically speaking, very few women kill, but those who do generally fall into two categories: killing for lust or visionaries. Since we have both male and female victims, that makes killing for lust less likely which means we are probably looking for a visionary."

"What's a visionary?" Bubba asked.

"Someone who kills because they think someone told them to or because they see it as getting rid of the scourge of society.

Generally, visionaries have had a psychotic break which makes them harder to catch because they lead a normal life the rest of the time. If our killer is a visionary, she could be anyone."

"What would cause a psychotic break?"

"Abuse generally, especially in childhood. Breaks generally form early in life but lay dormant until something triggers them like a death or a-"

"A breakup?" Bubba asked, interrupting her.

"Maybe." She narrowed her eyes at him. Something was clearly on his mind. "Why? What are you thinking?"

"It's probably nothing." His words held a note of dismissal, but the nervous tell of his hand rubbing across his chin told her it might be something. "Felicity came over for dinner the other night, and she just seemed," he paused as if searching for the right word, "agitated. Plus, remember my mother said she broke up with her boyfriend shortly before the first recent murder. She said they had been together for years."

"Okay, but that's not much to go on," Makenna said, wondering where this accusal was coming from. Having been falsely accused himself, she couldn't imagine Bubba doing the same unless there was more he wasn't telling her. "People break up all the time, and maybe she was agitated about the breakup."

"Maybe, but remember how she didn't come over the night I returned? She also left in a rush the night she came for dinner saying she had something she had to attend to. She's a receptionist. What work could she have at ten o'clock at night?"

"What night was that?" Makenna asked.

"The night the insurance guy was killed."

"Okay, that's a bit of a coincidence, but the fire didn't start until after midnight, so why would she have to rush out?" Makenna had her reservations about Felicity - she had found it odd that his sister hadn't come to see him the first night - but she was not about to accuse someone else in Bubba's family unless the proof was there. So far, there were just some odd coincidences and a general feeling of unease.

Bubba shrugged and shook his head. His hand ran across his chin again. "I don't know. To prepare? Plan it out? Maybe these visions come on suddenly and once she gets one, she has to plan her attack right then."

"It's possible." Makenna chose her words carefully. She didn't want him to think she was dismissing his concern. "However, that's a huge accusation to place on your sister."

Bubba sighed and ran a hand through his hair. "I know, but she also had a rough childhood and sometimes when she looks at me, it just feels wrong. I hate saying that about her, especially since she's family, but if the killer could be anyone, don't you think we should at least consider the possibility?"

Makenna stared at him. Did he really think his foster sister could be capable of arson and murder? She couldn't quite read the emotion on his face, but she thought it appeared to be a sad determination. "You're right, we'll look into her, but I want to look into the victims first. And I want to go back over the women. Maybe there was something other than you that tied them all together that we missed." She desperately hoped there was something they had missed. Swallowing that would be a lot easier than throwing his family into disarray again.

Half an hour later, they sat at a table with officer Cook who had pulled everything he could find on Dr. Hayworth.

"You might be right, Captain. Dr. Hayworth has some interesting discrepancies between what he charged clients and what he billed to insurance companies. If the companies don't know already, they'll probably be opening an investigation into him soon."

"Wasn't the insurance guy doing a similar thing?" Bubba asked.

Makenna nodded as she thought back over the scene. "Yeah, he was intercepting checks and telling clients they were denied.

Is there any evidence of Peter overcharging clients? We know his ex-girlfriend Skye said he cheated on her, and his mother said he was asking for money."

"Nothing yet, but we're still looking. However, it was his shop. He could have charged people extra and few would realize it."

"Okay, and how about the women?"

Officer Cook shook his head. "I'm not finding anything with money issues or relationship issues with the women. Is it possible we're looking at a copycat?"

Copycat murders happened, but Makenna had a hard time believing they would happen in this small town. They were already dealing with an insanely rare situation. "I won't discount that possibility, but I think it's much more likely that our woman is a visionary who is getting dreams or messages to kill certain people."

She turned to Bubba. "I still think you're the link for the first round, and if so, we could be looking for someone who was interested in you. Maybe someone you turned down or possibly you didn't even know was interested."

Bubba cocked an eyebrow at her. "No offense, but that makes it a pretty impossible list. I can give you the names of the few women I dated, even the ones who I thought were interested that I turned down, but if I didn't know they liked me then, I certainly won't have any idea now."

"That is true. We'll start with what we do know and work backwards from there."

"We better get some coffee then," Bubba said with a smile. "I have a feeling this might be a long day."

## 15

Bubba kept his eyes peeled for Rachel as they walked to the coffee shop. He still couldn't place how he knew her, but the vibe she had given off the first day combined with the fact that she appeared to be following him made her a woman he wanted a word with.

Unfortunately, she didn't materialize before they reached the shop. Nor did she appear to be inside. Daphne was though, and her face lit up when her eyes landed on Bubba.

"Matt Fisher, back for more?"

"Hey, Daphne." He didn't know why her uber chipper attitude affected him the way it did. Perhaps it was just because she still looked at him the way she had in high school - like she was already picking out curtains and china patterns for their life together - and he didn't want to do anything to make her think there was a future there.

"You want the same coffee you had the other day?"

"You remember what I drank?" He turned slightly to catch Makenna's eye. Was she hearing this?

"Of course I do." She flashed him another wide, flirtatious smile.

"I, uh, think I'll just have an Americano today."

"With two sugars?" she asked, unfazed by his order change.

"Yeah, how did you know that?"

"That's what you drank in high school, Matt. I told you, I remember everything." Her smile was still bright, but for a moment, he thought he saw her eyes flicker. Change. As if for just an instant, something dark crossed her mind.

"Right, of course." He grabbed his wallet to pay for the drink, but as she rang up the order, he noticed the bandage on her hand. "What happened to your hand, Daphne?"

"Oh, this? Burned it on the coffee machine this morning," she said with a laugh. "I'm such a klutz sometimes."

He did remember Daphne being klutzy occasionally in high school except when she was cheering or performing on stage which he always found odd. She could trip over a speck of dirt in the hallway, but when pom poms were in her hands or lights were on her, she seemed to have the focus of a surgeon. Still, was she telling the truth? He couldn't imagine Daphne hurting anyone, but it was odd that her hand was injured the night after someone bled on a rock at a crime scene. He wondered if Felicity would have a cut? Or Rachel?

Shaking his head, he handed over his money and shuffled down to the end of the counter to wait for his drink. He had to stop thinking about Felicity like a suspect. She was probably completely innocent and he was simply chasing shadows that didn't exist.

As he waited for his drink and for Makenna, he scanned the room again. He felt eyes on him, and there by the door, he saw her. Rachel. The mystery woman. His eyes widened, but before he could move, she bolted out the door.

"Where are you going?" Makenna called after him as he made his way through the crowded tables to the door.

"Be right back." He pushed open the door and scanned the area. To the left were the other businesses but no sign of the woman. He turned right, but it too was void of people. It was like she had vanished into thin air. Where could she have gone?

With a sigh, he returned to the shop. Makenna stood at the end of the counter with two drinks in her hands. "What was that about?" she asked, holding out his cup.

Bubba glanced back at Daphne who appeared engaged with a customer. She probably wasn't listening, but he didn't want to take any chances. He shook his head and whispered softly, "Not here. Come on."

She followed him out of the shop and to a bench a few feet away. "You want to tell me what happened in there?"

"I don't know. Maybe I'm going crazy. First there was Daphne who still seems obsessed with me, and for a moment, I thought I saw something in her eyes. Something strange. " He wasn't sure he could put into words the exact feeling. "Plus, did you notice her bandage?"

"I did, but she said she burned it on the coffee machine."

"Maybe she did, but you have to admit, the timing is odd. Then there was that woman, Rachel, but when she saw me, she ran out of the shop. When I got outside, she was nowhere to be seen."

Makenna placed a hand on his arm. "First off, you aren't going crazy. This case has us all tied in knots, and this new information is a lot to process."

He glanced down at her hand on his skin and then back to her eyes. The desire to kiss her burned within him again, but she'd said they had to remain professional. Easy to say but much harder to do. How long had it been since a woman had ignited these feelings in him? But were they real? Or did they simply feel real because of this crazy situation? And even if they were real, what then? He didn't plan to stay here once this case was complete. His life was back in Fire Beach. And did he think she would come back with him? Her life was obviously here. He supposed they could do a long-distance relationship, but he'd been alone for so long that he didn't want to be with someone and not be able to see her. No, kissing her would be a bad idea. He knew that, but then why did he keep thinking about it?

"You're right. I don't know how you do this every day."

Makenna chuckled. "Well, not every day is like this thankfully. Most days, I'm issuing traffic tickets or breaking up fights after a football game or at The Hop. I don't think I'd want to do this every day, but I think you might be onto something. I do want to talk to Daphne and Rachel."

"And Felicity," Bubba added. He still couldn't get the uncomfortable dinner out of his mind.

Makenna removed her hand, and Bubba immediately missed the warmth. "Tell me more about Felicity," she said as they stood and began walking back toward the station. "I don't know her well."

Bubba sighed as he thought of where to begin. "My mom and dad felt a calling to help kids after my brother and sister and I graduated from high school, but they were older, and they knew they couldn't handle small children, so they took in teenagers. Most of the kids didn't last long because by high school, they are generally either too messed up to want a home or they're so independent that they go off on their own as soon as they can.

"Felicity was different. She wanted a home. Evidently, her father had been an alcoholic and beat her and her mother when she was young. Her mother eventually turned to drugs, and her father was killed in a bar fight. She went from one foster home to another until she landed with us.

"She was quiet at first, and because I was older and out of the house, we weren't that close. But when Jacob and Rebecca moved away, I spent more time with her. Still, something was always off. Once or twice, I brought a woman home to meet my parents, and Felicity would issue snide remarks about them under her breath. It almost felt as if she had a crush on me, but maybe she was just looking out for me. Those women didn't last, obviously."

Makenna shook her head as if wanting to make sure he understood. "It wouldn't be the first time a foster kid has developed a misplaced attraction for a sibling. A lot of them mistake romantic feelings for security, which is what they're really craving. Still, given where we're at, it's worth looking into. You said she just broke up with a boyfriend too?"

Bubba nodded. "Yeah, her boyfriend, Roger. She doesn't seem especially torn up about it either which I find odd because Mom said they were together for years."

"Maybe we should talk to Roger."

Bubba nodded. He'd like to meet the man who had dated Felicity himself, see what kind of person he was.

It took a stop at Bubba's parents' house to find out who Roger was. Even in this small town, Makenna didn't know everyone's name. Roger turned out to be Roger Ellison who ran the only bed and breakfast in town.

"Felicity? Why are you asking about Felicity?" he asked as he placed the breakfast dishes in the sink.

Makenna looked to Bubba. She wasn't sure just coming out with their suspicions would be the smartest way to handle this. Bubba, thankfully, seemed to understand and took the lead.

"She's my sister. I'm not sure we ever met, but I'm Matt Fisher."

Roger turned to face them, his eyes wide. "I thought you were dead. That's what Felicity told me."

"We needed people to think that," Makenna said, stepping in. "I'm sure you must have heard about the recent fires."

"Yep, kinda hard to miss that." Roger turned back to the sink and turned on the faucet. "Especially in a town of this size."

"Well, we had a similar string of arsons five years ago. Matt here was one of the victims, but he managed to get away. However, to test a theory, we let everyone believe he died."

Roger shut off the water and turned back to them, leaning against the sink. "I assume your theory turned out to be true?"

"It did. Until the fires started again. I asked Matt to come back to help." Makenna was having a hard time reading Roger. Was he guarded because of his feelings for Felicity or was he hiding something?

"I know I've been away from Felicity for several years, but she seems off. We were hoping that maybe you could fill us in on her behavior the last few years you were together and why it ended," Bubba said stepping in.

Roger folded his arms across his chest and sighed. "I'm not sure anything I have to say will help you, but I'll try. Felicity and I met about six months after your "death." I guess I moved to town a month or so after the fires ended, and I worked at a crisis hotline in the evenings while I was getting this place ready. Felicity was grieving and became a regular caller. It's not generally recommended to meet the people you talk to on the phone, but she begged me. I said no at first, but after about a month of phone calls, it appeared she really needed a friend, so we agreed to meet at a coffee shop.

"It was sort of attraction at first meet, I guess you could say. Though I think some of that was because we had shared so much over the phone. Anyway, we started dating, and for a time, everything was great. But then, about a month ago, something changed. She began talking about all the people who came into the office and how she wished she could help them. I think she was reading the doctor's notes on them because she had way too much information."

"Wait," Makenna interrupted him as puzzle pieces began turning in her head, "doesn't she work for a local doctor?"

"Yep, Dr. Bloom, the psychiatrist. She's the receptionist

there. Now, maybe these people were sharing while they waited for their appointment, but I don't think so. When I asked her about it, she got defensive and told me to mind my own business. It just went downhill from there, and I finally had to call it off for my own sanity."

Makenna exchanged a glance with Bubba. She didn't want to think his sister could be the arsonist, but she now had motive, odd behavior, and a troubling history.

Roger caught the look and shifted his eyes from Makenna to Bubba. "Is she okay? I mean I couldn't take the negativity, but I still care about her, you know? I know she had it rough growing up."

"We're going to find out, Roger," Makenna said, putting out her hand. "Thank you for your help."

He shook it, but his eyes were on Bubba. "I wish I could do more."

"Thank you, you've helped a lot."

Makenna knew those words were hard for Bubba to say. She thanked Roger again and led the way out of the house. When the front door closed behind them, and she was confident they were out of earshot, she turned to Bubba. "I think you're right. We need to question Felicity." Her list of suspects was growing, but Felicity was at the top of the list right now.

His face was pale, but he nodded. She couldn't imagine how hard this must be on him. If Felicity was the arsonist, it meant not only had she murdered five people but that she'd tried to kill him as well. That had to be hard to swallow.

## 16

The ride to Dr. Bloom's office was quiet, uncomfortable. What would his mother say if she knew he was on his way to pick up his sister on suspicion of murder?

"What can you tell me about Rachel Hanes?" Bubba asked, trying to get his mind off the task at hand. He still couldn't shake the feeling that he knew her somehow and that she was important.

"Um, I don't know much about her. She's a little odd, but she stays out of people's way. She's been here as long as I can remember, so maybe you crossed paths with her before?"

"Yeah, that's what I've been trying to figure out. She doesn't look familiar to me, but the name does." He ran again through the list he had started in his head. He didn't remember saving her, but he certainly didn't remember every victim's name from five years ago. Sometimes he never even knew their names. He'd never dated a Rachel, and he was sure he would remember her if he had.

So, that left high school. Had he known a Rachel in high school? He ran through the names and faces he did remember, but there was no Rachel Hanes. But there had been a Rachel. Rachel....Rachel Jones? He hadn't known her well, but he remembered the name from a musical program. He'd only ever been to one and only then because his best friend had asked him to go because he was dating one of the actresses. It had turned out to be a nightmare because Daphne had also been in that cast, and she'd been convinced Bubba had been there to see her. It had taken weeks to convince her otherwise. Could it be the same Rachel? Could she and Daphne be in on this together?

"Do you know if Rachel Hanes is married or was married?"

"I don't know for sure, Bubba, but I promise you if Felicity turns out not to be our suspect that we'll look into her, okay?"

Bubba nodded, but he couldn't shake the feeling that held on with claws and wouldn't let go.

"You sure you want to come in?" Makenna asked when they reached the office. She turned off the engine and shifted so she was facing him. "You don't have to."

He appreciated her concern, but he had to know. If his sister had really tried to kill him, he needed to be there when she was confronted. "No, I'm good."

Concern flashed in Makenna's eyes, but she nodded. "Okay, let's go."

Bubba's heart pounded in his chest as they approached the office door. Would Felicity have a cut? Would she try to run? Turn herself in? Questions and scenarios flashed through his mind, but he had no way to prepare for the unknown.

Makenna pulled open the door and entered first. Bubba almost ran into her when she stopped short in the room. He scanned to see what had made her pause and realized the woman manning the receptionist desk was not his sister, but a petite blond.

"Can I help you?" she asked when she ended the call she was on and looked up at them.

"We're looking for Felicity Fisher," Makenna said.

The girl shrugged. "Sorry, she's not here today. Called in sick. I'm Becky, the temp. Is there anything I can do for you?"

"Is Dr. Bloom available? You can tell him it's Captain Drake," Makenna asked.

"Her, you mean. Dr. Bloom is a woman."

"Of course, my mistake." Makenna recovered nicely, but Bubba could see that this information had thrown her. It had thrown him too. He wasn't sure why, but he had also assumed Dr. Bloom was a man.

"Let me check." The woman punched a button on the phone and waited. "Dr. Bloom, there's a Captain Drake and a man here to see you. Do you have a moment?" She looked up at them and nodded. "Yes, ma'am." She replaced the phone and motioned them toward the door. "She said to go on in."

"Thank you." As Makenna led the way to the office, Bubba wondered what she had up her sleeves. Was she just hoping to get more information or did she think Felicity might be hiding in Dr. Bloom's office?

"Captain Drake, what can I do for you?" Dr. Bloom was a smart looking woman with her dark hair pulled back in a severe bun, and a pair of cat-eyed glasses that accentuated her thin cheekbones. She sat behind her desk, and Bubba found it odd that she didn't rise to greet them.

"I was hoping to ask you a few questions about your employee, Felicity Fisher."

Dr. Bloom's eyes shifted to Bubba and a tingle ran down his spine. Why was she looking at him like that? Did he know her? He certainly didn't remember ever meeting her before.

"This is my friend and Felicity's brother, Matt Fisher," Makenna said.

"Ah, yes, Felicity told me about your faked death. You know it took quite a toll on her. Losing you." Her eyes bored into his, and the concern she was projecting felt a lot more like blame to him.

"I know, but we thought it was the right move at the time," Bubba said.

"Fair enough, so how can I help?" She leaned forward and placed her hands on the desk, one on top of the other.

"Did you speak with Felicity today?" Makenna asked.

"No, we have a temp agency who fills her spot when she is sick. She must have called them directly."

"Is she sick often?"

"Rarely. She's very punctual and efficient."

"She recently broke up with her boyfriend and he said her behavior had changed recently. Have you noticed anything different lately?"

Dr. Bloom shrugged. "This can be a challenging job. Felicity has to listen to people in the waiting room and deal with customers on the phone. She handles it well though perhaps she's been a bit more short tempered than normal."

"Does she have access to your files? Her boyfriend also stated she seemed to have knowledge of cases."

At this Makenna finally seemed to find the chink in the doctor's stoic demeanor, and her laid back attitude disappeared. "No, I do all my notations online. She would have no reason to know anything about my cases unless the clients told her themselves. I'm assuming you're not just here about that though, am I right?"

"No, I'm afraid Felicity is a person of interest in a current case."

A person of interest was putting it mildly in Bubba's mind. She was their number one suspect, but perhaps Makenna was downplaying it for a reason.

"You think she's the arsonist?" The doctor shook her head slowly as if she were considering this option for the first time. "She does have some of the markers: abuse in her past, a recent trigger, but I think you're wrong about Felicity. I don't know why she was in my files, but I don't believe she's your arsonist."

"With all due respect, ma'am, that's for me to determine. Do you have Felicity's current address?"

"Of course." The doctor turned to her computer and tapped a few keys, but Bubba noticed she only used her left hand. Strange. Someone who typed as much as she claimed to surely didn't chicken peck the notes. Perhaps she used voice to text? "Her address is 1214 Sway Ave. She's not your killer though."

"I hope you're right. Thank you." Makenna nodded at the doctor and led the way out of the office.

Bubba followed, wanting to hear her take on what had just happened, but he held his question until they were back in her car. "Did Dr. Bloom seem a little off to you?"

Makenna shook her head. "Off how?"

"I don't know. The way she looked at me, the fact that she only typed with one hand. What kind of a doctor only uses one hand to type? Did you see her right hand at all?"

"She placed both hands on the desk," Makenna said.

"Yes, but she had the left over the right."

"Bubba, I think you're hoping to find something that proves it's not Felicity, but blaming Dr. Bloom is a bit of a stretch. What's the motive? She's a psychiatrist who helps people."

"Maybe they were all clients. Did you look into that?" He didn't want Felicity to be the arsonist, but that wasn't what this was about. Something about Dr. Bloom had seemed wrong to him. Maybe it was just them showing up unannounced and maybe it was learning about Felicity. But maybe it was something more.

Makenna opened her mouth and then sighed before speaking. "Okay, we didn't look into counseling. We can check that. After we talk to Felicity."

"The doctor seemed certain Felicity isn't the suspect. She's a psychiatrist. Wouldn't she know?"

"It's possible, but she's not her psychiatrist, Bubba. She's

Felicity's boss which means she has a different relationship with her."

"So, what now?"

"Now, we go to Felicity's house and hope we can find her before anyone else ends up dead."

She paced around the room, trying to calm her rage. Failure was not an option and yet she had failed. Again. She pulled out the pictures of her victims, landing on Matt Fisher. This was his fault. His appearance in town had thrown her off her game. He was not supposed to have survived. No one was supposed to survive. So, the only thing to do was get rid of him. Then she would see clearly again.

But how? How could she take out Matt when he was always with Captain Drake? The station? They were bound to be spending time together there, but could she set the station on fire? The station would have surveillance cameras. If she did this, she would have to leave town, which meant she might not be able to finish the Dr. Hayworth mission.

"What do I do?" she asked aloud. The voice had been curiously silent today. Was he angry that she failed?

"Let it go," the wimpy voice whispered.

"Shut up," she yelled at the voice. "You are a coward. You are worthless."

The voice stilled, and while she felt satisfaction at that, she still wasn't getting the orders she needed. But that was okay. She could wait. If she'd learned nothing else over the years, she had learned patience, and she could wait. But not here. She couldn't think with the two men smiling at her. Mocking her failure. She had to get out and clear her head. Then he would tell her what to do. She was sure of it.

Makenna wished she had the words to say to Bubba as they drove to Felicity's house, but what did you say to someone when you were about to arrest his sister?

"You don't have to go in with me," Makenna said when she pulled the car to a stop in front of the small rambler. "I could leave you here and get her without you."

Bubba shook his head, but his eyes remained fixed out the window. "No, if she is responsible, I want to be there. In some weird way, I feel like I owe her, like I failed her somehow."

Makenna touched his arm and waited to speak until he turned to face her. "You did not fail her, Bubba. If she is the arsonist, her parents failed her long before she ever met you."

He squeezed her hand and held her gaze a moment. "Thank you."

His touch sent a tremor down her spine, and her throat dried up as if she'd swallowed a cotton ball by mistake. "You're welcome," she said softly, pushing the words past the cotton. "I guess we better go." It wasn't what she wanted to say. She wanted to tell him she enjoyed his company, that she hoped they could have a future, that she didn't want to be just friends. However, now was not the time. It could wait until they found the killer.

He let go of her hand, and with great reluctance, she dropped her hand from his arm and opened her car door.

The house was dark as they approached, and Makenna wondered briefly if they were walking into a trap. Would Felicity lure them here and then set her own house on fire? Makenna's hand touched the butt of her gun, but it wouldn't be much help against a fire.

Her blood pulsed in her ears like a rhythmic beating of a drum, but she forced her breathing to stay even. It wasn't dark yet. The killer always struck after dark, so surely they would be safe. She hoped they would be safe. She'd promised Bubba's parents she would protect him, yet here she was dragging him along to danger.

The porch creaked under her feet, and the hairs on her neck lifted, but then she felt Bubba's calming presence behind her. He placed a hand on the small of her back, and her heart began to slow. After a deep breath, she pressed the bell. The chime echoed throughout but then silence fell again.

"Maybe she's not home?" Bubba asked as the silence drew out.

"Do you know where she might go?" Makenna didn't have a warrant, so she couldn't just bust into the house, and the blinds were pulled, blocking visibility.

"No, but my parents might."

Makenna sighed. "I didn't want to get your parents involved, but you're right. They're probably our best hope." She just hoped they would talk to her when they found out what she wanted.

## 17

B
ubba shivered as he opened the car door and stepped out into the cool evening. Night was approaching, sending shadows across the streets, and he felt eyes on him. He looked down the street, but he could see nothing. He must just be on edge.

There was no need to knock, but Bubba paused a moment at the door anyway. What would his parents say when they told them why they were here? Would this damage the relationship he had just begun to rebuild?

"You okay?" Makenna asked. She might have said she wanted to remain strictly professional but her eyes brimmed with concern. They would have to revisit this relationship when the killer was safely behind bars.

"Yeah, just wishing she wasn't a suspect."

"Me too, but it will be all right." She placed a hand on his arm, and Bubba forced himself to focus on the task at hand and not how much he wanted to kiss Makenna. After, he told himself. When everyone is safe again. Then we can think about the future.

He pushed the door open, calling for his mother as he stepped over the threshold.

"Captain Drake, nice to see you again," his mother said as she rounded the corner, but her tone didn't match her words. She sounded about as happy to see Makenna as she would be to invite a tax collector in for an audit. Bubba couldn't blame her. Makenna seemed to bring bad news whenever she showed up around here.

"You as well, Margaret. Mind if I come in?"

"Well, you're here already." His mother turned and led the way into the living room.

"Felicity, what are you doing here?" Bubba asked as he rounded the corner and saw his sister curled up on the couch.

"She's been here all day," his mother said as she reached down to touch Felicity's head. "She called a little after you left this morning. She's running a fever and needed someone to take care of her, so I brought her here. Why?"

"We were actually looking for Felicity," Makenna said. "We need to ask her a few questions."

His mother crossed her arms, and her mouth pulled into a tight line. She moved as if to shield Felicity. "Don't tell me you think Felicity is the arsonist now."

Oh no, this was going downhill quickly. He could see the 'mama bear' instincts taking over, and he needed to pacify her if they had any hope of getting their questions answered. "There's some information that needs clarifying, Mom."

"I'll answer their questions," Felicity said, struggling to sit up a bit.

Bubba scanned her for any sign of a cut, but he could see nothing. He shot Makenna a look hoping she would notice the same.

"You don't have to," his mother said. "I'm sure Captain Drake knows you have the right to an attorney."

"It's fine, Mom." Felicity placed a hand on their mother's

arm which seemed to quell her intensity. For the moment at least. Bubba nodded to Makenna. It was now or never.

Makenna cleared her throat, obviously nervous having to ask these questions in front of their mother. "Felicity, we spoke to Roger earlier, and he said you changed in the last month, grew more negative and began talking about helping the people who came into the office. Can you tell me why the sudden change?"

Felicity took a deep breath and let it out slowly. "A month ago, I got a call from a doctor in Richmond. I guess my biological mother ended up there a few years ago. I hadn't heard anything from her since Child Protective Services pulled me from her house so long ago, but I guess they found her unconscious on a park bench. She never woke up, and this doctor was calling to tell me that she passed away. So yeah, things changed for me a month ago. I had a lot of memories dredged up."

"Why didn't you tell us?" his mother asked as she sat on the edge of the couch next to Felicity.

"I didn't want to bother anybody with it. You all have been so good to me, but when the memories came flooding back, I just felt like I needed to help the people I saw everyday. I mean they come in once a week, and it doesn't seem as if Dr. Bloom is doing anything for them.

"Sometimes they would tell me their stories as they waited for their appointment, and sometimes I would hear things as I walked by the room. I didn't mean to look in their case files, I just thought maybe I could help them if I knew more about their issues. If they had backgrounds like mine."

"Felicity, I have to ask, where were you last night?" Makenna still sounded all business, but Bubba could hear the compassion in her voice.

"I was home all night. Why?"

"There was another arson last night, and we think the person was injured. Can I see both of your arms?"

Felicity held her arms up, but there were no cuts, no bandaids. Where did this leave them now?

"Satisfied?" his mother asked.

"Yes, ma'am. I'm sorry, but I had to ask. Felicity, I know there is a lot in your past, but I'm sure Dr. Bloom would help you process your feelings or find someone who could help you."

"Roger wanted to let you know that he still cares for you as well," Bubba added. "Maybe if you talk to him, explain things, you guys can work it out."

"Thank you both," Felicity said.

Suddenly Bubba wondered if Felicity might know about Rachel Hanes. Maybe she had been a patient or maybe she had just been privy to some gossip. Either way, he figured it was worth a shot. "Felicity, do you know Rachel Hanes?"

"Rachel Hanes," she appeared to think for a moment before nodding. "Yeah, the odd one, right? Always hanging around coffee shops, but never speaking to anyone?"

"Sounds like her. Do you know her story?"

Felicity cocked her head at him. "You don't remember her?"

Bubba blinked at the tone in Felicity's voice. It was obvious she thought he should know her, so why couldn't he remember her. "No, should I? She seems familiar, but I can't place her and I don't remember her name."

"Her husband was the one killed at the construction site. You told me you watched him die and felt badly you all didn't reach him in time."

Bubba fell into the nearby recliner and ran a hand across his forehead. He'd forgotten all about that incident. Or maybe pushed it from his mind was more like it. It wasn't the only death he'd ever seen, but it had certainly been one of the more gruesome.

"I'm afraid I'm not following," Makenna said. "Can someone fill me in?"

Bubba sighed as the memories flooded his mind. "About a

month before the murders started five years ago, the fire department was called out to a construction incident. A worker had been working on the top of a building when the scaffolding he was standing on broke beneath him. He was still holding on when we arrived, but before we could get a ladder to him, his fingers slipped, and he fell to his death. We all watched as the life drained out of him. It was horrible."

"Was Rachel there?" Makenna asked. "Why would she blame you and not the other firemen?"

"I was the one extending the ladder. The story was in the newspaper for the next week, and an investigation was even opened, but I was cleared."

"Well, that is definitely a reason to ask Rachel a few questions," Makenna said. "What could have triggered her now though?"

"I'd have to look to be sure, but I'm fairly certain that the first recent death would be five years to the day that her husband died."

Before Makenna could respond, the sound of glass shattering carried through the house.

"What was that?" His mother's fearful eyes glanced toward the front of the house.

"Wait here." Bubba raced toward the utility room where the fire extinguisher was stored. He couldn't smell the gas as he rounded the corner, but he knew the fire would not be far behind.

"I'm going after her," Makenna called as she pulled her gun and raced past Bubba and toward the front of the house.

"Be careful," he called, but she was already out of earshot.

Makenna rounded the corner just as the flame erupted. The force of the heat lifted her and flung her back against the wall. Though she didn't lose consciousness, for a moment she also couldn't move. Shock. It had to be shock.

She watched as the flame crept closer to her. Was she going to die here? She needed to get up, but her body refused to cooperate. Then she saw the white foam of the fire extinguisher and Bubba wielding the nozzle with an expert touch.

The fire danced and darted as if trying to avoid capture, but Bubba had been quick, and he had the flame out before it could destroy more of the house.

"Are you okay?" he asked after setting the fire extinguisher down. He knelt down beside her and placed his hands on her cheeks. "Makenna, are you okay?"

Makenna could see his lips moving, enough to make out the words, but all she could hear was ringing. "I'm fine, I think." She felt her mouth moving, but she couldn't even hear her own words. She hoped that he could.

"You need to see a doctor." The words were muffled but she could make them out as the ringing subsided. Bubba's eyes brimmed with concern as his fingers touched her face and then slid down her neck and arms as if searching for injuries.

She knew she did, but she also needed to see if the arsonist was still outside. The chances were slim. Makenna had probably missed her window, but she had to be sure. "Not until I see if she's still here."

Bubba shook his head, and his hands returned to her face. He held her gingerly, and Makenna warmed at the look in his eyes. They were failing miserably at this professional only relationship. "You're in no condition to chase anyone down, and she's probably long gone by now. Let me call an ambulance. None of us can stay here tonight anyway."

Makenna wanted to argue, but her body still wasn't responding the way it should. Instead, she nodded and tried to stand. Bubba moved his hands to her shoulders and pressed gently. "You're not moving until an ambulance arrives to check you out."

A small smile touched her lips. She had suspected he was a protector, and she couldn't deny that it felt nice having someone take care of her. If only he lived closer. If only she could convince him to stay. "Okay, I won't move, but can you click on my radio, so I can call dispatch?"

"Of course." He grabbed the radio from her belt.

Makenna prayed it hadn't been injured in the blast and would still work. Relief flooded her at the sound of the familiar squelch when he pressed the call button. He held it to her mouth. "Dispatch, this is Captain Drake. I need an ambo and a squad car to 353 Fir Street."

"Captain Drake, Matt, are you two okay?" Bubba's mother's voice carried in from the other room.

"We're okay, Mom, but we can't stay here. Pack some clothes and things you and Dad need. We'll find a place to stay for tonight."

"You can stay with me," Makenna said although she wasn't sure Bubba staying in her house was a good idea. Not with him looking at her like that, and her heart racing the way it was.

He smiled and brushed a strand of hair behind her ear. "I appreciate the offer, Makenna, but I don't think your place will be any safer. If she knows where I live, she probably knows where you live too."

"You're right," Makenna agreed, placing her hand on his. She really wished she wasn't injured because the desire to kiss him right now burned throughout her body. "She attacked much earlier than usual, and not in the normal way."

"What do you mean?" Bubba asked.

"Molotov cocktail. The flame exploded when I walked in the room. I bet if you look around, you'll find glass shards. Maybe if we're lucky, we'll find fingerprints on those shards."

Bubba stepped away from her and scanned the floor. A

moment later, he leaned over and, using the hem of his shirt, he picked something up from the floor. "Looks like you're right."

Makenna marveled at how careful he was with the evidence. He had good instincts. She wondered if she could convince him to cross into police work and stay here with her. "Tad and Kelsey should be here soon. We'll let them deal with the evidence, but we have to figure out somewhere to go."

"You're going to the hospital to get checked out. Maybe we can get some hotel rooms after that."

The front door opened then and Tad and Kelsey burst in. "Captain? Are you okay?"

"I think I'm just shaken up, Tad, but I need to get looked at. Did you see her outside? The arsonist?"

Tad shook his head. "No, there was no one out there."

Makenna nodded. "I figured. We'll find her another way. She used a Molotov cocktail this time. Bubba found one glass shard, but I'm sure there are more. You and Kelsey see what you can find while I'm getting checked out."

"Of course, Captain. And then what?" Kelsey asked.

"Then we need to find a place to stay. No one can stay here, and I don't trust my place or Felicity's."

"I have room at my place," Kelsey offered.

Bubba shook his head. "Kelsey, we couldn't impose."

"Yes, you can. I insist. I'll take you and your family to my house while Captain Drake gets looked at."

Makenna exchanged a glance with Bubba. It wasn't her first choice, but right now, their options were limited.

"No, you can take my family, but I'm going with Makenna."

Tad and Kelsey exchanged a glance, but before they could say anything, the EMTs entered and began strapping Makenna to the board. As they loaded her in the ambulance, she prayed that her injuries weren't serious enough to keep her off the case. More than ever, she needed to find this woman and stop her.

Bubba climbed up beside her and grabbed her hand as the EMT began prepping her arm for an IV.

"We're going to have to talk about this soon," Makenna said, smiling up at him. Something had definitely changed between them, and though she had no idea where it might end up, she was going to enjoy it while it lasted.

He returned her smile and squeezed her hand. "Promise, but let's get you checked out first."

## 18

"You didn't have to come with me," Makenna said as Bubba wheeled her out to the waiting police cruiser a few hours later. He hadn't left her side except for when she'd been taken back for x-rays. She'd called Tad to come pick them up only because Bubba didn't have a car with him.

"Yeah, I did. You're tough, Makenna, but everyone has limits, and sometimes I wonder if you know yours. Also, in case you didn't notice, I'd like to keep you around."

Makenna's lips twitched into a lop-sided grin. How did he seem to know her so well in so short a time? "Okay, perhaps you're right. I don't always know when to stop, but all this time we've lost at the hospital?" She shrugged. "I feel like we're running out of time."

"I know, and I feel it too, but I have to trust that God brought us together to catch this woman and that He won't let us fail. However, we have to take care of ourselves to be useful to Him and that means rest and recovery, Makenna."

Makenna nodded at his sage wisdom. She'd been so caught up in following the evidence that she hadn't been bringing it to God, and maybe that was part of the issue.

Tad stepped out of the cruiser as they approached and flashed a tight smile. "Glad to see you're okay, Captain. We got everyone set up at Kelsey's house."

He held out a hand, and Bubba took her other arm. Together, they helped her stand, shuffle the few feet to the car, and slide into the passenger seat. "Good, I think a little sleep is in order, but then I want everyone looking for Rachel Hanes. We think she might be the arsonist, and we need to end this. Today." It was after midnight, so she was counting it as the beginning of the day.

"Understood. I've got Brayden checking on the glass shards. He'll alert us if any fingerprints pop up."

"Good, I'd also like you to find out everything you can about Kevin Hanes's accident from five years ago. I need to know if that's what started all of this, and if it is, what the recent trigger was. Bubba and I will pick up Rachel Hanes."

Tad's face pulled into a tight line. "No offense, Captain, but how about you let me pick up Rachel?" Makenna opened her mouth to protest, but Tad held up his hand to stop her and continued. "If she is the killer, who knows what she might do, and you're not in peak condition. I promise I'll bring her straight to the station so you can question her."

"He's right, Makenna," Bubba agreed. "You're going to need to take it slow for a few days."

Makenna knew they were right, but she hated being sidelined especially when she felt they were so close to finally ending it. "Fine. Bubba and I will research, but you ask her nothing without me there."

"Got it." He chuckled and shook his head as he shut her door and walked around to the driver's side.

Ten minutes later, Kelsey met them at her front door. "Welcome to my home," she said, gesturing to the open area behind her. "Patrick, Margaret, and Felicity are all upstairs. Are you ready to do the same?"

Makenna wanted to say no. She wasn't sure she would be getting any sleep tonight anyway, but she had promised Bubba she'd at least try. Who knew what tomorrow would hold. "Yes, let's get some rest, and we can debrief tomorrow morning."

"You got it." As Kelsey led the way up the stairs, Makenna grabbed the railing with one hand and let Bubba offer support with the other. Her eyes scanned the house as she made her way slowly up the steps.

The house was nothing like Kelsey. Filled with knick knacks and all sorts of kitchy paintings, it was a stark contrast to Kelsey's minimalist attitude. Had she inherited it then? Or had she purchased it this way and just been too busy to make any changes?

"It's a lovely house, Kelsey," Makenna said as they reached the landing. She hated that she was already out of breath.

"Thanks. It was my aunt's which is part of why I moved here. She and I had very different styles, but the structure of the house was so good that I couldn't sell it. One of these days, I'll renovate it though." She opened a door to reveal a pink flowery bedroom. "You can take this one, Captain. Sorry about the pattern."

"It's fine," Makenna said though her stomach was already turning from the assault of flowers on the walls. She squeezed Bubba's arm one last time before closing the bedroom door. They hadn't had their "talk" yet, both agreeing they would rather wait for the case to be over, but Makenna knew strictly professional was no longer an option. She'd felt the change in his touch when he assessed her injuries, and she'd seen it in his eyes both then and on the way to the hospital. The question was what did she do about it?

She changed into a spare shirt Kelsey had and brushed her teeth with an extra toothbrush before climbing into the bed. As she stared at the ceiling, her thoughts alternated between finding the killer and having a heartfelt conversation with Bubba.

She knew she felt something for him, but was it enough to leave her job? Would he ever consider moving here? The questions cycled through her mind, but there would be no answers tonight. Maybe after they caught the killer but not tonight. With a sigh, she closed her eyes and prayed for peace, for safety, and for help in closing this case.

Bubba stared at the ceiling in the guest room and tried to process his feelings. It had been a long time since he had opened his heart, but he wanted to. He was tired of being alone, tired of watching his friends find love and trying to live vicariously through them. He'd shut those feelings off for fear he would fall for someone and she would get hurt because of him, but when he'd seen Makenna lying against the wall, he'd been so afraid that she was dead. That she had died before he got to tell her how he felt. He knew his feelings for her had been growing, but he hadn't known how much until then.

And he knew she was feeling something too. He'd seen it in her eyes when he touched her, felt it spark between them, and she'd said they needed to talk in the ambulance. But where did that leave them? Could he come back and live in Woodville and be Matt Fisher again? Would she ever consider leaving? Could they make a long distance relationship work? It was easier with video chats and instant messaging, but they both had demanding jobs. Could they even find times to virtually meet up?

Bubba pulled out his cell phone and opened his Bible App. He usually preferred holding the Bible in his hands - there was something about the feel of it that always gave him comfort - but as he didn't have his Bible, his phone would have to do. He flipped to the book of John and began reading. As he did, he prayed for wisdom. His life had changed so much in the last few days, and he had no idea what he was going to do when the killer was caught. But he did know that God could offer peace, and that was exactly what he needed right now.

How could she have been so stupid? She never should have gone to Matt's house, and she certainly shouldn't have thrown the bottle in. She'd let her anger get the best of her, and that wasn't smart. She needed to be smart. She needed wisdom. However, the voice was still curiously silent. Had she angered him with her failures? Was he done with her now? What would she do if he stopped talking? Could she let the weak voice take over again?

"Help me," she pleaded with her empty room, but there was no answer. At least not from him.

"Let it go," the coward said. "It's over."

With a snarl, she ripped Matt Fisher's picture off her wall. "No, it's not over until I say it's over. Attacking the house with everyone there was stupid, but attacking one of his family members wouldn't be. And she knew just who to choose. It was almost too easy.

## 19

"Did we find anything on the glass shards?" Makenna asked Brayden when she entered the police station the next morning. Her body was still stiff and sore, but the sleep had helped a little. Even though it hadn't been enough. She could walk without assistance, but running would be out of the question as would tackling anyone if it were necessary.

Brayden set his coffee mug down and rubbed his eyes. He had been manning the station all night, and she would let him take the rest of the day off to sleep, but she needed an update first.

"Still waiting on the lab, Captain."

She turned to Kelsey and Tad. "Did you find anything else at the scene? Any usable footprints outside?" She had sent them back to Bubba's parents' house after breakfast to see if the killer had left any clues outside that had been missed in the dark the night before.

"Nothing," Kelsey said with a soft shake of her head. "I think we got lucky at Dr. Hayworth's because his sprinkler system had been leaking which made the ground wet. Everywhere else, it's hard and cold and covered with leaves."

Makenna sighed. She had been hoping for better news though she'd expected this outcome. "Okay, so that means it's time to pick up Rachel. Her husband was killed in a construction accident, and Matt was named in the story that came out about it. Kelsey, you and Tad go find her and bring her in. Brayden, go home and get some sleep. Bubba and I will start looking into the Kevin Hanes accident and see if it's the trigger."

"Copy that." Tad grabbed his car keys, and he and Kelsey headed out. Brayden followed a few minutes later.

When they were alone, Bubba touched Makenna's shoulder. "Can I get you anything? Coffee? Tea?"

"Coffee would be great," Makenna said, "but let's just make it here. I don't want to lose any time waiting at a shop."

"Sounds good. Where's the break room? I'll go put a pot on."

Makenna pointed down the hall and watched him leave before collapsing in the chair behind her desk. She sighed and rubbed her head. The hospital had cleared her last night, but she didn't feel quite right. A chill that she couldn't seem to shake grew inside her, her head still ached, and her back was sore from hitting the wall.

Rest would probably cure all of that, but there was no time for rest now. Their killer was obviously escalating. Four attacks in less than a week and the addition of Molotov cocktails meant she could be spiraling out of control, and if that happened, who knew what she might do next.

Makenna turned on her laptop and began searching for any information on Kevin Hanes.

Bubba returned a few minutes later and held a steaming mug out to her. "I put a little cream and two sugars. I think that's how you drink it, am I right?"

"Right as rain." Makenna took the mug and smiled up at him. It had only been a week, but he already seemed to know her inside and out. She wrapped her hands around her mug to infuse the heat into her hands.

"You have a laptop for me?" Bubba asked as he pulled up a chair to the other side of her desk and sat down.

"You can grab Brayden's. It should be ready to use."

He nodded and returned a moment later with Brayden's laptop. For a few minutes, there was only the sound of tapping keys and the occasional sip from a mug. Makenna marveled at how comfortable she was around Bubba. There was no need to fill the silence with idle chatter.

"It seems I was right about the date," Bubba said. "Here's the original story and the date of the construction accident was five years to the day that the repair shop owner was killed."

"Okay, so that could have been the trigger. Let's see if we can find anything else about Kevin or Rachel." Her hand shook as she picked up the mug again.

Bubba tried to keep his focus on the research, but he couldn't help his eyes wandering to Makenna every few minutes. Though she said she was fine, he could tell she wasn't quite herself.

Not only did she still have the dark circles under eyes, but she shivered every few minutes. Was she even aware she was doing it? In addition, she kept picking up her mug and cradling it in her hands even though she didn't always drink it, and occasionally her hand would shake enough to send the coffee sloshing over the lip of the mug. She needed rest, but she was stubborn. He knew she wouldn't take any until this case was over. So, he needed to make sure this ended. Today.

He clicked out of the story of Kevin's accident and focused on Rachel instead. Who was she? There wasn't much on her other than the fact that she used to be a teacher at the local school before Kevin died. After, it appeared she stopped teaching and withdrew from life. Their marriage certificate showed they hadn't been married long, and he could find no birth certificate for children. Bubba knew death affected people in different ways, but he just couldn't find anything other than Kevin's death that would point to Rachel's behavior.

The door opened, and he looked up to see Kelsey and Tad leading Rachel into the station. She appeared to be calm and collected. At least until she saw him.

"What's he doing here?" she shouted as she charged his direction.

Tad managed to grab her before she reached Bubba, but she struggled against his grip.

"Let me go. He killed my husband," she said as she twisted and writhed.

Tad pulled out his handcuffs and secured her wrists. "Is that why you tried to kill him?"

"Kill him? What are you talking about? Are you listening to me? He killed my husband."

"I didn't kill him, Rachel," Bubba said. His heart broke for her even though he knew he wasn't at fault. "We just didn't get there in time."

"You lie," she spat. "She told me you would, but you were supposed to be dead." Rachel's voice quieted, and she began to rock from side to side. "She told me you were dead."

Makenna and Bubba exchanged glances. He had expected crazy, but this was beyond what he had imagined.

"Who told you Matt was dead?" Makenna asked.

"She told me it would be okay. That he got what he deserved." Her voice was even softer as if she were speaking more to herself than any of them. "But he didn't. He didn't get what he deserved."

"Who, Rachel? Who told you he would get what he deserved?"

Rachel lifted her head and looked at Makenna, but her glazed eyes were clearly seeing something else far away. "Iris."

"Who's Iris?" Kelsey asked.

What was going on here? They'd all thought Rachel was the killer, but now she was rambling about some other woman.

"Rachel," Makenna shook the woman's shoulders. "Who's Iris?"

Rachel blinked as if seeing Makenna for the first time. "His sister," she said before she floated away again.

"His sister?" Tad asked. "Who's sister?"

"Not mine," Bubba said. "Felicity is my foster sister and Rebecca is my biological sister. Could she mean Kevin?" He looked back at his laptop screen and pulled up Kevin's birth record. "Makenna, come look at this."

Makenna leaned over Bubba's shoulder to read the screen. "He had a twin sister?" Her mouth pulled into a tight line, and though she said nothing, Bubba could read the thought in her head. A twin sister would have a close tie to Kevin and therefore a high chance of wanting revenge on his killer. The question was where was Iris now?

Makenna pulled her gaze away from the screen to issue orders. "Tad, take Rachel to an interrogation room. See what you can find out. Kelsey, Bubba, find out anything you can on Iris Hanes. I need to know where she is."

Silence invaded the room as everyone focused on the task. Bubba typed Iris Hanes into the search bar and began scanning the stories for any clue, any picture.

"I found something, Captain," Kelsey said. "It's a few years old, but this appears to be a picture of Iris Hanes at some conference a few towns over."

Kelsey turned the screen around, and Makenna sucked in her breath. "Bubba, is this who I think it is?" The hair was down and flowing in the picture and the face was younger and graced with a smile, but she would bet her job it was the same woman.

Bubba stared at the picture and nodded. "It sure looks like her."

"Can I buy a clue here?" Kelsey asked. "I feel like I'm missing something."

"Kelsey, I want you to find out everything you can about Dr. Bloom. I want her history all the way back to birth."

"Wait, Dr. Bloom?" Kelsey asked. "Why are we looking into her? I thought we were focused on Iris Hanes."

"Bubba and I are pretty sure that Dr. Bloom is Iris Hanes."

Kelsey's eyes widened and without another word, her face returned to her laptop screen.

"Makenna." Bubba's serious tone grabbed her attention, and she turned his direction. "Did Felicity go to work today?"

A cold sensation flooded Makenna's veins. If Felicity had gone to work today, she could be in real trouble. "Kelsey, keep looking. Call me with anything you find. Bubba, you're with me. Let's go pay Dr. Bloom a visit."

"Makenna, should we bring Tad?" Bubba whispered as they neared the front door.

She knew his words were coming from a place of concern, but they annoyed her all the same. She was fine, and they had no time to bicker about her health. "I'll call him on the way. Let's go."

As they pulled up to Dr. Bloom's office though, Makenna wondered if she had made a mistake not waiting for Tad. There were no other cars in the parking lot which led her to believe that Dr. Bloom was expecting them. Plus, she had no idea what the woman might be armed with, and as much as she wanted to believe she was, Makenna knew she wasn't functioning at one hundred percent. Still, time was of the essence. Especially if Dr. Bloom had Felicity. Who knew what the woman might do.

"You ready?"

Bubba nodded, his face set in a grim determination. Makenna was glad to have him with her even if he wasn't a trained cop.

Besides, she knew Tad was on his way. She'd radioed him on the drive over. All she had to do was either take Dr. Bloom in easy, if she acquiesced, or kill a little time until her backup showed up.

"Let's go."

Makenna pulled her gun as she led the way up the sidewalk. She dared a glance in the glass door before she opened it, but the lobby was empty. Either Dr. Bloom wasn't here or she was in her office. Makenna hoped for the latter; she didn't feel like tracking this woman down all over town.

She gestured for Bubba to follow her and then eased her way toward the office door.

"Come on in, Captain Drake. We've been expecting you." The voice that came out of the office sounded little like the Dr. Bloom they had spoken to the day before. Confidence and disdain oozed from this voice, and Makenna did not miss the use of the word we. So, she definitely had someone in there with her.

Makenna stepped into the office. Her gun found Dr. Bloom, but as she had feared, Dr. Bloom was not alone. Felicity sat in the doctor's chair, a knife to her throat and fear burning in her eyes.

"Matt, I know you're out there too. Why don't you join us?"

Makenna hoped Bubba would keep his calm when he saw his sister. The last thing she needed was for someone to get antsy. She felt him fill the space behind her and sensed his tension.

"Iris, this is over. It's time to let Felicity go," Makenna said, trying to take control of the situation.

Iris smiled a cold, calculated smile. "I don't think so. See, I made a mistake once when I didn't make sure Matt here was dead, but he forgave me and granted me a second chance."

He? Who was she talking about. "Do you mean Kevin forgave you?"

"No, not Kevin," Iris laughed, "though I'm sure he will thank me for bringing his killer to justice. There won't be a mistake this time."

Felicity winced as Iris pulled the knife tighter against her neck. Makenna had no shot. Not with Iris leaning so close to Felicity, but there was a window behind her. If only she could find a way to let Tad know their situation.

"I didn't kill him, Iris," Bubba said, stepping forward. "I was cleared in the investigation. We simply got there too late."

Iris turned her attention to Bubba, and hatred flashed in her eyes. "I felt him die. Did you know that? Twins are connected that way sometimes, and Kevin was my best friend growing up. I was in the middle of a session with a client at my old practice, and I felt this crazy fear come over me. Fear that I was going to die. My lungs closed up and my pulse raced just like his must have.

"And when his heart stopped beating-" Her hand shook and she paused to compose herself. "When his heart stopped beating, mine did too for just an instant, and then I knew that he was gone and this terrible vacantness settled on me."

As Iris got lost in her story, her face turned away from Makenna, and Makenna used that moment to click the talk button on her radio and wedge it into a locked position against her belt so that Tad, Kelsey, and dispatch would hear what was going on. Perhaps it would give them some edge.

"I am incredibly sorry for your loss," Bubba said, taking another step closer to the desk, "but those women you killed were also somebody's sister, somebody's daughter. Their families are now grieving the same as you are."

Iris shook her head. "I should have picked them better. Their deaths were supposed to hurt you. He told me they would, but I didn't choose the right ones. I should have picked Felicity here the first time and maybe your mother, but he wasn't clear. He should have been clear." The hand holding the knife shook, and Felicity whimpered again.

Makenna could see Iris unraveling. She wondered if the

doctor even recognized her own psychotic break. "Who is he, Iris? Who's been telling you to kill people?"

Iris turned back to Makenna, and for a moment she looked confused, but then she twitched and the icy face returned. "God, of course. God chose me as his angel. He showed me what to do and gave me the information on them. They were evil people, and they deserved to die."

Makenna shook her head. "No, Iris. They were children of God, made in His image. They might have been doing evil things, but God - the true God - does not condone murder, and He believes in second chances. Even for you."

"I don't need a second chance." Iris's voice rose in pitch and volume. "I was doing His will."

"No, you weren't. Have you heard of a visionary before, Dr. Bloom?" Makenna had no idea if switching to the woman's professional title would cause that part of her to take over, but she had to try.

"Of course I've heard of a visionary," Iris said. "I am a psychiatrist."

"Then you must know that usually those visions are the result of a trauma the patient has experienced. Abuse. Sickness. Death."

Recognition flashed in Dr. Bloom's eyes, and then she twitched again. "No, I'm not a visionary. I'm an angel. There's a difference."

"But you didn't become an angel until Kevin's death, did you?" Makenna pressed. She glanced over at Bubba who was watching, waiting for a sign. She nodded slightly at Felicity, hoping he would understand her message. If she could get Dr. Bloom back, they might have a second to take her down. But only a second.

"I…. no, that's different."

But Makenna could hear the confusion in Dr. Bloom's voice.

"Dr. Bloom, the anniversary of Kevin's death was your trigger. It's what brought the visions back. It's when he began talking again, am I right?"

And there it was. Makenna might have missed it if she hadn't been paying close enough attention. She saw the change come over Dr. Bloom a moment before she stepped back.

She stared at Felicity and then the knife in her hands. "What have I done?"

She didn't even have to signal Bubba. With those words, he launched himself across the remaining space, sending Dr. Bloom crashing to the ground and the knife skidding in the other direction. By the time Iris took over again, Bubba had her pinned to the floor, and Makenna was slapping handcuffs on her wrists.

"No, I can't fail him again. I won't."

"Iris Bloom, you have the right to remain silent. Anything you say can and will be used against you in a court of law." Before she finished the Miranda rights, Tad appeared in the doorway, and she passed the woman off to him so she could check on Felicity and Bubba. "Are you okay?"

Felicity was still rubbing her neck, and a thin trickle of blood oozed out of a small cut, but she managed a nod. "Yeah, I'm okay, but I think I'm going to need a new job."

Makenna felt the chuckle bubble inside her, and she caught Bubba's eye and smiled. "Yeah, it looks like you might."

As the three waited for the EMT to arrive and check Felicity out, Makenna breathed a sigh of relief. It was finally over. She could rest and return to her normal life. But did she want to? She loved her job, but her normal life meant evenings home alone with her cat. It meant paperwork, few dates, legal jargon, and death. And she was no longer sure that was what she wanted.

Watching Bubba with his sister and with his parents these last few days had reminded her of family - the importance of it and what she was missing. Could she give this up though?

Running a department had been her dream. Hadn't it? Or had she told herself it was her dream when she'd been shoved into it? She just didn't know.

Bubba turned to Makenna as the EMTs carried Felicity out. Though she'd stated she wasn't injured and just wanted to return to Kelsey's to rest, the paramedics had insisted she get her neck looked at. Evidently Iris had pressed hard enough to draw blood at least once, and they wanted to be sure she hadn't damaged anything underneath the skin.

"Reckon we should have that talk now?" he asked as he took Makenna's hand and pulled her to him.

She smiled and wrapped her arms around his neck. "I suppose we should."

Man, how he wanted to kiss her, but he needed to tell her what was on his heart first. "Makenna, after the first murders, I felt such guilt that I didn't think I'd ever open my heart to anyone again, but there is something about you that makes me feel complete, whole. My life isn't here any longer, and I know that yours is, but Fire Beach isn't that far. We could talk during the week and trade weekends."

She shook her head and placed a finger on his lips. "I don't want just weekends, Bubba. I worked hard to get to where I'm at, but I realized last night that my job, my title, means nothing if I don't have someone to share it with."

Bubba wasn't sure what she was saying. Was she telling him it would never work? Or was she saying that she would consider leaving Woodville? "Makenna, it's been a long time since I had to decode woman-speak. Can you just tell me what you mean?"

Makenna laughed and pulled his face down to hers. She placed her lips on his, and even though he still had questions, his arms wrapped around her waist. The kiss was everything he had imagined it would be, and while he had kissed women in the past, those kisses had never felt like this one. This one shook him to the core.

"What I'm saying," Makenna said as she pulled back, "is that this town holds a lot of memories for me. Some are good, but a lot of them I'd rather forget. Now, it might take awhile and I would certainly like to check the place out before I decide completely, but I don't think I would be opposed to transferring to a new police department."

Relief and elation flooded Bubba's body. "Like Fire Beach?"

"Like Fire Beach," she said with a smile, "or anywhere close to it."

"Yes." He picked her up and spun her around before setting her back down and finding her lips once again.

Makenna shivered as Bubba kissed her again. She wasn't sure if it was from the blast the night before or the heat racing through her from his kiss, but she knew that as much as she wanted to stay right here in his arms, she needed rest.

"You're still shivering, Makenna." Bubba's eyes were full of concern as he pulled back this time. "Are you okay?"

"Honestly, I think it's just my body realizing it's all finally over. What do you say we go tell your parents the killer is behind bars and then catch up on the sleep we've been missing this last week?"

"I can't think of anything I'd rather do," he said with a smile.

As they walked out of Iris Bloom's office hand in hand, Makenna thought about all the things she still had to do. She needed to inform the families of the victims that the killer had been caught, she needed to make sure Iris Bloom was processed correctly, and she needed to look into a replacement. Tad seemed like the obvious choice, but would he want the position? It was definitely a lot of work, but he was young enough and still single. And she couldn't think of anyone else she'd rather pass the mantle off to.

"Captain Drake, Matt, can I get a word?"

Makenna sighed at the sound of Natasha's voice. She was definitely not up to dealing with the reporter. "What are you doing here, Natasha? How did you even know we were here?"

Natasha rolled her eyes and shook her head. "You really don't know what a valuable asset you have, do you? Old Henry is almost always sitting outside your station, and he sees and hears a lot. I paid him a hundred bucks to come find me whenever you left. He wasn't sure where you'd gone, but he remembered the name Felicity, so I figured this was worth a shot."

Old Henry. Makenna should have known. Though the man often had a bottle in hand, Makenna had seen the sharp focus the few times she'd seen him sober. Natasha must have as well and used that to her advantage.

"Is it true then? Dr. Bloom is the killer?"

"It certainly appears that way. Of course, we still have to question her, but she had a knife to Felicity's throat, and she didn't deny the accusation. There's still a long road ahead, but I think the people of Woodville are safe again."

Natasha's eyes dropped to the ground, and she cleared her throat. "It would seem, then, that I owe you an apology, Matt.

I'm sorry I threatened to print that first story, and for what it's worth, I'm glad to know it wasn't you."

Makenna stared at the woman in front of her. Had Natasha Kingston actually apologized? By the shocked expression on Bubba's face, she could tell he was having a hard time processing it as well.

"Uh, thank you, I think," he said.

"You're welcome." And then suddenly her apologetic demeanor was gone, and her vicious, cutthroat side reappeared. "Don't think you're getting off so easy when it comes to your relationship though. It's clear there's something going on between the two of you, and I think the people of Woodville could use a feel good story, don't you?" With that, she snapped a picture of the two of them, smiled, and clopped away.

"What just happened?" Bubba asked as if he had just received an unknown error message on a computer.

"I think the world might have just ended," Makenna said with a laugh. It felt good to laugh, to finally relax, and to do it with Bubba.

"**A**re you sure you can't stay a little longer?" his mother asked as Bubba zipped his bag up. He knew that she was asking because she missed him, but he'd already been in Woodville much longer than he'd intended. Thankfully, his captain had agreed to the extra time though Bubba was sure kitchen duty would be on his plate for the next month to make up for it.

"I have to get back, Mom. My life is in Fire Beach now, but I promise I will call and visit." He had stayed the extra few days to make sure their window was repaired and the damaged floor replaced.

"I know it is. It's just been so nice having you here, and there's this part of me that fears if you leave, I'll never see you again."

He stepped away from his bag and took her hands in his. "Mom, I promise that you will see me again. How about you, Felicity, and Dad come out this weekend to Fire Beach? I'll show you around and you can meet all of my friends. Maybe we can even convince Jacob and Rebecca to come. It can be like a mini family reunion."

His mother sniffed and nodded. "I'd like that. I know you're not little any more, but you'll always be my little boy."

And he wouldn't have it any other way. It was nice to have his family in his life again. "There's just one thing, Mom. My friends all call me Bubba or Billy since that's how they've known me for the last five years."

His mother's nose wrinkled. "Bubba? What kind of a name is that? What's wrong with the name we gave you?"

"It's a nickname, Mom, and I couldn't go by Matt when I first got there. I had to be someone else, remember?"

"Can I still call you Matt?"

"Of course, Mom. You can always call me Matt."

"How about me?" Felicity asked, poking her head in the doorway. She too looked like a new woman. After the hospital released her, Roger had come by to see her. They still had a lot of work to do, but once he heard the reason for her behavior, they had agreed to attend counseling and give their relationship another shot. She still didn't have a new job, but Kelsey had promised to help her find one that would allow her to go to school and get the counseling degree she'd decided she wanted. Bubba had no doubt she would make a fantastic counselor, especially with her ability to relate to people from challenging backgrounds.

"Yes, you can call me Matt too."

"I can't thank you enough, Matt, for saving me, for bringing Roger back into my life, for everything really."

"Hey, that's what big brothers are for," he said as he pulled her in for a hug.

"Yeah, well, don't be a stranger."

"I promise," he said before picking up his bag again. His mother and sister followed him to the front door where his father was waiting. He was not one for embracing his emotions, but Bubba would miss him all the same. "Dad, it was good to see you again."

Bubba stuck out his hand to shake with his father, but his father stared at his hand and then pulled him in for a hug instead. "Be safe, son," he said and then the hug was over.

Bubba blinked as he tried to process the emotions running through him. "I will, sir."

And then a knock sounded at the front door. Makenna. She hadn't officially resigned from her post yet, but she had agreed to drive him back to Fire Beach and spend a few days talking to the police department there and looking at rental properties.

"That will be Makenna. I love you guys, and I promise to come back soon."

Makenna smiled as she glanced over at Bubba. The last few days with him had been amazing. He'd come with her to talk to every affected family and then let her cry on his shoulder when the emotions grew too heavy.

Kelsey had let him and his parents stay at her house until his parent's house was fixed, and Makenna had spent every evening there with him. They'd done devotions together and talked about their plans for the future. It had felt like a family, but now he was leaving, and she would hopefully be following soon.

She'd discussed her decision with Tad, and he had agreed to take the job if she resigned. That only left getting him trained and selling her small house if she decided Fire Beach was for her. She planned to do both after driving Bubba back to Fire Beach and spending a few days there. He'd said his friend Jordan might know of an opening in the force, and Cara had offered to let her stay at the bed and breakfast while she was in town. Makenna was excited but also nervous. Woodville had been her home for the last several years, and though it held a lot of bad memories, it held some good ones too. And she would miss it.

"You ready to be home?"

"Am I ever," he said. "It was nice to see my family, and I'm glad they're back in my life, but this is my home." He smiled as they passed the sign welcoming them to Fire Beach.

Makenna swallowed her nerves as she parked the car in front of Cara's bed and breakfast. Bubba had offered to get her settled before she took him home, but she was still a little nervous about staying with Cara. What if they didn't get along? What if she didn't fit in here?

She pushed the thoughts aside as she opened her door. That was fear talking, and fear was a liar. She would be fine. Things with Cara would be fine. She simply needed to trust that God's hand was in all of this.

Bubba rang the doorbell, but when no one answered, he turned the handle and opened the door. "She must be where she can't hear the bell," he said as he led the way inside. "Cara? It's Bubba and Makenna. Are you here?"

His voice echoed in the open room, and the hairs on the back of Makenna's neck stood up. Something felt wrong. She pulled her gun and motioned Bubba to let her lead the way. This wasn't her jurisdiction, but at least she was armed.

She cleared the current room and then followed the hallway to the right. The bedrooms lay to the left, so she assumed the kitchen and dining room would be the other direction. She wanted to clear those areas before opening bedroom doors.

As she stepped into the kitchen, the sound of moaning reached her ears. She quickly crossed the room, dropping to the floor when she spied Cara laying on the floor.

"Cara, are you okay?" Bubba had joined her and was carefully touching Cara's shoulder as Makenna pulled out her phone.

"This is Captain Makenna Drake of the Woodville police," she said when the 911 operator picked up. "I'm at Cara Hunter's bed and breakfast, and she's been injured. Please send an ambo and a local unit to 212 Whistler Avenue."

"Yes ma'am. I'm contacting them now. Please stay on the line until they arrive."

"What happened here?" Bubba asked as he looked up at her.

Makenna had no idea. What she did know was that the rest and relaxation she had been hoping for would have to wait. She may have just finished one case, but suddenly she found herself smack dab in the middle of another one.

Want to find out what happened to Cara? Be sure to read Secrets and Suspense.

The End!

# IT'S NOT QUITE THE END!

Thank you so much for reading *Never Forget the Past*. This book was inspired by my readers who told me Bubba needed his own story. Boy, did he ever, and now there are so many new characters to bring back around.

I hope you enjoyed the story as I really enjoyed writing it. If you did, would you do me a favor? If you did, please leave a review. It really helps. It doesn't have to be long - just a few words to help other readers know what they're getting.

I'd love to hear from you, not only about this story, but about the characters or stories you'd like read in the future. I'm always looking for new ideas and if I use one of your characters or stories, I'll send you a free ebook and paperback of the book with a special dedication. Write to me at lorana-hoopes@gmail.com. And if you'd like to see what's coming next, be sure to stop by authorloranahoopes.com

I also have a weekly newsletter that contains many wonderful things like pictures of my adorable children, chances to win awesome prizes, new releases and sales I might be holding, great books from other authors, and anything else that strikes my fancy and that I think you would enjoy. I'll even send you the first chapter of my newest (maybe not even released yet) book if you'd like to sign up.

Even better, I solemnly swear to only send out one newsletter a week (usually on Tuesday unless life gets in the way which with three kids it usually does). I will not spam you, sell your email address to solicitors or anyone else, or any of those other terrible things.

God Bless,
    Lorana

## ❧ 22 ❧

# NOT READY TO SAY GOODBYE
# YET?

Your favorite characters from Fire Beach are never far away. Readers voted to read Cara's story next, so be prepared for ….

### Secrets and Suspense

**Bubba and Makenna found Cara on the floor...**
**She's ex-military...**
**What exactly is she hiding from her friends?**


**Pre-order Secrets and Suspense today!**

## ❧ 23 ❧

# A FREE STORY FOR YOU

Enjoyed this story? Not ready to quit reading yet? If you sign up for my newsletter, you will receive The Billionaire's Impromptu Bet right away as my thank you gift for choosing to hang out with me.

**The Billionaire's Impromptu Bet**

**A SWAT officer. A bored billionaire heiress. A bet that could change everything....**
Read on for a taste of The Billionaire's Impromptu Bet....

# THE BILLIONAIRE'S IMPROMPTU
# BET PREVIEW

Brie Carter fell back spread eagle on her queen-sized canopy bed sending her blonde hair fanning out behind her. With a large sigh, she uttered, "I'm bored."

"How can you be bored? You have like millions of dollars." Her friend, Ariel, plopped down in a seated position on the bed beside her and flicked her raven hair off her shoulder. "You want to go shopping? I hear Tiffany's is having a special right now."

Brie rolled her eyes. Shopping? Where was the excitement in that? With her three platinum cards, she could go shopping whenever she wanted. "No, I'm bored with shopping too. I have everything. I want to do something exciting. Something we don't normally do."

Brie enjoyed being rich. She loved the unlimited credit cards at her disposal, the constant apparel of new clothes, and of course the penthouse apartment her father paid for, but lately, she longed for something more fulfilling.

Ariel's hazel eyes widened. "I know. There's a new bar down on Franklin Street. Why don't we go play a little game?"

Brie sat up, intrigued at the secrecy and the twinkle in Ariel's eyes. "What kind of game?"

"A betting game. You let me pick out any man in the place. Then you try to get him to propose to you."

Brie wrinkled her nose. "But I don't want to get married." She loved her freedom and didn't want to share her penthouse with anyone, especially some man.

"You don't marry him, silly. You just get him to propose."

Brie bit her lip as she thought. It had been awhile since her last relationship and having a man dote on her for a month might be interesting, but.... "I don't know. It doesn't seem very nice."

"How about I sweeten the pot? If you win, I'll set you up on a date with my brother."

Brie cocked her head. Was she serious? The only thing Brie couldn't seem to buy in the world was the affection of Ariel's very handsome, very wealthy, brother. He was a movie star, just the kind of person Brie could consider marrying in the future. She'd had a crush on him as long as she and Ariel had been friends, but he'd always seen her as just that, his little sister's friend. "I thought you didn't want me dating your brother."

"I don't." Ariel shrugged. "But he's between girlfriends right now, and I know you've wanted it for ages. If you win this bet, I'll set you up. I can't guarantee any more than one date though. The rest will be up to you."

Brie wasn't worried about that. Charm she possessed in abundance. She simply needed some alone time with him, and she was certain she'd be able to convince him they were meant to be together. "All right. You've got a deal."

Ariel smiled. "Perfect. Let's get you changed then and see who the lucky man will be.

A tiny tug pulled on Brie's heart that this still wasn't right, but she dismissed it. This was simply a means to an end, and he'd never have to know.

Jesse Calhoun relaxed as the rhythmic thudding of the speed bag reached his ears. Though he loved his job, it was stressful being the SWAT sniper. He hated having to take human lives and today had been especially rough. The team had been called out to a drug bust, and Jesse was forced to return fire at three hostiles. He didn't care that they fired at his team and himself first. Taking a life was always hard, and every one of them haunted his dreams.

"You gonna bust that one too?" His co-worker Brendan appeared by his side. Brendan was the opposite of Jesse in nearly every way. Where Jesse's hair was a dark copper, Brendan's was nearly black. Jesse sported paler skin and a dusting of freckles across his nose, but Brendan's skin was naturally dark and freckle free.

Jesse flashed a crooked grin, but kept his eyes on the small, swinging black bag. The speed bag was his way to release, but a few times he had started hitting while still too keyed up and he had ruptured the bag. Okay, five times, but who was counting really? Besides, it was a better way to calm his nerves than other things he could choose. Drinking, fights, gambling, women.

"Nah, I think this one will last a little longer." His shoulders began to burn, and he gave the bag another few punches for good measure before dropping his arms and letting it swing to a stop. "See? It lives to be hit at least another day." Every once in a while, Jesse missed training the way he used to. Before he joined the force, he had been an amateur boxer, on his way to being a pro, but a shoulder injury had delayed his training and forced him to consider something else. It had eventually healed, but by then he had lost his edge.

"Hey, why don't you come drink with us?" Brendan clapped a hand on Jesse's shoulder as they headed into the locker room.

"You know I don't drink." Jesse often felt like the outsider of the team. While half of the six-man team was married, the other half found solace in empty bottles and meaningless relationships. Jesse understood that - their job was such that they never knew if they would come home night after night - but he still couldn't partake.

Brendan opened his locker and pulled out a clean shirt. He peeled off his current one and added deodorant before tugging on the new one. "You don't have to drink. Look, I won't drink either. Just come and hang out with us. You have no one waiting for you at home."

That wasn't entirely true. Jesse had Bugsy, his Boston Terrier, but he understood Brendan's point. Most days, Jesse went home, fed Bugsy, made dinner, and fell asleep watching TV on the couch. It wasn't much of a life. "All right, I'll go, but I'm not drinking."

Brendan's lips pulled back to reveal his perfectly white teeth. He bragged about them, but Jesse knew they were veneers. "That's the spirit. Hurry up and change. We don't want to leave the rest of the team waiting."

"Is everyone coming?" Jesse pulled out his shower necessities. Brendan might feel comfortable going out with just a new application of deodorant, but Jesse needed to wash more than just dirt and sweat off. He needed to wash the sound of the bullets and the sight of lifeless bodies from his mind.

"Yeah, Pat's wife is pregnant again and demanding some crazy food concoctions. Pat agreed to pick them up if she let him have an hour. Cam and Jared's wives are having a girls' night, so the whole gang can be together. It will be nice to hang out when we aren't worried about being shot at."

"Fine. Give me ten minutes. Unlike you, I like to clean up before I go out."

Brendan smirked. "I've never had any complaints. Besides, do you know how long it takes me to get my hair like this?"

Jesse shook his head as he walked into the shower, but he knew it was true. Brendan had rugged good looks and muscles to match. He rarely had a hard time finding a woman. Jesse on the other hand hadn't dated anyone in the last few months. It wasn't that he hadn't been looking, but he was quieter than his team-mates. And he wasn't looking for right now. He was looking for forever. He just hadn't found it yet.

Click here to continue reading The Billionaire's Impromptu Bet.

# THE STORY DOESN'T END!

You've met a few people and fallen in love....

I bet you're wondering how you can meet everyone else.

**Star Lake Series:**

**When Love Returns:** Can Presley and Brandon forget past hurts or will their stubborn natures keep them apart forever?

**Once Upon a Star:** Now that Blake has gained confidence and some muscle, will he finally be able to reveal his feelings to Audrey?

**Love Conquers All:** Now that Azarius has another chance with Laney, will he find the courage to share his life with her? Or will his emotional walls create a barrier that will leave him alone once more?

**The Heartbeats Series:**

**Where It All Began:** Will Sandra tell Henry her darkest secret? And will she ever be able to forgive herself and find healing? Find out in this emotional love story.

**The Power of Prayer:** Who will Callie choose and how will her choice affect the rest of her life? Find out in this touching novel.

**When Hearts Collide:** Amanda captivates his heart, but can Jared save her from making the biggest mistake of her life? A must read for mothers and daughters.

**A Past Forgiven:** Can Chad leave his bad-boy image behind and step up and be there for Jess and the baby?

**Sweet Billionaires Series:**

**The Billionaire's Secret:** Can Max really change his philandering ways? Or will one mistake seal his fate forever?

**A Brush with a Billionaire:** Will Brent and Sam's stubborn natures keep them apart or can a small town festival bring them together?

**The Billionaire's Christmas Miracle:** Drew Devonshire is captivated by the woman he meets at a masquerade ball, but who is she?

**The Billionaire's Cowboy Groom:** When Carrie returns to town requesting a divorce, can he convince her they belong together?

**The Cowboy Billionaire: Coming Soon!**

**The Lawkeeper Series:**

**Lawfully Matched:** Will Jesse find his fiancee's killer? And when Kate flies into his life, will he be able to put his painful past behind him in order to love again?

**Lawfully Justified:** Can Emma offer William a reason to stay? Can William find a way to heal from his broken past to start a future with Emma? Or will a haunting secret take away all the possibilities of this budding romance?

**The Scarlet Wedding:** William and Emma are planning their wedding, but an outbreak and a return from his past force them to change their plans. Is a happily ever after still in their future?

**Lawfully Redeemed:** Dani Higgins is a K9 cop looking to make a name for herself, but she finds herself at the mercy of a stranger after an accident. Calvin Phillips just wanted to help his brother, but somehow he ended up in the middle of a police investigation and caring for the woman trying to bring his brother in.

**The Still Small Voice Series:**

**The Still Small Voice:** Will Kat be able to give up control and do what God is asking of her?

**A Spark in the Darkness** coming soon!

**Blushing Brides Series:**

**The Cowboy's Reality Bride:** Laney Swann has been running from her past for years, but it takes meeting a man on a reality dating show to make her see there's no need to run.

**The Reality Bride's Baby:** Laney wants nothing more than a baby, but when she starts feeling dizzy is it pregnancy or something more serious?

**The Producer's Unlikely Bride:** Ava McDermott is waiting for the perfect love, but after agreeing to a fake relationship with Justin, she finds herself falling for real.

**Ava's Blessing in Disguise:** Five years after marriage, Ava faces a mysterious illness that threatens to ruin her career. Will she find out what it is?

**The Soldier's Steadfast Bride: coming soon**

**The Men of Fire Beach**

**Fire Games:** Cassidy returns home from Who Wants to Marry a Cowboy to find obsessive letters from a fan. The cop assigned to help her wants to get back to his case, but what she sees at a fire may just be the key he's looking for.

**Lost Memories and New Beginnings:** She has no idea who she is. He's the doctor caring for her. When her past collides with his present, can he keep her safe?

**When Questions Abound** A companion story to Lost Memories, this book tells the story from Detective Jordan Graves's point of view.

**Never Forget the Past**

**Secrets and Suspense coming soon!**

**Stand Alones:**

**Love Renewed:** This books is part of the multi author second chance series. When fate reunites high school sweethearts separated by life's choices, can they find a second chance at love at a snowy lodge amid a little mystery?

Her children's early reader chapter book series:
The Wishing Stone #1: Dangerous Dinosaur
The Wishing Stone #2: Dragon Dilemma
The Wishing Stone #3: Mesmerizing Mermaids
The Wishing Stone #4: Pyramid Puzzle
The Wishing Stone Inspirations 1: Mary's Miracle
To see a list of all her books

authorloranahoopes.com
loranahoopes@gmail.com

# ABOUT THE AUTHOR

Lorana Hoopes is an inspirational author originally from Texas but now living in the PNW with her husband and three children. When not writing, she can be seen kickboxing at the gym, singing, or acting on stage. One day, she hopes to retire from teaching and write full time.

www.ingramcontent.com/pod-product-compliance
Lightning Source LLC
Chambersburg PA
CBHW030747030726
47497CB00001B/165